On the Eighteenth of May

Jordan R. Samuel

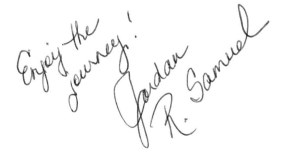

ARCHWAY
PUBLISHING

Archway Publishing books may be ordered through booksellers or by contacting:

Archway Publishing
1663 Liberty Drive
Bloomington, IN 47403
www.archwaypublishing.com
1 (888) 242-5904

ISBN: 978-1-4808-8935-4 (sc)
ISBN: 978-1-4808-8936-1 (e)

Library of Congress Control Number: 2020904868

Print information available on the last page.

Archway Publishing rev. date: 04/09/2020

For my family. My husband, my children, and my extended family close and far away.

Family is important, and I am blessed that you are mine. This story is for you.

Prologue

The girl is sitting in a chair, with an opened textbook on the desk. She is sitting among many others who have the same textbooks and the same desks and the same chairs. It is her English class. It is her final semester of high school. The teacher is reading a poem aloud, a poem by Robert Frost.

A voice said, Look me in the stars
And tell me truly, men of earth
If all the soul-and-body scars
Were not too much to pay for birth

The teacher is speaking. "What is the question the poet is asking?"
A student is answering. "Is it worth bearing the suffering of life just for the opportunity to live a life?"
The teacher is nodding and sharing more about the poet and the poem. The students are listening and taking notes and raising their hands.
But the girl is still thinking about the question. And she is smiling. Her smile is wide and full of happiness. She knows the question is an easy one, for her life is filled with joy and family and love.
She knows.
She knows the answer to the question.

Arrival

One

$\mathcal{A}$s she brushed the strand of wet hair from her forehead, she felt a sense of gratitude for the sudden cool breeze that swept under the overhanging oak trees. It brought a brief reprieve from the stifling mid-morning heat.

She continued walking, keeping her eyes on the trajectory of the sun. She sensed it was slightly after ten o'clock, but perhaps it was earlier than that. She could not know. She did not wish to know. She wished only to be in the middle of nowhere, with no idea what lay behind her and no anticipation of where she was headed. So far, the day had transpired uneventfully. She had walked the entire morning, and as she did so she had welcomed the passing of the day.

She continued walking throughout the afternoon. As dusk began settling in around her, she found herself passing through a place named Hendersonville and heading east. A few miles beyond she walked over a bridge, one that crossed over the Broad River. It was there, at the bridge's end, that she found there a choice to be made. Left offered places by the name of Gerton and Fairview. Right offered Lake Lure and Chimney Rock.

She had been among the mountain ranges the entire day,

and imagined at this late hour that she was now fully immersed in the winding roads of the Blue Ridge Mountains. She felt this instinctively, not just through the coolness of the tall, leafy trees along the curved roads, but in the ache in her muscles from managing steady inclines and predictable dips throughout the day's trek. As she paused her walking to consider her choice, she reminded herself that she would end up somewhere. Her tightening legs told her to start moving again.

She turned to the right and proceeded on a slight decline headed east, noticing never-ending forests and very few houses. She approached then passed a darkened *town limit* sign. The rushing Broad River was her constant companion, with sounds of the water crashing into and over its masses of rocks.

She realized as she walked that the place she was now entering would most likely be the place in which she would stop walking. Accepting this reality, she shifted her attention to actively finding the perfect place to serve as her *peace*. She already knew her criteria for this discovery. It had to be small, remote, and alone. Whether it was new or old or falling down around itself did not matter. She just wished to know that in *this place*, the town where she would live for now, that a *peace* existed. A place where she could mentally imagine herself and escape. She knew not what she was escaping from, only that she wished to be ready.

The special place or house or structure would have to be discovered in *this place* because there were no other places before *this place*. The place she had been in this morning, its people and her experiences there, they were all now safely shielded from her. She would have no memories of them. *This place* would be her new memory.

Having determined to find her *peace* as quickly as possible, before full darkness engulfed her, she began peering with serious eyes to the right and the left, back and forth, on either side of the road. Still walking, she saw several mountain homes scattered on both sides, but none appeared to be what she was seeking.

She then noticed a clearing ahead, on the right, amongst the curtains of forestry that lined the road. She passed a particularly massive tree, with huge limbs and large leaves, and then caught sight of a splotch of white. It was a house, sitting alone atop a faraway hill and gleaming subtly in the muted moonlight. It looked abandoned and quiet, even starkly quiet compared to the vast silence around it. There was a dark bridge that led over the river and merged again into a long winding driveway that led to the house. She glanced back up, and she knew.

This house is the most peaceful ... in this place.

She took out the single piece of paper and pen from her backpack. Over the span of a few rushed moments she sketched out the little she could see under the growing canopy of darkness. She wanted to draw the house right away, for there was no predicting what awaited her tomorrow or whether she would actually even see this house again. She had not found it to live in it, or even to visit it. She needed only to know that it existed. She would have the drawing as a reminder. A reminder that there was *peace*, and it was here.

Upon completion of the drawing, which she determined was a fairly accurate depiction, she folded and tucked the paper safely into the right pocket of her shorts while advancing further into the town in whose borders she was now fully immersed. She did so in full darkness, with no visible creature in sight and no available lodging to be seen. She saw a playground ahead and finally allowed herself to accept the weariness that had been gradually creeping into her mind and joints. Her last memories of the day were a slide, the sound of crickets, and a makeshift backpack pillow.

—⁓⁓—

Slowly opening her eyes, Cass felt a strange sensation of someone in close proximity, a light breath in and out, inhaling and exhaling close to her face and ear. As she gradually opened one eye, she was met by an eye looking straight into hers, one that blinked several times then withdrew with a youthful squeal. This jolted her to full wakefulness as she quickly sat upright and felt her head hit hard against a ceiling of some sort. She registered subtle giggling coming from somewhere beside her, yet, when she turned her head, she saw nothing but red. *Oh, Cass,* she thought with disappointment. She knew better than to sleep in a covered slide. She grabbed her backpack from behind her head and shimmied her body out of the opening at the bottom.

Once out, she turned to the source of the laughter. A little boy and a little girl were standing together, holding hands and shaking with apparent joy. As the pair stopped laughing they stared at Cass in wonder. Still holding hands, they began an approach towards her. They both looked to be six or seven, with blond curls that appeared lighter on the girl's longer hair.

"Juney. Jacob."

The children turned towards the voice as Cass saw a third person approaching from a bench nearby.

"I'm so sorry if they disturbed you. Their curiosity sometimes gets the best of them." The woman quickly glanced at Cass and then away as she took the children's hands. She appeared to be trying not to stare.

"No, they didn't disturb me at all," Cass responded. "I'm just sorry I was in the way." Cass looked directly at the children. "I'll be going now, so you two have a fun day."

Cass arranged her backpack firmly on her shoulders and started towards the road, then unexpectedly heard the woman's voice calling behind her.

"Would you like one?"

An hour later, Cass was sitting on the playground bench enjoying her second banana-nut muffin with the woman, whose name she had learned was Margie. As the two watched the children play, Margie shared a bit about the place in which Cass had stopped walking the night before. It was a small village named Chimney Rock, with a population of a little more than a hundred people and mountains on all sides. This population figure was a little misleading, as this little village partnered up with a small town, Lake Lure, which had a population of several thousand. Together, these two places operated and lived harmoniously and seamlessly. They shared utilities and schools, and the small village actually received fire and police services from the larger municipality.

While listening to the descriptions of the town and its inhabitants, Cass asked for ideas on places to live and work and was pleasantly surprised to hear of several promising options. She decided that there were a few that she would actually look into immediately after finishing the unexpected meal.

The friendly dialogue continued, with Cass asking all of the questions and Margie readily answering. Margie was a single mom who actually lived on the Lake Lure side of things. She worked in a local real estate office and sewed upholstery on the side.

Cass was enjoying her final bite of muffin when Margie asked her own question. "And are you here in Chimney Rock visiting someone, or are you moving here?"

Cass replied truthfully, "I don't know anyone here." She paused, then added, "I won't be staying too long."

After exchanging more pleasantries and general conversation, Cass thanked Margie for the muffins and for the helpful information, then turned and walked away. Glancing upward towards the sun, she determined that it was now mid-morning and well past time for her to get on with her Day One activities, including finding a legitimate lodging option and maybe even a job. As she approached the road, she remembered something she had been slightly curious to know but had forgotten to ask.

Turning around but still walking, backwards now, she called out to her new acquaintance. "I forgot to ask you, Margie. How old are your children?"

Margie grinned as she looked at the playing, giggling kids. "They're seven, getting ready to turn eight."

*How are they **both** getting ready to turn eight?*
Cass was suddenly struck with a jolt of understanding. She quickly turned and began walking briskly away, hoping to be out of range before Margie could say anything else.

CHAPTER

Two

Sitting on the restaurant's outdoor deck, Lucas looked out over the water of the lake. He had spent this time at lunch mentally planning for the upcoming weeks, or the time known as the "tourist season" in Lake Lure and Chimney Rock. Starting in a little over a week with Memorial Day weekend and until the colorful splendor of fall, this entire area would become busy with activity. Perhaps he should dread it, but the thought of a little break from the norm of this small town brought him a feeling of excited anticipation.

He took another sip of the cold, sweet tea and leaned back in his chair. He relaxed his tense shoulders and allowed himself a full minute to just sit in silence and enjoy the view of the lake and the breeze, without the nagging temptation to check his phone for notifications.

The lake was still. The reflection of the mountains created a mosaic of calming colors on the water. This water's color was different, though. Different from the water of his college years. This water was the flat lake water of his childhood.

Lucas had been home now for a little over six years, having returned here immediately following his college graduation from

Pepperdine University, a place that was 2,900 miles away. A place with crashing waves and sea breezes, white sands and memories. He had gone there to play baseball and had unexpectedly fallen in love with the Pacific.

Returning his attention back to the present, he wondered whether those images were even parts of this current lifetime. It seemed as if the memories were of a different person, a young man being remembered by an old man. Over six years had passed between that youth by the ocean and this man by the lake.

No, he thought. *This lake is not that ocean. This lake is darker and calmer and smaller. It is quiet. Always, always, quiet.*

After his father's passing, a few months after his graduation, Lucas had lived for a while with his mother. Then, when she had nudged him, he had found his own small ranch style home a few miles away. And here he had remained, for these past six years. Working. Living. Being. Twenty-one years of age had somehow turned quickly into twenty-three. He had joined the local police force. He had endured training drills and rookie taunts. Twenty-three turned into twenty-four, then somehow he found himself at twenty-six.

He had been seen as a hard worker with a level head and an ability to speak, to lead, and to navigate through small town politics and drama. He moved himself up in rank over the years, to Sergeant, then Lieutenant, then Deputy Chief. And now, at twenty-seven years of age, he was the Town of Lake Lure Chief of Police. The Chief of a force of ten, a town, a lake, and some mountains.

His life was unfolding so differently than he had thought it would. At times he even considered it wasn't unfolding at all, but rather folding, in and upon itself.

He left a twenty on the table and finished off the last of the tea, all while taking one last look at Chimney Rock Mountain. The mountain was named for a chimney-shaped rock formation that prominently jutted out from its side. At the top of this chimney was an American flag waving gently back and forth. There were numerous groups of people on top of the chimney, tiny as ants from this distance.

So far, it was shaping up to be another calm day. An early cup of coffee at his mother's café had started his morning, followed by a forty-minute meeting with the mayor, a few conversations here and there with some of the locals, and a few patrols around the area. The remainder of his morning had been spent in his office working on paperwork. Other than a lone woman he had seen walking along the side of the road earlier today, all had been predictably normal.

He headed back to his car, although the Police Department was close enough that he could have easily walked. He pulled onto the main road and headed back towards Chimney Rock, intending to make one more pass through before returning to the station, where more paperwork awaited him.

Driving into the village, he noted that there were more people on the sidewalks now than had been when he was leaving the café earlier this morning. Most of these he assumed to be tourists. There were families with small children, older couples peering through windows, and a few groups of motorcyclists perched next to their bikes.

On his left, up ahead, he could see the sign announcing his parents' place. Observing souvenir shops and more pedestrians along the way, all looked well. He drove further up the road, turned around, and headed back in the direction of Lake Lure to return to the station. As he again approached the downtown area, Lucas looked to his left and saw her again. The lone woman.

A drifter.

Glancing quickly again and getting a better look, he felt his senses become more alert and his scrutiny accelerate. She had just exited one of the restaurants and was now headed towards a crosswalk painted in the road. He approached slowly, stopped, and motioned for her to cross. She looked squarely into his eyes and nodded slowly, then held her head down for another second or two in a gesture that

Lucas found strange. An objective observer may mistake it for some type of show of respect. Lucas, however, found it to be troubling.

He watched intently as the drifter lifted her head and proceeded to walk quickly across the street towards the shops that ran along the riverside. She looked young, and he considered the possibility that she was a runaway teen. As soon as he considered this possibility, he rejected it. She was young, he decided, but she was not that young. He concluded that she was more likely a college kid, fresh off her spring semester and exploring the world. That could certainly be the case, as she had a backpack tightly secured around her and an indifferent, almost resigned expression on her face. Her hair was pulled back in a messy ponytail. Her face had patches of dirt across it that appeared to be made from sweaty hands brushing against sweaty cheeks.

Other than her disheveled appearance, Lucas determined she was most likely harmless. He anticipated that she would probably spend the afternoon in Chimney Rock, take a few selfies by the river, and then move on. He watched as *the drifter* completed her trek across the road, then he proceeded to his department, without another glance her way.

CHAPTER

Three

Walking along the main road of Chimney Rock, Cass found herself curious about the hokey charm of the place. Dotting both sides of the road were one, two and three story structures, all of which housed a variety of establishments. Massive mountains on each side of the village provided the perfect backdrop. She imagined the mountains as a protective wall, keeping the little village secure and safe from the outside world, all under the watch of an American flag flying high above on a rocky perch.

She was sweaty and tired of feeling day-old moisture on her t-shirt. She had been wearing the same clothes for over twenty-four hours now, and she desperately wanted a shower and a fresh bra. She hoisted her backpack straps firmly back up on her shoulders and kept walking, now focused on a search for lodging.

She carefully surveyed her surroundings for any sign of availability. Seeing none, she started to wonder if this village was too small to accommodate her. As she passed a few hotels along the river, she began contemplating the option of renting a room for a year. She had a roll of cash in her backpack, but knew the hotel option would most likely prove too expensive in the long-term.

While processing her lodging dilemma, she approached a sign indicating that she was now passing into the Town of Lake Lure. She decided that exploring Lake Lure would have to wait until tomorrow. There were still plenty of things that she wished to get done and the day was progressing quickly. She headed back towards Chimney Rock's small downtown area.

Having tried to address her immediate needs on her own, she now accepted the inevitability of relying on locals to help with her search. Finding herself once again in the heart of the shopping district, she began entering one after another.

Eight or so businesses later, she felt the early tinges of disappointment beginning to creep into her mind. While all of the salespeople were extremely friendly, none were aware of any available lodging or employment.

As she continued on, she gazed through the window of a souvenir shop and noticed busy patrons examining the shop's offerings. Watching them for a few minutes longer, she was suddenly and silently jolted by an image.

The boy's hand is shaking the snow globe, and the snow inside is frozen in mid-flight. The boy's voice is speaking. He is saying, "Here, it's your turn now…"

Cass felt her pulse accelerate and her breaths quicken. She steadied herself and reached into the right pocket of her shorts, pulling out the rough sketch she had drawn the night before. She unfolded the paper and looked at the tiny house placed high on the hill, beyond the long driveway that led over the river. She looked at the sketched porch and she pictured herself there.

Peace.

She closed her eyes and saw only this place, this small tiny house. She felt her breath slowing. She felt her mind clearing and memories returning to where they belonged. She opened her eyes and took one last look at the sketch before returning it to the safety of her pocket.

Turning away from the shops, she spied a small building across the street, neatly tucked in between two larger businesses. She crossed the road and saw a hand-painted sign hanging from the building's rafter. *Walt's Bakery and Café.*

Pushing the front door open, she heard a little bell ring from above her head, a pleasant sound that announced that a customer had just arrived. She saw what she assumed to be the last of the lunch crowd, two couples engaged in their own conversations and too occupied to notice her. She approached the counter but noticed that no one else seemed to be in the café other than herself and the four customers.

A small bell sat on the counter with a neatly written sign that read **Ring Bell for Assistance**. Cass touched the bell lightly and was a little startled when a silver mop of wispy hair appeared out from underneath the counter.

"Oh, I'm sorry, dear. I didn't hear you come in," said the silver-haired person, blowing a breath upward to remove a flop of hair from her face. "Time to get my hearing aid checked again. What can I get for you this morning, or is it afternoon already?"

Standing fully upright now, the woman behind the counter barely came to Cass's shoulders. She had a full head of wavy hair that came to her shoulders paired with silver-rimmed glasses perched on her nose. She was wearing bright orange lip gloss and rosy rouge on her cheeks, a combination that may have looked a little much on others, but on her, appeared to be a perfect match.

Cass began her usual introduction, just as she had for the previous eight businesses.

"Good afternoon, ma'am. My name is Cass and I was wondering if the owner or manager might be in today?" She grinned politely and stood quietly waiting for a response.

The older woman behind the counter grinned in return and appeared to be taking a few seconds to assess what she could about this stranger standing before her. Then, she took Cass's hand in her own.

"Hello, Cass. It's nice to meet you and welcome to my café. I'm the owner, Ella, and it's a pleasure to have you here." As Ella continued with her introduction, she held Cass's hand in her own. It was a soft, reassuring hold that was entirely unexpected.

"Now you may be wondering why this place is named 'Walt's' when my name is Ella," the older woman continued. She had placed her other hand over her chest as she had said this. "Well, dear, Walt is the name of my precious husband, the love of my life, and this bakery and café was his pride and joy for forty-one years." Ella paused, cleared her throat, and continued. "We spent those many years here running this place, living this quiet mountain life, and just being together. And now that he is gone, I carry on the traditions of Walt's Bakery and Café on my own. And I cherish every minute of it." Ella looked down at the counter now, but continued to hold onto Cass's hand.

Cass remained still and quiet. She sensed that Ella had more to say. She decided she was willing to stand there, in silence, for as long as Ella needed.

Ella finally looked up again, patted Cass's hand a few times and then released it. "So, Cass, let me guess why you were looking for the manager of this place? Could it be that you are looking for a little summer employment?"

"Yes, ma'am," Cass replied. "Actually, I'd be happy for seasonal employment, but it would be even better to find something for a little longer." Cass stopped there and continued looking at Ella, now with a hopeful optimism that seemed to radiate from Ella herself.

"Well, Cass, you may be in luck. Last week my friend, Sal, who's been my right-hand woman since my dearest Walter departed, decided to move to Florida to be closer to her daughter and grandkids. I've been trying to manage everything on my own, but, to be honest, I'm an old woman, and waking up at five o'clock in the morning to make biscuits and scones is not my idea of easing gracefully into my golden years."

Ella paused while glancing at Cass's backpack, then seemed to focus a little more carefully on Cass. "Just how long are you planning to be here in Chimney Rock?"

Cass answered quickly, "Until the eighteenth of May." Ella's arched eyebrows suggested that she was contemplating this response. "May eighteenth? Isn't that today? Oh wait, today's the nineteenth. My goodness how the days all flow together in this place." Ella was shaking her head now and slightly chuckling to herself. "So, you have your date of departure set? That's good. That's good. I like people who have a plan." Ella looked back at Cass and regained a semblance of seriousness as she asked the next question. "Cass, have you had experience working in a café or restaurant before?"

Before? Before what? Yesterday? Before here? Before now?

Cass projected her friendliest grin and responded, "I'm a quick learner," then added a little more softly, "and I would be grateful if you could just give me a chance."

Their eye contact was interrupted by a lyric from a song that Cass did not recognize. It was blasting loudly from Ella's phone, which was sitting a couple feet away on the counter.

"Excuse me a minute, dear," Ella said as she moved to retrieve and silence the loud music. "I set the volume on high so I can hear it in the back, but it dampens the café mood when I accidently leave it here. When will I learn?"

Ella checked the notification on the front and smiled. "My son… probably checking to see what I'm serving for dinner tonight. Even though he's turning twenty-eight soon, he still loves his momma's chicken and dumplings." She said this with a tenderness and laughter in her voice, one that conjured up for Cass an image of Margie and her children from the playground earlier in the day.

Cass had glanced around a little while Ella had been checking her phone, and had noted the light green and dark coral colors that adorned the café, along with paintings of wildflowers in ceramic vases and woven rugs scattered around the floor. The café appeared to be its own little sweet spot, hidden in a world of wood and rock. Cass looked back at Ella, who was now retrieving a folded apron from under the counter.

"Can you start employee training later on this afternoon?" Ella asked as she extended the apron towards Cass.

Cass couldn't help but grin with a mixture of relief and gratitude. "I could start right now, except for the fact that I'm quite sweaty and I'm sure I look and smell disgusting." Cass paused briefly and then continued, unable to hide the excitement in her voice and hoping to sound as reassuring as possible. "But as soon as I can locate a place to live for a while, I'll take a quick shower and grab a change of clothes. Then, and I promise this, Ella, I'll be back. I'll be back very soon."

Cass grinned again, held out her hand for a quick handshake, and then turned to depart. As she neared the door, she heard Ella's voice call out from behind her.

"So, you're looking for a place to live, huh?"

Cass stopped and turned around to see Ella smiling from behind the counter.

"Well, Cass, it's looking like today really is your lucky day."

Four

$\mathcal{A}$fter a relatively uneventful afternoon at the station, Lucas packed up his laptop, thanked the few members of his team who were still left finishing up, and headed out to welcome the weekend. Other than the meeting with the mayor earlier in the day and the lone drifter he had briefly encountered twice, this day had shaped up to be quite mundane. It was the perfect transition into the off duty weekend he had planned in order to catch up on all his projects. His mother had several items that needed fixing on her back deck, and there were his own chores that needed addressing as well. He felt an urgency to get these things done, before the busy season arrived.

First, however, there was the issue of his hair. Arlene was waiting on him at her salon, and he was already ten minutes late. He grinned as he drove slowly towards Chimney Rock, feeling grateful in knowing that Arlene would never fuss at him for his tardiness. Arlene had moved to the village over five years ago, and had opened up her beauty salon shortly thereafter. In her first few days of living in Chimney Rock she had visited the police station and had shared her history of domestic abuse at the hands of her now estranged husband, Mike. She was a battered wife on the run, and she had chosen this place to restart her life. Over the years, Arlene had developed a deep connection to the police force, and to Lucas in particular.

He had always assumed that Arlene was in her mid- or late-thirties, although he knew better than to ever ask. She had short, fiery red hair which she paired with consistent heavy makeup and heavier perfume. At first, those many years ago, he had sensed Arlene's favoritism and had mistaken this attention for flirting, but then he had realized that she was simply grateful. Somehow, Lucas and the police force had given her a sense of safety, which was all she had wanted.

Lucas pulled into a parking space in front of Arlene's salon, locked the door to his squad car, and jogged in to give the appearance that he had hurried as quickly as possible to get there. Arlene was standing at his chair, with his robe in one hand, a pair of scissors in the other, and a faux look of disappointment on her face.

Sitting down with the beauty salon robe now secure around his neck, Lucas took a glance at his reflection in the mirror. His hair had grown quite long since his last visit, now well past his ears and encroaching on his neck.

Arlene began her methodical trim, starting first with a close cut up the back and sides, then transitioning nicely into longer strands on top, shaping his thick hair into a professional style that was fitting to his role as Police Chief. She trimmed around his ears, checked the length and overall shape a few times, and then exclaimed the same phrase she used upon each of his visits.

"Goodness, Luke, you could be a movie star." Arlene gazed at him in the mirror from her vantage point behind him, not with the admiration of a lover or a potential love interest, but with the pride of someone who had become more like a family member. "I mean it, Luke. With your tan skin, your jaw line, your dark hair, not to mention your height and build. Have you ever thought about modeling?"

Lucas was ready with his reply. "No Arlene, since the last time you asked me that two and a half weeks ago, no, I have not joined the modeling world nor the Hollywood Actors Guild. I'm still just Lucas Montraine, your friendly, neighborhood Police Chief."

They locked eyes in the mirror with a serious stare down, then both started chuckling at the same time. Arlene brushed the cut hairs gently from his neck, removed the robe, and then brushed again for "safe measure", as she liked to put it.

As he stood, Lucas reached into his wallet for a twenty-dollar bill, then removed an additional ten for good measure. He handed both to Arlene and hugged her endearingly. Heading for the door, he suddenly heard her voice call after him.

"Oh! Did you find it? The croquet set?"

He turned with a puzzled look, then suddenly registered what she was talking about.

"Geez, Arlene, I completely forgot to look. I told you to remind me." He had promised her on his last visit he would scour his old room for the set he used as a child. Apparently, Arlene had discovered a newfound interest in the game. "Listen, since you're obviously terrible at actually reminding people of things, I'm going to go home and look for it right now. If I don't return with it in ten minutes that means it no longer exists." He gave a slight, sarcastic bow and headed out the salon door.

Moments later, as he walked down the street towards his mother's place, he realized that there was a distinct possibility that the croquet set was not there. He had not lived in his childhood home for almost six years, and there was no telling how much had been given away in the interim. Still, he had promised Arlene that he would try.

He crossed the street and caught sight of his parents' cafe as well as certain parts of the home. For a split second, he felt like a middle schooler again, having just hopped off the school bus and now heading to his house for an afternoon snack and some homework time.

Remembering school days hit a raw nerve for Lucas. He pictured his father helping with math and coaching him in baseball, taking him fishing and teaching him about Native American folklore.

His memories included the phone call that had changed everything, that had led to his hurried move back home after graduating from college. His mother had been the one to call, on that evening during his final semester. She had been the one who shared the unexpected news. His father had not had the strength to share with his only child that the cancer had returned.

Lucas made his way along the side of the café building, foregoing the locked front door of the business even though he had a key. He proceeded around the back, walking along the carefully laid pavers until he came to the back porch steps. He walked up to and across the back porch and to the back door of the home, his childhood home. As he did so, he remembered his mother's words, those many years ago. He remembered the care and quiet assurance of her voice from thousands of miles away. He remembered his dad then picking up on the other line, and the three of them crying and talking.

They had wanted him to know, but they also had not wanted him to come home. They had wanted him to remain and finish college. They had told him not to change plans. They had encouraged him to go for the interviews he had lined up in various locations along the southern coast of California, to pursue the job opportunities and dreams that he had cultivated for the four years prior. They said then, those many years ago, that they had called simply because they wanted him to know, they wanted him to be prepared, and they wanted him to pray.

And so, twenty-one-year-old Lucas prayed. Initially he prayed for a miracle, for the cancer to leave and never return. Then he prayed for comfort, for some relief from his sleepless nights filled with worry about his parents and about himself. Finally, in the end, after he packed up his worldly belongings, traveled back to his hometown and moved back into his room behind the bakery and café, he prayed for something different. Then, he prayed for peace.

Taking his keys from his pocket and unlocking the back porch door, Lucas returned to the present. He was well aware that this was his mother's favored napping time, a time she lovingly referred to as her "pre-supper beauty sleep", so he was careful to open the back door quietly. After entering, he softly stepped through the kitchen and headed straight for his old bedroom.

The bedroom door was closed, which seemed odd. He quickly shrugged it off and proceeded to walk towards it, intending to find the croquet set and leave the home so quietly his mother would never even know he had been there.

As he turned the doorknob, the bedroom door slid slowly open, offering him a small and then increasing slice of vision. As the opening grew wider, Lucas suddenly saw. There was a stranger in his bedroom.

The stranger was looking out his window. Her face was fully turned away. However, he did not need to see her face to realize the stranger was *the drifter*. The very same drifter he had seen earlier in the day. The same clothes, the same sweat, the same hair.

He thought back to the questions he had considered earlier in regards to her age. Whatever her age, she was old enough. Old enough to know how to break into an older woman's home and steal her blind.

Quietly, and in the most controlled voice he could muster while feeling as enraged as he currently did, Lucas slowly stated, "Against the wall." And then he added, with anger in his tone, "And hands behind your head."

CHAPTER

Five

Which wall?
Cass assumed the police officer was referring to the wall closest to the window, so she proceeded to move her body against it and to put her hands behind her head. As soon as she did she wondered if her hands were placed where they should be. She proceeded to move them even lower to a location behind her neck. She awaited further instructions but heard nothing, aside from the steady intake of his breath moving closer.

After taking her hands and separating them, the officer moved them briskly down to her lower back. She stood still, with her arms and hands exactly as he had placed them, and felt the cold metal of handcuffs as he began to speak.

"You have the right to remain..."

"Lucas Walter Montraine! What EXACTLY do you think you're doing?" Ella's voice was loud and authoritative as she called out from the hallway.

The officer held Cass's hands tightly while he called over his shoulder. "Stay out there, Mom. Don't come any closer. Go back in your room and shut the door."

But Ella was already approaching. "There are times, Lucas, during which I am grateful for the fact that you're in law enforcement, but this is not one of them. This young lady is my guest. So, please, son, please, quite manhandling her!"

Ella took Cass's hands from the officer's and turned Cass around to look straight at her. She stroked Cass's hands affectionately as she continued.

"I'm so sorry, Cass. This is not his fault, but my own. I failed to let my one and only child know that I had a new tenant in my home. And my one and only child happens to live close by and happens to carry a badge and a gun."

Ella rubbed Cass's hands a few more seconds, a gesture that, Cass had to admit, felt reassuring and warm. Ella then released the hands and turned to speak to the officer.

"Lucas, I'm sorry. I had no idea you were coming over this early or I would have forewarned you…"

While Ella continued her explanation to the officer, Cass noticed that this particular trio of individuals, of which she was included, were all diverting their individual attention in contrasting directions. Ella was looking at the officer, Cass was looking at Ella, and the officer was glaring at Cass.

Cass turned slowly and stared back at him, this person whom Ella kept naming as Lucas. Standing mere inches from him, Cass could readily make out the finer details of his features. His tan skin, his dark eyes, his black hair. He was taller than Cass by what she guessed was four or five inches. He was slender but broad-shouldered, thin but seemingly muscular. She decided quickly that he was a study in contrasts. His full lips seemed gentle, as if they may utter soft words, but his eyes were hard and piercing. The black of his hair and his eyebrows seemed to bring a deep darkness to his overall countenance.

Cass knew that he was scrutinizing her, and she felt confident that he had already assessed her as a pathetic and perhaps dangerous person. He continued staring as he returned the handcuffs to his belt.

She looked down at his badge, and then at his name tag.

Chief Lucas Montraine.

She looked away and back at Ella, who was finishing up something she was saying about the current predicament.

"So this is all my fault and hopefully we can all just laugh it off and have dinner together tonight." Ella chuckled lightheartedly as she said this.

The officer moved his gaze to his mother, then said with an agitated voice, "Could I please see you in the hallway for a minute?"

Allowing his mother to proceed ahead of him and closing the door behind them, the pair soon disappeared from Cass's sight and hearing. She waited a few minutes, then hearing nothing further she proceeded to the private bathroom to finally shower.

The warm water felt refreshing and soothing as Cass stood still under the showerhead and allowed herself a few minutes to think. She knew she needed to scrub every dirty inch and remove the sweat-filled stubble of hair from her body, but for now all she wished to do, for just a few minutes longer, was to rest in the warm water and reflect on the day so far. This was Day One for her, and she had already found a place to sleep at night and a method of earning money.

The remainder of the day now seemed fairly set as well. Cass would finish cleaning up, put on some clean clothes from her backpack and the *Walt's* t-shirt Ella had given her, then head back to the café as quickly as possible. Ella had explained that since the café was now closed for the day, this would be a perfect time for employee training.

Once her training or anything else Ella needed was completed, Cass planned to take off straight from there and get a few hours of walking in before complete darkness. Ella had also mentioned something about eating dinner together, and Cass had already determined that she certainly wouldn't turn down such an offer.

She reluctantly turned the warm water off and proceeded to grab one of the three towels Ella had loaned her to wrap her washed hair. She wrapped another around her body and stepped out of the shower. Wiping the steam from the sink mirror she took a brief glance at her reflection, still a little glossy on the glass, then quickly looked away.

Stepping now out of the bathroom, Cass entered into the remainder of her living space in this small bedroom in Ella's home. The home itself was actually a two-bedroom attachment on the back of the bakery, one that included a living room and a kitchen. Much of it was decorated in the same coral and green that adorned the café.

The second bedroom had belonged to Ella and Walt's only child, a son whom Ella had described as her "beloved boy". The room was small, with a single twin bed, a nightstand and another larger table placed in the corner. A few trophies and plaques were scattered around the room, but for the most part it appeared to Cass that the previous inhabitant had taken most of his personal belongings with him. There was a dresser along the side wall, a couple of small lamps, a tiny private bathroom, and a large window which faced the massive mountain of Chimney Rock.

Cass now stood in her towel, remembering other details of the early afternoon interactions with Ella, including Ella's gifts of fresh towels, trial-sized shampoo and conditioner, and other items to hold Cass over until she had time to go shopping. She remembered Ella's words about providing home-cooked meals and access to a laundry room, and that Cass could keep any tips she made in addition to a couple hundred dollars that Ella insisted that Cass be given for her monthly "payroll". Even as she was reflecting on this earlier conversation, Cass heard a gentle knock on the bedroom door.

"Cass, honey, did you find everything you needed?"

Cass began actively drying off and then hurriedly put on her fresh set of clothes, calling back to Ella through the closed door as she did so. "Absolutely, Ella. That shower felt fantastic. Thank you for the soap and shampoo."

Moments later, she opened the door to find Ella on the other side. Cass smiled softly and gestured towards the room. "This is a lovely room, Ella. I will take great care with it during my year living here. Thank you so much."

"Sweetie, you don't have to keep thanking me," Ella said while patting Cass's arm. "If this whole arrangement works out, I'm the one that will be thanking you! Do you know how hard it has been on me, getting up early each morning and basically manning the whole kit-and-caboodle on my own? Lord, I'm too old for that."

Ella walked towards the twin bed and plumped the pillow enthusiastically while continuing. "This might be just exactly what I need, and maybe you were brought to my doorstep this morning because I'm too hard-headed to realize when I need help. You help me run my bakery, and I trade you room and board in return."

Turning towards Cass and pausing as if to consider her next words carefully, Ella continued in a hushed tone.

"My son is very protective, and I am so sorry for what happened. I can't imagine how upsetting that must have been for you."

"Ella, please don't ever think about it again," Cass responded softly. "Please. I am not upset, and I believe your son was completely right in everything he said and did." This statement seemed to lighten the mood a little and return Ella to her happy and positive demeanor.

The two women shared a quick cup of coffee and then proceeded back to the bakery for "employee training", as Ella had described with a giggle. Cass was quickly getting the impression that it had been quite a while since Ella had actually had an employee or any kind of formal help for that matter, so Cass decided to remain quiet and dutiful and to allow Ella this opportunity to play boss.

Standing in the kitchen area of Walt's, Cass couldn't help but be impressed. Ella had arranged this small space with the utmost of efficiency and organization. As Cass listened intently, Ella took her time in explaining where each item was located, what it was used for, and why it was important. Ella then pulled out a large drawer and retrieved a small cardboard box. With a touch of sadness in her expression, she laid her hand atop it and seemed lost in thought.

"I remember when we only had a few recipes in here," Ella whispered as she removed the top and placed it to the side. "During those early days, we only made a few things – croissants, scones, and our very own mountain blueberry muffins, which still happens to be our best seller. And then, as business picked up and we realized how much we loved our little bakery, we decided to add a café and about forty more recipes."

Ella was looking through the pile of index cards in the box, some handwritten and some with cut out magazine recipes taped neatly to the card. Ella continued as she found one that appeared to be of particular interest.

"I haven't opened this box in several years, Cass. Walt and I both discovered that after we had baked these same treats thousands of times over thousands of days, we tended to memorize every detail of each one of them. Thank goodness I kept these, though, because you're going to need them." Ella handed the card to Cass.

Cass read the title, *Freddy's Froggy Biscuits*, which was printed a little off center. Reading the brief description beneath, Cass was surprised to find only five ingredients were needed. She looked back up at Ella and awaited further instructions.

Ella stared a little longer at the back of the card in Cass's hand, then looked up. "Let's start here and see what level of baking skills you have," Ella said kindly. "This particular recipe was the result of a creative writing assignment that Lucas had in third grade. The assignment was to create and write about a new invention. Having grown up in a bakery, our boy decided he would invent a new cookie. In fact, the recipe you now hold is one written with his own eight-year old hand, and named for his favorite character from a storybook I used to read to him at night."

Ella paused and smiled with what seemed like a touch of

melancholy. "The funny thing is, he decided that instead of just turning in the card with the recipe he had written, he would actually bake his new invention for his classmates. And when we tasted it for the first time, low and behold, it was actually quite tasty."

Ella chuckled lightly as she pointed to the card with her finger. "This particular cookie is my son's favorite, even to this very day." Ella raised her eyebrows in a curious but encouraging way. "So, Cass, how about you whip us up some Froggy Biscuits, sort of as your new employee exam?"

Cass looked again at the card. She didn't know if she could bake or not, but she felt ready to find out. With a slight grin, she placed the card on the counter and reached for the flour bin.

Twenty minutes later, as Cass's Froggy Biscuits baked in the large oven, Cass wandered out to the café area where Ella was seated at a table, speaking on her cell phone and looking out the window. Cass spotted a clean, dry dishcloth on the same counter where she had met Ella earlier in the day. She took the dishcloth to the bakery sink, where she dampened it with warm water and grabbed a clear spray bottle labeled as Clorox solution.

As Ella was still engaged with the phone call, Cass proceeded to clean the tables and chairs placed around the café, sanitizing and wiping down each, except for the one currently occupied by Ella. Returning the spray bottle to its proper place near the sink and rinsing and wringing out the cloth, Cass then returned to the service counter.

She picked up one of the menus from a neat wooden display case on the counter and perused the items made and sold at Walt's Bakery and Café. There were the mountain blueberry muffins that Ella had referenced earlier, which were featured in their own text box with fancy scrollwork emphasizing them as the bakery's specialty item. Other items from the bakery sounded equally delightful, with names like cinnamon apple butter scones and glazed blackberry biscuits. On the lunch side of the menu, she noticed a limited but appetizing selection of sandwich and soup varieties. She glanced at the bakery display case and noted that while there were a few scones and muffins still remaining, most other items had sold out.

Cass returned to the kitchen and then back to the café a few minutes later with a tray of the freshly baked Froggy Biscuits. Ella eyed the tray from across the room and promptly but politely concluded her phone call.

After a quick approach towards the tray, Ella picked a warm cookie and handed it to Cass, then picked up another for herself. As they both took a bite and chewed, Ella took the tray from Cass and headed towards the door that led to the attached home.

"Well, I'd say we've done enough for one day. Think I'll get started on supper and …." Ella stopped mid-sentence as she turned to notice Cass still standing at the service counter. "I'll see you for supper around a quarter past seven?"

Feeling a little confused, Cass asked, "Did you want me to stay here and practice some more baking, or mop the floors?"

Ella smiled sweetly and opened the door. She appeared to be waiting for Cass to walk through to the home.

"No need for any more practice or training, Cass. I would say, from what I just tasted and from what I've already seen, you're going to be just fine."

CHAPTER

Six

7:15. Please, son. Be polite.

*L*ucas stared at the text message. It was a response from his mother, the answer to his question about what time she was hosting the supper. A nice little meal for the two of them…and *the drifter*. He shook his head as he hurriedly laced up his sneakers and stood from his living room couch. The scalding hot shower he had just taken had helped, but the agitation and anger lingered. He felt his jaw clenching and his pulse quickening.

Quit thinking about it and start doing something about it.

He returned to his bedroom and found the belongings that he always kept in his pockets when wearing his uniform, including a small spiral flip pad and a ball point pen. Though he was young, he preferred paper to electronics. He sat on his bed and flipped the pad open to the next available blank page. Flicking the ball point out, Lucas started with an entry on the first line.

Drifter – May 19

He stopped and stared at the page. He recalled the images of her throughout the day. Walking along the side of the road this morning, crossing the road this afternoon after lunch, and standing in his old bedroom later in the day. Clenching his jaw again, he poised the pen over the pad and resumed his list.

Walked here (from where?)
Late teens, early 20s
5'8" (app.)
Unkempt
Backpack
Hiding something (missing persons? parole? check with other towns)

Lucas flipped the pad closed and returned it to his dresser. As he did so, he said aloud and convincingly to himself, "Hopefully you're not planning on staying long, *Cass the drifter*, because this list will get longer. I can assure you of that."

He grabbed his keys and exited his home, heading towards his truck and reflecting further on the sudden turn of events. He was anxious to see his mother, to hear her voice and to try again to reason with her. Their conversation in the hallway earlier had ended in a stalemate, with Ella reminding Lucas that she was a "grown adult", and that she was free to determine who she employed and who she took in as a tenant.

For his part, Lucas had attempted to use the obvious persuasive tools, including facts like Ella had no idea who this stranger was, what her history or intentions were, and why she had decided, of all places, to pounce upon an older, unassuming bakery owner for a job and a place to live. Lucas had also brought up some of Ella's other past attempts at helping the supposed outcasts of the world. Two years ago, Ella offered to tutor a young juvenile through his senior year of high school, only to find that he was sneaking money out of her purse while she was turning the pages in the workbook. Before that, Ella had raised money to buy toys for a divorced mother who had just moved into the village, a pitiful figure who had a sad story of lost custody and three young children she never got to see.

The young mother just needed some help buying toys so she could surprise them at Christmas, as she had described it. After giving the toys to the mother, Ella found out later that the mother had returned the toys at the local Walmart, taken the cash, and left Chimney Rock, no doubt to find a new gullible victim.

Even after reminding his mom of her good-hearted attempts that had ended in disappointment, the earlier conversation ended exactly as Lucas predicted it would. Ella assured him that her choice was *her* choice, and that he should stop worrying. His mother had also added, apparently just for good measure, that if he tried, he may even get to make a new friend.

Lucas thought for a moment about what his new friend's name would be. *What was it? Cass? What kind of name is that?*

He wondered if perhaps it was a nickname for a fugitive, or a pseudonym for a wife running from an abusive husband. He even considered that it may be an assumed name for someone who had just escaped from the mental ward at the local hospital.

As he reached his truck and proceeded to start the engine and depart from his driveway, he recognized that he was feeling a little more controlled now. More aware with a clear assessment of the situation. He considered that maybe Cass was her actual name and perhaps she was living an honest life here. He conceded that, yes that was a possibility, but a remote one. Years in law enforcement had taught him to be aware of and expect the worst of scenarios.

He drove the four minutes to Chimney Rock and parked along the front of the bakery. Making his way to the back porch, he walked up the steps and then remembered with frustration that he had just walked up these same steps a few hours earlier, only to find a stranger in this house. He pushed open the back door and walked into the kitchen, spotting first his mother and then Cass. They were both hovered over a plate at the dining room table, giggling.

What the hell?

Ella turned at the sound of his entrance and immediately jumped out of her chair to hug and greet him. Lucas returned her affection. Even though he was still upset and disappointed in Ella's decision, he couldn't show any visible signs of anger or disappointment, not to her. He would handle this his own way, without upsetting her or getting her involved.

Hugging his mom tightly, Lucas stole a glance over at the drifter. She was watching them with what others may have interpreted as envy, but what he believed to be a clever attempt to appear as someone she wasn't. A trustworthy figure. The look on her face grew stranger, almost as if she were mesmerized. He assumed she was enamored with thoughts surrounding whatever scheme she was planning, watching them even as she prepared for her next step or steps.

Lucas sat down at the dining room table and Ella proceeded to retrieve several dishes out of the warm oven, hushing and leading Cass back to the table as she offered to help. As Ella turned towards the oven, he looked straight at Cass.

Her hair was pulled back into a messy braid and she wore a wrinkled t-shirt, but she appeared to have removed the dirt and sweat from her body. He made it clear through his expression and his unyielding glare exactly how he deemed her presence at his mother's dinner table. After a few seconds, she spoke quietly.

"I'm so sorry that I alarmed you today, Chief Montraine."

After what seemed like an eternity of silence in which Lucas was determined not to waver in his expression, Cass continued speaking, this time to Ella.

"Ella, are you sure I can't help you with anything?"

"No, Cass, but thank you," Ella replied cheerfully. She carried the first dish, clasped in two potholders, and placed it in the middle of the table. "Everything's ready. It's just a matter of bringing it over here." Ella proceeded back to the oven for another round of readied food.

A few minutes later, Lucas found himself eating his mom's homemade chicken and dumplings, along with buttered peas, creamed corn, and a hot buttermilk biscuit. This was exactly the kind of meal that Lucas would normally devour with great satisfaction, but tonight he was unable to find any appetite. He found the presence of the drifter off-putting, no matter how harmless she tried to appear. The home-cooked meal tasted stale, and he struggled to eat even half of what Ella put on his plate.

Something was off, way off, but it was difficult to even begin to connect the dots with so little information. Earlier in the day, Ella had shared with Lucas the few details that Cass had already willingly given, but those were scant at best. Lucas listened intently to the supper conversation as it unfolded, adding nothing of his own but making mental notes of words and expressions. All were clues to add to his flip pad.

To Ella's question about where Cass had lived prior to coming to Chimney Rock, Cass replied politely.

"Thirty or so miles from here."

Ella, appearing to Lucas to be somewhat confused by this evasive response, shifted her topic slightly.

"And do you have family or friends nearby?"

"No, I don't know anyone here." A split second later, Cass added another phrase to her response. "I won't be staying too long."

The conversation proceeded as such, with Ella asking light-hearted and generally harmless questions and Cass providing respectful, polite answers with little to no substance. Lucas continued his pretense of eating while considering Cass's responses, including her latest, which had been a "no" to Ella's question of whether or not she was tired from her journey yesterday.

Lucas lifted his eyes and watched the drifter move her peas around and then choose three or four to add to her spoonful of creamed corn. He had already noticed a few things about her during their encounter in the bedroom that afternoon, but now, sitting three feet away and across the table from her, he was able to add greatly to his mental picture.

The strongest descriptor that came to his mind was *rough*. Her hair was apparently freshly washed, from what he could gather from comments made earlier between she and Ella, yet appeared just as unkempt and unattended to as when he had seen her earlier in the day, crossing the street. The color itself was a light brown, with splotches of natural highlights woven throughout. Her hair was long, probably well past her shoulder blades. There were loose wisps falling about her face, around her shoulders, and down her back. All of these gave the impression that someone had tried to braid her hair and then had decided to place her head in a clothes dryer right before coming to supper. If she had looked in a mirror, she would have known this, which suggested to Lucas that either she knew it and didn't care how she looked, or she hadn't cared enough to even look in a mirror in the first place.

As he was considering these two possibilities, he lost track of how intently he was staring at her hair, until he shifted his eyes to her face and found her staring back at him. Their eyes locked for a brief second. He saw in hers a cautious readiness, and he was sure she had seen in his a resolute scrutiny. Whatever secrets this girl had, he was convinced now that they would not be kept for long.

Not here. Not under my watch.

As Cass slowly looked down at her plate, Ella continued with some chitchat about the village, including directions to some shops that Cass may want to visit the following day. Ella's banter somehow successfully filled the gap left by lack of information and inability to converse with this stranger. Cass had made it clear from her answers that the totality of her life that she would, or perhaps could, discuss included only the present, including the current day and the day prior. The years that had passed before those two days had been artfully kept out-of-bounds for discussion.

As Ella continued sharing a lesson in Chimney Rock history, Lucas continued his examination. Later, after leaving, he would scour the missing persons and wanted files, so he knew he needed to remember her features in order to compare. He also knew that asking her for a quick picture was definitely out of the question.

A few moments earlier, when their eyes had locked for those few seconds, he had noted her eye color. Her eyes had been a light teal, the color of waves, of the ocean, and of memories. But now, looking at her eyes again as she directed them towards Ella, he realized they were actually darker. Not light teal but a deep topaz blue. The color of impending storms. The color of secrets.

Her face was lightly sun-kissed, with a few scattered freckles about the bridge of her nose and her upper cheeks. Her teeth were straight and white from the little he could tell, for she only showed these when speaking, never revealing more than what was needed. Even when thanking Ella for the vast number of things Cass had thanked her for over the past hour, this gratitude was never delivered with a broad smile, but more so with a tight-lipped, subdued grin.

Pushing his chair back and lifting his plate, Lucas turned to Ella. "Dinner was delicious. Thanks, Mom." He proceeded to walk towards the sink with his plate, utensils and glass in hand. He wanted to leave as soon as he was able so he could return home and begin looking into the police database for clues as to exactly who she was and what she was doing here. As he set the items down in the sink, he noticed a plate of what appeared to be freshly baked Froggy Biscuits sitting on the counter.

She is the absolute best mother in the world.

He wondered how she had known that today, of all days, this was exactly what he needed. He took one of the cookies in his hand and proceeded to begin munching on the crunchy exterior while making his way to the moist gooeyness of the middle.

"Oh, Lucas. Do you really have to be in such a hurry?" Ella looked disappointed at his abrupt attempt at departure.

"Sorry, Mom. I just want to hit the hay a little early tonight so I can get an early morning jumpstart to all my weekend projects around the house. But I'll be back tomorrow." And then, looking squarely at Cass, he added, "In fact, I might be back tonight. In a few minutes or a few hours. I'm just down the road so you never know when I might show up."

Lucas continued chewing the cookie and grabbed a couple for the road. He again looked at Ella and added, "Bless you for having these little treats baked up for me, Mom. What a great way to start the weekend. And might I say, they are especially delicious tonight." He finished the first cookie and readied to begin eating a second.

"You can thank Cass," Ella shared proudly. "She made them."

Lucas froze and looked over at Cass. He put the pair of uneaten cookies back on their plate. "Really, Mom?" he whispered with a touch of frustration, then added more loudly, "I'll be going now."

With that declaration, he turned to depart, then paused and turned back around to find Ella and Cass still looking at him. He directed his attention towards the drifter.

"I almost left without asking *my* question of you," he said impatiently. He arched his eyebrow and stared directly. "What is your real name?"

Cass looked over at Ella and then back to Lucas.

"My name is Cass," she said hesitantly, as if anticipating a follow-up question. But Lucas had decided - he was in no mood for games.

"Well, *Cass*," he said with frustration. "I hope you have a restful night in Chimney Rock." With those parting words, he once again turned his back on them both and walked out the kitchen door.

CHAPTER
Seven

*A*s she lay alone in the cool darkness, she lifted her hand up in front of her. She was surprised to find that the hand was difficult to see, with just a dark grey outline of her palm and fingers visible against the faint starlight of the night sky. She had been reclining here, on this lounge chair on Ella's back porch, for what seemed like a long time.

At first she had tried to rest in the strange bed in the strange bedroom, but it had soon become obvious that sleep would not come. She had proceeded in her shorts and t-shirt and sock feet to the porch behind Ella's home and had been lying here since.

When she had first come out onto the porch, there had still been enough light, natural and artificial, for Cass to make out the cracked cushions on the lounge chair and the spider webs woven among the chair legs. Now, however, with the surrounding porch lights turned off and the moon retreated behind a cloudy sky, darkness enveloped her and all of Chimney Rock.

She wondered if it was now late at night or early morning. At some point, she would return inside and try again to sleep. She would curl up in that bed and try to close her eyes and allow the mechanical timekeeper to alert her in time for her new job. But she knew instinctively the time to go inside was not yet here.

The darkness felt thick, and Cass felt hidden. She was alone, cushioned between the layers of black and dark grey on all sides of her. She tracked the stars above her that were visible amongst the clouds, moving only her eyes while the rest of her body remained frozen and still. She heard crickets and frogs and wondered if they were near or far away. They, too, were invisible, hidden, and alone.

And then, there was another sound that reached Cass's ears, the sound of someone approaching. Footsteps that were making their way up the back porch and towards the kitchen door. A dark grey silhouette against the black backdrop, a man who had returned to check on his mother.

Even as Cass remained still, it appeared that the Chief had been alerted to her presence. He stopped walking and stood two feet from her. She could feel his glare. She wondered if he might speak, but knew there was nothing left to say. She knew why he was here.

She sat up, placed her legs over the side of the chair, steadied her balance, and then stood. Still in silence, she turned and fully faced him. She looked towards his face, which was shrouded in shadow. She imagined that his dark eyes were glaring into her own, so she turned her face as if looking at something of interest beyond Ella's porch.

Lucas turned and opened the door that led into the kitchen, then quietly walked into the home and headed towards his mother's room, using his cell phone to illuminate his pathway through the dark house. Cass watched him, first through the kitchen window, and then through Ella's bedroom window, his sparse illumination marking his progression as he stopped to watch his mother's peaceful slumber. After a few minutes, Lucas retreated from Ella's room, retraced his steps back to the outdoor porch, and softly closed and locked the kitchen door behind him.

Cass had remained standing in the same place this entire time and now watched him, still with the illuminated cell phone in his hand, approach her. He stopped a few feet from her and stood facing slightly away from her, looking off toward the mountain that hovered behind and over the home and the village. He turned the cell phone light off and stood still in the shadows.

"Why are you outside at one forty-five in the morning?" he asked quietly with a hint of suspicion in his voice.

She sensed that he had turned and was now looking her way. "I can't sleep," she shared softly, and truthfully.

Cass could make out his hand as it ran through his hair, could hear his breath as he exhaled loudly, as if in frustration. He turned away from her without another word and proceeded towards the stairs and then down, walking quickly now around the side of the porch to return to his home and to what Cass predicted might be his own sleepless night. As his steps retreated further from her, the sounds of crickets and frogs returned. She wondered if they had all been silent while he was here.

Then, for no reason that she could think of, Cass spoke.

"Cass," she said, loudly and clearly. She heard his footsteps stop. "Cass is my name," she continued, into the dark night. "And I promise, I *will* be gone, on May eighteenth. I will only stay until then. No longer. I will try not to be a burden. And between now and then, I won't hurt anyone. Especially your mom."

After a few seconds, she heard the footsteps resume, and then they were gone entirely. She unlocked the back door with the key that Ella had placed under the door mat and closed it behind her. She had no cell phone to light the way, nor moonlight through the windows to guide her footsteps. Nevertheless, she found safe passage through the strange home and into the bedroom which had once belonged to the beloved son. She turned on the reading lamp beside the bed and prepared to crawl under the covers, when suddenly she caught sight of her backpack in the corner.

Cass then remembered all the things she had meant to do this afternoon but hadn't done, due to almost being arrested. She retrieved the backpack and placed it closer to the side of the bed. She unzipped it and found several items that had made the trip with her, including a new, small stand-up calendar. She took off the plastic wrapping from the calendar and flipped it open to the month of May. She noticed that the picture that accompanied this month was of a cute, pure white kitten playing with a ball of yarn.

She found the date of "May 19" on the calendar and used her pen to place an X through it. In the corner of the May 19 square she wrote a small *1*, and then whispered quietly to herself.

"Day One."

She clicked shut the pen and set the calendar upright on the nightstand. She stared at the calendar a few seconds longer, then crawled into the bed, still wearing her shorts and t-shirt and socks. She checked to make sure the alarm clock was set for 4:45 a.m., then turned off the lamp.

She turned on her side, pulling her knees close to her chest and forming a tight ball with her long frame. She closed her eyes and drifted...

The little boy and the little girl are playing in the resort pool. It is a holiday weekend. The splash of water is suspended in mid-air. The children are in mid-laugh, looking at one another. They are loving. They are laughing. The sweet giggles of children.

The sounds are not frozen as is the image. The sounds are of voices, children's voices. Laughter and sweet giggles. The sounds change now, to those of a grown-up.

"You two get out of there. What did I tell you? It's time to get ready for the cookout."

The frame changes now to a new image. The woman has dark hair and green eyes, with magazines in one hand and two large pool towels in the other. She is standing beside the pool. She is frozen in a broad smile, a loving smile, filled with pride. The sounds are changing, the laughter becoming disappointed whines.

"We want to stay in here, Mommy," the children are now saying. "We're having fun."

The frame now dissolves into a picture of all three, the two children and the woman, and then a fourth person. A man. The children are wrapped in towels, hugging the woman, one on each side. The man is standing behind her, smiling as he gazes down. The woman's hands are around each of the little children, one around the little boy and one around the little girl. The woman's nose and face are nestled deep into the sweet neck of the little boy, giving him sweet kisses.

The woman is speaking now. "Don't worry, you'll have plenty more time in the pool. After all, it's a long weekend, and today is just day one."

Cass opened her eyes in the dark room and sought out the lamp. With hurried breaths she quickly turned on the bulb and proceeded to reach deep into her short's right pocket. She found the folded piece of paper and pulled it carefully out. Propping herself upright, she unfolded and gazed upon the drawing.

Peace.

She stared at the house. It was a small house that sat atop a hill, with a river flowing in front of it and mountains and hills behind it. A porch where she pictured herself rocking in a chair, looking out over the grassy hill, watching flowers as they bloom around her.

Focus. Peace.

Soon, the freeze frame images were no more. The faces and voices of someone in some time and in some place were gone. She was again hidden and alone.

"Good morning, Ella," Cass exclaimed as Ella entered the bakery through the home's connecting door. Ella looked almost startled at hearing another person's voice at this early hour of half past six in the morning, and looked equally out of sorts at having slept so late. "May I get you a cup of coffee?" Cass asked, as Ella began surveying the progress in the bakery.

Cass had woken up along with the alarm clock and had easily made it to the bakery by five, needing only a few minutes to brush her teeth and splash some cold water on her face. She had thrown on some clean undergarments along with her outfit from the night she had arrived, all now clean and fresh thanks to Ella's laundry room. She had pulled back her hair into a loose ponytail, secured it roughly with a hair tie, then washed and dried her hands. She had slipped on her cleaned socks and her one pair of shoes, and headed out of her bedroom. After walking down the hallway quietly, she had entered into the kitchen of the bakery and tied on her very own Walt's Bakery and Café apron.

Ella had left a detailed list on the bakery counter of the items to be prepared, along with the corresponding recipes and a very brief reminder of where everything was located. By half past five, Cass had found herself mixing up ingredients for the mountain blueberry muffins, with several items already made and several others in pans and ready for baking.

Cass continued working on the muffins as Ella responded to her question. "Yes, dear, I would absolutely love a cup of coffee, but only if you'll take a little break and enjoy one with me."

Ella was smiling so sweetly that Cass, who actually wished to keep working, couldn't say no. Cass found and poured two mugs full of piping hot coffee while Ella flipped the *Closed* sign to *Open* and unlocked the front door.

"I need to show you the ins and outs of the register today so that you can go ahead and open the café yourself," Ella called back over her shoulder. "After this morning, I may just be able to get used to this whole 'sleeping later' deal." Ella gave Cass a little wink and a chuckle, then led her to a small table near the front.

Only as she sat down did Cass notice the flour all over her apron, but Ella had apparently noticed it first. She was smiling again, but this time it was one filled with melancholy and memory.

"You're just like my Walter," Ella shared softly. "He put more flour on himself then he did in the batter. But, Lord, that man could bake. And cook. He just knew how to make everything taste so delicious, so I never really minded about the mess he made while doing so."

The two sat together and drank coffee and watched as more

people appeared along the sidewalks in front of the café. As the first customers of the day entered, Ella took their orders and processed their payment while Cass watched over Ella's shoulder. Before too long, Cass was back in the kitchen finishing up the last batch of buttery biscuits.

Ella had stayed busy during the early morning hours in the cafe, and now that Cass had completed Ella's baking list, she proceeded to the front counter to help Ella with customers. One such customer was Chief Lucas Montraine, who arrived on the sidewalk in front of the café a little before eight with a large, empty mug in his hand. He was not in uniform, and Cass was reminded of his discussion with Ella last evening. He had said something about working on her back porch or fixing things around her house or his house. He was dressed in blue jeans, a t-shirt, work boots and a Pepperdine ball cap.

Cass happened to see him before he actually came in the front door. She decided to retreat to the kitchen again, checking on the dishwasher and double-checking her cleaning job. From this vantage point, she could no longer see the café or its customers, and they could no longer see her.

While she proceeded to wipe down the counters, she could overhear Ella's enthusiastic greeting to her son. Both of their voices soon became hushed, but Cass could still make out a few phrases, such as his "didn't sleep a wink" and her "why do you worry so much about everything?" and his reference to a "drifter". Cass moved to the counter further away. She didn't wish to hear any more.

The morning progressed, the customers came and went, the sign was flipped back to *Closed*, and the first day at her new job was concluded. Leaving out the front and hearing Ella lock it behind her, she headed in the direction of The Treasure Chest, a local shop that Ella had recommended to her during their early conversations the day before.

The Treasure Chest was a quirky consignment shop housed in a small yellow building just a few blocks from the café. Entering through the front door, Cass found herself surrounded by shelves and racks of various items, most of which appeared at least gently worn or used. She scanned the shelves and saw glassware, intricately carved woodwork, pottery, and jewelry in locked display cases, all while noting the pleasant lavender smell of the room and the soft symphony music playing in the background.

Her vision landed on one particular jewelry case sitting atop a counter, and even as she attempted to look away, her eyes rebelliously resisted. They were locked on something, something that was sparkling. A pair of something shiny and glamorous.

The woman is following the teenage girl's gaze to the locked case, where teardrop earrings are on display. They are glimmering. The girl's gaze is fixed, fixed upon the lovely earrings. She has never seen them before. But she thinks they are very pretty. The woman is speaking. The girl is listening, even though her head does not turn.

"You already have earrings, and the ones you have will look just fine with your dress." Another voice is speaking now, but it is not the girl's voice. And it is not the woman's voice.

"Ah, c'mon, Mom."

The image changes, dissolves and evolves, and now the teenage boy is there with the woman and the girl. "You can see how much she likes them, Mom. She's practically hypnotized."

The image changes again. The girl is laughing at the boy. She loves his teasing, his sweet way of defending her even when no defense is needed. She loves his protection. She cherishes his love. The girl and the boy are laughing at each other, but the woman is not laughing. She is watching just one of them. She is watching just the girl. And the look on the woman's face is not laughter. It is something else.

Cass jolted as a middle-aged woman entered from a doorway towards the back of the large room and interrupted Cass's remembrance with a bellowing welcome.

"My goodness, I'm so sorry about your wait. How are you today?"

Cass was so grateful for the well-timed interruption that she enthusiastically replied, "I'm doing very well, thank you. I was told you may have some used clothing on consignment." She noticed the woman's bright pink nametag with "Justina" written in block letters. "We sure do," Justina stated as she turned towards a side door and motioned for Cass to follow. "Some really pretty things, in fact."

Several minutes later, Cass was checking out with four pairs of shorts, four t-shirts, two pairs of athletic leggings, and a fleece, hooded jacket. Pulling out a twenty-dollar bill from her cash roll, she handed the money to Justina and waited for her change. She was pleased that the entire lot of her newly acquired clothes had totaled just over sixteen dollars, primarily due to the shorts being marked on sale for fifty cents each.

As Justina began bagging the items, she paused with the jacket in her hand. "I know this is probably real warm and cozy," she stated gently, "but this fleece will soak up rain in no time. You may want to fetch one of the umbrellas we have for sale in that basket over there, just to be safe." She was pointing to a tall basket near the front door where umbrellas of every variety were gathered. "We tend to have afternoon showers pretty frequently," she added.

Cass looked at the basket then back to Justina. "I think I'll pass for now," Cass said, not unkindly, "but I'll certainly remember where to come if I find myself needing an umbrella." She took the bag and thanked Justina for her help.

Back on the sidewalk, Cass removed one of the pairs of leggings and looped it through the bag handles and around her waist, securing the bag and freeing her hands for the walk ahead. She then headed onward, down a slight decline, around the curves, beyond the village limits, and into the town of Lake Lure. She stayed on the main road, walking along the side and well away from the busy traffic that seemed in a hurry to go somewhere.

She was feeling tired from only a few hours of sleep last night. But more than physically, she felt the exhaustion mentally. She realized that *this* was why she was remembering, why the images were coming at her too frequently. She knew she was too weak. She determined that she had to be stronger. She had to focus.

She inhaled the cool air that she imagined drifted straight to her from the tops of the mountains. She studied the lines on the leaves, the pine needles on the ground. She looked up at the sky, at the shapes of the dark clouds approaching. She looked out at the lake, up ahead and getting closer. She noticed the waves being whipped up by the strengthening wind and then watched as those same waves formed patterns in rhythmic order across the beach. She saw the rain ahead, advancing in a dark curtain of downpour that left the road behind it dark and sleek. She saw people scattering, on the beach and in nearby parking lots, trying to find shelter in order to escape the impending storm.

She predicted that she was now three or four miles from Ella's home, and knew she would soon need to turn around to arrive back at Ella's before dark. There, she would eat a protein bar for her dinner, mark an X through May 20 on her calendar, and conclude her Day Two in restless, sleepless solitude.

She decided, however, that she wouldn't turn around yet. Not quite yet. Her legs continued their walking, and she soon felt the cool rain upon her face and her shoulders. The rain intensified all around her and the storm made its presence known with a thunderous boom that echoed across the rocks and throughout the gorge.

She walked on, keeping her eyes on the mountains that surrounded the lake. These were great mountains that had stood for generations and had transcended history and family. As she witnessed their grandeur, she also accepted her own state of being. She was entirely alone now, for all others had found shelter from the storm. They were all somewhere that they thought would be safe.

Alone, she again looked out towards the mountains. But now, even these were hidden from her, behind an unyielding curtain of dark mist and water.

Summer

CHAPTER

Eight

Lucas aimed carefully, took a deep breath, and then propelled the dart forward. The bursting sound of the targeted balloon was followed by the squeals of young children. This was his third balloon in a row, which meant he was now the proud recipient of a small, stuffed purple snake. He turned and saw the crowd of children who had been intently watching his throwing prowess and cheering him on every step of the way. In the front, smiling broadly, were two of his biggest fans. Juney and Jacob.

"Is that purple snake for me, Chiefth?" Juney's missing teeth made for a most unusual greeting each time she saw Lucas. He looked around and saw that the other kids, aside from these two, had scattered off to their families or to other games. He decided to happily grant her request, with conditions.

"Well, Juney, I would love to give you this snake, but first you have to promise me that you two will stop wandering off into the woods. Your mom told me that she had to come looking for you yesterday, when you both went exploring, looking for a windmill or something. You know that's very scary to your mom, right?" Lucas paused for effect and noticed that both of the children looked a little hurt by this gentlest of reproaches, Juney to the point of soft tears forming in her eyes. Lucas knelt down and hugged her, then brought Jacob in for a hug with the other free hand.

"Chief's not mad, okay? I'm just asking if you both will be careful. And not wander off?" He saw both of them look at each other and then sweetly nod their heads in affirmation. This gesture made Lucas smile, which in turn led to smiles on the children's faces. All was well again.

Handing the snake to Juney, Lucas looked at Jacob. "I'll try to win you one later on, buddy." Jacob was hugging Juney and looking along with her at the purple snake, so lost in the enjoyment of her gift that he didn't even react to Lucas's offer.

Lucas watched them and remembered when they were born. He had been home then, on his summer break from college. Margie and her husband, Ray, had traveled back and forth, to Asheville, where the twins lay for months in the prenatal unit. By the time Lucas had moved back home, Ray had already abandoned Margie. Apparently he couldn't handle the stress and exhaustion of family life.

Lucas had enjoyed watching these two as they had grown and still had distinct memories of both of them as they started talking in sentences, saying his name, and running to him for hugs. They were affectionate to everyone they met, but seemed especially so towards him. They had even chosen him to write about for their Kindergarten assignment on "A Person I am Thankful For." He still had the two pictures they had drawn and rudimentary sentences they had written, framed and on display in his house.

Leaving behind the sweet memories, Lucas looked up to see Margie approaching and prompted the two children to turn around. As they did so and saw their mother, they both went running off joyfully, leaping with delight as they showed her the purple snake.

Lucas called after them, "Remember what I said about staying close to home." Margie grinned and looked up, waving appreciatively towards Lucas, then walking off towards the rides with the bubbly siblings in tow.

Now looking around the entire field, Lucas noticed how large the crowd had grown in just the last hour. The annual Lake Lure Founder's Day Festival appeared to be in full swing. He predicted that many of the town's residents, as well as lots of visitors and tourists, were now enjoying the games, rides, live music, and food trucks that were all crowded into the modest community area near the lake.

He had scheduled most of his police force to be here, not just because of the large crowd, but primarily because it was great for building a sense of community. He now had ten officers on his force, including himself, but anticipated a vacancy in a month or two. Officer Rebekah Rinehart, one of his best officers, would be getting married over the winter. Lucas predicted that she and her new husband would be returning to her hometown, which was somewhere in Kansas, to help care for her aging parents. He anticipated that filling her spot would come with the usual challenges associated with recruiting the best officers to this small mountain community.

In addition to Officer Rinehart, there was Sargent Tim Sturgis, Sargent Randall Goodall, Officer Sam Abernathy, Officer Joe Alexander, Officer Liya Henderson, Officer John "Tank" Nixon, Officer Michael Craig, and Lucas's Deputy Chief, Farley McSwain. He and Farley had known each other since middle school, and even though they were nothing but professional while executing their professional duties, while off duty they often hung out as the best friends they were.

Scanning the crowd, Lucas spotted a few of his team members easily. Officers Henderson and Craig were walking near the food truck row, intermingling with visitors and monitoring the crowd. Farley, meanwhile, was busy trying to win his toddler, Austin, a toy guitar from the "ring the bottle" booth. Lucas continued scanning to his right, across the festival field and along the public beach and over towards the inn. He spotted Officer Nixon out in the road, directing new arrivals as to where to park and aptly navigating other traffic that was simply passing by. Lucas turned his attention back to the left, back across the field and the crowd of thousands, back towards the western tip of the lake that happened to point towards his police department.

And then he saw her. Cass.

The last three weeks since her arrival had been a time of significant stress for Lucas. In those early days, he had been confident that he would quickly discover who Cass was and why she was here. Disappointingly, he had been unable to track down anything about her. Back when she first arrived, he had stayed up all night for several nights in a row, scouring law enforcement databases, reaching out to fellow police chiefs, searching through missing person reports, and all to no avail. He had even gone to the trouble of contacting local hospitals for any information on patients who may have abruptly left the psych ward, but all had appeared to be counted and present.

And so, here she is.

Standing alone on the outskirts of the festival, she appeared to him to be watching the activity, moving her vision to the game booths and then to the stage where young tap dancers were now entertaining the crowd. He noted as he watched her that she was wearing the same general outfit that she was always wearing whenever he had seen her during the past few weeks: a t-shirt, a pair of shorts, and her sneakers. At this point, he was fairly convinced that these were the only outfits the stranger owned.

He assumed she had worked at the bakery early that morning, just like every Saturday since she had been here. He also assumed that after work she had proceeded to have her usual protein bar for lunch before setting out for her walk, which on most days appeared to last somewhere between six and eight hours.

Many of the details he now knew about Cass he had learned through Ella. For example, although Ella often offered to cook Cass breakfast or dinner or to whip her up a quick lunch at the café, Cass rarely accepted these offers. She appeared to prefer a meal of a protein shake or bar while walking by herself along the road. The few times Cass had accepted Ella's offer of a meal, Lucas had made it a point not to join.

Other details he now knew about Cass, however, he had discovered on his own. In the few brief encounters he had had with her, he had noted that she spoke very little. Ella described her as quiet and thoughtful. Lucas tended to think more in terms of suspicious and secretive.

Another thing he had noted quite early on but had refused to believe until he could confirm it was that Cass did not own a cell phone. Or, as Lucas preferred to consider, did not let anyone know that she owned a cell phone.

Lucas had added these observations among others to his note pad list, which had gradually grown in length over the weeks since he had first met her. Even so, he was disappointed to have to admit to himself that he was no closer to answering any questions about exactly who she was and what she wanted than he had been on that first day.

He turned his attention from her and focused again on the crowd. Someone with a megaphone was announcing something near the contest area.

"Chief! They're calling for us," shouted Farley from quite a distance away. "Time for the race."

Great, Lucas thought to himself. It was time for his most dreaded part of this weekend. Some Police Chief many years ago had thought it was a grand idea for the Chief and his Deputy to participate against other citizens and even children in the festival's three-legged race competition, which had led to a request for the same pair to participate the following year, and the year after that. This race entry had been such a hit that the Police Chief's participation in the event had become somewhat of a town tradition.

This would be Lucas's second time racing as the Police Chief of Lake Lure, and third time overall, counting the one time he had done so as the Deputy. He honestly wanted to be a good sport, but wondered if there was any organized race in the whole world that made two people look goofier than a three-legged race. And having to "hug" Farley as they made their way down the racing field was, to Lucas, just a perfect icing on the cake. As he started walking towards the race area, he had just one thought on his mind. *The sooner I get there, the sooner this will be over with.*

Lucas reached the competition area and put on a cheerful grin, giving every outward appearance that he had waited all day just for this opportunity. Farley was already at the starting line with a Velcro leg wrap in hand, ready for his partner to join him and sporting a silly smile across his face.

As the other racers gathered around their respective lanes, Farley and Lucas sized up the competition. Most were teens and children, but there were also a few serious-looking adult pairs, all of whom appeared to be sizing up the two police officers as the team to beat.

If only they knew, thought Lucas with a muted chuckle. He and his deputy had come in last place last year as they had attempted this endeavor. Apparently they both had two left feet and a general lack of coordination to boot.

Farley secured the Velcro strap tightly around their lower legs, Lucas's right and Farley's left. The two stood side by side at the start line, waiting for the other teams to ready themselves in the same fashion. It appeared the race may be starting in a minute or two.

Lucas heard Farley's phone ding with a text alert, then watched as his friend read it. Farley's smile disappeared, replaced by a look of concern. Suddenly, Farley was crouched, unlatching the Velcro strap and readying to depart.

"Sorry, Luke. Kaley just called. Austin fell coming off the bouncy slide and busted his lip. He's pitchin' a fit and she needs my help." Farley finished disconnecting his leg from Lucas's leg, dropped the Velcro to the ground, and anxiously jogged away towards the children's play area.

The megaphone announcer was readying the competitors now. "All teams to the line, please. I'll count down from three to one, then listen for the horn as your start signal."

Lucas watched as the other pairs approached the line where he now stood alone. He looked down at his right leg where the Velcro strap lay. He started to bend down to retrieve it so he could move aside and out of the way, when suddenly he saw another leg appear beside his. A person was crouched down, securing a left leg to his right one, pulling the Velcro tight and fastening the hooks.

The megaphone announcer shouted, "Three!"

The person was standing upright now, looking straight ahead towards the finish line. Lucas, however, was looking at the side of her face. He felt her left arm reach around his waist, felt her hand as it clasped onto his shirt.

"Two...," the announcer called. The spectators appeared fully enthralled with the drama of the countdown.

She was silent, looking straight ahead, and now, he too, looked straight ahead and readied himself for the race. Without thinking, his right arm reached up and over her shoulders, found her waist, and settled there in a loose embrace of her shirt and skin underneath.

The announcer yelled, "One!"

Cass turned her face slightly upward and towards his and whispered softly, "Outside legs first."

The horn blasted. The race started. And the Police Chief, surrounded on all sides by dust and racers and noise, sprinted towards the finish, moving in perfect tandem with his racing partner.

Crossing the finish line in first place, Lucas was not prepared for the reaction from the crowd, one that seemed a mixture of disbelief and euphoria. He realized immediately that he had greatly underestimated the degree to which he was a "hometown hero" of sorts, a person for whom people naturally rooted.

After crossing the finish line, several people had congratulated him, hugging him and patting him on the back. When he had looked down to unleash their Velcro tether, he had found that she had already done so and had departed. The announcer inquired where the rest of his team was, but she had disappeared after the race as quickly as she had appeared prior to.

The Mayor made a big deal of the trophy presentation, calling Lucas up on a medal dais and giving him the small team trophy. He was their Chief, and now their three-legged race champion. He would have laughed out loud if not for the fact that children were watching him, seemingly in awe of him. Many adored him, he felt it now, and finally they had seen their Chief win this silly competition.

The remainder of the festival activities proceeded without a hitch. Farley's son calmed down and eventually went back to playing, having suffered a little of a swollen lip but nothing more. Juney and Jacob got their bellies full of cotton candy. Singers and dancers wowed the festival-goers. Lucas won a green stuffed frog for Jacob, and the whole day ended with a nighttime fireworks display over the lake.

As Lucas headed towards his house on Boys Camp Road, he felt the exhaustion that was a result of this full day at the festival. He had arrived at the festival site around eight that morning, and was now approaching his driveway at a few minutes past ten. He couldn't wait to shower and collapse in his bed. Except...

He had been thinking about the race all evening. He had been wondering why Cass had done that. He was confused as to what could possibly compel a stranger to place herself in that position, with someone she barely knew. He had questioned where she had even come from and had even contemplated the creepy possibility that she had been watching him all along.

He pulled into his driveway, sat for a few minutes in his squad car, then backed up and out, driving back down the road and then turning right towards Chimney Rock. A few minutes later, he was parking his truck in front of the café. He grabbed the trophy, stepped out of the car and proceeded to the back porch steps.

Even before walking up onto the porch, he knew she was there. The moon was bright this evening, and he could clearly make out Cass laying on the lounge chair, one arm behind her head and the other across her abdomen as she gazed, stone still, at the night sky.

He walked towards the chair and she turned her head towards

him. His plan was to stand beside the lounger and question her, but he couldn't bring himself to begin. It was something about her position, the arm behind her head, and the expression on her face. She looked *peaceful*.

He hesitated.

Cass sat up and draped her legs over the side of the chair, apparently ready to stand. Before she could do so, however, Lucas pulled a chair over from the table behind him, and, placing it a few feet from her, sat down.

She watched him now, the *peaceful* look on her face replaced by her normal one, a look of polite and cautious indifference. He returned the gaze and held eye contact with her in silence, then held the trophy towards her.

"You left before the awards ceremony," he said, with a friendliness in his voice that surprised even him.

She looked at the trophy, then reached out to take and hold it. She stared at it, then at him, then outstretched her hand to return it to him. "Congratulations, Chief Montraine."

Lucas stood. "You keep it," he said gently. "I'm pretty sure you're the reason we won." He was actually pleased that she didn't argue with this decision. Instead, he watched as she grinned a little to herself and stood up.

"Then in that case, thank you." She said these words nonchalantly, but also with enough sincerity that it appeared she was almost touched by the gesture. She turned and walked towards the door that led into the home.

Lucas then remembered that he had come here for one specific reason, one particular question.

"Why did you do it?" he called, as she made her way towards the door.

She stopped and turned around, and he watched as her eyes took on the kindest and gentlest of expressions. He could tell that she was thinking of how to respond, and then finally, she did.

"You were alone," she said, with a tinge of sadness. She turned and opened the door to retreat into the home with their trophy, stepping over the threshold and allowing the screen door to close behind her. But before it closed completely, Lucas heard an additional statement, one that she said quietly as if speaking only to herself. "In this world, a police officer should never be alone."

CHAPTER

Nine

*C*ass awoke earlier than the alarm sounded, adjusting to the darkness of the room before turning on the bed lamp. She sat up and then remembered something significant from the evening before. Turning her attention to the corner table she noticed the small trophy, with a plastic statuette of two golden runners atop it. She smiled slightly while looking at the trophy but then felt the smile fading as an image approached.

The teenage boy and the teenage girl are sitting at a table, dressed up in church clothes. The girl is wearing a lilac dress with high wedges on her feet. She has light pink painted toenails peeking out from the front of the new shoes. The boy is in a white shirt, a navy jacket and lilac tie. They look like a matching set. The woman and the man are sitting at the table as well, and in the frozen frame all are smiling. The voices are talking all at once as the group of four admires two trophies sitting in the middle of the table. The male high school athlete of the year. The female high school athlete of the year. It is the first time in the history of the school that two siblings have won the two prestigious awards. There is pride in the father's voice.

Cass reached under the covers to find her pocket, then reconsidered. She quickly retreated from her bed and went to the trophy, holding it up and focusing her mind on the events of last evening: the excited crowd, the quartet she had heard singing on the stage, little children with stuffed animals clutched in their arms, and the three-legged race. She focused on the details of each of these, her immediate memories. The ones that were allowed. Quickly the frozen image dissipated.

After showering and dressing in a clean t-shirt and shorts, Cass headed to the bakery. Even though it was Sunday and the bakery was closed, Cass wanted to take a careful inventory for Ella and help her with the shopping list for the upcoming week. This was a function that Ella usually performed, but today was the third and final day of the Founder's Day Festival Weekend and there was some type of auction for which Ella had signed up to volunteer.

Having completed the inventory less than an hour later, Cass returned quietly to the bedroom. She retrieved the small book of short stories that she had found in the dresser near the bed and departed the house. Walking away from downtown and towards Lake Lure, Cass soon found herself sitting on a small bench at the bridge garden, a little area that was contained entirely on an old bridge that once was used to connect the village to the town. It was summertime, and the garden was adorned with a lovely variety of evergreens and annuals. Groups of butterflies danced around the blooms and the old bridge was covered in vibrant splashes of color and motion.

Eventually, she left the solitude of the garden and quickly walked back to Ella's. Entering the kitchen door, she saw a huge picnic basket sitting on the kitchen counter, tied with a shiny blue ribbon that was secured on the top with a golden bow. She walked around the small home and, noticing that she appeared to be alone, concluded that Ella was still at her own church and would most likely return a little past noon.

Cass decided to use this time just as she had on the other

Sundays since her arrival. She started with the furniture, dusting and polishing each piece in the living room and two bedrooms. She stood on a chair and dusted the ceiling fan, then vacuumed the carpet in the living room. She went outside to the back porch, swept the leaves and twigs from the deck, neatly arranged the chairs and tables, and watered the plants that were scattered here and there around the porch's perimeter. She was careful to give extra water to the vibrant pink and orange impatiens that Ella had planted in boxes attached on the porch railings.

Cass returned inside and continued a steady progression of chores and general cleaning until the moment came shortly after noon that the kitchen door opened. A few minutes later, the two women were together on the back porch, enjoying Ella's homemade pimento cheese sandwiches, coleslaw, and chilled, sweet tea.

Ella used the first few minutes of their lunch together to exclaim several times her appreciation for Cass's Sunday morning cleaning. "I just can't tell you enough what a delight it is to come home from church to a sparkling clean house, but you don't have to do that. You know that, right?"

"Yes, Ella, I know that." Cass grinned a little as she recalled having this exact same conversation with Ella each Sunday for the past three Sundays. "So, tell me about this festival event that you're involved in today."

Ella finished chewing and replied, "Well, you know the Founder's Day event is a weekend affair. It officially kicked off Friday evening with a bicycle race up Chimney Rock Mountain. Then yesterday, of course, was the big festival."

Ella paused briefly, looking to her side and over the porch railing. She seemed deep in thought, but soon placed her sandwich on her plate as if readying to continue her sharing. "Even though I've never actually lived in the Town of Lake Lure, we're so close by and have been for so many years that my family and I have always participated in the different activities at the festival. When our son joined the police force, and, of course, Walter had passed away by that point, well, I just wanted to do my part to help out. And now my son just happens to be the Police Chief, so I try to volunteer in any way I can. That includes organizing the auction today, which, if my watch is telling time correctly, is going to be starting soon." Ella took a sip of tea, wiped her mouth, and pushed her chair from the table. "Since I'm the person in charge, I better head over there."

Cass stood and started gathering the dishes. "Here, let me take care of these so you can go ahead and leave for your event," she said, but Ella was working to clear the table as well.

"What do you mean 'so you can leave'?" Ella asked as she took a pile of dishes hurriedly to the kitchen sink. She gave them a quick rinse and left them to air dry. "I counted on your help at the auction. If you don't have other plans, I sure could use it."

Moments later, Cass found herself again at the festival grounds, where another large crowd had gathered to enjoy the same games and rides and food trucks that were in place the day before. Today, however, there was a special area designated as the "Sunday Picnic Auction", where Cass was now helping Ella in placing lovely pastel tablecloths on long rectangular tables. The tables themselves had been arranged in the shape of a gigantic square, with the ends butted up lengthwise for all except one table. It was within this square that people could walk and view the contents placed upon them. As the tablecloths were laid down, participants soon began approaching, setting down picnic baskets tied up with ribbons and bows.

As Ella explained, this was a tradition that had begun just a couple of years ago, but one that had quickly grown into a crowd favorite. As Cass understood it, bidders would have the opportunity to bid on a particular basket without knowing the contents of the basket. The winner of each basket's auction would then be treated to a Sunday picnic, on that very day, by the sponsor of the basket. The sponsor's job included not only packing a great picnic, but also standing on stage with the basket during the bidding process.

Ella also explained that there were three rules that applied to this affair. First, there was absolutely no peeking allowed. Second, a bid of five hundred dollars would automatically secure the bidder the basket of their choice. And finally, all picnics were required to be completed on that very day, come rain or shine. All proceeds from the auction were earmarked for the Lake Lure Police Department Scholarship Fund, a small but growing scholarship that was given each year to local high school students who had future aspirations to pursue a career in law enforcement.

Cass could see that, already, most of the tables were covered with baskets. Ella was busy with a clipboard making note of the entries and placing numbered tags on each. In looking around, Cass spotted Ella's large picnic basket across the square viewing area, complete with the giant blue and gold ribbon and bow.

At three o'clock sharp, the Annual Founder's Day Sunday Picnic Auction began. First up was the basket that had been randomly selected for the initial slot, sponsored by an elderly man named Edward Manning. Mr. Manning quietly picked his basket up from the table and proceeded to slowly walk up onto the stage. The Lake Lure Parks and Recreation Director, Todd Somerville, turned a mic on and, from the side of the stage and behind a podium, began the auction.

"Do I hear twenty dollars?" the auctioneer asked enthusiastically. "Twenty dollars for a Sunday picnic with Mr. Manning?"

Cass heard someone in the crowd yell, "Twenty!" to a scattering of excited laughter. Then there was a "twenty-five" and a "twenty-seven".

Cass reached into her shorts' pockets. In the right was the drawing of her *peace*. In the left, a small container of Vaseline for her chapped lips and a pair of sunglasses. She regretted not bringing along a few dollars from her backpack cash. Not for the purpose of bidding or picnicking, but simply for a donation to the cause.

Gradually, the picnic baskets on the tables dwindled as entry after entry made its way to the stage and was secured by a winning bidder. Margie had a beautiful basket up for bid, adorned with purple and pink ribbons and a giant unicorn stuffed animal on the top. As her number was called out, Margie took the basket onto the stage with Juney and Jacob walking beside her, a clear indication that bidders were bidding on a picnic experience with all three. The basket was soon won with a bid of forty-three dollars by Shirley Cannon, Margie's colleague from the real estate office.

Cass was surprised that the crowd around the auction had stuck around in such large numbers for the entirety of the event. Eyeing the tables, she could see that only a few baskets remained. One by one, the last few baskets were claimed, until only one, a large basket with a blue ribbon and a gold bow, remained.

The crowd seemed excited. Cass was as well. Because she had lived in Ella's home for close to a month now and had eaten some of Ella's home-cooked meals, Cass could understand why it now appeared that Ella's sponsored basket was the premier auction item to be won.

"And now, for the last basket of the day, the one many of you ladies have been waiting for." Todd announced this to the muted squeals of several females in the crowd. "Basket number twenty-four, sponsored by ..."

Cass watched as Ella picked up her large basket and handed it off to a man dressed in black dress slacks, with a starched white shirt and black tie. He walked up the steps, onto the stage, and faced the crowd.

"Chief Lucas Montraine!"

"One hundred dollars!" yelled a voice from the crowd.

"Well, that was quick," followed Todd with a chuckle. "We have a bid of one hundred. Do I hear one twenty-five?"

"One hundred twenty-five dollars," yelled another bidder. Then, "One hundred forty," from yet another.

Cass listened to the various bids and watched the excitement grow as the amount increased. She turned and looked at the Chief, still standing on stage, as he peered out over the crowd. She noticed how the white shirt drew contrast to his tanned skin. She noticed how his black hair was combed to the side, slightly onto his forehead, which Cass determined made him appear younger. She thought he looked uncomfortable, but willing to be so.

"One eighty." This latest bid had been called out by a woman standing with a group of young women near Cass, all of whom had pooled their money and intended on joining in together on the picnic. The crowd oohed and awed at this latest bid.

Todd announced, "We have a bid of one hundred eighty dollars. Going once, going twice..."

"Five hundred," a soft voice called out, not from the crowd but from the side of the stage. The crowd silenced as Ella stepped forward, with cash in hand, ready to claim her own basket.

As Cass would learn a few minutes later, what had just unfolded was a little bit of a tradition in and of itself. Even before Chief Montraine was Chief, even back in the days when he was still Officer Montraine, Ella would make Lucas Montraine's basket then, more likely than not, find a way to win it.

Cass had noticed the Chief's relieved expression as Ella made the winning bid. He had smiled widely, showing straight white teeth and a slight dimple on his right cheek.

Why have I never noticed his smile? She realized she had never noticed it because he had never smiled, at least when she was around.

Now that the auction was over, Cass quickly got to work on the tablecloths, folding each one carefully and placing them in a plastic tub. Afterwards, she began breaking down the rectangular tables, carrying each to a trailer that was hooked up behind a tractor.

"Cass!" Ella called out from near the stage. "Leave the rest of those to the others and come over here for a minute." Ella was still standing near the stage, sealing up the money and checks from the auction bids and smiling widely as Cass approached.

"We made over sixteen hundred dollars today," Ella exclaimed.

"Sixteen hundred!"

"That's amazing, Ella. And it looked like everyone had a great time."

"Oh, the good times are just starting, Cass," Ella shared with excitement and a little exhaustion in her voice. "Now all of the picnic basket winners are getting treated to their picnics. They will be spread out all over town by this point, some sitting on blankets on grass, others at picnic tables, and still others on boats or in canoes. I just love hearing the stories afterwards of what the food was and where the locations were." Ella looked sweetly out over the festival grounds and beyond as she shared the description, and then went back to packing up some supplies into a box nearby.

"I suspect you already know what food you'll be having," Cass said with a subtle grin, "but do you have any idea where the location might be for your special picnic with Chief Montraine?"

Ella stopped her packing and looked up at Cass, taking her hand and patting it softly. "I have no idea as to the location, but I'm sure you'll tell me when you get back. I have a Women's Club meeting this evening that I can't get out of, so I actually bought the picnic basket for you."

Ella released Cass's hand and began walking away. "Oh, and you best get going," she called over her shoulder. "It looks like Lucas is waiting."

CHAPTER

Ten

What the hell, Mom?

She was approaching his truck, and his mom, in the distance, was driving off in her grey Camry. Lucas brought his attention again to Cass and followed her progression towards him. He put two and two together and took a deep breath.

So this is who I will be picnicking with? That's just great.

Cass stopped a few feet from where he was standing. She was wearing a t-shirt and shorts and her usual sneakers.

What a shocker, he thought, feeling suddenly ridiculous in his dress slacks and white collared shirt and dress shoes. He decided he didn't care. The auction had done incredibly well, and his "dress up" was part of the expected drama. He had thought he would be picnicking with Ella, *as they had agreed,* but there was nothing he could do about that presently. Cass had been sent in her place, and with only two choices before him, to proceed on the picnic or to blow her off, he decided his parents had raised him better than to do the latter.

This is going to be so awkward.

She stood in front of him, waiting silently. He thought about his note pad back at his house and the growing list of descriptors and clues. But his thoughts were interrupted by memories of the day before, of running down the field tethered to her leg, with her hand tightly about his waist. She had gone so fast and pushed forward with such strength, he had found it exhausting to even keep up.

Lucas looked out over the water of the lake, beyond her. This could be miserable or it could possibly be almost bearable. He decided to get through it, in gratitude for her help the previous day and for the potential information he might gather about the person herself.

"Well, it looks like you and I will be celebrating our race win yesterday in grand style," he said abruptly and a little uncomfortably, holding up the picnic basket for emphasis. She, on the other hand, didn't appear to him to be uncomfortable at all. In fact, as he said this, she looked slightly curious. She grinned a little as she looked at him, then his truck, then the picnic basket in hand.

After some polite conversation regarding what each had done that day and the weather and the general sights and sounds of their drive, Lucas was soon parking in downtown Chimney Rock. The conversation so far had felt to Lucas a bit forced, but he was relieved that at least it hadn't been silence. They both exited the truck, and with the picnic basket in tow he led the way down a dirt path. The path led them behind shops and restaurants, away from the road, and towards the roaring river below.

This particular area beside the river was one of his favorite spots, and had been since he was a little boy. *That's why I chose it for my mom's picnic,* he thought, with a twinge of disappointment. In planning the picnic he had thought of somewhere that might be special for his mom as well as for himself, which had made this spot, at which he had so many special memories with both of his parents, the ideal location for this year's picnic.

Growing up with the river flowing behind his home, Lucas had always just assumed that the river was actually part of his backyard. After the vigorous rain storm that had come in the middle of the previous night, the river was now high and flowing with great speed. He watched as it crashed over and around the huge rocks laid throughout it, creating a thunderous yet calming noise. He found the sight and sound of it mesmerizing, but also haunting.

He glanced behind and saw that she was following him. She looked up and their eyes met, but with her eyes now drawn from the path she veered too closely to the bushes that bordered it. Suddenly she grimaced as her fingers caught on something in the bushes. She was visibly upset at first and then, noticing him watching her, she seemed to quickly regain her composure.

Looking ahead again, he spotted the small round table he had set up earlier in the afternoon on the flat bank of the river, with two folding chairs propped up against it to hold down a plaid tablecloth. He placed the basket on the table and proceeded to open it, randomly removing items and placing them on the table.

He was surprised when she stepped up beside him and started setting the table even as he was placing the items out of the basket onto it. She took the plates from his hand and distributed them in front of each chair, followed by the silverware and napkin placement. She removed tops of Tupperware dishes and placed a serving spoon in each. She lifted the pitcher of tea and poured it into each of two cups while he held them in mid-air.

She's acting like we're long-lost buddies. Wait, does she think we're friends?

He knew it should feel weird, the way she was helping him and the close proximity in which she was standing near him. But he wasn't feeling weird. He realized that what he *was* feeling was... relaxed. She sat down in a chair, and he sat as well.

Ella had gone all out with her preparation for the picnic. Lucas appreciated that she had made many of his favorites, including chicken salad croissants and Froggy Biscuits for dessert. Cass appeared to enjoy the food selections as well, but was more focused on what Lucas was saying rather than what food he was offering for the meal.

An hour passed and they were still eating their food. He was perplexed as to why this picnic was taking so long, then realized that the progression in eating was being so steadily interrupted by conversation that it was almost impossible to get one bite down. Cass had started the meal conversation with a question about his childhood in this village, followed by questions pertaining to where he had attended school, what his interests were, and what life had been like growing up in the bakery. As soon as he answered one question, she would ask another.

During his responses she was highly attentive, apart from the three or four times that he found her staring at her pricked finger from the bush incident earlier. She seemed somewhat consumed with dabbing blood gently from it and rubbing it as if to comfort herself. It seemed to Lucas like a disproportionate amount of attention for such a small prick on one's finger. The fourth time she did this, he paused his response mid-sentence.

"You know, you probably caught your finger on a Firethorn Bush. They're all over the place around these mountains." Lucas pointed towards the bank for emphasis. "Those thorns hurt like a bitch when ..." He trailed off as he remembered to whom he was speaking. The informality of his statement seemed suddenly very out of place.

For her part, however, Cass seemed amused by his choice of words. "Your description is spot on. It really, really hurts." She dabbed at it again, looking more perplexed than in pain. "Also," she continued as she studied the tiny prick on her finger, "I tend to overreact when anything cuts into my skin. I'm not sure why." She tore her eyes from her finger and appeared to regain her focus on their conversation.

As they reengaged in the active dialogue, Lucas was surprised to find that Cass didn't shy away from questions about his father. So often people did, but not her. She knew he had died, but she still wanted to know as much as Lucas was willing to share, and he was surprised to learn that he was actually willing to share quite a bit. At one point she took a bite of pasta salad and Lucas figured this was his opportunity to pose his own questions, and to finally add some new information to his note pad.

"So, what school did you attend?" Lucas asked.

Cass looked out over the water and responded in a friendly tone. "It would be quite a ways from here. I doubt you would have heard of it." She grinned in a way that said *I answered your question but please don't ask for more detail.*

Shockingly to Lucas, he didn't.

After their meal was concluded, they worked together to pack the dishes and food containers back into the basket. Cass folded up the chairs while Lucas packed the tablecloth and folded up the table. He knew the picnic was now over and felt relieved that their time together would soon end.

Then he heard himself say, "Would you like to walk across the rocks and hang out in the middle of the river for a while?"

What the hell?

She was looking out at the water, grinning ever so slightly. He took that as a yes. He walked a few feet towards the river and found a good spot to reach a huge rock, one of hundreds that bordered the river bank and were spread throughout the water. He stepped across several smaller rocks well into the water, then reached a slightly larger one. He stepped off the rock onto a second, then onto a third. He knew he could do this in his sleep, but then wondered.

How long has it been since I've actually been out here. Before college? Maybe during middle school?

He stepped up onto another huge rock, then another. He was now on a rock that was almost to the midway point of the river's span. It was then that he remembered someone else, a person he had forgotten to check on during his hurried progression over the rocks. He looked back to find that she had made it over the first and second larger rocks and was now on the third, appearing to be confused as to how to safely get to the fourth. She seemed focused on gaining her balance enough to spread one leg safely across the distance between the rocks.

He recalled that even though she was tall, he was taller. His legs were longer. He silently chastised himself for not thinking of that beforehand. He went back to the fourth rock. She looked up and saw him and seemed relieved. He held out his hand and she took it eagerly. Soon they were on the fourth, then the fifth and final rock together.

He sat, and she sat as well. Even though this rock was broad enough to hold ten people, she sat down very close to him. He assumed she was a little worried or even scared. He assumed it was her first time being on a rock in the middle of a river.

They sat in silence and looked out over the river as it headed east. It would wind its way through the village and then beyond to join somewhere in the distance with Lake Lure. The sun was now beginning its gradual descent across the western sky behind them, reflecting against the mountains and producing lovely splotches of orange and dark yellow. These colors appeared to be sitting atop the mountain ranges ahead, adding halos of majesty to the already majestic.

Lucas's thoughts drifted to his father.

Did we sit on this same rock, Dad?

He became lost in memory. Not the happy kind of memory that would sometimes make him shake his head and laugh. This was the crippling kind, the kind that paralyzed, that hurt in places rendered hollow and empty.

"This is a special place for you."

He had forgotten there was another person on the rock, forgotten until he heard her voice whispering, somehow completely detectable and clear over the rushing water mere feet below. She had said it not as a question, but as a statement, with a quiet reverence of someone who wishes another to know that they have discovered a secret. He turned to look at her and found she was looking straight ahead, at the water. He did not respond to her statement. It was too raw to acknowledge. He had no wish to start feeling melancholy, and certainly not while stuck on a rock with her.

Her.

Who the hell is she? And why is she here, on this rock? With me?

He suddenly felt tired of always having questions that never seemed answered. She was here with him now. And there was nowhere for her to go, not without his help.

Perhaps I should know a few of your secrets as well.

"This is your first time in Chimney Rock," he stated nonchalantly, still looking at the side of her face while she looked out over the water. He saw her head nod slightly, and took this as her affirmation. He also noticed her right hand, which had been spread flat against the rock, was now slightly tensed and beginning to ball up, almost nervously. He sensed that she was anticipating, was preparing to dodge and to avoid. He thought of how to make her as uncomfortable as he could, how to catch her off guard. Interrogation with lawbreakers was easy enough. This would most likely be a cakewalk.

He looked away from her, back to the water. He waited. He glanced over and watched her hand relax again against the rock. There were no rings on her fingers, no polish on her fingernails. The nails were clipped down and clean, but nothing else adorned her, nothing other than her plain yellow t-shirt, her black shorts, and her tennis shoes. The shoes themselves looked relatively worn, which seemed reasonable considering how much he saw her walking every day. His eyes made their way back up her arm and to her face, a face that was now turned towards his.

He looked into her eyes, the deep topaz catching the hues of the river below her, giving the illusion of a river of sorrow and pain running beneath her weary eyelids. He looked quickly away.

"Tell me something about yourself, Cass. Something that has a specific detail and something that I don't already know or can't already guess on my own." They were both looking at the water now, but he sensed that she was thinking about his request and probably formulating a way to avoid it altogether. Instead, he heard her inhale deeply. And then, she started.

"I arrived in Chimney Rock twenty-eight days ago, late at night. I slept that night in a playground, in a red slide. Juney and Jacob were the first people I ever met here. And then I met their mother, Margie. The most difficult part about arriving in a new place is always..."

She stopped speaking. She seemed to be reconsidering something she had said. She continued with a revised version of the sentence.

"I anticipated that the most difficult thing about arriving in Chimney Rock would be finding a place to work and live, so May nineteenth was devoted to exactly that. I met your mom, and she needed help and I needed work, so that particular task was taken care of."

Cass continued talking, providing Lucas with a play-by-play of every day since the day of her arrival. She described people she had met, her trip to buy used clothes at The Treasure Chest, and the many times she had looked through the souvenir shop windows but had never actually entered. She described where she walked each day and what her favorite spots were. She told him about seeing his Police Department and wondering how he could focus on his work being in such close proximity to the lake and mountains. She shared with him sounds she heard late at night and how she had wondered what wild animals might live around Ella's home. She described her daily work schedule to him and talked about how much she enjoyed her early morning hours all alone in the bakery. She shared her impressions of Ella and her appreciation for Ella's overwhelming kindness.

"How far do you walk each day?" he asked, when Cass had taken a pause from sharing. He was surprised to realize that he actually was curious to know this.

"I'm not sure. I walk primarily on the main road, back and forth between the village and the town. I usually leave right after my work shift at the café and try to return by the time it gets dark."

"So you walk about six hours a day." He stated this as fact, then added, "Why?"

She looked at him with a confused expression, so he elaborated.

"Why do you walk for so long and so far? And every day at that?"
She was still looking at him. "Because I have to be ready for the
day I'll walk out of here. On that day, in May."
She's in training.
"What do you do while you're walking? I mean, I've noticed
you never have your phone with you when you walk, so you're not
listening to music or podcasts or anything. Don't you get bored?" He
already knew she didn't use a phone when others were around, and
she had told Ella she didn't own a phone. He turned and watched
her, waiting and curious for her response.
"I don't carry a phone because I don't have one. And I don't have
one because…well, I really just don't want…I really just don't need
songs or pictures or a way to get me in touch with anyone. I mean…"
She paused and cleared her throat. "I don't really know anyone
here and I won't be staying for too long. So I just walk and look at
everything around me, and, no, I never get bored." She paused and
looked out at the banks of the river. "I try to notice different things
each time I walk on the same road, but sometimes I try to remember
the exact same things, just to see if they have changed since the day
before. I try to listen to the sounds around me, notice the people
around me. That's how I happened upon the festival yesterday. I
heard the sounds. I wanted to see what was making people happy,
what was making people laugh."
As he watched and listened, Lucas realized it was becoming
more difficult to make out the features of her face. It was getting
darker, and he anticipated that soon it would be too dark to travel
back across the rocks without the help of a flashlight. He felt that
he should have been eager to depart, to end his forced picnic and his
time with her. But he wasn't ready…not quite yet.
"What's the most interesting thing you've ever seen on your
walks?" He asked this quietly, then wondered, *why am I whispering?*
"Mailboxes," she replied rather quickly. She turned and they
were both now looking at one another.

"How so?" he asked while holding her eyes a second longer, then looking away.

She pulled her knees up then wrapped her arms and hands around them, weaving her fingers together and locking them in place at the front of her bended kneecaps. "I've never understood why mailboxes are just mailboxes," she shared in a serious tone. "To the rest of the world, who happens to just be passing by in a car or riding a bike or just walking, a mailbox is the only thing they might see. It's the only thing that tells them that someone is there, that someone lives in that house. A mailbox is the part of that family or that person that people see first, yet it says nothing about anything." She stopped and looked over at him, then seemed to decide that she would finish her thought.

"All the mailboxes I've passed are white or brown or grey or black. They usually have numbers on them, sometimes a last name. But that's it." She paused a minute and swallowed hard, seeming to steady herself for what she might say next. "I mean, for someone who is lucky enough to have a home, shouldn't they want to tell the world who they are? Shouldn't they want to paint their mailbox with their favorite colors? Or add things that tell the world about them? Like neon shapes or sparkles and glitter, or gemstones and pictures?" Her words stopped abruptly, as if she were exhausted from even thinking about it.

He looked out over the water, towards the mountains. She had mentioned *home*, the word itself spoken from her lips as if it was both a curse and a long sought-after treasure. *Home.* This was *his* home. These mountains, this valley, this rock. He felt something stir inside him.

Pity? Empathy? Sadness?

Without rationalizing what he was feeling, he decided he wanted to share. He wanted to share this place. With her.

"Hundreds of years ago," he began. He saw in his peripheral that her face had turned towards him. He kept his eyes on the river. "This very river and the valley and the gorge around it, they all belonged to Native Americans. The Cherokee Nation."

He paused and noted that she had stretched her legs back out and was leaning back on her hands, staring out at the water. She seemed to be waiting and listening. He continued. "The Cherokee are a people whose history is steeped in legend and lore," he said, remembering conversations that had happened many years ago. "My grandmother, whose father was full-blooded Cherokee, would take me by the hand and lead me out behind her home high up in the mountains, over there." Lucas pointed to his left, towards the mountains on the other side of Chimney Rock. "Back to where her apple trees grew. I loved picking them from the branches. I would eat so many my stomach would hurt all night." He chuckled at this, remembering the feel of holding small red apples in small hands. "My grandmother was my dad's mother, so he always used to say that I got my darker skin and black hair from his side of the family, from the Cherokee blood in me." He unconsciously ran a hand through his hair.

"My grandmother and I had many days together, and she spent most of those days telling me about her people, or *our* people, I should say. About their past and their way of life. She told me about how the Cherokee cherished this place, the very place where I was born and where I grew up. The Cherokee believed this whole area had a certain mystery to it, and in many ways they considered it as sacred." Lucas pointed up to the "chimney" of Chimney Rock Mountain. "If you look up there, you see the stone pillar. The land beyond that pillar is what my people would call Suwali-nuna, where they believed little people lived." He stopped and looked over at her, hoping to gauge her reaction or level of interest. Cass was staring out at the water, but in the silence, she turned.

"Your people," she repeated.

"Yes," he replied. "They lived their lives and passed down their traditions all throughout these mountains of western North Carolina. This was their home. My grandmother taught me about different ceremonies they would use for different occasions. About their reverence for nature. For example, this very river and all rivers and lakes. They considered water to be full of wisdom."

She was now looking past him, at the water behind him. She blinked and brought her attention back to his eyes.

"What ceremonies did she teach you about?"

Lucas took himself back, to those many afternoons spent on the shores of this river with his grandmother. Listening. Learning. "I remember one day she told me about how they would show love to one another, through gifts of corn and venison. How they would conduct a wedding. You see, her own grandmother and grandfather were married in the Cherokee way. They exchanged the gifts of food and then the groom and the bride each had their own blanket. A blue blanket. And the bride, if she actually wanted this man, would add her blanket to the blanket already draped about his shoulders. And then, if the groom agreed to choose the woman, he would bring her under both blankets, under his blankets."

He looked over at the embankment, suddenly remembering these very stories being told to him on that very spot. He wished, at that moment, that he had listened more carefully. He wished he could remember more accurately the precious details and history that he had been told. He decided to continue, despite now feeling inadequate as a storyteller.

"There were so many times that my grandmother visited me and my mom and dad here. She would walk down the path to this river, and she would hold my hand. She would recite an old Cherokee prayer as she gazed out over the water. I remember hearing the rush of the water over the rocks, just as I'm hearing it now." He felt something painful just beneath the surface. "My grandmother would repeat it, over and over. Teaching me the prayer of my people. But now she is gone."

As he concluded this final thought, he couldn't overcome the deep sense of loss and regret he was feeling. Loss of his grandmother. Loss of his father. But it was something else. Another person or part of a person that was lost, a youth whose time had come and apparently gone just as swiftly. A boy who no longer walked to the river nor sang the songs of the Cherokee. A boy who was now a man, a man who had all but forgotten.

Lucas stopped, then looked across at her, embarrassed that he had been rambling on for so long. He found her staring, not at him, but out over the water of the river. She seemed lost in thought. He considered that perhaps she had quit listening a long time ago. Perhaps she was bored out of her mind.

"Do you remember it?' she asked, in a whisper.

"No, that was so long ago." Then, looking out at the water, words and phrases began washing over him, and he added, "Maybe a small part of it."

"What is it?" she asked quietly.

"What is ... what?" he asked.

"What is the part you remember ... of the prayer?" She sat still. Waiting. Watching. Seemingly mesmerized by something in the water.

Lucas thought for a minute, sure that he wouldn't remember now that he had been asked. He looked to the water and it came to him, quickly and confidently. He put words to memories and found a part of the prayer, a small part that he would now share with her.

"We honor water, to clean and soothe our relationship, that it may never thirst for love. With all the forces of the universe you created, we pray for harmony and true happiness." He paused and, inexplicitly, turned back to look at her. "As we forever grow young. Together."

Eleven

Water. Stories. People from long ago.

As Cass walked along the road, images from the night before continued to interrupt her thoughts. She walked by a huge tree, limbs drooping with purple flowers. She wondered if anyone ever picked these flowers to enjoy in their homes. She thought about veering from her walking route and heading over to the tree, to pick a bloom or two for Ella to enjoy on her kitchen table. She thought about it, then felt pain as a memory approached, uncalled and unwelcomed.

The young boy and the young girl are smiling and looking ahead in anticipation, each with a bouquet of flowers wrapped in their ten-year-old arms. The father has given each of them some money, some money to pick out flowers for the woman, who is their mother. It is the mother's birthday. Their voices are excited and happy as they whisper to one another and ready themselves.

The two children are standing in front of the mother now. The mother is smiling as she sees the white roses in the boy's arms. The mother's face is happy. She wonders at the beauty of the white roses. She knows they are very expensive. She thanks the boy for picking out the most special of all flowers for her.

The girl is also presenting her bouquet. It is one filled with daisies, yellow and white on long, thin stems.
The mother's face is different now. These are flowers that can be found growing along the side of the road. There is nothing elegant nor special about these. They are not cultivated or sought after or cherished. All they do is live.

Cass sat down under the tree and quickly pulled the drawing from the pocket of her shorts. She transported to the porch, rocking in a rocking chair. The freeze-framed images with the faces and voices were soon gone.

Now that her mind and conscious were rightfully focused on the present, in this place, Cass considered standing and resuming her walk, yet she remained sitting. She was still looking at the drawing. She was still lost in the steady rocking of the chair.

Her rocking was interrupted by the sense that she was being watched, that there was someone else here, on this porch with her. As she looked up from her spot under the blossoming tree, she saw the police car driving past, much too slowly. The driver was looking her way, curious as to what she was doing, or maybe curious about what she was holding and staring at. She caught his eyes. They were different than before, different from what they had been on the other days of her time in this place. They were not worried or mad or questioning. They were just eyes. Brown eyes. Curious brown eyes.

Her mind wandered back to the evening before, to the picnic by the river. She and the Chief had sat out on the rock well past sunset and into full darkness. He had shared many stories about ceremonies and traditions, about land and family and sacred things. When he had indicated that they should probably call it a night, they had found it difficult to make it back over the rocks, even with the help of the light from his phone. He had taken her hand to help her, to bring her behind him as he navigated these rocks from his childhood. He had lost his balance and almost fallen, but she had taken his hand and guided him back to steady footing. When their feet had become firmly planted on land again, they had started for the path. Then the

Chief had asked if she wanted to sit for a while longer, talk a little more. She did, and they had. Later still they had both gotten chilly as the night air fully engulfed them. Leaving behind the river that had morphed into a darkened shadow before them, they had walked the winding path back up to Ella's house. There, she had returned to her bedroom at Ella's home and had quickly fallen asleep from exhaustion, a fatigue that was laced with an unexpected calm.

She stood from her spot under the tree and resumed her walk. As she did so she noticed Mrs. Stampshed's small white house up ahead on the left. Mrs. Stampshed was not only a regular at the café, but also one of Ella's dearest friends. Cass knew this to be Mrs. Stampshed's home because she had walked on this route almost every day and had seen the elderly woman on several occasions checking her mail or watering her flowers. Today, Mrs. Stampshed was nowhere to be seen as a delivery man hauled a large box onto her small front porch. Cass continued walking.

A few hours later, she turned and headed back towards the village, having walked the entire late afternoon and early evening along the mountainous roads. She was actually looking forward to getting back to Ella's, feeling oddly exhausted in both her mental and physical capacities. As she progressed towards Ella's home and the downtown area of the village, Cass once again passed Mrs. Stampshed's house. She noted the shipping box still on the front porch, now with Mrs. Stampshed standing beside of it. The woman appeared to be trying in vain to open it.

Cass looked ahead, at the encroaching twilight. She noticed the moths making their nightly journey towards the street lights that were now dotting the path towards her destination. She was sweaty and hot, and her long hair was sticking to her neck through its loose braid. She pictured her bed, and her body falling down onto it in welcomed rest.

She turned and proceeded up the sidewalk towards Mrs. Stampshed and her box. She called out as she approached the porch steps. "Can I help you with that, Mrs. Stampshed?"

The older woman seemed a little startled at first as she turned to see Cass. "Oh, dear, where did you come from? Are you still out exercising this late at night?" Mrs. Stampshed stopped fidgeting with the box and turned towards her unexpected visitor.

"Ella's house is right up the street so I'm not that far," Cass replied. "Are you wanting to open that tonight?" Cass studied the box, which was actually taller and wider than the elderly woman attempting to open it.

"My granddaughter, Jordan, is coming to visit tomorrow, along with her boyfriend. So I ordered a new display cabinet for my living room just for her visit. You see, there are all of these little pieces of pottery that Jordan made for me when she was just a little girl, and I wanted to surprise her with having them on display when she came. I ordered it last week, but it just arrived today."

Cass noticed how flustered and disappointed Mrs. Stampshed appeared, a demeanor that seemed out of place for the usually chipper woman. "How about I help you?" Cass asked. When she saw Mrs. Stampshed readying for a protest, Cass added, "Just for a little while?"

Surprisingly, Mrs. Stampshed agreed to this arrangement and assured Cass that once they pulled the display case out of the box and moved it into the house, the work would be done. It was at this moment that Cass noticed the printing "Assembly Required" on the side. She chuckled softly to herself then proceeded to open the box, cutting through tape with the knife and scissors that Mrs. Stampshed had retrieved from the kitchen. As she did so, dozens of thick boards and thin slats fell out and scattered around the women. A sealed bag full of nuts, bolts, and screws hung loosely by tape from the inside flap of the box.

Assembly required, indeed, thought Cass. Then she bent down to begin the process of organizing the parts.

Moments later, Mrs. Stampshed was bringing two glasses of apple juice to the porch, where Cass had just completed organizing the fifty-seven separate pieces that must now be assembled together.

She had the nuts and bolts and screws in their own piles on the
top of a small porch table and the pamphlet titled "Instructions for
Assembly" in her hand. "Do you happen to have any tools here, Mrs. Stampshed?" Cass
asked hopefully. "Like a small screwdriver?"

"No, dear. I'm sorry to say, I don't. I usually just call Lucas when
I need help with things like this." Mrs. Stampshed took a sip of juice
and Cass noticed the worried look had returned to the woman's face.

Cass grinned reassuringly, then decided to get to work. She
knew instinctively that the sixteen-page instruction manual might
be a little complicated. She also knew from looking around the porch
that while the project itself might not be that difficult, it would,
no doubt, be time-consuming. The only tool she had was the one
currently in her hand, a small L-shaped piece of metal that would
apparently pass for a screwdriver in this endeavor.

As she worked, she occasionally checked the little clock that sat
atop the wicker table on Mrs. Stampshed's porch. As the minutes
and then an hour passed by, the initial structure of the cabinet started
coming together. The elder woman had sat on the porch in a wrought
iron chair the entire time, sharing stories of bear visits, icy roads, her
family members, a new recipe she was trying, and life in general here
in the mountains. Cass listened intently while never ceasing work
on the display case.

"Cass, are you sure you wouldn't like something to drink besides
that water?" Mrs. Stampshed asked this while eyeing the mostly
empty glass of water that she had given Cass earlier, right after the
juice had all been consumed. "Perhaps some more juice or a soda? Or,
I keep beer in the fridge for when Lucas comes over to fix things. I
can bring you one of those."

Cass kept working as she asked, "By Lucas, do you mean Chief
Montraine?"

"Of course," replied Mrs. Stampshed. "What other 'Lucas'
would I be referring to? He lives just a few blocks from here, so he's
always dropping by to fix this or to check on that. He won't take

money or gift cards or any type of compensation for his time, so a few years ago, I started stocking my fridge with his favorite beer. I figured the least I could do was keep him hydrated while he's here." She laughed a little to herself and looked back at Cass as if waiting for a response. But before Cass could speak, a third voice interjected. He must have walked here from down the street and approached from the road, unnoticed and unheard. It was soon obvious, however, that he had certainly heard them.

"How dare you offer someone else my beer stash?" Lucas declared as he neared the front porch. He walked up the steps and then stopped to survey the piles of parts and hardware. "And what's all this? Have I been fired from my handyman job?" He was smiling at Mrs. Stampshed as she stood from her chair to embrace him.

Cass continued working, her eyes diverted away from the tender moment, her attention back on the work. Back on turning the L shape over and over and over.

Unexpectedly, Lucas addressed her. "Hello, Cass."

Cass looked up and found that he was fully facing her, with a friendly look upon his face. "Good evening, Chief Montraine," she responded, looking at him long enough to nod, then returning to the assembly. As she did so, she saw a hand enter into her vision, coming close to the place where her own hands were busy, where her wrist was turning and rotating the L-shaped tool. The hand laid a screwdriver on the porch floor, then retreated back into the pocket of the Chief.

Cass picked up the screwdriver and let out an exasperated sigh, perhaps too loudly. "Thank you so much. This will make a huge difference."

"I drove by earlier on my way home from Mom's," Lucas shared, sitting down near her as Mrs. Stampshed retreated into the house to get more beverages. "I saw you two out here and thought maybe you could use a hand." He was pulling another screwdriver from the pocket on his shirt and looking around the porch as if getting an assessment of the situation.

Mrs. Stampshed returned with two cans of Miller Lite in her hands and a bag of Lays Wavy Potato Chips stuck underneath her arm. She set all three items gently upon the table and shared, "Sorry, kids, but these are the only snacks I could find."

"It's perfect," replied Lucas. Then, as Mrs. Stampshed approached her chair to sit, he added, "Cass is no longer alone. I'm here now, and I won't leave until she's safely back at Mom's house. So you can go on to sleep, Mrs. Stampshed." He smiled sweetly. "I know from my many evenings here that you are now about two hours past your bedtime."

As Cass watched him, he glanced over at her, and added, "We've got this."

Mrs. Stampshed looked from Lucas to Cass. Cass nodded her head in support and wiggled her hand in an indication to "go".

After Mrs. Stampshed had vigorously shared multiple words of gratitude and had finally retreated back into her home, Cass and Lucas worked together on the furniture, consulting on the instructions, finding parts for one another, and delegating who would do what. Cass was genuinely surprised to see how quickly they were making progress, no doubt in large part to the existence of the screwdrivers and the extra pair of hands.

Abruptly, Lucas laid down his screwdriver and announced, "Let's take a little break." He stood up and proceeded to the small table, retrieving the beer cans and chips and seating himself on the porch steps.

Cass readied herself to stand, then eyed the scissors that she had used earlier, close by on the porch. She was reminded of something she had meant to do a few days ago but had forgotten. The summer heat, even in these waning hours of evening, brought the needed task again to her mind. Lifting the scissors, Cass pulled her braid around to the front of her shoulder. It reached past her breasts at this point. She considered the length that was needed to pull her hair well off of her face in a ponytail or braid, then assessed the length she currently had that was not needed for this purpose. She took a handful from the bottom and quickly cut if off.

As she glanced up she found that Lucas was watching her, a look of disbelief spread across his face. She shifted her legs and stood, then proceeded to the front porch garbage pail and threw the thick clump of hair into it.

She headed for the porch steps, then sat down not far from him. As she did so, Lucas took the bag of chips and opened it, along with a can of beer. He looked over to her empty water glass from earlier, then took the second beer can and held it out to her.

She studied it for a moment, then reached to take it. As her hand clasped around the cold can, Lucas continued to hold it tightly. With both of their hands on the unopened can, his lips turned up in a mischievous smile.

"Since I *am* a police officer," he said with a formal hint to his voice, "please verify you are actually old enough to drink this alcohol."

He paused and their eyes locked. It was then that she saw things she hadn't seen before. The color of his hair seemed darker this evening, contrasting with the black stubble emerging against his smooth skin. His jawline was tensed. His brown eyes seemed to be changing in front of her own.

Looking straight at her, he rephrased the question. "How young *are* you, Cass?"

How young am I?

Have I ever been young?

She chuckled quietly to herself, then offered up the answer to his question. The cold, pathetic truth. "I'm twenty-seven," she said, as she pulled the beer from his grasp. "I'm pretty much the same age as you."

CHAPTER

Twelve

T wenty-seven?

"Earth to Chief," Farley called out from across the road. He had headed back to the squad car to get two reflective vests and was now interrupting Lucas's thoughts about the front porch, the display case, and the beer with *the girl.*

The girl? The woman?

He still could not reconcile the fact that she was twenty-seven. In looking at her more closely last night, all the clues were there that she was telling the truth. He had again seen the weariness behind her eyes. He had seen the fine lines about the corners of her lips, the roughness of her hands. At the same time, however, he had also confirmed why he had thought she was twenty or twenty-one, why he had assumed she was much younger. He had detected a naivety about her, an innocence that didn't seem to fit with the new reality that she was a grown woman.

A grown woman who wanders into a village. Without a real possession to her name, without relations or connections, without a resume or a history. Yeah, that makes perfect sense.

"So why the license check today, Chief?" Farley was handing him one of the vests and placing his own about his shoulders.

"Some of the residents are complaining about erratic driving through here," Lucas replied as he secured his vest around his chest. "I just want to make sure the tourists as well as the locals continue to understand that we have people who actually live along this road." He took his place behind his deputy along the double yellow lines.

Car after car proceeded through the checkpoint, with most in compliance. After writing tickets for three expired tags, Lucas appreciated the welcomed surprise as Margie pulled up in her green Ford Explorer. He heard Juney yelling an enthusiastic greeting from the back seat.

"Where are you going, young lady?" Lucas called back to Juney through the open back window. "Don't you have piano lessons today?" Margie readied to retrieve her license as Lucas chuckled and waved her off.

Juney brushed a few blond curls from in front of her eyes and responded in a pitiful voice that contrasted drastically with the excitement she had portrayed mere seconds earlier. "I'm sick and I have to go see the doctor." She added a cough for extra effect.

The twins were two of his favorite people in the world, but even Lucas had to admit that they could be a handful. For the most part, they listened. But there were also times that they tested the boundaries too far. Lucas had once had to help Margie after a particular "exploring adventure", one that had only ended after an hour-long search and the discovery that the twins had been quietly sitting in a tree, a mere sixty feet from their own house.

Lucas looked back at Juney. "As soon as you feel better, Juney, I'll come over and take you and Jacob for ice cream." As he was finishing the sentence, Lucas noticed a shift in Juney's demeanor. He knew that he had gotten her attention, and dipped his head slightly to shield his grin.

An hour and two tickets later, Lucas entered the back door to the station and headed towards his office. He still had a smile on his face from the unexpected surprise of Margie and Juney, and was generally pleased with how the day was shaping up.

"You have a visitor, Chief," Sam said nonchalantly as Lucas passed by his desk.

Lucas maintained his quick pace as he called back, "Who is it?" He was still finishing this question as he opened his office door. It was then that he realized that he had asked the question too late.

Sitting behind his desk, checking her phone as if she owned the place, was Jana. He felt his breath catch as he froze.

After a moment that seemed to go on forever, he proceeded to close the door as if he wasn't flustered at all, and then stood in silence in front of the desk that held his name plate. He watched as she punched something into her phone, then lowered and placed it on the desk. It was at this point that she looked up and cast her eyes upon him. The same eyes he had looked into thousands of times before. In anger. In love. In lust. And in disbelief.

She looked very different than she had six years ago, when last he had seen her. More polished. Classy. Rich. She was wearing an expensive looking suit, which hugged her in all the right places and demonstrated to the world just how much time she spent in the gym. Her face could have been straight off a magazine cover. Makeup perfectly applied, smoky eyes, glowing skin. Her full lips had a dark red tint to them. She smiled, not sweetly, but teasingly, showing her perfectly white teeth. She was what most men would consider as sexy. Sexy as hell.

Lucas stared at her and recognized the old attraction welling back up in him. The memories of intimate times with her, times during which he had felt that they would be together for a very long time.

"What are you doing here?" he asked. The words came out quickly and sounded demanding once he heard them spoken.

Jana stood and walked slowly towards him. She was wearing heeled boots.

Really, Jana? It's summertime.

He remembered that she had always been more concerned with fashion over function, with impressions over logic. He assumed that she had dressed today to impress, no matter how ridiculous the outfit looked for the weather. She was smart enough to know that the overall impact of the outfit would outweigh any logical thoughts from the male species.

"Well, since it's obvious you're in the mood to cut right to the chase, I'm here because I've missed you." Her voice was soft and deep, a sound that most would find sultry. "And I wanted to see you. I wanted to see twenty-eight-year-old Luke, on his birthday, and compare him to twenty-one-year-old Luke. Compare him to that boy I spent my California days with."

As she shared these words, she continued walking towards him. She was now in front of him, assessing him fully.

If you think I'm going to flinch or look away...

She smiled and reached out as if to hug him. He stood stoically and she, seeing that he would not return the gesture, stopped midstream and returned her arms to her sides.

"Well I can see this is not a welcome surprise. How disappointing." She walked over to one of the arm chairs placed near his desk and sat, crossing her legs seductively. "I'm in Asheville this week for a conference that my law firm sent me to, and thought I would drive up here and see…." She trailed off, no doubt noting that he was rifling through papers on his desk, giving the obvious impression that he wasn't listening.

Why is she here?

He stopped busying his hands. He sat behind his desk and looked at her. He realized he was being rude, maybe even obnoxious. He wouldn't allow the discomfort he felt at seeing her these many years later make him into something he didn't want to be. The angry ex.

"I'm sorry, Jana," he said with sincerity. "I'm just a little thrown off by seeing you here, so unexpectedly." He mustered a smile. "It's good to see you again."

He sat and listened over the course of the next twenty minutes to all she wished to share. He listened to her describe how she had gone on to law school in California, just as she had always planned. How she had landed a job with a top-notch law firm in San Diego. How she was working her way up in reputation and savvy. She shared that she had just bought her dream condo, with views of the Pacific and close proximity to an amazing spa. She shared on two separate occasions that she was still single. And she shared that she was happy. Life was proceeding just as she had hoped.

As she continued talking, Lucas glanced out the window of his office. A small group of geese were waddling across the road, slowly making their progression towards the lake. A person was also on the road, not too far behind them.

She's a twenty-seven-year-old woman. And there she goes on her mid-afternoon six-hour walk.

He watched Cass for a few seconds. She was on the main road now, as she usually was. She was looking all around, at the tree branches, at the sky, at the road. Now she was touching a flower. Walking, never stopping. Always walking.

"And you, Luke? What's been going on in your life all this time? Are you married? Kids?"

He diverted his eyes back from the window as Jana asked this with equal parts interest and anticipated disappointment.

His voice was softer than he had intended when he began his reply. "It is as you see. I am the Chief of the Town of Lake Lure Police Department. I live in a small ranch a couple miles from here. My mom lives a couple miles from my house and ... and ...." He looked up and saw her staring at him, a strange look on her face.

Is that pity in her eyes? Sadness? Or, perhaps, regret? Should I tell her? I'm saving up. I almost have enough to buy a bigger house, to move back to California, or to a large city. To join a larger force, or to pursue other interests. I've saved a lot. I'm almost ready...

"And that's about it," Lucas added. There was an uncomfortable pause now, a chasm of silence between them that indicated both were thinking and remembering.

"It can still happen." She said this with the self-assurance of someone who knows what she wants and how to get it. "It can still happen for us. Between us." She said this with the same self-confidence and demand that she had always possessed, even as that young woman in California. The Political Science major. The president of her sorority. The Homecoming Queen. The girl of everyone's dreams. She had been his, and from what she was saying now, could be his again.

As he listened to the words, it all came back, in full color and smells and sounds and emotions. His father had been sick. After graduation, Lucas would be returning home. *For how long?* She had asked him. He hadn't known. *But what about our plans? Your job? Law school for me? I can't do it without you.* She had wanted him to stay. He hadn't known what would happen in a month or two months. It might even be as long as a year before he returned.

She could have come with him, just for a while, just during the summer as he headed home to prepare for the worst scenarios. Just to help him through the heartbreak that had awaited him. He had been afraid. He had asked her, almost begged her. But she had looked forward to a summer break. To fun times at the ocean with friends. Bonfires at night on the shore. An ocean breeze through her hair.

She had told him that she had no intention of spending the summer in North Carolina, in the shadows of mountains. She had asked him to keep in touch. To let her know when his father got really bad. Maybe she could fly out for a few days for the funeral. Maybe she could help him pack to return to California and to her.

She had told him, the last time she had seen him, *Hurry back.* She had told him, *I will wait all summer.*

Lucas had never really taken the time to dissect what had happened between them. Why she had been his whole world one minute and completely voided from it the next. Perhaps he had always considered it to be too painful to revisit. But now, with her unexpected presence in his office, he had been forced to do so. And he now knew exactly what she had been, what she was now, and how they both had come to this point.

"Jana." He paused to consider his words carefully. "Those last days together …"

She had tears forming in her eyes, but she remained silent. Still.

"Neither of us was wrong," he continued. "Well, actually, I was wrong. I assumed, because we loved each other, that you knew what I needed. But I never really said it, Jana. I never really said the words. And that's on me."

He stopped. He was glad he had shared with her what had happened to them. To him. He was glad to finally hear the words, if only from his own mouth.

"And what was that, Luke?" she asked impatiently, using the nickname from their youthful days together. "What was it that you needed so desperately that I wasn't already providing? Please enlighten me, finally, after all this time." She stopped, seeming frustrated now.

He considered her question, but only briefly. He already knew the answer. "I needed to know that I wasn't alone. That's all, Jana. Just that."

He looked at her and saw the pained expression on her face. She was watching him, but the tears that had appeared to be forming were now gone, replaced with a steely glare.

"Thank you for taking the time to come see me today," he said kindly. "It was great having the chance to catch up. You were an important part of my life," he added, nodding his head and conjuring up a gentle smile. "You really were."

He stood and she followed, appearing to take his lead that the conversation was wrapping up. He walked towards the door as if to escort her out, but as he opened it, she stopped and stood in front of him. Her eyes were boring into his. Those stunning, dark green eyes, made the more dramatic today with heavy eyeliner and long, false lashes.

She was shaking her head. "Damn, Luke. You're still the most handsome man I've ever seen. And there are lots of handsome men in California."

With this declaration she leaned forward and kissed him gently on his lips. It was the first time he had been kissed by a woman since the last time he had seen this same woman, six years ago. He felt her breath exhale on his skin as her soft lips grazed his own. He felt her gaze upon him as she hesitated there, allowing her lips to linger a little longer.

Yet, even as he felt all the physical sensations of the kiss, his heart felt nothing. It was as if he was standing alone on the top of a summit, and the wind had blown across his cheek.

It was there, then it was gone.

CHAPTER

Thirteen

*T*he sun began its descent over the western prong of the lake as Cass gazed out over the glistening water. She was viewing this particular sunset from the grassy edge of land on the lake's outskirts. This particular spot had become one that she returned to often, serving as a perfect vantage point to take in the eclectic sights. There was the public beach, the old inn, the mountains, and scattered homes and cabins. She determined that, on this particular day in late July, the weather and the scenery and the light breeze all made for a truly picturesque encounter.

Her days in Chimney Rock were now pleasantly predictable. She worked, she walked, and she attempted to sleep. Then, she repeated those same three steps the next day and the day after that. She had now been here for over two months, and the routine and mundane schedule of her days left her feeling very much at ease. She saw and spoke with Ella on a daily basis, but, for the most part, the rest of the locals, including Chief Montraine, were infrequently encountered.

While the main road remained her preferred walking route, she sometimes chose to explore a side road or trail. When she did so, she was always pleasantly surprised at the gems of unexpected wonders she found. A deer wandering near a brook, a tree filled with unknown flowers, or a rotten log filled with a continent of ants busy at work – or play. She never quite knew which one.

And so it was, on this day, that Cass decided to try a new road, one that was not far from Margie's road and one that she had not walked before. Leaving the main highway, she soon found herself on a narrow winding road with no structures in site. She assumed this was one of those remote mountain roads that appear to be uninhabited until you reach the turn with the million-dollar views and the houses to match. She kept walking, feeling a slight incline as she did so. She was thankful for the strain on her hamstrings and for the sweat breaking out on her forehead. She knew she needed to work hard, to train and to get ready. Her day of departure would come, and she couldn't be unprepared when it did.

She continued walking, noting up ahead and on her left a break in the overgrowth that lined the sides of the road. In the partial clearing, she could make out something grey and set back in the woods. As she neared, she could now see that it was a chain-link fence, one that she assumed was old from the rust formed around its base and among its joints. She glanced upward towards the fence's top, where each link ended in jagged points. She could see a good thirty or forty feet of the fence in both directions, the jagged pointed tops appearing as an ancient fortified wall. She imagined what dread or hidden secrets must be protected by such a fearsome display of guarded warning.

Tearing her eyes away and continuing her walk, she looked ahead at the unexpected straightaway of asphalt road that was now visible. While it included an additional incline, she believed she could see a house far ahead, one that no doubt enjoyed amazing views of the lake and the mountains. She heard a bird call out, and peered up in the giant trees to find it. In doing so she noticed two squirrels playing on the trunk of a tree, frolicking or chasing. A butterfly gracefully fluttered by, and she watched it for as long as she could, wondering where it was headed or when it might return. In noticing all of this beauty, she had never once stopped walking.

She smiled to herself as the butterfly winged its way beyond her view. She imagined it flying amongst the trees and flowers, stopping here or there but mostly content just to be on its own, alone. Unseen. Unknown.

A faint cry from behind her caused her to look back. It was a sound she did not recognize. But then again, it was so high-pitched, it was difficult for her to tell. She stopped walking and stood very still. She listened.

The sound came again.

Now, with a full concentration on it, she knew it was coming from a person. It was pain, desperation and fear, all combined in an unmistakable pitch.

Cass turned in the direction the sound seemed to be coming from, back down the road. She quickly walked seventy or so feet, then stopped to listen. She heard it again, and this time she understood.

"Help, please ... help ...." The words were followed by fearful screaming.

Cass suspected she was much closer now and hurriedly walked to one side and then the other, back and forth as she continued progressing down the road. She looked feverishly for signs of the source of the voice, but found no trace or clue. There was no one else on the road. There were no houses, nor cars, nor people.

She noticed that she was now back at the chain link fence. With a strange dread now infiltrating her spine, she heard the voice crying out. This time there were no words, just guttural screams and sounds filled with panic and despair.

She rushed to the fence and looked through it, and then down into the embankment below it. She frantically searched in all directions for signs of anyone. She moved now a dozen feet along the fence to the left, as it wound into the thick of the forest. She kept following the cold steel, steady under her hands as she stepped over logs and ducked under overgrown bushes. She maneuvered through limbs and vines that were now intertwined into the links of the fence, an indication of years of abandonment.

She felt a chill as the warmth of the day's sunlight vanished under the canopy of the forest. While still moving and searching, she began feeling the early tinges of failure. The voice had not made itself known for several minutes now.

As she peered through the fence links, all she could see was a steep ravine filled with a small pond. The pond was dark. The embankment that led from the chain-link fence was overgrown with green vines, all growing uncontrolled on all parts of the slopes downward. Still grasping the fence and moving further now into the darkness of forest, she felt the twilight encasing her, playing with her vision and blanketing the forest in encroaching shadows.

She heard something and froze. Not screams or pleading, as before, but a whispered weeping of a tiny, heartbroken soul. She squinted her eyes to focus more clearly with the limited light now, peering down into the abyss of the ravine. She saw the dark pond again, rendered almost black in the limited light. At its edge stood a small building. On the top of the building was something similar to a fan, with a shape that resembled a windmill. She looked beside the make-believe windmill and saw a little person crouched there, on the pond's edge. Alone.

Juney looked so very small and frail from Cass's vantage point high behind the fence. The little girl was crying and staring at something in the pond. Cass's eyes followed and spotted immediately the head of a small figure coming up from under the water. The head was gasping. And now arms were emerging and flailing, and then the head and arms were going under again.

Cass readied herself to scream, to yell out for help, but she already knew. There was no help. She considered the best path, to get quickly up the hill to the house she had seen from afar, or down the street to the main road, where so many people would be passing and driving. These would be able and strong people. People who actually had the strength to save other people.

And then she heard it. Juney's weak voice. Trying, struggling, to call out with one last breath. One last appeal. "Please, help him...brother...please...somebody." Cass looked upward at the fence, the nine or ten or twelve feet of the chain link. She saw the jagged points of the links as they sat atop the fence, points that looked like they could cut. Like they would tear. She felt her breaths coming quickly, her chest rising violently as she looked down at Juney, and at Juney's brother, struggling in the darkened water.

She stood on her toes and reached and grabbed the intersection of two links. She propped her foot in a space and began pulling herself upward. She was gritting her teeth tightly as she pulled with her arms and pushed with her legs, tensing every fiber of her muscles and willing her body to move and to climb. She cursed inwardly at her stupid, useless weakness as she fell down and landed on the damp ground.

She rose to her feet and repeated her effort. This time she pulled harder, with desperation in every grasp of a link. She neared the top and reached her fingers towards it. Her right forefinger grazed one of the spiked points and she cried out in shock. She looked at the blood now dripping from the open rip on her finger. The localized pain she felt was soon replaced with an unwanted dread.

Horrid memories began moving towards her. Blood. Cuts. Burning. Memories of desperation and sorrow.

Youth. Crying. Pain.

She again slipped from the fence and landed hard on the ground. Her leg twisted awkwardly underneath her and her finger was burning in pain. The painful memories were threatening to engulf her as she struggled to get up. All air had been knocked from her but she heaved anxiously and fought to stay conscious.

As she lifted her body from the ground, she alerted her ringing ears for any sounds. There were none. No voices were coming from beyond the fence. No tearful pleas nor desperate cries. The twins were all alone, and so was she.

Alone, except for the memories. They were gaining the strength needed, to sweep her away once and for all. She felt for her short's pocket. She reached inside and readied to retrieve the drawing.

She hesitated. She listened.

She left the drawing in its place and removed her hand. She turned her face to the fence. She stood upright from her crouched position, ignoring the pain now throbbing in her finger and her leg. She quickly grabbed the fence and started pulling and pushing herself upward. With every inch she climbed, it felt as if another two had been added.

Using the strength of her legs to propel her, she threw her left arm to the top. As she did so, she saw her hand reach for the pointed tips. She felt the searing pain as the jagged points pierced through. Her hand was now trapped by the piercing. And her body was now scraping its way slowly over the exposed tips.

Despite the pain, her mind was fighting onward. It was telling her something that must be done. Something that she, alone, must do.

Fourteen

*R*ounding the corner into the private family waiting room, Lucas searched for and then spotted Margie. She was rocking back and forth on a bench, with her hands clasped tightly in front of her. Her face was visibly wet and her eyes were swollen and red.

A priest was beside of her and Lucas could make out, even from this distance, that it was the hospital's chaplain, Father Jeremiah. Lucas remembered some difficult days spent here, and Father Jeremiah had been present for all of them. Now the chaplain was with Margie, whispering something while tapping his hand lightly to her shoulder.

Lucas mentally checked himself. Since hearing the emergency call come across the radio an hour earlier, he had sought through all channels to get some update on the children. The little he did know was enough to make his pulse quicken.

He had been told by his EMT contacts that both children had been brought here, by ambulance. They both had been found near the old, abandoned retention basin, an eyesore that had been part of an abandoned plant from the 1950s. The plant itself had since been torn down but the fenced and dirty water trench had been left behind, mostly hidden amongst a forest of overgrowth. Somehow the children had found a breach in the fence, most likely made by some animal that had dug its way underneath and disengaged the links above ground. The radio alert had also referred to someone else, someone who had intervened and somehow helped.

This was the extent of what Lucas currently knew. What he didn't know, however, was the current condition of any of these three people. The two children he adored, and the person who had somehow found them.

As Lucas walked slowly towards her, Margie looked up and saw him. She leaped from the bench and ran, embracing him tightly as she reached him. He patted her gently on the back, waiting as a fresh round of tears emerged from her upturned face. He remained silent, giving her time to speak first. He tried to avoid it, but could not shield his mind from considering the possibility. He shuddered as he thought about Margie, about all she had endured when her husband had abandoned them, about all of her struggles and sacrifice in raising the two children on her own. He fought against the picture of their sweet little trio being ripped apart.

Margie caught her breath in between sobs and slowly gained her composure. As she pulled away from him, Lucas retrieved a handkerchief from his back pocket. As he did so he felt the note pad dependably in its regular place. He handed the handkerchief to Margie, and he waited.

"Juney says they just wanted to see the windmill, whatever that means. Juney says he was drowning, Lucas. Drowning." Margie choked this out tearfully, holding the handkerchief to her face. "My baby boy, all alone in that filthy water." Margie blew her nose, then folded the handkerchief and blew again. She took several deep breaths, looked again at Lucas, then continued. "The doctor says he has some water in his lungs, but he was conscious. He never lost consciousness. His foot was weighted down in the mud or tangled up in something. But he fought and he fought." She coughed, on the verge of hyperventilating. "My baby boy fought until she could get there." At this point, Margie collapsed her head into her clasped hands, no doubt weeping at the reality of what was and the possibility of what might have been.

Lucas felt his eyes close. He felt as if he might faint with relief. He stood by Margie for a few minutes, rubbing her back shoulders. He whispered and said, "It's okay. It's going to be okay, Margie," even while he knew that she and the children would not be okay for a very long time. But they would survive. Both of the children would survive.

Father Jeremiah approached and attempted to lead Margie back to the bench, to a place of rest for the weary mother. Lucas patted her back and encouraged her to follow the chaplain.

As she did so, she called back to him. "Pray, Lucas. Pray for her."

"Of course, Margie," he replied gently. "I'll pray for Juney and for Jacob. Always."

"Not just for them, Lucas. Pray for the one who saved him." Lucas saw that she was again weeping, her shoulders heavy with worry and despair. "Pray, Lucas," Margie whispered through trembling lips. "Pray for Cass."

Margie walked slowly away with the chaplain as Lucas processed the words she had just spoken. He felt himself transition into a trancelike state while reconciling this new information. The name Margie had just shared was a name that he knew. He had seen her, Cass, walking around the town just this morning.

I was in my office. Talking on the phone. I saw her, starting up a side road. She was looking up into the trees. She was kicking pine cones into the grass.

He walked to the nurse's station and then found himself in the hallways of the Intensive Care Unit. He asked a few questions and quickly ascertained that Cass was presently in the room marked IC329. He took a right turn, and then another, and soon found himself on her wing. He walked slowly down the hallway, proceeding towards her door but stopping short of reaching it. He stood and waited, and eventually saw a nurse walking towards him.

"I'm Chief Montraine from the Lake Lure Police Department," he stated in an official tone. "If possible, I'd like to speak to the attending physician for the patient in 329."

Moments later, Jodi was standing in front of him. She had a large tablet in one hand and a Sprite in the other.

"Hey, Lucas," she said in a casual tone. "I figured I might be seeing you at some point this afternoon." Jodi had been a family friend for about twenty years, and had been a true angel during those final, tough weeks of his father's illness. She was retired from private practice now, but worked at the hospital a few days a week just to stay active.

"Any updates on the two little ones?" Jodi asked with concern.

"It looks like they're both going to be okay," Lucas shared, still feeling gratitude that the words could even be spoken. "If I'm understanding correctly," he continued, "the patient in 329 is the one who helped them out. I've met her a couple times before so I thought maybe I would check in, get a quick statement from her, see how she's feeling. Thank her on behalf of the family and community. You know, the usual." As he completed the statement, he noticed Jodi's expression dramatically change.

"So, you know her?" Jodi asked.

"Yes, I know her...somewhat," Lucas replied. Memories of a picnic passed through his mind. "She lives with my mom and works at her bakery." He turned and looked towards the room door.

"Then can you give us some information on her, like where we can get her medical records, her birthdate, her insurance carrier, her family or emergency contact, things like that?" Jodi waited, too serious in her request, and seeming quite hopeful at his ability to help. "We most urgently need to know what her and her family's wishes are on DNR, Lucas. And, well, we just need to get our hands on some information. And quickly."

DNR? Do not resuscitate? Family?

"What are you saying, Jodi?" Lucas asked, surprised at the unexpected lack of calm or professionalism in his voice. He was

starting to sense an uneasiness creeping into the conversation. Softer
and steadier now, he turned back to Jodi and continued. "Is she really
hurt? I mean, is she hurt really badly?"

Jodi exhaled softly. "I'll piece it together for you as best as I
can, Lucas. And, keep in mind, I am piecing this together from
two different sources. The first being what the children told the
nurses who were working with them. And the second being what
the EMTs, who arrived at the scene, shared with me. From what
I can tell from looking at the patient's wounds, and from all that
other information from the EMTs and the children, the picture
has become pretty clear. She must have seen the children from the
other side of the fence. She must have decided, probably correctly so,
that to make it around the perimeter of the fencing in order to find
whatever opening they had found, well, that would probably have
taken more time than the little boy had. So, from what I can gather,
she climbed the fence."

Lucas turned again towards the door, the door to room 329.

*I can see her. Her strong legs, climbing. Her arms, reaching. She sees
the children. She hears them. She is going to try to climb the fence.*

He continued looking towards the door as Jodi continued
painting the horrific picture.

"From the wounds on her left hand, specifically the two holes,
one of which pierced one of her middle carpal from the anterior side,
we can assume that her hand was probably impaled upon the open-
tipped chain links on the top of the fence. The EMTs described the
fence itself as about ten or eleven feet high, so I would imagine she
probably lunged her left hand on top of it to try to get some type of
grip, to help as she pulled herself upward."

*Two rods through her hand, with one against bone. I can see her
pulling her body. She is coming, children. She hears you.*

"You may be wondering how she was able to keep climbing
with the pain from her left hand. But," Jodi continued, "I don't need
to tell you that our bodies are able to do amazing things once that
adrenaline kicks in. I would imagine that was the case for her. That's

the only thing that could explain how she was able to keep her left hand in place. Anyway, judging from the cuts along her abdomen and her upper thighs, and even a few on her face, she did her best to propel her body over the edges of the top without further damage. It really is a miracle, the more I think about it, that she didn't puncture any of her vital organs. Of course, she still got significant cuts and abrasions, but, it could have been much worse."

Lucas closed his eyes, then opened them as he heard Jodi's voice continuing.

"Along her upper right arm and the upper right part of her back she has a significant bruise, which is in the current state of still forming and will probably get much worse. I believe this most likely is related to some kind of free fall, probably after she had made it over the top of the fence. The release from the top also resulted in a deep rip in her left hand, which will be a significant challenge that we may need to address later on if...."

Lucas interrupted. "Why later? Why wait?" As soon as he said it, he knew the answer. There were other, more pressing concerns. Doctors knew how to prioritize.

"I think the bruise is from something she hit when she landed," Jodi added. "Perhaps a rock or a tree trunk. In any case, it's obvious she landed with force on her right side. It was at this point that she apparently got up and made her way to the pit where the retention pool was, where the children were. The EMTs shared with me that the embankment around the water and leading up to the fence, in the general area from which the little girl indicated this woman came from, is about forty yards, all downhill. When they brought her in, her clothes were completely shredded, her shorts to the point that they were barely hanging off her. Whatever shirt she may have had on was gone completely. Her undergarments and shoes were still intact while still pretty tattered."

Lucas noticed Jodi's pause. He tore his eyes from the door to room 329 and looked back at her. He noted concern in her gaze.

"Are you okay, Lucas?" she asked.

"Of course I'm okay," he said, suddenly sounding and feeling weary. "I'm just listening to your account. I'm taking it all in so I can write it up in my report later." He looked back at the door. "But why were her clothes so torn?"

"According to what the EMTs shared with me, the entire embankment is covered in Firethorn bushes. By the time she got to the water...."

We had a picnic. She pricked her finger on a Firethorn. She pricked her finger one time.

"She would have been bleeding profusely," Jodi continued. "We counted over one hundred and eighty-five cuts to her skin, and, quite frankly, there are probably more. We just quit counting." Jodi stopped and took a sip from her soda, keeping her concerned eyes on Lucas as she did so. "The most serious cuts, the ones that ripped into muscle, were clearly from the fence top. But most of the other abrasions were probably from the thorns. Some are very shallow, Lucas, while others are a little deeper. I'd imagine the thorns on that unchecked vine growth are out of control. With the embankment covered in hundreds of them, well, I can imagine how going through that could rip a shirt from a person's back."

Lucas exhaled deeply and turned to the doctor. "What are you trying to say, Jodi? I mean, how...?" He ran his hand through his hair and looked to the floor. He had no words to match his thoughts.

"Thankfully, the really deep ones on her face missed her eyes," Jodi said gently. "So her vision and other senses for that matter shouldn't be affected. That's the bit of good news I have, Lucas." She reached out and tapped his hand lightly. "The bad news is, from what I can predict, she entered the standing water, which the EMTs described as dark and dirty, with close to two hundred open wounds on her body."

Lucas started slowly walking towards the door to room 329. He heard Jodi's voice behind him, saying something of importance.

"That's the real issue, Lucas. The potential for Cellulitis or Sepsis are real, but what we are most concerned about is the possibility of Necrotizing Fasciitis, which, as you probably already know, is fatal."

Why were you all alone, Cass? Why are you always alone?

Jodi was still talking behind him. "The next seventy-two hours are critical ... infection ... the old scars ...."

Lucas stopped with the door a mere foot away. He turned back to Jodi. "The old scars?"

"What I was saying, Lucas, is that although she'll have an uphill battle, she's obviously a fighter. You can tell from the other scars, the older ones. She's been through something, and she somehow survived. Maybe she can do it again. This time." Jodi was smiling, a gentle smile meant to encourage. Lucas had seen the same smile during his father's last weeks and days.

"What old scars are you talking about?" Lucas asked. But Jodi was already walking away, into another room to care for another in need.

He was alone now, in front of her room. He opened the door and entered, keeping his head lowered and looking towards the floor as he did so. Closing the door, he turned and faced what he assumed was the general vicinity of the bed, then raised his eyes to look upon her. The person who had saved Jacob's life.

He walked closer and stood beside her bed. Every bit of skin that was exposed was covered in red, raw marks. On her face, on her neck, on her arms and elbows and wrists. He saw the IV inserted into her left arm and the pulse monitor strapped to her forefinger. There was a nurse close by, keeping notes on the patient's status with an anxious alertness.

There was a table by the bed. On it was a piece of paper. The nurse explained that the paper had been in the pocket of the ripped shorts. The nurse told him that the shorts were long gone, taken out along with other bloodied and ruined things.

He reached for the paper. The nurse shared that the paper had been opened from its folded state because they had hoped to find some kind of information on it. Something, anything, that would help them identify the patient. He picked it up and saw, for the first time, what was on this paper that he had seen in her hand so many times. As she sat along the road, or under a tree, or sometimes even as she was walking.

He saw a drawing of a house. A house on a hill. There were splotches of dried blood splattered across the paper, but overall the drawn image was untouched.

He returned the paper to the table and turned again to the patient. He looked at her. At this woman lying still in the bed. This woman he had shared a beer with while building a display cabinet. This woman he had won a three-legged race with and had taken on a picnic.

Why are you alone in this world?

He stood there for a very long time. He remained there after the nurse left, and was there when another came in. He watched as she breathed in and out, her body fighting internally in a battle he could not see. With no family to hold her hand, no friends to whisper comfort. No one who knew her, or her medical history, or why there were other scars that told of her life long ago.

He watched her. And then he turned his gaze to look out the window at the darkened sky. He remembered another darkened evening. A time when they had sat on the rock in the middle of the river. He remembered, and then finally faced a truth that he had known for quite a while. A truth he had known but would never allow himself to acknowledge. A clue that he had gathered, but had never written in his note pad. Not until this moment.

He retrieved the pad from his back pocket and pulled the pen from his shirt. He opened the pad to his list, started over two months ago on the day he had first seen her. He clicked open his pen and put the tip to the paper. Then he slowly, finally, added the word.

Beautiful.

CHAPTER

Fifteen

The image was in color, not the usual black and gray and white. It was a frozen frame of two young people, teenagers, gazing across a glass counter.

The display is full of sparkling jewels. Diamonds and gems with gold and silver accents. The look on the boy's face is one of pride, and love. The girl's face is filled with gratitude and awe. The shimmering hues on her eyelids accentuate her blue eyes. Her hair is loose, long and flowing, down her back and around her shoulders. The boy's hair is golden, roughly combed across his forehead. His blue eyes are twinkling with happiness. They are there so he can buy her a pair of earrings.

The frame remained frozen as she wakened from her deep slumber. The two faces of the two teenagers were clear and sharp, but they began to fade, ever so slightly. Her eyelids struggled to remain open, but they were heavy and weary and soon closed again.

She was being assaulted now, by sensations of jolting, scraping pain. The pain was coming from her arms, her legs, her back, and her face. She fought to open her eyes, to see if she was surrounded by porcupines who were rolling around her, or if, perhaps, she had fallen into a vat of sharp nails. Whatever was causing the sensations, she was thankful. The memory was still with her, the faces of the two young people were still there, fainter but still present. She needed the pain, needed it to distract her. Needed it to push away the memory that was hanging on, that wouldn't leave, that threatened to bring along other, stronger memories. She struggled to open her eyes and finally did, even as she pushed the image back and away.

Cass realized, instinctively and immediately, that she was lying in a hospital bed. She stared at the ceiling, allowing her vision to come into full focus, then slowly turned her head towards the slow beeping sound close by her. In one glance she saw a monitor and an IV hooked into her arm. She turned her head in the other direction, towards a door. There was a nurse and a police officer standing there, whispering to one another and oblivious to the newly awakened patient.

She looked again at the ceiling as a bolt of recognition intruded on her thoughts. She felt nauseous, then, inexplicably, she felt hopeful. Hopeful at what this might mean.

Where is he?

In one swift gesture, she ripped the IV from her arm and quickly moved her body to place her feet on the floor. She was weak, too weak to stand. She collapsed to the cold, hard tile, landing with a thud.

How long have we been here?

She began crawling, inching her way towards the door. Even as she was doing so, she was calling out, calling out in a voice that she wished to be loud but was horse and scratchy and soft. "Where is he? Tell me, please. Where is he?" She continued pulling herself by her hands on the floor, her wobbly legs and knees slipping on her hospital gown underneath. She called to the nurse, who had noticed her now and was hurriedly approaching her.

The nurse was saying something, urging her to return to the bed. "Please, Miss, let me help you back up. You have serious injuries and you've been sick for over two weeks. You're too weak."

Even as the nurse talked to her, and tried to persuade her, and tried to console her, Cass continued. Her eyes were on the door, and beyond the door. She was seeking beyond to where *he* was, somewhere in this hospital.

He will be wondering where I am, she thought.

I am coming. I am coming.

"Please, Miss. We have to get you back in the bed," the nurse was saying. There was concern in the nurse's voice. There was another nurse now, and a third coming through the door. They were holding her, gently pulling her up, back towards the bed.

Why aren't they answering? Can't they hear me?

Cass continued, calling out louder now. "Where is he? I need to get to him. Please, just tell me where he is. Just tell me where Tristan is."

The nurses continued their tugging and their pulling. They were forcing her, but she was resisting. She could be strong, and they could not. She was pulling her arms from their grips. She was talking louder now, screaming.

"Why won't you answer me?"

Why won't they answer me?

She felt herself growing frustrated, and anxious and upset. As she continued to struggle, she looked closely at the nurse who was holding her shoulder. The nametag read **Asheville Mission Hospital**. Just as suddenly as the feeling of the familiar had come upon her, it was gone.

Tristan.

She knew now - *he* was not here. This was not *that* hospital. This was not *that* time.

She ceased her struggle. Her voice no longer screamed. She collapsed upon the hard floor. She sat and pulled her knees up tightly, dipping her head down. She held her head against her kneecaps and placed her folded arms around her face and head.

She was preparing, preparing for the wave even as it approached. It was strong, and it would not bring frozen images in black and white or color. It would bring with it something more, something horrid.

They are walking now, through the front door of the jewelry store, together. They are smiling and giggling. The boy is so proud that he has pulled this off. That he has surprised her. They walk up to the counter, and he immediately points out the earrings.... They are standing together, waiting for a sales person to come out to help them. The boy, Tristan, is looking at the watches, which are displayed in a glass cabinet next to the earrings. "Mark this day and time. May the eighteenth at 10:21 in the morning. This will be the day and time that you will always remember...."

Cass's shoulders started shaking. She struggled to regain control and to escape the wave of memories and pain that had found her. She tried to steel her mind. She tried to prepare her soul. She would escape this memory and transport herself to her *peace.* She knew how to do it, was taught how to do it in some place and time before this place and time. She would do it quickly, before the impending memory developed further. She would soon be rocking in a rocking chair, on a peaceful front porch. She reached for her right pocket, but the pocket was not there. The shorts were not there.

"Excuse me." Cass whispered this without lifting her head, keeping it shielded from the world with her folded arms. She had meant to be louder, but a whisper was all her dry throat would provide. "May I please have my shorts?"

She started to extend her left hand, then realized for the first time that this hand was completely immobilized, heavily bandaged and throbbing with intense pain. She had been crawling with it just moments earlier. She had not realized then that it was so useless. She kept the left hand wrapped about her dipped head, and extended her right hand slightly, ready to take the shorts as they were given. She waited in silence for a response. She heard a whispered exchange close by.

A gentle, female voice answered her. "I'm sorry, Miss. Your shorts were, well, they were completely destroyed. We had to get rid of them."

Cass returned her right hand to her body and wrapped it tightly around the top of her head. She heard the door open and close, and heard the voices of the nurses fade away with the closing door. She was alone.

The wave is coming. The memories are coming. I am not strong enough.

She felt an unexpected touch. The touch of a hand, upon her own hand. As she kept her head bowed, covered and shielded, the hand remained. The hand was bigger and rougher than her own. But gentle in its touch and in the slow manner in which it was taking her right hand, taking it into a tender grasp. The hand was pulling softly on her fingers, opening her right hand to expose and flatten her palm. This hand was now holding her hand on the bottom, supporting it for what may come next.

She felt paper. A folded paper placed onto her palm. And then she felt the strong fingers of that hand gently folding her own fingers over. The hand covered her own clasped hand now, holding it securely for a second or two. And then, it was gone.

Even without unfolding the drawing, as she had so many times, she could feel herself sitting on the porch of the tiny house on the hill. She could feel her gentle rocking, with the cool breeze brushing against her face. She imagined wind chimes. There were chimes all across the porch, and they were accompanying her rhythmic rocking with a sweet melody of beautiful sounds. Her breath calmed.

All was now quiet in the room. She kept her head downward, her body in a cocoon. The paper was still clasped tightly in her hand. And although the room and the world were silent around her, she felt it. A presence.

He had stayed when others had left. Even as she had felt herself drifting in and out of consciousness, opening her eyes for mere seconds on random days, she had seen him. Slouched over in a chair asleep, or staring out the window. He was here even now, somewhere in this silent, cold room.

And in the silence, deep inside her soul, there was an echo. A hint of something she had not felt before. Had not felt for any time that she was able or willing to remember.

She felt it. She knew.

I am not alone.

Fall

CHAPTER

Sixteen

There is more orange today than yellow. And more yellow than brown.
Lucas gazed out the office window and continued to study the leaves. He enjoyed keeping daily tabs on the subtle changes of the trees around the mountains. For all its beauty in the spring and summer, it was fall that often brought the most enthusiastic tourists to this region of North Carolina, visitors who enjoyed sipping warm apple cider while taking in the splendor of the Blue Ridge Mountain range in all of its autumn glory. He had seen the annual uptick in tourist activity during the latter weeks of September, and now that it was the first day of October, the area was bustling with excited visitors.

The cooler temperatures partnered with the smells of pumpkins and chrysanthemums all made for the perfect season to be in these mountains. The children were now back in school and the familiar pace of school and work life had settled in. The summer gardens around town had all been tilled up for cool weather plantings such as cabbage and turnips, and the autumn apple harvests were being enjoyed in apple fritters and pies. Lucas tore his gaze from the window and his mind from the thought of Ella's homemade apple dumplings, warm from the oven with vanilla ice cream on top.

"I'm always interested in how people are led to become police officers. What first got you interested in this line of work?" Lucas was still jotting down some notes from the last question even as he asked this one, but glanced up at the candidate to indicate he could go ahead and begin his response. These softball questions at the beginning of interviews were his least favorite, but necessary in their own way. Now that Rebekah Rinehart had officially announced her resignation from the force, it was time to get serious about filling the impending vacancy. After interviewing three candidates last week, none of whom he would ever hire to join his team, Lucas was getting some good vibes from this applicant, Colby Melton. Officer Melton was a recruit from a South Carolina town about a hundred miles south of Lake Lure. Lucas kept writing as Colby commenced with his answer.

"Well, Chief Montraine, I had always been somewhat interested in being a police officer, I guess for the same reason as lots of young boys. You know, looking up to policemen as community heroes and all that. I was raised to know that policemen and policewomen and firefighters and all of the community service people, well, my parents raised me to know how valuable and important they are. So, yes, I always sort of had that as an aspiration as I was growing up."

Lucas smiled slightly and stopped writing. He set his pen down and looked up at the young officer, who had cleared his throat and looked ready to add to his response.

"But all of those were values or perceptions that my parents helped to instill in me." Colby stopped and seemed to be considering something carefully, proceeding with a more formal and subdued tone in his voice. "It wasn't until my senior year in high school that I really became serious about police work and the potential for me to be a police officer as a career."

Lucas nodded encouragingly as the candidate paused. "What happened your senior year in high school?"

"It's rather strange when you think about it, the fact that something so unrelated to me would have such a profound impact. My senior year, there was an incident in a town that was located in the same county as my town but was actually not very close to my home at all. Anyway, a police officer was killed, killed in the line of duty. He was trying to save some young people, some high schoolers. I remember how that made me feel, since I was in high school as well." Colby paused and looked down at his hands in his lap. "Anyway, it just really hit home with me, and after that I just thought about police work more seriously and, you know, the rest is history, as they say."

Lucas nodded his head. "I'm glad you shared that, Officer Melton. I think it says a lot about your maturity at such a young age." Lucas added a few notes to his interview form. "And where, exactly, was home back in those high school days?"

"A small town in Alabama called Springville," Colby answered. "But my family moved away a few years back, so I haven't visited there in quite a while."

The interview continued with the usual questions and responses, both general and technical. Lucas found through the conversation that he had high marks for Colby Melton. He appreciated Colby's humility, his smarts, and his common sense answers to situational questions. He just basically liked what he considered to be Colby's youthful enthusiasm for the work of law enforcement.

Why do I keep thinking of him as youthful? He and I are the same age.

Lucas shook his head self-mockingly, then determined with seriousness that Colby Melton may very well be the perfect new member to join the Lake Lure Police Department. After thanking Colby for his interest and walking him out to the parking lot, Lucas joined Officer Alexander on afternoon patrols around town.

As was most often the case, all was calm and in order. They checked by the high school, where the principal had reported some vandalism the weekend before, but apparently the rivalry with a nearby high school had calmed down on its own. They rode up and down many of the side roads of the town, including the side road that led to the location of Juney and Jacob's incident and Cass's injury. As they slowly drove up the road and past the tall, rusted fence, Lucas felt a slight shudder. Turning the squad car around at the top of the dead-end street, Officer Alexander proceeded back down the road. This time, Lucas kept his eyes straight ahead.

After returning to the station with Officer Alexander and then confirming all was in place with the officers who had second shift, Lucas proceeded in his own squad car towards Boys Camp Road and his house. Showering and changing quickly into some jeans, a t-shirt, and a light hoodie, he then did what he had done several times a day, for every day, for the last two months. Since the day Cass had been dismissed from Asheville Mission Hospital. He headed to Ella's.

Because of the damage to her left hand, and the cuts spread about her body, and the significant and deep bruising along the right side of her back, those days had been quite difficult for Cass. She was weak. She had struggled to push herself up or to even balance herself when her walk was unsteady. During that time, it was Lucas who had lifted her gently to sitting position, or had placed her arm around his shoulder to help her in walking to the bathroom or to the kitchen. The first few times Cass had protested and had stated she could do it. She had insisted that she didn't need help. But then, as the days turned to weeks, and as her strength seemed to seep back into her bones and her muscles and her resolve, she appeared to also come to terms with the fact that Ella and Lucas would not be deterred. She had seemed to accept that she was sore and weakened.

During her time of healing and through all of the physical limitations she encountered, the scabs had appeared to present the greatest challenges for Cass. Lucas had watched as she had scratched and rubbed, despite Ella's chastising about leaving scars. Ella had continuously dabbed ointment over as many of the cuts as she could, telling Cass repeatedly that this would stop the itching and would help the red slices to heal. There was a rather deep gash on Cass's upper right cheekbone, and another along her right jawline. These, along with several on her arms and legs, would most likely leave lasting marks on her body. Nevertheless, Ella continued rubbing on the ointment as Cass continued her slow but steady recovery.

And while Cass had healed, Ella had jumped into action. She organized community leaders across the area, propelling many with money and some without to pitch in for Cass's hospital bill. Within a week after the incident, Ella had raised seven thousand dollars beyond what was even needed to pay the medical debts. What was obvious from this community outreach was that Cass's act of heroism had captured the attention and gratitude of people far and wide, both those who knew her on a familiar basis, like the regulars in the café, and those who had never met her but were now curious to do so.

About two weeks after Cass had left the hospital, she had insisted on returning to her job at the bakery. But Ella had been ready.

"Once you are completely healed and back to normal," Ella had said, "I promise I will work you double or maybe even triple shifts." This assurance that all debts would be paid and all time accounted for had seemed to put Cass more at ease.

And so it was, on this first day of October, that Lucas found himself back at his mother's home and the home of his childhood. As he walked up the steps of the back porch, he was a little surprised to find Cass sitting in one of the plastic chairs around the porch table.

"Hey, Chief," she said as she watched him approach. "How was your day at work?"

"I'm not answering that until …." He stopped walking and waited.

She grinned a little then amended her salutation. "Hey, Lucas. How was your day at work?"

"Well, let me see. How was my day?" Lucas pulled a chair up across from her, then sat and relaxed into it, looking upward at the stars that were faintly appearing in the sky. "We actually had an emergency today. At first I thought Mr. Tiller's garage was on fire, but once we got there, along with our buddies from Bill's

Creek Fire Department, it actually turned out to be a giant pile of burning leaves. Apparently the concerned neighbor down the street had not really checked things out very thoroughly before calling in the emergency." He chuckled a little then looked towards her for a reaction.

She was grinning, and almost smiling. It was ever so slightly and with no teeth showing. She never smiled with her teeth showing. It was just a trace of a smile, but he could tell she was a little amused. While looking at her, he noticed her shiver a bit. Standing, he removed his hoodie and placed it about her shoulders.

"Oh, no, Lucas, you don't have to …." She left the sentence incomplete as she began wrapping herself in the hoodie. He noticed a strange look on her face.

Shit. Did I even wash that hoodie after the basketball game yesterday?

He suddenly felt self-conscious as she sat quietly, encased in the hoodie he had been wearing just a minute before. He sat back down and try to act nonchalant.

"It's still warm," she said, wrapping the garment tighter around her chest. Her head was down and her cheek was pressed against the material. She added, "Thank you, Lucas."

At that moment, Ella burst through the back door onto the porch, bringing a platter of hot ham and cheese sandwiches, a bowl of cantaloupe slices, some leftover potato salad from Sunday's dinner, and all the plates, forks and napkins needed for an impromptu evening supper. Their meal together was filled with small talk about Ella's morning at the bakery and the mishap with the pumpkin scones she had made. Lucas then shared, for Ella's enjoyment, another recounting of the emergency call to the leaf burning at Mr. Tiller's house. As he did so, he noticed how intently Cass appeared to be listening to all of this meaningless nonsense. She ate slowly and methodically, as if she didn't want to miss a single word.

Well into the meal, Cass finally broke her silence and interjected herself into the conversation. "Will you share a story, Lucas? About the Cherokee?" Cass asked this with what seemed like hopeful anticipation. Lucas noticed Ella's surprise. He had never shared with his mother the conversation between himself and Cass on the evening of the picnic, the evening they had spent hours sitting on a rock in the middle of a river.

"Sure, Cass. What kind of story do you want to hear?" Lucas asked this while putting down his sandwich and giving her his full attention.

As Cass appeared to consider this, Ella piped up.

"I have a beautiful story to share, Cass. It's the story of Lucas's great-great-grandmother's wedding day. The Cherokee that once lived on this land had such lovely rituals for meaningful times in people's lives. Such as weddings. Oh, I wish I had some kind of recording of Sunny telling it. She was such a beautiful storyteller. Anyway, the groom would have a blanket...." Ella stopped and looked towards Lucas, who himself was looking and snickering at Cass.

Cass teasingly inquired, "A blue blanket?"

Lucas could see that Cass found this as amusing as he did, but Ella was a different story.

"Well, if you've already told her this particular one, why'd you let me ramble on, son?" Ella was pretending to be mad, but Lucas could tell she was anything but.

"How about a story of something sad?" Cass asked, looking first at Ella and then at Lucas.

Lucas took a deep breath and considered which sad story he might share. The sun had fully set now, and with these shorter fall days the darkness was fast encroaching. Ella took a book of matches and lit a candle on the table, then excused herself to the warmth of the inside of the house.

"Well, I could share with you some of the stories my grandmother used to tell me about rituals for the land and for the harvest, or for the children. But since you asked, I do remember something very sad that my grandmother shared with me once." Lucas paused and turned his head towards the river below. "It was what the elders had taught her father about what happened when a loved one died. How they mourned."

Lucas turned back to her to see her reaction. Because he knew so little about her past or about her life, he wanted to give her a chance to pass on this if the subject was just a little *too* sad. But Cass was watching and seemed to be listening, and as he hesitated she nodded ever so subtly.

"The Cherokee that lived on these lands were a very spiritual people," he started. "They really believed that death was just a transition to a life beyond this one. But they also loved and cared for one another deeply, so the death of any member of the tribe was a significant event." He stopped, realizing he had been looking upward towards the summit of Chimney Rock. He brought his gaze back down to her, and found that her eyes were boring deeply into his own. They had a troubled shimmer to them, as if they were a mirror, and the object of their reflection was pain.

He silently chastised himself for picking such a morbid topic. *You're such a jackass. Why did you choose this to talk about?*

"Let's talk about something else, Cass. Like some very special people I happened to see today. Three of your biggest fans. Can you guess?" He was acting over-the-top cheerful, attempting to distract her from the previous discussion and focus her on a more jovial image. He was shocked at her eventual response.

"I don't really know anyone here, so I'm not sure who it could be." *You don't really know anyone **here**?*

"It was Margie. And Juney and Jacob. Margie brought the kids by after their school day. They keep asking me when they can see you. They want to talk to you, Cass. They want to see you."

Cass had been too weak in the hospital for any emotional visits, and once she had returned to Ella's house, she had kept asking for more time before facing the two children and their mother. Lucas had respected this, had respected how this interaction or meeting might affect her, emotionally or mentally. But now, after she had put it off for so long, he was starting to wonder if it would ever happen.

Cass replied with a determined voice, almost as if she was convincing herself. "I have to start walking again. So, I'll walk and visit their house sometime soon." She nodded her head slightly, then stopped.

Even as he was digesting what she had just said, she spoke again. "Lucas?"

"Yes?"

"Please finish the story. The story of your people when they were sad."

He thought back to the times that it was just he and his grandmother, sitting by the river. He regretted that he hadn't known then what precious moments those were. He felt sure, if he had, that he would have approached them more seriously, would have been sure to have been the kind of young man who could be entrusted with treasured memories from long ago. Now, sitting here with Cass, the stories and lore somehow came back.

"The Cherokee believed in a quick burial. Actually, it would happen the day of the death or, at the latest, the day after." He looked at Cass and found that she was hanging on his every word, willing him to tell the story. "But they were also aware of the pain and suffering that this could bring to those loved ones who were left behind. There was a time of seven days, set apart after the burial, that was designated as a time for mourning." He paused and looked away briefly. Their eye contact had become intense and he was finding it hard to focus. He wondered why she appeared so mesmerized by this history, by the traditions as he recounted them.

He kept his vision on a faraway grouping of trees as he continued, unable to look at her even though he was sure she was looking at him. "During this time of mourning, the family of the departed couldn't be angry, nor could they show happiness. They ate and drank very little, just enough to survive. But no more. And then, after those seven days, those mourning family members were taken by their tribe to the water, where they were told by the tribal leader to immerse themselves." Lucas paused, working his mind to remember if there was something after that. Something important.

He looked back at Cass. She was leaned back in her chair, relaxed and peaceful. His hoodie was still wrapped around her, but now, instead of perched on and around her shoulders, her arms were in the sleeves, and the jacket was zipped up to her neck. She had placed the hood up around her head, where it was presently balancing lightly around her hair.

"Why did they need to immerse themselves in the water?" she asked quietly.

"It was part of the cleansing. The whole seven days of mourning was considered cleansing in and of itself, and then, this final act was the conclusion. The mourners would not just immerse themselves one time, but actually seven times, alternating the direction in which they faced." He looked down at his hands in his lap, feeling her eyes upon him. "First, they would face east, I think. They would face east and dip down into the water. Then, they would face west and do the same, over and over, for a total of seven times. Afterwards, their cleansing was complete and they were welcomed back into the tribe, to resume the true living of their lives."

Having concluded his sharing of what he could remember from his grandmother's teachings, he scooted his chair a little closer to the candle. The little bit of heat emanating from it was welcomed as he started to feel a chill in his bones. It was the kind of chill from which a hoodie would perfectly protect him.

I need to just get up and go inside. Why am I sitting here freezing?
He didn't get up.

"Why did they face east, then west, while they were dipping into the water?" She was staring at him, two dark eyes under the shadow of a grey fleece hood.

"I suppose...." He realized his grandmother hadn't shared this part, or perhaps she had and he had long forgotten it. He started again. "I suppose it has something to do with beginning and end. The sun rises each morning in the East, and with each new day babies are born and life begins anew. But the sun sets each day in the West, and the day is ended, and to each life there is a time that it ends as well. So I guess east and west are symbolic in several ways. But, most likely, the Cherokee used them to emphasize one important thing. Something that all mourners must remember."

"What is that?" she asked, softly but seriously.

"That just like the setting sun, at some point, the mourning ends." Lucas looked up and met her shadowed eyes. "It means that no one should mourn forever."

Seventeen

*C*ass switched the wet rag to her weak left hand and finished cleaning off the last few tabletops. She knew that despite its damaged appearance, she needed to use the hand as much as she could in order to build it back up to a fully functioning level. She wiped down the counter once more, pushing and pulling the rag rigorously despite the strain and ache.

It had been two weeks now since she had been back at the bakery and things were finally starting to feel normal. She was once again contributing to Ella's business and pulling her own weight, or at least partially pulling her own weight. She was keenly aware of how indebted she was to Ella – and to Lucas – for all of their care during her slow healing process. She knew that no matter how hard she worked or how vigorously she scrubbed and cleaned, some debts would never be reconciled.

She had tried to find out how much the hospital care had cost, so that she could put together some kind of plan to pay it off before she left. But Ella had only been willing to tell her, "It's been taken care of, Cass. You are cherished more than you know."

Hearing these words had made Cass feel ill at ease, as if she were surrounded by people who thought they knew her, or who thought she knew them. The reality was still as it had always been. She planned to leave this place in two hundred and nine days. It was important to her that no one have the wrong idea about who she was in their lives.

I won't be staying too long.

She hung her apron on the peg near the door and turned off the lights. Ella had already left the café for the day to go home and lay down. Cass knew, without Ella saying it, that the weeks she had been unable to work had been challenging for Ella. She regretted having put the older woman in that position and vowed to stay healthy. She would work doubly hard to somehow make it all up, before it was time to go.

Cass walked towards the door that led to the home. Lucas was standing in the door frame.

"My mom is out cold. Like, snoring. You two must have worked hard today." He said this with a friendly tone as he walked towards the display case and helped himself to a peanut butter cookie. "I'm headed up to the state park to check out their emergency plans and stopped to see if she wanted to come along. She loves it up there, but hardly ever goes anymore." He was sharing this in between bites. Upon finishing, he wiped the crumbs that had fallen on the counter into the palm of his hand and disposed of them in the trash can. "When you see her this evening after your walk, just let her know I stopped by." Lucas turned and headed towards the front door.

He had been right to assume that Cass was getting ready to go on her walk. She needed to, desperately. She had missed out on too many days of training during the time she had been weak. Now that she was back in her routine, she couldn't afford to miss any more opportunities to build her endurance. Knowing this, and being fully aware of this intention on her part, Cass was perplexed at what she then heard herself ask.

"Can I tag along?"

Lucas stopped in his tracks and turned around slowly.

I didn't mean that I wanted to. Actually I need to walk.

"Sure," he said. His face showed no emotion, but she was sure hers was showing mortification and disbelief.

Why did I ask that?

Yet, as he exited through the door, she found herself following behind, locking the front door behind her. She made her way to the passenger side of his squad car. There she found him waiting, and then watched as he opened the door for her.

Several times over the past months, Ella had shared how much she and her husband had emphasized three things with their son as he was growing up. *Faith, family,* and *respect.* And Cass had often noted how attentive Lucas was to carrying out what his parents had taught him. Opening the door for café customers. Waiting to begin eating his meal until Ella was seated at the table. And now, Cass was surprised to see that he was opening his car door for someone he barely knew.

It felt strange.

A few minutes later, Lucas was pulling into the Chimney Rock State Park entrance, which led to a bridge that took them over the Broad River. Peering out of the window as they did so, Cass thought she saw the same rock they had sat upon on that evening long ago. She also reflected, as they drove over the bridge, that this was the same river that she had crossed over to arrive in this place, and the same river that ran in front of the house known only as her *peace.*

She thought quickly about it, the drawing of which was currently tucked safely away in the right pocket of her shorts. She had only seen the actual house that one time, the evening that she had arrived. She realized as she thought back to that moment, the moment in which she had seen it and drawn it, how strange it was that she had never once returned back to that part of the little village.

I always take my walks in the other direction. Towards the lake.

She already knew that in two hundred and nine days she would be walking out of this place in the opposite direction from which she had come. She drew the logical conclusion that she may very well never see her *peace* in person again.

I don't have to see it in person. I just have to know it exists. In this place.

She was riding up the mountain now, in his squad car. The road was narrow with lush canopies of autumn leaves on all sides. He had rolled down the windows and she felt a cool breeze blowing across the front seat, circulating through the car and bringing in scents of pine and dried leaves. The sun was glimmering through the gaps in the leaves, creating a splash of light and shapes across the dashboard.

This seemed to bother Lucas. He fumbled in his console for a second and retrieved a pair of aviator sunglasses. Putting these on, he then looked over at Cass.

"I have another pair. Would you like them?"

He was looking at her now. Looking at her from behind the dark sunglasses. The addition of the sunglasses, against his black hair, his tan skin...

I wish he would take those off.

She nodded in silence as she once again looked ahead to the road.

—⁓—

Arriving at the top parking lot and securing a parking space right below the chimney, they both emerged from the squad car. As they rounded the corner and was exposed to a clearing, Cass found her breath catch. She could see the tops of trees and the peaks of mountains, as well as the glistening blue of the lake well below her. She stood there and looked, while Lucas walked off to find the park ranger for his safety discussion. She remained, silent, taking in the autumn splendor as it spread as far as the eye could see.

After Lucas conducted his official business, he suggested they go to the chimney itself. "If you think this view is something, wait till you see it up there."

He led the way towards the stairs, five hundred and twenty-four of them.

And I was worried about my training for the day.
He started up the steps and she followed close behind. By about
a third of the way up, their pacing had slowed. She felt sorry for
Lucas, who was dressed in his full uniform, complete with weapon
and bulletproof vest. But he never complained. In fact, he seemed
rather eager to make it to the top.

Eventually they reached the final step. Walking from there and
following him, she soon found herself standing upon the rocky ledge
shaped like a chimney. She then saw the reason for Lucas's insistence.

She was standing above the mountains, and could see for miles
in all directions. The mountains were all plastered in tiny dots of
yellows and oranges and browns and reds and greens. She now
understood how artists could name yellow so many different names.

They stood there, together, and took in the majestic view. At
one point she turned to look at him and found that he was already
turned towards her. They both were wearing his sunglasses now, so
she couldn't see his eyes.

"Is something wrong?" she asked.

"I'm just enjoying seeing it all again for the first time. I'm seeing
it through your eyes," he shared, then he turned again to take in the
view on his own.

He led her to an open space on the rocky perch where other
tourists were now seated or gathered taking selfies. He sat and she
followed, sitting closely beside him. Here they were again, on a rock.
Together. And just as it had before, the conversation came easily.
Calmly. Gently. He shared memories of growing up and visiting
this very place, sitting upon this chimney and looking out on these
mountains. She added thoughts that were more currently grounded,
observations on the vibrancy of the mountain leaves and the blueness
of the sky.

I could sit here forever. I could sit right here until the day I leave.

"I can't believe I haven't shown you the Opera Box yet," he
suddenly announced, rising to his feet quickly. He reached his hand
downward to help her, but she had already risen on her own.

"What is an Opera Box?" Cass inquired, following his quick pace off the chimney and towards a path nearby. He didn't respond to this question, only glanced back at her and grinned a little. Soon they had come to the end of the short path and were entering into a natural indentation on the side of the mountain. It appeared to be a boxed bench, eroded just so by nature for the enjoyment of humans. He walked slowly to the end of the rocky bench and she followed, sitting down next to him in this strange natural wonder.

After a few moments of silence, Lucas chuckled a little. "You know, I feel obliged to tell you the dark secret of this Opera Box before you find your reputation around the village totally ruined." He smiled as he said this, still looking forward. "When I was in high school, and quite honestly for generations before me, this is where the kids on field trips snuck off to just for the purpose of making out."

He shook his head, seeming embarrassed. She assumed he was remembering a particular moment with a particular person in this very box.

He then appeared to reconsider what he had just said. "Just a peck," he quickly added. "Innocent stuff, like that whole first kiss thing. This was sort of an iconic place in that way. Nothing too serious. You know, teenager stuff." He stopped and looked towards her, waiting for a reaction.

She looked out at the expansive view ahead of her. "I'm happy for them," she said. She was speaking quietly now, almost solely to herself. "I'm happy for all the teenagers who got to have their first kiss right here, at this spot." She tore her eyes from the beauty and looked down at her hands, still streaked with pink, tender lines. Scarred and damaged. "I'm glad they got to do that while it was still important. While it still seemed like something that would actually matter, even if it did happen."

She paused and looked back at the mountains. "It's funny how things like anticipating your first kiss feel so normal to the young. "But then …" She stopped to take another breath. Her chest was moving in a stronger rhythm as she breathed more rapidly now. She felt as if she were fighting something, pushing and pulling against something painful and hidden.

She felt the image approaching, peeling back a wall and another and another. She felt it coming towards her in all its monstrous form, even in this most beautiful of places.

The teenage girl is looking in a full length mirror. She is wearing a long pink satin dress. It is strapless. The girl's strong shoulders and lean arms are made the lovelier by the tight fit of the dress, around her bodice, flowing down to the ground. It ends in a slight train trailing behind her. There is a slit in the skirt of the dress, one that comes from the floor up and beyond her knee. Her leg and open-toed high heels can be seen emerging from the slit. Her ankle has now healed and she is standing with confidence in the heeled shoes. She is looking at herself in the mirror.

The teenage boy is slightly behind her. He is smiling with pride. He loves her and is glad that she is happy. He is speaking now. He is saying something about his friend, who will be her date. Something about a "first kiss".

"Cass." Lucas had removed his sunglasses and was looking at her. Concern was splashed across his face.

"I'm sorry, Lucas. I guess I'm just a little tired." Cass had thought she may have to retrieve her drawing and retreat to a place of solitude. But somehow, looking at him now, the image had escaped her psyche just as quickly as it had assaulted.

Lucas smiled and stood up. "Let's get you home," he said as he reached out his hand to help her up. And this time, she took it.

CHAPTER

Eighteen

He wondered why everyone assumed it couldn't be stifling hot in late October. Even with his trusty Braves t-shirt and a pair of basketball shorts, he was sweating from the morning's work in his garden. The garden's dirt had stuck in spots to perspiration, creating nasty streaks of grime across his face and arms and legs.

Lucas pulled some weeds from around his young cabbages and added these to the growing pile next to the garden. He then turned to assess his turnips. He personally didn't care for them, but Ella loved the bitter vegetable. He eyed the row of turnip plants with their leafy greens already several inches tall and felt particularly satisfied at their progress.

He stood to head inside. As he walked towards his back door from the garden plot, he glanced up to see the back of a familiar pedestrian. She was walking hurriedly on the road that ran in front of his house, at a point that was visible from his back yard.

If he hadn't known Cass from the long ponytail down her back or her familiar thrift store orange t-shirt, he would have definitely known her from her skin. Most of the scrapes and cuts on her legs and arms had already fully healed. But some of the deeper ones, while long ago shedding their scabs, still held the pinkish-reddish tint of tenderness. This gave the impression of crisscrossed stripes across her appendages. From behind her, he could make out several across the backs of her calves.

This was the first time he had ever seen her on Boys Camp Road. He wondered if she was exploring or had actually walked up and down this road before. The two of them had never discussed where, exactly, he lived. Lucas considered the possibility that perhaps his mother had mentioned it at some point in time. If so, Cass had never let on like she knew.

He diverted his attention back to his door and proceeded inside. He grabbed one cold beer from his fridge, then, without really thinking it through, grabbed another. He walked through his small living room, then through the front door onto his front porch. There he set the beers down on a small table, then relaxed in an old rocking chair passed down from his paternal grandfather.

And then Lucas waited.

Twenty or so minutes later, he saw her coming back towards him, around the curve farther up the road and walking at a steady pace. She never seemed to slow down when she was walking. She was a fountain of endurance, from what he could surmise.

As she neared his home, he stopped rocking and sat still. He felt a little strange, almost like a stalker. He was watching her but she had no idea he was there, or that his home was close by. He decided to remedy his uneasiness immediately.

He stood up and waved to get her attention. She seemed to notice the hand waving off the porch and, once she did, he waved again, this time as a greeting and not as a notification. Cass stopped in her tracks.

Does she know it's me?

She continued staring as she stood there, a hundred feet or so from his front porch. He suddenly felt awkward. He felt ridiculous, and vulnerable. Until...

Is she smiling?

From this distance it looked as if she just might be. It was always hard to tell with Cass, since she never *really* smiled. Any sign of anything positive for her was always indicated with the slightest of grins. But now, as he focused on her from his perch on the porch, it appeared that her facial expression was one worn by a person who has just been given an unexpected surprise.

She started walking again, this time in a straight trajectory leading to his front porch. She crossed the distance quickly, then stopped at the bottom step as he remained on the top.

"Is this where you live?" she asked, seeming eager to hear his response.

"Yep. Been here about six years," he shared, glancing around the porch as he did so in a sign of modest pride.

She remained standing at the bottom step. He reached over to the table and retrieved the two beer bottles.

"I can drink both of these myself, or, I guess I could share if you're up for it."

She dropped her head and put her hand over her mouth, muffling a sneeze, or maybe a chuckle. When he saw her face again, he knew, she was pleased.

They sat together on his porch. He drank the cold beer while she asked him about the Cherokee and his job and his family and his home. He asked her about her day, about what she had seen on her walk. He asked her how she was feeling and how the bakery had been this morning. He asked her whether or not she liked turnips.

Turnips?

Thinking about the turnips reminded him that he was covered in sweat and dirt.

What a sight I must be.

He shook his head slightly, wondering why he hadn't thought to at least wipe off a little before waiting for her on the porch. As soon as he thought it, he quickly checked himself.

Why would I bother to do that? It's just Cass.

During their conversation, he noticed she had hardly touched her beer. "Is it not cold enough for you?" he asked, concerned at his apparent lack of hospitality. "I can get you another one."

"To be honest, I just don't like beer," she said, gently as if to shield his feelings from being hurt. "The one I drank at Mrs. Stampshed's was, I think, the first time I had tried it. I didn't want to be rude and waste it, and I was really thirsty. But I knew that evening that my first bottle of beer would also be my last." Cass concluded this confession, then handed the beer to Lucas. "But you look like you could perhaps use a second one."

Having retrieved a cold bottle of water for her from his fridge, the two of them enjoyed more conversation on his front porch. She brought up the turnips that he had mentioned earlier, and he shared reflections on his fall garden and his favorite things to grow. She seemed extremely interested in this, so they decided to take a walk to the back of the house so she could see his garden for herself.

He showed her the rows he had planted and the sprouts of leaves that indicated something growing underneath. He explained why he had planted the selection he had, with the vast majority of his choices made simply because Ella loved this or that. As he was talking about the cabbage and the collards, Cass bent down and pulled a few weeds from around the emerging plants, adding them to the pile he had formed earlier. He crouched down close to her and resumed his garden work alongside her.

"Do you like it here?" Cass asked as she started working on the next row over, the one where green heads of cabbage the size of softballs were growing.

"Here in Lake Lure?" he responded, stopping his work momentarily to look at her.

"Here in this house, on this street, in this town. I was just wondering if you're happy," she added. "You seem like you are, but I was just wondering." She continued with her work, keeping her eyes on the dirt and plants.

"Well, I'm close by my mom, I have a great job with an amazing team, I'm living in one of the most beautiful locations in the world, so, yeah, I'm happy." As soon as he said it, he wondered why it felt like he was trying to convince someone.

"Good," she said. She moved on to the turnip row.

Resuming his work, he felt compelled to say something. Something that had been missing from his earlier response. "I won't be staying here, though. Someday soon I'll save up some money. Enough for a nice down payment for a house somewhere else, possibly in a place where real estate prices are a little different from around here." He sensed her looking up from her work, taking a pause to fully hear what he was saying. "I won't be here forever. There will come a day when I will know and my mom will know that she'll be okay without me. At that point, I'll somehow be ready. Ready to go back to California. To the coast. To the Pacific."

Will that day ever come? I had this same plan six years ago.

He looked at her, but her own attention was now diverted again to the garden.

"And what's your plan?" he asked abruptly.

She continued pulling weeds but he knew that she had heard him. He wondered if she would respond, or wait it out, as she had on occasions before. She was a master at simply staying silent until the conversation moved to a different topic.

"My plan for what?" she asked. She had added another weed to the pile, then had stopped. She was looking beyond him, at the mountain peak that could be seen from the garden.

"Your plan for the rest of your life, or at least the next decade or so of it." He watched her as she watched the mountain, then he followed her gaze to the mountain peak. He decided to add to his question, to push the envelope a little. They had built a certain trust between them over recent weeks, but he had not yet attempted to explore the degree to which she was willing to truly trust him with answers.

"What are your hopes and dreams, Cass?" He asked this with a gentle encouragement in his voice. "Or at least the aspirations you had on the day you walked into Chimney Rock and decided to live there for a year? How does this year fit into your vision for your life?" They sat side by side, with their gazes upon the mountain. He waited.

She took a deep breath then stood up. Now, after the work in his garden, she had the same streaks of wet dirt across her face and arms as he had.

"I think we did a great job weeding," she said, with a tinge of pride in her voice. She was looking out over the rows of plants, and a slight grin had formed on her lips. "It's a wonderful garden, Lucas. I can't wait to try one of your turnips someday soon."

She looked at him, grinned gently, and turned to walk towards his driveway. This would lead her back to Boys Camp Road, then back to the main road and to her endless walking.

As she departed from him, however, he sensed a hesitancy. She had left his question unanswered and unacknowledged. He was going to allow for this, as he had so many times before. He was ready to watch her walk away. But she didn't. Instead, she stopped as she neared the driveway and turned to face him. She met his eyes.

Something has changed.

"At some time, at some point, I was told to do three things," she said, quietly and almost painfully. While her voice was steady, her body seemed to be trembling slightly. Her jaw looked clenched and she seemed to be working hard to calm herself. This was difficult for her.

As she stood before him, he felt ashamed that he had asked, ashamed that his question was causing her turmoil. He wondered if he should tell her "never mind" or attempt to change the subject, but decided to do so would be an insult to the resolve she had mustered to stand before him now. He pushed himself up from where he was still seated near the garden, and stood in place quietly.

She swallowed, then coughed, then swallowed again. Still looking at him, she continued.

"I was told to be strong. To survive. And to do it on my own." She looked down and brushed some dirt from her leg. She looked back over at the garden then back at him. She smiled sweetly at him, not with teeth showing or with any exuberance of joy, but with acceptance, and with sorrow. Her subdued smiles were always for others, but seemingly never for herself.

"So, that's the plan, Lucas," she said softly. "That's the plan for the next ten years. And the ten beyond that. I'll be strong. I'll survive. And I'll do it on my own."

CHAPTER

Nineteen

"Wonder what that boy has gotten himself into now?" declared Ella as the two women readied the café for business. Cass had all the day's bakery items prepared and Ella was prepping the register and wiping down the counter. Cass enjoyed this time of day, the time when it was just the two of them, surrounded by the smells of fresh baked yumminess.

"A few years ago it was an old motorbike." Ella continued. "Lucas had found it sitting out in front of Mr. Runyon's barn with a "for sale" sign tied to it and had decided it would be the perfect project. He worked for months replacing every part, removing the rust, sanding and painting. He didn't even tell me about it, just kept declining my many invitations to supper. Before that, it was his back porch on his house, which, I'm proud to say, he built with his own two hands."

Hearing about his back porch led Cass to memories of a particular walk she had taken that had ended up in a location she hadn't planned. It had been a week since her visit down Boys Camp Road and since her conversation with Lucas over weeds and turnips and beer and bottled water. She had thought about their time together several times since then, wondered why she had shared so openly when she shouldn't have. She had chalked it up to the heat and exhaustion from walking.

I need to get stronger. Build my endurance so I can stay sharp. Be focused.

It had also been that long since she had last seen Lucas. During the time of her healing, he had joined them almost every evening for supper, and on the weekends he had often come over for breakfast as well. He had spent those many days fixing things around Ella's house or doing chores. For some reason, however, these visits had appeared to cease over the last few weeks.

Bringing herself back to the present, Cass realized that Ella had stopped talking and was now looking out the front windows, as if hoping that Lucas might walk by at any moment. Cass sensed that the older woman may be feeling a little melancholy, or perhaps a little lonely.

"Cass, I just had an incredible idea!"

Moments later, as Cass was placing the last of the warm blackberry scones into the display case, Ella was explaining her plan.

"There's an annual event held each November on the first Saturday of the month. It's called The Community Service Memorial Dinner." The excitement in Ella's voice resembled a child's. "There's a silent auction, a dinner, a dance. There's people from all over the region. Lots and lots of comradery and remembrance. And this year, Cass, the whole thing will be held at a resort just twenty minutes away."

As Ella described it, this event was attended by an eclectic group of community leaders. Politicians, police officers, firefighters, EMTs, family members, and philanthropists, all of whom wished to gather in order to pay tribute to those who serve and to those who had fallen while serving.

"And I always get to drive alone to the event and spend most of the evening by myself." Ella shared this while restocking the menus. "Lucas goes with members of his squad, which he should do, and is always so busy talking to other Chiefs and politicians that I hardly even see him. But I also don't want to skip it outright." Ella went to the front door and flipped the *Closed* sign to *Open*. "After all," she continued, "these are the people who keep us safe. Of course I want to go and show my support. It's just that I'd love to have a little company?" Ella had a sly smile on her face as she ended her sentence as more of a question. She was eyeing Cass with a hopeful expression.

"I'm sure there are many people who will be happy to go with you, Ella. And I would love to give some money, as a donation. Here." Cass reached into her shorts' pocket and pulled out some bills. "I have more, in my bedroom. I'll get it for you tonight."

Ella took the bills from Cass's hand and nodded gently. "Thank you, Cass," she said softly. "I'll be sure to add this to the donation box once I get there." Ella quietly got busy on refilling the napkin holders for the day's business.

I don't want to go. I want to walk that day. Up and down the road of this village.

Cass looked at Ella. The person who had reached out and taken her hand. The person who had opened up her home and had given Cass a place of shelter.

She sighed gently. "Thank you for asking, Ella. It would be my honor to go."

Later that afternoon, after closing up the café for the day, Cass and Ella headed to The Treasure Chest. Ella had originally suggested that they travel together to Asheville to find a new outfit for the event at a specialty shop. Cass had insisted, however, that she could quickly pick out something appropriate to wear on her own, at the thrift store located on the other side of the lake. They both had agreed to a compromise. The outfit would come from The Treasure Chest, and Ella would get to tag along.

The two women walked slowly down the road, slowly because Ella was forced to stop every few feet or so to greet the shop owners and locals along the sidewalk. Cass was amazed at how many people rolled down their windows to yell "Hey, Ella" or came running out of their shops just to get a chance to converse for a minute. Cass knew from her own experience how kind and giving Ella was, but now it was apparent that Ella was also the most popular person in the village.

The two women finally made it to the lower outskirts of the main road where The Treasure Chest sat alone by the rushing river. Upon entering, both women were immediately greeted by the energetic owner.

"Well, my goodness. Look who the cat dragged in!" Justina came walking quickly over to Ella, giving her a strong hug and then turning to extend a similar hug to Cass. "I haven't seen either one of you since my visit to the café last month. What an unexpected surprise!"

While Ella and Justina were busy getting caught up with the latest on family news (Justina's brother and his wife were coming to visit in two weeks), village gossip (Margie was getting a promotion to senior sales associate at the real estate office), and general friendly banter, Cass walked around the shop. She recognized some of the same t-shirts she had perused through on her last visit. She made her way over to the leggings basket, wondering if she should get one more pair for the winter.

"So, you're here to find a dress?" Justina called out to Cass as she walked past on another aisle. "How delightful!" No doubt this meant that Ella had filled her in on all the details of the event and the fact that Cass would be going.

Justina was now at a rack near the back wall, one filled with skirts and dresses. She called back over her shoulder to Ella. "I tried to tell her, last time she was here, that she needed to grab at least one nice outfit." Justina reached to grab a dress from the rack, then stopped abruptly. "What exactly is your size, Cass? I'm guessing a four?" Both Justina and Ella were looking at Cass now, and from the looks in their eyes, they were halfway waiting for her response, and halfway sizing her up with their own guesswork.

"Sure," Cass responded.

"I thought so," Justina shared as she nodded her head. She turned back towards the rack, replacing the dress that had apparently been a different size and moving herself down one section to an area labeled with a plastic white "4" marker. Justina and Ella simultaneously started fumbling through the dresses hanging on the rack, commenting on the colors and styles.

Cass watched them for a brief minute, then quietly walked over to the rack. She reached for the very first dress behind the "4" marker, then announced, "This one is perfect."

In truth, she hadn't even looked at the dress beyond knowing that it was the first one on the rack. She followed the horrified looks on Ella's and Justina's faces and took a closer look at the item in her hand. It was a satin dress. A deep-yellow dress. It resembled the color of mustard. The length suggested it would come about mid-calf. It had puffy sleeves with taffeta cuffs that would come right around the wrist. There was a light orange fringe sewed around the waistline and a large bright orange silk flower pinned to the upper bodice.

Cass headed towards the check-out counter. Ella and Justina stood frozen in place, then quietly followed her.

In her usual upbeat manner, Ella broke the silence. "She'll look lovely in anything, really. Now, how about shoes?" Ella started glancing through the used shoes on the rack near the counter. "Size seven and a half. Right, Cass? I think I remember that from the day you and I went to get more sneakers at the thrift shop."

Cass hadn't thought about shoes, other than the walking shoes she intended to get while she was here. She was beginning to regret her decision to go with Ella to the event. This shopping was getting out of hand, causing her a general discomfort. The whole experience was disturbing, and seemed to be pushing her towards images best left undisturbed. She just wanted this to be done. To have the outfit. To go to the event and show her respect.

But even as Justina started speaking, Cass sensed she was already too late. A memory was approaching. Slowly. Stealthily.

"You help her with the right shoes, Ella, while I look for the perfect jewelry. Cass, how about these dangling earrings, which would actually…."

Justina's voice started to fade, even though her lips continued to move. She was smiling and excited and seemed so happy to be a part of making Cass look beautiful. Cass heard Justina's voice continue in a faded, muted echo, as if the sound was reaching Cass's ears through a long tunnel.

"And a little gold eyeshadow and just the right tint of coral on her lips. Oh no! It looks like that dress might have a little stain. But don't worry, Cass. I think maybe…."

Cass laid the dress on the counter along with a ten-dollar bill and backed away. She turned towards the front door and started a hurried progression towards it, then remembered the other women who were with her.

"I'm so sorry," she said quietly over her shoulder. "I just need to step out for a minute. I do appreciate everything. Please just get a dress, any dress, and some shoes. I don't care what they look like. Just please, nothing else. Please." With that, Cass left the store.

She turned right on the sidewalk, then took a hard right and took the path down to the river. She found a rock in a spot where no one else was visible. Her head was starting to ache, her breath coming quickly. She reached to find her right pocket and the contents within, even as the image found her.

The girl is standing in front of a full-length mirror. The long dress has a slit that reaches beyond her left knee, showcasing a tanned leg in an open-toed high-heeled shoe. The boy is standing behind her, looking at her in the mirror. He is proud. He is speaking, even as their smiles are frozen in place. She is admiring the pink satin gown perfectly fitted to her lean stature. She hears what he is saying and it makes her happy. "Once he sees you in that tonight, you're sure to finally get your first kiss." He is making

fun of her, and laughing, and she loves it. They are giggling together,
happy that she looks so pretty in her brand new dress. They both are ready.
Ready for their senior prom. Ready for tonight. The day is finally here. It
is finally the eighteenth of May.

CHAPTER

Twenty

"How are things in Lake Lure, Chief Montraine?" Chief Thomas Trull of the Sylva Police Department was shaking Lucas's hand, one of dozens of handshakes Lucas had already encountered in the thirty minutes since he had arrived. He always enjoyed this annual event, particularly reconnecting with fellow officers, such as Tommy, from across the southwestern region of the state. Tommy's town was a good seventy miles or so from Lake Lure, a little much for a frequent friendly visit.

"Very quiet, Tommy. As usual, very quiet." Lucas gave the older man a gentle pat on the shoulder and they spent a few minutes catching up. As they did so, Lucas took another casual glance around the venue for this year's event. The resort located on the north shores of the lake proved to be a perfect setting. It included a private beach, an impressive restaurant and reception area, and stunning views of the mountains and the water.

He walked outside to the open-air deck, and noted how warm the air felt. Since the event was always held the first Saturday of November, the weather was always a wildcard. But on this day the temperature was wonderfully mild. The band started playing inside, sending rhythmic vibrations of classic pop and show tunes echoing across the entire building. The annual Community Service Memorial Dinner was officially underway.

As he stood looking out from the deck, Officer Nixon joined him. Each year Lucas paid for one of his officers and a plus-one to join him at this special event. This year was Tank's year.

"Hey, Chief. Having fun?"

"So far, so good," Lucas replied. "And you and the Mrs.?"

"Lower your voice, please. I don't want her getting any ideas," Tank replied jovially. "Oh, that reminds me. I saw your friend a few hours ago. She was down near the park. Acting strange as usual." Tank took a sip of his beer and looked out over the water.

"What friend?" Lucas inquired.

"You know, that girl. Cass. She was just sitting there, all crouched up like she was hiding, or in a trance. I didn't bother her or anything. But I did make it a point to drive by a few times, just to make sure she was okay. Each time, she was just sitting there, staring at a piece of paper. Still as a statue."

Tank provided a little more small talk then left to find his girlfriend. Lucas decided to stay on the deck and wait on his mother to arrive. Ella had called him earlier to share that she had a "little surprise" she was bringing to the dinner tonight. He was curious as to what surprise she had in mind. He predicted it was a goofy school picture from third grade, or some other memento with which to embarrass him.

He looked out over the blue waters of Lake Lure. The lake was still this evening, appearing like a glass floor at the base of Rumbling Bald Mountain. His eyes left the water and fell upon the beach of white sand, and then grass, and then the wooden walkway that led from the water to the reception venue. He saw people standing there, gathered in small groups, talking and enjoying the view. His eyes shifted to a lone figure.

She was wearing a blue dress with a sheer blue wrap held loosely about her shoulders. The wrap, and her long, loose hair, blew softly in the gentle wind. She was turned to the lake, standing as still as the water.

He felt his breath catch in his chest as her head turned slightly to the side. Her face continued slowly turning, until she was fully looking back. Over her shoulder.

At him.

The soft breeze lifted strands of her hair again, and a wisp played lightly across her forehead. He felt unable to move. He couldn't think. He wasn't prepared, not for this.

"There you are!"

Ella's voice abruptly drew Lucas's gaze away as he rotated around to find his mother approaching. She was dressed to the hills in a lovely brown gown and matching long jacket, accented with a large gold necklace draped around her neck. Her trademark orange lipstick was applied generously for this special evening.

He embraced Ella in a tight hug as she reached him. He held her there for a long time, enjoying the sight and presence of her, as he always did. He could smell her perfume now, that combination of lavender and jasmine that fit her personality so well.

"Goodness, I thought I would never find a parking space," Ella exclaimed, brushing out the few wrinkles in her dress and tapping down her wispy hair. "What a crowd there is tonight!"

"I know, Mom. I think we may actually break an attendance record this year." Lucas glanced back over the deck nonchalantly, trying to locate the object of his earlier attention.

"By the way, Lucas, have you figured out my surprise yet? I happened to drop the surprise off while I went to park the car, but I'm having a little trouble finding her…I mean *it*." Ella snickered at this correction, trying her best to conceal the big secret.

He was glancing again towards the walkway. "Yes, I think I know what your surprise is, Mom." There were dozens of people there, and over a hundred more on the same deck where he was standing. Women with lovely cocktail dresses and sparkling jewelry.

Coifed hair held in place with clips and spray. Makeup applied to eyes and lips. Nails polished and shimmering.

Among them all, however, he no longer saw her.

"I still can't believe she agreed to come," Ella said as she looked around the room. "But now I can't seem to find her." Ella paused then continued, her voice now suddenly taking on a somber tone. "Poor thing. She already had a little bad luck on the ride over here." Ella dropped her voice to a whisper and leaned in closer to Lucas. "Apparently, she was planning to wear her hair pulled back, like it always is. But as she tried to tighten her ponytail the hair tie snapped. She kept trying to retie it in knots and get it to hold, but it just wouldn't work." Ella scanned the room again, seeming anxious. "Of course, I didn't have any spare hair ties in the car. You know I haven't worn those things in years. I personally think her hair looks lovely, but she seemed pretty upset by it all."

Ella continued scanning the crowd while Lucas excused himself, promising to find his mother again in a few minutes. He proceeded to the exit that led to the grounds and the beach. He opened the door.

She was there. Standing before him, just a few feet away. He could see that the blue of her dress was almost the exact color of her eyes. It showcased her lean body and her feminine curves and her shoulders and arms and legs. She was standing comfortably in heels that strapped around her ankles. She walked a few feet towards him now, as if off a runway.

He noticed her hair, the hair that Ella had just referenced and the hair that was supposed to be up, in the usual ponytail. Her hair was falling around her neck and shoulders like a cascading waterfall of golden and light brown water. It was touching her skin in lovely waves.

Her lips were glossy and a natural pink, as they normally were. As far as makeup or jewelry or any other adornment, there was none.

She bent her knees and slowly lowered herself enough to touch a flower that was growing along the sidewalk. It was a daisy. She picked the flower and then raised up again to stand before him, placing the flower behind her right ear.

He knew he was staring, but was unable to take his eyes from her. He decided to break the silence.

"I must say, I wasn't expecting to see you here tonight." He stepped a little closer to her, attempting to lessen the air of formality that seemed to be surrounding the two of them.

"As you well know," Cass replied, "your mother is a hard person to say no to. It seemed to be important to her, so...." At that, Cass made a sweeping gesture down the length of her dress, as if to indicate *so here I am*.

She turned then and looked out over the lake, but his eyes remained on her. Seeing her like this was distracting, confusing. He wasn't ready. He had received no forewarning.

He heard himself say, "Well, I'm glad you came. Enjoy your evening." With that he turned to walk away and noticed that Ella was walking towards them.

Good. She won't be alone.

Lucas made his way back into the throng of people and filled the next hour of his evening with eating, socializing, and reconnecting. At one point, he was speaking with the new Deputy Chief of Rutherfordton when he saw Tommy standing near the bar, motioning for him. As he walked towards his old friend, he noticed Tommy was actively scanning the crowd, as if searching for someone.

"Hey, what's up, Tommy?" Lucas asked as he approached.

Tommy ceased his visual searching and lowered his voice. "Earlier in the evening, I happened to see you speaking with a woman in a blue dress right outside the deck area. I knew she looked familiar, but I couldn't quite place her until it hit me, just a few minutes ago. By any chance, was that Cass?"

What?

"Yes," Lucas replied softly, in partial shock. "It was Cass."

Over the next few minutes, Chief Trull answered Lucas's many questions on how exactly he knew the woman in the blue dress. From what Tommy could remember, she had visited and actually lived in his town two years ago. He was able to remember this timeline due to a bad flood that had occurred during the fall of that year and Cass's assistance in filling sandbags to help protect some of the local businesses. He remembered that Cass had lived in the basement of a local church, and had exchanged this room and board for custodial work she did in the church facility. The church congregation had actually grown quite fond of her and had considered this exchange of services part of their mission work. Tommy also thought, from what he could remember, that she had worked part-time in a local bar, cleaning tables and washing dishes. According to Tommy's recollection, she had lived quietly, caused no trouble, and then, one day, she had just left. She had walked out of town without saying goodbye to anyone and had never been heard from again.

"I'll never forget the afternoon that I got to actually talk to her," Tommy shared. "I mean, I had greeted her in passing, of course, but there was this one day that I actually had a few minutes to converse with her." Tommy paused to take another sip of beer. "I had been patrolling some of the roads on the outskirts of town when I had happened upon her, sitting on the side of the road. She was just sitting there, staring at this old house that's down in a valley. Anyway, I hadn't known at the time if everything was okay. She may have been in distress or had a snake bite or, who knows. So I pulled over to check on her and we ended up talking for a while."

Tommy stopped, seeming to have ended the remembrance. Then, almost as an afterthought, he continued. "She's actually a sweet person. Talking to her, I just remember thinking how kind and gentle she seemed. But she also seemed to have some great weight on her shoulders. She never shared what that was, and to be honest, I don't think anyone ever asked."

Lucas was taking this in, comparing it to what he already knew and the clues already written on his note pad. There seemed to be some similarities, and he suddenly felt more intrigued.

"So what was the deal with the house?" he asked.

Tommy looked confused. "What house?"

"The house she was staring at. Why that one?" Lucas asked this as he pictured Cass sitting in the grass, silent and alone.

"I asked her that same question," Tommy replied. "From what I can remember, she just liked it because she thought it looked peaceful. In fact, I remember her saying that she had chosen that house as the most peaceful place in our town. Which I had thought was sort of sweet. I guess that's why I remember that part of our exchange so vividly."

The two men stood in silence, Tommy enjoying his beer and Lucas trying to process what he had just learned. Suddenly, Tommy turned to Lucas with a chuckle.

"I almost forgot to tell you the most unbelievable part," Tommy said with excitement. "Before I drove off that day, after talking to her, I remember that I told her to take a picture. That if she loved the house that much she should take a picture. That way she could look at it whenever she wanted. And you'll never believe what she said."

Oh, I think I can guess.

"She said she didn't a cell phone!" Tommy said this with sincere disbelief in his tone. "Can you believe that, Lucas? What young person nowadays doesn't have a phone?" Tommy took a drink of his beer and then resumed his recollection. "But anyway, it didn't seem to bother her. She told me that day that she already had a picture of it. Of the house. And that was that."

Lucas nodded his head in understanding. Tommy was accosted by some colleagues from a neighboring city and Lucas was left alone to consider all that had been shared. He heard the band in the adjacent room begin a new ballad, one that was slower and more solemn.

He realized that he should be shaking hands and making connections. But he felt locked in place, his mind attempting to connect dots in some logical pattern that continued to elude him.

What does it matter?

He walked from the bar towards the music, towards the crowd

that was gathered around couples slowly dancing. The music was sad but in a beautiful kind of way. He glanced nonchalantly around the room and his eyes found the familiar. Ella and Cass were standing near the corner. Ella was engaged in a conversation with the Fire Chief from nearby Hendersonville and Cass was standing quietly. Her hands were holding the shoulder wrap and were folded in front of her.

He walked towards them, never taking his eyes from her. She appeared as just a woman, a beautiful woman. A woman that anyone in the room would have noticed. From this angle he could not see her eyes, the eyes that tried to hide the constant companionship of pain.

He patted Fire Chief Sutton's back and shook his hand. He blurted a quick, "Hey Chief. Hey, Mom. I don't want to interrupt," and then turned to Cass and took her hand. "Dance with me, Cass?"

He knew without looking that Ella's mouth had gone agape, but he was more focused on Cass, more interested in her reaction. She glanced down at her hand, now in his, and then back to his face. She glanced over to the dance floor and appeared to be processing what her response might be.

She nodded her head gently and then whispered, "Why not?" She handed her wrap to Ella and then turned to walk towards the dance floor, with her hand still in his own.

Lucas had known all of his adult life that dancing was not his strength, but attempting to dance with her made him feel like a professional. He got the sense from their early steps that perhaps she had never danced before. It took her a little while to get the rhythm of the back and forth and side to side. He saw her glancing frequently at her feet and then his.

But by the end of the song, she had started to get the hang of it and even seemed to be enjoying it. He asked if she would dance the next song as well, and she agreed.

He looked up and glanced around the room.

Is everyone looking at us?

He was sure he was imagining things, then tried to perceive

how they might look right now. Perhaps they were just dancing so awkwardly that others could not help but look. Or perhaps, with his black suit and black tie, and with her...

He stopped thinking about why people were watching them. She had moved a little closer, or perhaps he had moved closer to her. They were swaying to the rhythm of the instrumental in perfect tandem. Her left hand was till clasped in his right. He was careful not to hold it too tight. This was the hand that had been damaged and had required surgery. This was the hand that had ripped apart and had been put back together again. He knew not the pain or tenderness that still lingered there.

Her other hand at first had rested gently on his arm. But gradually she had moved it, and it was now on his shoulder and close to this neck. His hand rested softly on the narrow waistline of her open-back dress. He was careful to keep his fingers from touching her skin.

They continued to dance. The lovely music surrounded them as they swayed in a silent trance.

He didn't know how it happened, but the space between them had lessened even further. She was looking straight ahead, but her cheek was mere inches from his own. In her high heels she was almost his height, which meant as he cut his eyes sideways her own eyes were almost parallel. Their bodies were so close they were almost touching. Their hands had somehow lost the formal grasp, and his hand was now encircling hers. He felt her skin as his other hand spread out on the small of her back in a strong grasp. He wanted to pull her even closer. But there was no need, for he sensed she had moved closer on her own.

He felt intoxicated, then remembered he hadn't had any alcohol the whole evening. In truth, he wanted the song to play for a very long time.

But it won't. It won't last. She won't be staying too long.

He thought back to Tommy's words, spoken just minutes before. She had left Tommy's town without saying goodbye. She would be leaving Chimney Rock as well. She had made that clear. He willed himself to stop dancing, to walk her back to Ella. He told himself to find a distraction or someone he needed to speak with. But none of those things happened.

He danced with her, and as he did so he thought back to the afternoon they had spent on Chimney Rock Mountain. He remembered the things she had said to him that day. The words of this woman who he now held dangerously close. His thoughts veered to them sitting in the Opera Box. Of her melancholy as she talked about youthful joy as if it had been voided from her life. He moved his hand a little further up her back, feeling the sudden urge to hold her and protect her.

Why were you never kissed?

He bent his head slightly, so his lips were almost touching her ear. He was realizing it, even as he continued the gentle swaying with her close to him. He was understanding, and he wasn't afraid.

"It will be me," he whispered, so only she could hear. "You're going to be kissed, someday soon, for the first time. And if it's okay with you, the person who will kiss you ... will be me."

He looked straight ahead and could tell that she was doing so as well. Then she slowed her dancing and turned her head to look straight at him. He slowed as well, turning to face and accept her gaze. Other couples continued their swaying around them, but the two of them were barely moving now. She had not taken her hand from his nor removed her hand from his shoulder. His hand remained on her back, pushing softly to keep her close.

He bent his head again and brushed his cheek lightly across hers, whispering now again in her ear.

"On the day and at the time of your choosing."

He stood straight again and looked straight ahead, feeling confused and unburdened all at once. He started to let go of her hand, to move himself from her, but she grasped his hand tightly as it started to slip away. The song had ended and the dance floor was clearing. Yet she was still standing firm, still looking at him, now into his eyes as he turned to face her again.

Her face was filled with beauty, and her expression filled with wonder. She leaned forward and went up slightly on her toes, bringing her face very close to his, now whispering with her own lips into his ear.

"Now is all I have." She leaned back slightly, with her face mere inches from his own.

"I choose now."

CHAPTER

Twenty-One

*O*pening the Bible that she had borrowed from Ella, she turned to the page marked by a dried leaf, one she had picked up from this garden bridge just last week. The natural bookmark led Cass to a page deep into the book of Psalms. She started to read the words aloud, then swallowed against the dryness of her throat. It had been sore for several days now, and she wished she had remembered to bring a bottle of water. She began again, reading silently now, focusing on the words.

The cords of death entangled me.

The anguish of the grave came upon me;

I was overcome by trouble and sorrow.

She closed the Bible gently.

I will read Psalm 116 another day. But not today.

She stood and walked through the garden, among the dark evergreen bushes and the wilted flowers with dried blooms. She was the only one on the bridge today, so she took her time as she walked along the winding pathway.

She tried again and again to swallow, to alleviate the dryness of her throat. But with each attempt there was a shooting pain that stole her focus from the quiet garden around her. She gently rubbed the skin on her neck, knowing as she did so that it wouldn't help. The soreness was all-consuming. The soreness.

The girl is at the start line. There are others on either side of her. Challengers who know that she is the one to beat. Competitors who know that she is injured. She is weak. Their vision is frozen in place as they glance at her heavily taped ankle. Her foot is poised in a way to barely touch the black asphalt below it, appearing too tender and sore to even stand upon.

She is not looking at them. She is looking at the finish line two hundred meters away, around and up the asphalt track. The girl and the others are frozen in this image. These are the moments of time prior to the call for runners to "take their mark" and to "get set". These are the moments in which the competitor must decide. Decide how much she is willing to give. How much she is willing to endure.

A voice is speaking now, the voice of her coach. He is calling out to her. He is telling her how to endure. "Take yourself away from here. Pick a place that gives you peace. A place from your childhood or from your time with your family. A place at which you feel nothing but calm. Then picture that place in your mind, and put yourself there."

The coach's voice is confident. He is wise. He is telling her the way. He is preparing her for the pain ahead. "This is the State High School Championship," he is reminding her. "The one you have worked so hard for. Once you begin the race, the pain will be immense. But keep your mind in your place of peace. Calm your heart. Lock away all of those senses that will be telling you to stop."

The girl and the competitors have all crouched now, with their fingers at the start line. They are frozen at the start line with one second before the race will begin. Her injury is throbbing, filling her body with pain and fear.

She wants to cry but she will not cry. She wants to scream but she will not scream.

The coach's voice can still be heard.

"Keep telling yourself 'I am there. I am there. I am at that place of peace'. See the finish line. See it. And somehow find a way."

"Find a way," the coach is yelling. "Find a way. And, then…just go." She looked for a nearby bench, then decided to just sit on the pavement, with her back against a wooden planked fence. She reached into her legging pocket and retrieved the worn and bloodied paper. The one with hundreds of wrinkled indentations from folding and unfolding and folding.

Her *peace*. She focused and calmed her breathing, then willed her heartbeat to slow. A distant voice was still calling…

"Find a way…"

And then the memory was gone. She exhaled slowly and calmly.

She stood again and continued walking. There were birds nearby in the trees overhanging the garden. Their chirps and songs provided a perfect symphony to this cool, quiet morning. She saw a lone daisy, sticking out haphazardly from a pot of pruned rose vines. She considered picking it, then decided to let it stay. It had somehow stood resiliently into late November. It had somehow survived.

Seeing the daisy had reminded her of a few weeks earlier, when she had a daisy in her hair. When she danced with Lucas to a slow, sad melody. He had whispered in her ear, had told her that she would be kissed. This had made her feel strange, had made her feel warm. She had been very close to him, had seen his smooth neck up close. Had seen the pulse beating in the veins under his skin. She had imagined how it might feel, to rest one's head against that neck. She had wondered how it might feel, to take solace in that embrace.

He had turned his face towards her, had lowered his lips closer, towards hers. Their eyes had been locked, and in his she had seen something unexpected. An invitation. One that said *I can be trusted*.

They had stood still on the dance floor, even as others walked and danced and conversed around them. She had felt his hands move up her back, pressing against her skin to move her closer to him. She had felt her own legs inching their way in his direction, on their own.

She had felt his fingers find something unexpected, something out of place. It was something raised on the skin of her back. Something thick and deep. Something ragged.

She thought back to that moment, the moment at which she saw the change in his eyes, those eyes that were staring back into her own. He had watched her even as his fingers lightly traced the scar for an inch. Then two inches and more, up her back. And then he had stopped, perhaps unable to will himself to go any further.

He was a police officer. He would know exactly what could make such a scar, even if she did not. There had been recognition in his eyes, those eyes that had been mere inches from her own. Sorrow and concern had quickly replaced the intimacy. She had seen the understanding. She had known this would lead to questions. As his hand remained on her back, she had seen the questions forming, behind his dark eyes.

They had continued to look at one another, frozen in place, until suddenly he had made the slightest movement towards her. With his warm hand still on the scar he had found, he was bringing his face towards hers. His lips were nearing her own. She had seen in his eyes no evidence of the suspicion she had seen just seconds before. His eyes had held some emotion, and she had found the word to describe it even as she felt it well up inside her.

Longing.

His lips, however, had not met their target. Ella had appeared, seeming embarrassed by her timing. Then a colleague from a nearby police force had bumped into Lucas while walking by. Before long, all thoughts of the offer made just moments before had dissipated.

In the weeks that had passed since then, life in the quiet village had resumed to its normal patterns. Cass woke early each morning to bake, then worked in the café until a little past lunchtime. She then walked alone for hours along the roads that weaved in and around the gorge. Now that the days were shorter, she often found herself walking in darkness.

Ella had continued to look for Lucas's visits in the evenings and on the weekends, but these were still few and far between. He had been working on what he described to his mother as projects, and Ella had become visibly saddened with the vastly reduced contact with her son. The few times he had stopped by, he had been cordial and kind towards Cass, but always with a formal distance between them.

Cass reached the part of the garden that crossed over the river. She stopped and leaned over the railing to look out over the calm water. There were no rocks here to interrupt the water's progression, so the river flowed gently underneath.

Unexpectedly, she heard footsteps behind her. Turning her head, she saw Lucas approaching with two Styrofoam cups clasped in his hands.

"Hey, Cass," he said with a smile. His voice was relaxed and friendly. He was wearing a white long sleeve thermal shirt that fit his chest snugly. He had on dark brown khakis and work boots and a ball cap turned backwards that covered most of his black hair. It was Sunday afternoon, his day off.

"I was coming home from Mom's earlier and thought I saw you out here," Lucas continued. "I went home and made us a couple of hot apple ciders, just in case you were a little chilly." He held one of the cups out towards her and she took it eagerly.

"Thank you, Lucas," she said with hoarseness as she took the cup. "I needed this." She was genuinely grateful as she took her first sip. The warm spiced concoction warmed her throat and instantly soothed the scratchiness. "So, what might you be up to today?" she asked, glad that he had already taken the time from his busy home improvement schedule to spend some time with Ella.

"Oh, just the usual," he said as he looked out over the river. "I think I'll try to do a little painting today since this is probably the last nice weekend we have left before winter."

"Would you like some help?" she asked. She considered herself a decent painter and had even helped Mr. Campwell just last week in painting his barn.

Lucas appeared to contemplate this offer seriously, then answered.

"I think I'll let you sit this one out, but thanks for the offer just the same."

She nodded her head slightly in comprehension. A comfortable silence followed as they stood on the bridge watching the river.

After some time had passed, Lucas turned towards her. "How about today?" he asked quietly.

She turned towards him and took another sip of the delicious cider.

"How about *what* today?" She thought she must have missed something he had said during her trancelike gaze over the water.

"How about you choose today?" he said quietly. "The day and time of your choosing, remember?"

Yes. I remember.

She stared but didn't speak. He was watching her. He was waiting.

There was a breeze blowing now, a cool breeze that tossed orange and yellow leaves from their branches and floated them down and around the two of them. The breeze loosened strands of hair from her loose ponytail and these now played lightly across her cheeks.

She shook her head gently and looked forward again. "I think I'm getting sick, to be honest," she said hesitantly. "We wouldn't want our town's beloved Police Chief falling ill, would we?"

She felt a hand upon her arm, felt herself being turned back towards him, gently but resolutely.

He looked deeply into her eyes, nodding his head ever slightly. "I can handle a sore throat."

He stepped forward. Their eyes were locked, unblinking, as he leaned and closed the distance between them. Gradually, slowly.

I won't be staying too long.

She could hear his breath, hear as he exhaled softly. His hand tightened slightly on her arm, and as he came closer, his hand became more tensed. Soon he was so close she could see the darker specks of black in his darkest of brown eyes.

He is everything good.

His lips brushed hers, ever so lightly, and then held in place. And when he retreated from her, and unclasped his hand from her arm, her face suddenly felt warm. But she did not turn away. She did not take her eyes from him.

She studied the expression on his face. He was either regretting what had just happened or contemplating why it had happened. Before the kiss he had appeared confident and at ease, but now he seemed confused, almost pained. He shook his head slightly, as if thinking to himself. He took one final, intense look at her, then went to turn.

"I'll see you around, Cass." He started to walk away, then turned again and called back to her, "And I hope you feel better real soon."

She watched him as he walked to the end of the garden bridge and got into his truck. The truck sat in place for several minutes, then finally pulled away.

Her mind was filled with the sight and sound and smell of him. She started to giggle, then made herself stop almost as quickly as she had started. She looked back over the water, leaning over the bridge as she did so. She thought she saw her reflection, but only briefly. It soon morphed into a reflection of his face, into an image of the expression he had worn as he had left.

His expression was telling her that he knew. He was smart. He understood.

She will not be staying in this place. She will leave. On that day, she will leave.

She was glad he had pulled away. Glad that he knew and understood. Glad that he had left quickly afterwards.

Yes. Go. Do not linger here. I won't be staying too long.

She thought ahead to the day that she would leave. That day that didn't exist, except for the purpose of leaving and walking and being nowhere with no one. On that day, when she left, this spot on the bridge and the man who had just stood here and the kiss…it would be as if they had not existed. As if none of it had happened.

After that day, the day when she would leave, the kiss would never be thought of again.

But for this day, she rubbed her finger gently along her lower lip. She rubbed where his lip had touched her own.

For this day, she remembered.

Winter

CHAPTER

Twenty-Two

$\mathscr{L}$ ucas took a final bite of his fried chicken and laid it back down on his plate in dramatic fashion. He hoped to give a clear signal to Ella that he was done. She had piled his plate unusually full to begin with, and then added extra servings of potatoes and peas as he was finishing the first.

Glancing at Cass's plate, he was happy to see that she had eaten much of her food as well. It had been very rare during the early months of her stay that she had agreed to join in on the home-cooked meals in Ella's kitchen. But now, it was more normal than not for Cass to interrupt her afternoon walk to return to the home for the supper gathering.

With the colder weather now fully upon them, Lucas's home improvement projects had slowed, leaving him less busy in the evenings and more available to accept Ella's frequent invitations. Something about his mom's cooking and the warmth of the kitchen made him anticipate these meals with significant enthusiasm.

He took the opportunity to steal a glance at Cass while she was busy with the food on her plate. Since their time together on the garden bridge a couple of weeks earlier, they had not discussed nor attempted to repeat the kiss that had occurred between them. He assumed she had refrained from doing so because it had meant very little to her. For his part, it was almost the opposite.

On that day, with that kiss, he had nearly lost himself in her eyes, in the softness and beauty and sweetness that was her. But it had taken only seconds for him to remember. Even as he had pulled away from her, with every intent of kissing her again, he had regained his resolve. He had recalled with great clarity what it felt like to be left alone by someone you trust, by someone you love. He had determined at that moment that he had no desire to engage in any further intimacy with her. He had no appetite for being forgotten, again.

She is leaving, he had thought, standing close to her on the bridge. *She is leaving,* he had remembered as he had released her arm and stepped away. *She wants only to be alone,* he had said to himself, as he had sat in his truck and fought against the urge to return to her, to embrace her. *I don't know her,* he had said out loud as he had driven away on that day. *I don't know anything about her. And most likely, I never will.*

Coming to this realization, Lucas had decided to recapture his earlier, more clinical viewpoint of the situation. He had driven straight home from the garden that day, with a renewed focus on the unanswered questions. He had retrieved his notepad and studied the clues written there, on the list that he had started almost seven months prior.

He knew that she was twenty-seven years old. He knew that two years ago she had been in Sylva, a small town exactly seventy-two miles from Chimney Rock. He knew that her existence there had been very similar to her existence here. He had methodically checked off all that he knew while he sat at his kitchen table. He had tried to solve the riddle, with the taste of her lips still lingering on his own.

He had devised a theory, based on the number of miles a healthy young person could walk in a twelve-hour span. Using basic mathematical skills, he had deduced that Cass could cover around thirty-five miles in one day, taking into account variables such as weather and restroom breaks. With this formula in his mind, he had spread a map out on his table.

And he had considered all that he knew.

Grounding his theory on the key number of thirty-five, Lucas had put his thoughts to paper. He had found Sylva on the map, and then calculated.

A year in Sylva. A day of walking around thirty-five miles. Another year in another town. A day of walking around thirty-five miles. Another year – in Chimney Rock.

It was a viable theory, but one that Lucas realized rested solely on circumstantial facts. Tidbits of information that he had patched together in some way that made sense. There were many other explanations that could fit, but he had questioned if these other theories were even worth the time to explore. She was leaving in a little over five months.

What exactly am I trying to solve? It doesn't matter.

And so, a considerate friendliness had settled over the two of them as he resolved to forget the kiss and also to abandon the riddle. They resorted back to comfortable interactions with one another, the kind they had experienced before the evening of the dance. Before the kiss. Before he had reminded himself of what would not be.

Bringing himself back to the present, he saw that Cass was busy thanking Ella for the meal, seeming oblivious to the fact that he was watching her. As she looked away from Ella and in his direction, he quickly looked down at his plate. He abruptly took the plate by the sides and stood up, grabbing his glass and silverware and heading to the sink. He volunteered to do the dishes, and Cass offered up her own assistance. With this chore aptly covered, Ella went to her bedroom to change into warmer clothes.

"So, how excited are you to finally go souvenir shopping in the famous Chimney Rock shops?" Lucas asked this as he handed Cass a washed and rinsed plate.

"You're saying that a little sarcastically, but I'll have you know I'm actually super excited," Cass replied as she dried and then placed the plate on an open shelf. She took another from Lucas's waiting hand.

"Well, you are definitely the only twenty-seven-year-old I've ever met who's excited about browsing through souvenir shops." He said this with a slight chuckle.

"I'm actually twenty-eight," she shared, keeping her eyes on the dish as she did so.

You had a birthday. At some point, you had a birthday.

"Well, you're in for quite a treat," Lucas announced as he rinsed off the last dish and started to hand it to her. He realized too late that she didn't quite have a grip on it. He released it and then watched as it began to spiral towards the floor. They both reacted quickly, with Cass grabbing it first. As the two reached for the same target, their heads butted loudly together.

Cass uttered a muted grunt as Lucas yelled out "Shit". She lifted her head slightly from the impact, then closed her eyes and grimaced.

He began rubbing his throbbing head, hoping to alleviate the impending headache before it fully materialized. He lifted his eyes and he saw her, bearing her own obvious pain with closed eyes and a quiet reserve. He took his hand from his own head and starting gently rubbing hers, more in a gesture of comfort than as an actual remedy.

She opened her eyes slowly and looked up at him. He continued, lightly rubbing his fingers in a circular motion on the spot on her forehead that now was a little pink.

He expected her at any moment to declare that she was fine, that she didn't need any help. But she stood there. Still. And slowly, a smile started to form. It was her usual subtle grin, the one where the corners of her closed lips turned up just enough to indicate that she wasn't unhappy. He watched as her lips turned up at the corners even more dramatically. There were the slightest traces of dimples showing now, in her cheeks. Her eyes were reflecting something,

something different from the constant worry that seemed to plague them at all times. And then, the lips parted, and the smile blossomed fully.

She was smiling. Really, truly, smiling.

As suddenly as it had come, it was gone. He retreated his fingers back and away as she dried the plate in her hand and placed it on the shelf. Now that the dishes were completed, she walked towards his old bedroom to add on a layer of clothing.

—⁓—

After perusing through two of the souvenir shops and stopping for some hot chocolate, Lucas and the two women were now headed for Billy's Bear Trap, one of Lucas's favorite places in the village. He remembered many weekend trips here with his father. The usual routine was that Lucas would do his chores all week long and then Walter would bring him to Billy's to spend his earnings, usually on hand-carved walking sticks or slingshots.

I wonder where all of those souvenirs are now? Did I throw them away in my haste to pack for college?

Pulling himself away from the melancholy, Lucas led the two women towards Billy's, glancing backwards occasionally to spy Ella and Cass as they walked and chatted behind him. He heard Cass's voice and remembered the image of her smiling at him. It was the first time he had seen her teeth in a smile, the first time he had noticed that she had tiny dimples. As he walked and listened to her voice behind him, he came to a somber conclusion.

I wish I hadn't seen her smile.

They arrived at Billy's and escaped the cold through the front door, only to find Billy himself behind the counter. As Ella and Lucas stopped to catch up with the shop owner, Cass proceeded to the tables filled with trinkets. Apparently, she had developed some kind of system for seeing every item on every row in every corner of every shop. Ella and Lucas wandered over to a nearby table, one filled with Daniel Boone hunting hats.

"We're going to be here all night," Ella whispered as she stood beside him. She said this with nothing but patience and love in her voice. Lucas suspected that Ella was thrilled that Cass was having such an engaging time.

"Well, we're the ones who promised her an evening of souvenir Christmas shopping, so I guess we'll just have to endure it." Lucas said this with feigned exhaustion in his voice. He looked over at Cass, who had just moved on to a table filled with hand carved boxes. *Will she buy one? To take with her when she leaves in May? To remind her of this place, where she lived for one year?*

He thought about the seven months she had already lived here, in his old bedroom in his mother's house. He wondered if Ella had ever seen, during those many months, any remnant of any existence spent anywhere else. He wondered if Cass had, perhaps, brought a souvenir with her. From wherever she had been.

Is there any trace from before?

Ella interrupted his thought. "Do you think it would be all right if you and I got one more hot chocolate while she looks through the other half of the store?"

Cass had overheard her from the short distance away at the pottery table. "Of course you can, Ella," Cass said with a touch of humor in her voice. "I'll be right here, safe and sound."

Lucas and Ella headed out the door and back across the street to the hot beverage tent. It was during the time that Ella was enjoying her second cup that she concluded it was simply too cold for her to be out.

"Take care of Cass, son, and make sure she makes it back okay. I'm sorry I'm wimping out on you two, but I sure had a lot of fun this evening." Ella patted her son on his broad shoulders as she gave him a tender hug. She held on a little longer than usual. "I sure thought a lot about your daddy tonight." She continued with her hug, and he embraced her in return.

"Me, too, Mom. Me, too."

He walked Ella back to her home and saw her safely in, then

crossed the street and followed the sidewalk back to Billy's. As he approached, he saw Cass through the window. She was at the counter with a bag that appeared filled with various items. He entered through the doorway and made his way to the counter.

"It appears your Christmas shopping is going quite well," he announced as he proceeded into the shop. He took a position on the opposite side of the counter from Cass.

She looked up and grinned. It wasn't the full smile as had been displayed earlier in the evening, but it was a content smile. She took the bag by its handles, saying, "Thank you, Billy," as she did so, then left the counter and headed for the door. As she turned, the bag grazed against a nearby table of small, glass vases. One of the vases toppled over the table's edge, busting on the floor below.

Cass froze for a split second, and then bent down. Lucas started around the counter towards her, but she had already begun to pick up the miniscule glass pieces even while apologizing repeatedly to Billy.

"Stop that, Cass," Billy called out nonchalantly, then came around from behind the counter with a dustpan and small broom in his hands. "Don't you dare feel the least bit bad about that vase. It happens all the time."

Lucas made it around the counter and noted the look on Cass's face. It was one of confusion, and loss.

Billy took Cass's arm and helped her up from her crouched position, then began sweeping the hundreds of broken glass bits into the dustpan. "We don't need to bother with picking up those pieces, Cass. After all, we sure as heck are not going to put that vase back together." He chuckled after saying this, attempting to lighten the somber mood.

Even standing, she continued to stare at the floor, at the broken pieces of glass that were now neatly swept up into Billy's dustpan. She seemed as if in a trance.

"Really, Cass, it's fine." Billy continued. "That's why we have dustpans. When something's too broken to fix, we just sweep it up, and toss it." Billy lowered the dustpan into the garbage pail beside the counter and replaced the broom and dustpan to its spot. "There," Billy said, with cheerful assurance in his voice. "It's as if that vase never even existed."

CHAPTER
Twenty-Three

*C*ass rubbed her hands quickly together, trying her best to remove the numbed feeling from the tips of her fingers. From the way things were shaping up so far, it was going to be another very cold day in the mountains.

The timer buzzed and she grabbed the mitts. She was thankful for the warm blast of air emanating from the oven as she opened the door and peeked in at the cinnamon muffins.

Now that winter had arrived, these early mornings by herself in the bakery had included those first ten or fifteen minutes devoted entirely to removing the chill from the bakery and her own extremities. There were mornings that she actually resented the alarm clock that woke her, regretted leaving the warmth of the bed and the blanket upon her. Nonetheless, she would rise to head to the cold, silent bakery. Eventually, she would be warmed by the heat of the ovens, the motion of whipping batter and cracking eggs, and the gently blowing warm air from the two vents located in the bakery ceiling. It was at this point, each morning, in the quiet solitude of her lone baking, that Cass would think about and anticipate the events of the upcoming day.

The days since late November had passed with consistent rhythms and predictable cadences. Her early morning baking duties came first, always followed by waiting on café customers. Around lunchtime, Ella would prepare three plates of a light lunch, always setting them at the same table, the one in the corner by the front window. At each place setting she would include a cloth napkin, silverware, and a glass of cold beverage. Then, as part of the normal daily routine, Ella would announce that it was Cass's break time, and would insist that Cass sit and enjoy her lunch while Ella tended to the café customers.

And, each day, shortly after Cass had sat down, Lucas would show up to the café. He always greeted his mother first, usually with a hug, and then headed over to the table with the lunch setting. Lucas and Cass would eat a little together, with him sharing tidbits about his morning at the station and her sharing tidbits of what had happened that morning in the bakery. After a short time enjoying lunch, Cass would resume her work in the café while Ella took a little rest to sit and eat with her son.

Lunches were then followed by a few more customers, after which the two women would engage in a thorough sweeping and cleaning of the café. Once the sign to *Walter's Bakery and Café* was flipped from *Open* to *Closed*, Cass would head out the front door to begin her walk while Ella locked up and headed home for her afternoon nap. Four or five hours later, Cass would walk back to Ella's home, where she would quickly shower and then join in for supper.

More often than not, now that the weather had turned so cold, Lucas would join them for the late evening meal. Afterwards, the three of them would sit in the living room and talk, or simply sit in front of the fireplace in silence. Lucas usually started yawning around eight o'clock, so many evenings it was just Ella and Cass who remained in the living room as bedtime approached.

On some nights Cass would do a little housework, vacuuming or dusting, just to keep Ella from feeling there was something that needed to be done. Around nine o'clock, Ella would announce that she was "calling it a night" and would bid Cass "sweet dreams". This was the point at which Cass would grab the blanket from her bedroom and head to the back porch, where she would recline on the lounge chair and look up at the stars until her eyelids were too heavy to keep open. After returning to her room, Cass would brush her teeth quickly, mark the day through on her calendar, note the number of days that were left, and then crawl into bed and hope for sleep to take her quickly.

Those were her days. Her days here in Chimney Rock.

On this particular morning, the baked items for the day were almost ready and Cass was expecting Ella to come bounding through the door at any moment. While she was wiping off the bakery counters, she heard the unexpected ringing sound coming from the front door of the café. As she rounded the corner of the bakery wall, she was greeted by a smiling Lucas. He was standing right inside the front door of the café and was dressed in his full police uniform.

"Mornin', Cass," he said enthusiastically.

"Good morning, Lucas," she replied back. "What in the world brings you out at this early hour?" She looked over at the wall clock as she said this and noted that it was not even six-thirty.

"Mom called me and asked that I stop by to see if you needed any help. Apparently, she had a rough time sleeping last night, something she described as 'just feeling uneasy'. She was wondering if you would allow her a little extra time to sleep in."

Cass found this idea amusing, that Ella would wonder if it was okay.

"Well, since she's the owner, and my boss, and my landlord, and the person who cooks and shares delicious meals, yes, I suppose I can approve of that proposal." Cass ended this proclamation with a little grin. "But you really don't have to stay and help, Lucas. Not that I don't appreciate your offer and willingness to help, but I'll be fine on my own."

He flipped the front door sign to *Open* and walked towards the counter.

"If there's one thing I know about you, Cass, I know that you'll be fine on your own. But the fact is, you don't have to be alone. Not this morning. I have a whole hour and a half that I can be here, helping you, and in a way, helping my mom as well. So, put me to work." Lucas finished the sentence as he was retrieving one of Ella's aprons from the wall hook.

And work he did. He swept the floor and cleaned the windows and prepared the register for the day's activities. He started a pot of coffee in the industrial coffee maker, and another once that one was ready and seated on the warmer. While the second pot was brewing, he took some holly leaves and berries that Ella had found a couple of days earlier and arranged them on the tables all around the café.

As Cass added the last of the baked items to the display case, they both looked around to find that everything was now ready for the day's customers. Lucas removed and returned the apron to its hook.

The two of them sat down at the front corner table with mugs of coffee and plates of fresh croissants. There were no customers yet, and the café was eerily quiet as they both looked out the window. Cass sipped her coffee slowly, savoring the warmth and aroma.

"I'm sorry you had to get up so early just to help me out." She continued holding the mug, warming her hands on the toasty ceramic.

"I was already awake, so no need to be sorry. I had already been on a run by the time my mom called." Lucas yawned quietly and then took another sip of his coffee. "And the reason I took an early morning run is because I somehow got Arlene to squeeze me in midday for a quick haircut, after the reception. And the reason why I needed Arlene to squeeze me in midday is because I have an evening meeting with the Mayor and Town Manager to look over some ideas for a bathroom renovation at the police department. So," Lucas looked at Cass with an expression of resignation, "I would imagine that by the time I make it over to Mom's for supper tonight, I'll be pretty worn out." He seemed fatigued just describing his full day.

"If it would help you, I could make you a sandwich and some sides to take with you, sort of like a boxed lunch?" She was looking out the window as she made this offer, at the little village as it gradually lightened with the rising of the sun.

When she looked back, Lucas was staring at her.

"Actually, that would be great," he said quietly. "If I could either eat on the road or at the office, that would help tremendously. Are you sure that's not too much trouble?" He asked this with what appeared as sincere concern. "Or I could fix it myself. I know you have things you need to do."

Cass considered his offer. "Let's just do it together."

She led Lucas to the pantry and then the cooler, where they found everything they needed. She retrieved two slices of the sourdough bread Ella had made the day before, and within minutes a boxed lunch consisting of a turkey and Swiss sandwich, chips, and cantaloupe chunks was packed and ready for transport.

Lucas refilled both of their mugs with fresh coffee, then grabbed a second croissant for himself. Sitting back at the table at the window, he was the first to notice the change in weather.

"Oh, wonderful. It's raining now. Nothing like a cold, rainy day to really drive away the customers." He looked back at her. "Which reminds me of something I meant to ask you a while ago."

"What's that?"

"I've noticed, on those occasions when I happen to see you out walking, that you never seek cover when it's raining. It's almost as if you enjoy walking in the rain, even when it's cold, like today." He glanced again out the window and then back at her.

Is he waiting for an answer?

She nodded her head. "You're right. I do."

Lucas sipped his coffee and watched her over the top of his mug. He seemed to be waiting again. Waiting for the answer to the obvious follow-up. She decided to be forthright, to share the truth behind what he was wondering.

"Have you ever noticed, when it rains, the things that people do, in an effort to keep from getting wet?" She waited a moment, but seeing no response from him other than his eyes looking into her own, she continued. "People will hold their jackets over their heads as they run towards their cars, or tiptoe on the sidewalk so water puddles don't splash on them. They will make every effort with every step to remain perfectly placed underneath their umbrellas."

She paused to sip her coffee. She looked into his eyes and saw the warm brown that seemed to want to hear more. He seemed to want to understand, about the rain.

"They rush to find shelter or to put hoods up to cover their heads," Cass continued. "They put so much effort into it, whatever it is they do. But it's all in vain, Lucas. It doesn't matter. Because they can't protect themselves from getting wet. Whether it's a whole bucket or just a drop. Some way, the rain will still find them."

She set her mug down. "So, now you know why I walk in the rain."

"Not really," he replied. "I know that people get wet in the rain. But I don't really know any more than that." His voice sounded neither accusatory nor disappointed. His voice sounded simply like it was searching.

She turned to look out the window at the rain that was falling harder now. She was looking forward to her walk that afternoon and hoped the rain would continue drenching the village. She started to stand, but decided there was something more to be said. Some words that might help him to understand.

"Even with the largest umbrella," she said, still turned towards the window, "no one is safe."

They finished the rest of their coffee in silence, then Lucas took the mugs and plates to the sink while Cass wiped down the table and deposited the few crumbs in the trash. With no customers in sight and the outlook that there may not be any while the rain continued,

Lucas gathered up his boxed lunch and pulled one of Ella's umbrellas from the basket near the counter. He wished Cass a good morning, and headed towards the front door. Before turning the door handle to leave, he hesitated and turned back to face her.

"You know, Cass, I do happen to be the Chief of Police," he said. He looked down at his hands, appearing to ready himself to say something else. "Perhaps consider that you just might be safe. Here, in this place. Safe with us."

She watched him look up now. He held her gaze.

"Safe with me." He said it softly and slowly, hesitating slightly after each word. Then he turned and headed out, closing the door quickly to keep the cold air from intruding upon the warmth of the cafe.

He is everything good.

She watched him head towards his car to start his long, busy day as Police Chief of the Town of Lake Lure. The tall, strong hero who would keep them all safe.

Her eyes followed him as he walked away, with a black umbrella held carefully over his head.

CHAPTER

Twenty-Four

*L*ucas looked out the window of his office at the sheets of hard rain falling outside. The downpour had not let up since it had started earlier that morning, and the grey, overcast skies, coupled with the chill in the air, had seemed to cast a dreary mood on the entire town. This day was going to be challenging anyway, just on its own, with the farewell party in honor of Officer Rinehart. Now, with the additional headaches that came with rainstorms, such as the usual fender benders, he was anticipating an even more exhausting day than what he had described earlier to Cass.

Cass.

He glanced at the calendar. It was the eighteenth day of December.

Five months from today...

"She's leaving," Lucas whispered quietly. He formed the words out loud intentionally. He meant to shake himself free of any thoughts of anything beyond that date. Anything that involved her. She was a visitor, someone just passing through for a year.

And then a thought occurred to him, one he found himself considering more frequently with each passing day. He considered that perhaps, maybe during the holidays or even in early spring, Cass would think about staying a little longer, beyond her predetermined year. Perhaps she would find whatever it was she was searching for, or solace from whatever it was that haunted her.

Maybe.

But that opportunity would not come today. Not on this day where the rain was falling and blowing in gusts against the Hickory Nut Gorge. As she had told him, just a few hours before, on this day the rain would call to her, would remind her that she and all she knew were vulnerable.

"Yes, I am leaving," a familiar voice said from behind him. Lucas turned to see Officer Rinehart standing there, with two plates of white cake in her hands. "Are you just now coming to terms with that, Chief?" Rebekah asked, with an exaggerated look of pity on her face.

Both of them leaned against his desk and ate, laughing and remembering the five years they had worked together on the force. Lucas was reminded of how level-headed and calm Rebekah was, in all situations, and knew the force and the town itself was losing one of its finest.

"I'm so sorry I can't make the wedding, Rebekah. I'm just not able to currently pull off a trip. I'm a little low on funds, if you know what I mean." Lucas shared this with sincere regret. He would love nothing more than to be there to support his amazing friend on her special day, but the wedding was going to be in just under two weeks, and in Denver.

"What do you mean, 'low on funds'? I thought you were saving for your dream house in your dream location?" Rebekah said this with a little curiosity in her tone.

"That's true," he said, then decided to change the subject. "Hey, did you get to meet Officer Melton last time he was here for his second interview?"

"I sure did," Rebekah replied. "And I think he is going to fit in perfectly. I really liked him." She finished off her final bite of cake and placed the paper plate in the recycling bin beside his desk. "When does he get started?"

"As you may already know, he's moving here from South Carolina. I agreed with his current Chief for him to work out a couple months there, then transition up here to us. I think he's going to start moving his stuff in late April and then hopefully start the first of May. That's the plan, at least." Even as he said it, Lucas realized the hardship it would put his team under to be down one person for a few months. Such were the recruitment and retention challenges often faced by a small town police force.

The farewell reception was part fun and part melancholy. After Rebekah had said her goodbyes and left, the officers currently on duty resumed their patrols and desk work. The others, who had simply visited to see Rebekah off, returned to their time of leisure. The rain continued to pour.

Shortly after noon, Lucas found himself still on a conference call with Mayor Culbertson and Town Manager Chris Cottinger. The call had started shortly after eleven thirty, which Lucas had logically assumed would be plenty early enough for him to get on the road towards Arlene's by twelve. He was now realizing that perhaps he had underestimated the complexities of discussing a bathroom redesign for the dated police facility.

"Mayor Culbertson? Manager Cottinger? I'm going to hang up now for just a brief minute to switch over to my cell phone." Lucas shared this over his desk phone and then proceeded to disconnect. He had decided that continuing the call while driving to Chimney Rock might actually get him to Arlene's at a time that she might deem as late but still acceptable.

Moments later, Lucas was listening to the Mayor and Town Manager discuss price points and timeline while driving quickly towards Arlene's salon. He opened up the boxed lunch and placed it on his lap, taking hurried bites of sandwich and cantaloupe. Every once in a while, one of the two men on the line would pause and ask Lucas his opinion. He wondered if these requests were actually a sign that they were interested in his input, or perhaps a test to see if he was listening at all.

Parking his squad car in front of the salon, Lucas did his best to avoid the puddles that had formed. The last thing he needed was to step in one and drench his uniform pants leg. He still had a long afternoon and evening ahead.

What was that she had said about the rain? About tiptoeing through puddles?

He noticed that his car was the only car parked in front of Arlene's business. He wondered if he had still somehow arrived during that exact time frame when Arlene had a lull between her morning and afternoon customers.

Perhaps I'm not in that much trouble after all?

Realizing he had left his umbrella at the office in his haste to leave, Lucas jogged to the front door and entered, still holding the phone to his ear. The waiting room was empty, which he assumed meant that Arlene was in the back. He imagined that she was probably making herself some hot tea or propping her ankles up in the break room recliner. He even considered that perhaps she was in the bathroom. He listened for any sound, but heard none.

He decided this was the perfect opportunity to make up for being late. He grabbed a black, nylon robe from the wall hook and began to maneuver it awkwardly around his body. This simple feat was made the more difficult as he held the phone to his ear. He put his arms through the armholes, then worked to snap the back shut with one hand.

He had purposefully chosen the robe with Marilyn Monroe posing on the front. He thought this one, in place of the plain one he usually wore, might bring a smile to Arlene's face, even as she was potentially fussing at him. Once the robe was secure, Lucas sat down in his usual swivel chair.

Listening to the two leaders go back and forth on the conference call, Lucas watched in the mirror. He anticipated Arlene coming around the corner from the break room any second now, gently scolding him for being so late. He waited a minute, then two.

She's really pissed this time.

He knew he had screwed up, had waited too long at the office before switching the conference call over to his cell. He felt frustrated at himself. He never wanted Arlene to feel that he took for granted the many times she accommodated his unpredictable schedule. He felt a heavy cape of guilt start to descend upon his shoulders.

Lucas took the phone from his ear and punched the mute icon. He rose from the chair and held the phone to his side.

They probably won't even know that I've stepped away for a minute.

He walked towards the break room, stopping short before rounding the corner.

"Arlene, I'm so sorry that ..."

Before Lucas could finish his apology, a man stepped out from behind the corner and greeted him with a friendly smile.

"Well, look at you all decked out in your beauty salon robe," the man said, staring at Lucas while he spoke. "I guess you're ready for your haircut?"

The man appeared to be in his forties or fifties, with a heavy build and a height that matched Lucas's almost exactly. The man was a stranger to Lucas, and appeared to be speaking in generalities with no knowledge of Lucas's identity.

"Anyway, man," the stranger continued, "Arlene had to step out a few minutes ago. Something about having to run out to get some headache meds or something. Why don't you come back in a few hours and maybe she can help you then?"

Lucas noticed a few of the words were slurred, and the man appeared to be struggling with focusing as he spoke. Standing very still and keeping his eyes on the man in front of him, Lucas calmly asked, "What time did Arlene leave?"

The stranger appeared perturbed that the conversation was continuing. He replied in a curt tone, "Like I said, man, a few minutes ago." And then, the stranger added, "So why don't you take off that stupid robe and go ahead and leave?"

Throughout this exchange, the cell phone held in Lucas's right hand had provided monotone background chatter as the mayor and manager continued their endless conversation, oblivious to the fact that the third person involved in the conversation had muted his own phone quite a while ago. Neither Lucas nor the stranger had seemed to pay any heed to this ongoing cell phone banter.

And then a voice from the phone, with great volume and clarity, asked, "Chief Montraine? Chief Montraine? Chief Montraine, are you there?"

The stranger's eyes departed from the contact they had held with Lucas's eyes, and drifted downward to Lucas's waist. The stranger seemed to be trying to see through the black salon robe, as if seeking for something underneath. While still searching, the stranger reached his hand towards his back. Lucas glanced in the mirror located on the wall behind the man and saw a pistol tucked into the waistband of the stranger's jeans.

The realization suddenly came to Lucas that a long, oversized, nylon robe was currently separating his hand from his own weapon. He dropped the phone to the floor.

The stranger kept his eyes on Lucas while beginning to back up slowly, taking small steps backwards towards the direction from which he had come. The stranger's hand was still behind his back, but closer now to his weapon.

Lucas determined that several things would need to happen, and all at once. He would need to keep the man from securing the gun tucked into his waistband, while at the same time removing the robe and finding and preparing his own weapon for discharge.

He lunged forward towards the man, catching him in his midsection with the force of his own shoulders and chest. As he plunged the man into the wall, he reached out to grip the man's arms, but his own arm became entangled in the robe. The two men grappled with one another, grabbing and slinging until Lucas felt his balance waver. As he hit the hard floor, he braced for a counter attack. But none came. He looked around and found that he was now alone in the room.

He quickly stood and fully removed the robe while also unclipping and removing his firearm in swift motions. He called for backup on his radio and considered waiting for their arrival before exploring or pursuing further, but then he remembered. There was another who may be here. A person he had come here to see.

Where is she?

He walked towards the break room, rounding the corner with his weapon drawn and his senses alert. As he entered the room he found the lights had been turned off. Even on this rainy, overcast day, however, the natural light through the window was enough for him to somewhat navigate his surroundings. He scanned the part of the room he could see most clearly, but saw no other living being. He carefully and slowly stepped forward and turned his head fully to his right.

She was seated in her favorite recliner, with a long length of duct tape strapped on her mouth and across her cheeks. Her eyes were wide and filled with terror. Her hands were pulled behind her, held there as if she couldn't move them. Her ankles were secured to the base of the chair, red and raw from the multiple layers of tape wrapped tightly around them. Her shirt was gone, leaving her in just her bra. *Bitch* was written in lipstick across her upper chest, and *whore* was written in the same across her abdomen.

Lucas saw all of this. Saw it in one second. Saw it and understood.

He heard a subtle sound emanating from the shadows behind her chair. Lucas's weapon was still drawn, loaded and ready. But his target was not yet found.

He watched as a hand came into vision. It was a hand with a gun, and the gun was now pointed to Arlene's temple. The stranger was crouched low behind Arlene's recliner, hidden in the grey darkness created by the storm's dark reflection. The stranger's arm protruded out enough to angle the gun towards her head, and the stranger's eyes propped up just enough to cruelly glare at Lucas.

Arlene was screaming now, screaming into the duct tape and producing a guttural sound as the cold metal of the gun rubbed up against her face. Her chair was rocking back and forth in her futile attempt at escape and freedom. The man started to stand, slowly and deliberately. He kept his gun aimed at the side of Arlene's head.

The attacker was tall and thick, and from the steely look in his eyes, completely unafraid. His glare was full of resentment and rage. Even so, the man's hand was shaking unsteadily as he raised his other hand and gulped from a bottle of dark liquor.

"Let me guess," the man said as he lowered the bottle. "You're the asshole this bitch left me for." His voice was hoarse as he laughed sarcastically. Arlene's screams continued, but Lucas kept his eyes on the invader.

The man dropped the bottle of whiskey in front of him. It bounced off Arlene's bare leg and shattered on the floor. Still holding the gun against her temple, the stranger yelled out, "Put your gun on the floor, asshole. Or she's dead."

A few seconds passed as the scene held frozen, with none of the three people moving. Then the stranger screamed with spit flying from his lips.

"Now!"

Lucas looked down into Arlene's eyes and their vision met. Her eyes were frantic and desperate. She was shaking her head as she cried and screamed into the tape. He looked back at the man and began to crouch down slowly, holding his left hand up in a gesture of surrender. "It's okay," Lucas said softly. "I'm putting it on the floor now. Let's just stay calm. Nobody has to get hurt, okay?"

Lucas saw the bullet leave the man's gun even before he heard the sound. He felt his right arm burst with pain as the bullet hit. Even so, he kept his grip on his weapon as he fired his own shot. He readied to shoot again, but struggled to do so, feeling the blood soaking his right hand and the weakening muscles and pain around it.

The stranger briefly touched his upper abdomen, where the bullet had hit. Then he shifted his stance and glared. The man was charging now, full of rage and yelling something that included "die" and "pig".

Lucas readied to take his firearm into his other hand, even as he maneuvered to fully stand back up and brace himself. He anticipated his next move and the next after that and then realized, just as quickly, that he had been one second too late.

His face took the impact of a fist. He felt his eyelid split open as his head propelled backwards. Blood poured into his eye as his head hit the floor. He moved his fingers on his right hand, which still rested on the handle of his gun, but these were trapped underneath the body of the massive man.

Lucas started hitting the man's face with his free hand, connecting with his nose and hitting that same target again. As he was doing so, he was taking hits himself, to his jaw and his chin and his already damaged eye. He aimed his left wrist for the man's neck and, grabbing it, attempted a choke hold. But the stranger's neck was massive, and Lucas's attempt made little impact.

As he continued to be pummeled and to hit back with all the force he could muster, he also focused his strength on his right hand and his gun. As he willed his wrist to pull and turn the weapon, his forefinger touched the handle. There was something moist on his finger, and now on the handle of his gun.

He thought that perhaps it was blood. Or sweat. Or liquor.

But he knew it was none of these.

He knew that somehow. Some way.

A raindrop had found him.

Twenty-Five

Now that Ella had arrived and the lunch crowd had filled in a little, Cass was starting to feel some semblance of normalcy. The rain had continued, unrelenting, since earlier in the morning when Lucas had been here with her, sipping on coffee and talking alone in the quiet café. She thought back to those early morning moments. Rather than conjure up the specific words he had said, she remembered instead his lips as they had said them. She remembered the friendly tone of his voice and the gentle reassurance of his eyes.

She checked the display, removing the decorated placards from the items that had already sold out. She rang up a couple of customers and then busied herself cleaning dishes and reloading the dishwasher. The sound of the rain and the grey pale of the outside made her feel a little sleepy, but only momentarily. She looked forward to the end of her shift, to walking out the front door and down the road.

As she was wiping down the table near the front window, the same one she had sat at this morning, she looked again out the window. The rain had intensified. Loud thunder accompanied the rain, thunderous sounds that seemed to bounce between the mountains and then echo continually in a haunting, rhythmic pattern.

A car with sirens suddenly raced by. Then, she heard more sirens, in the distance, all of which seemed to be coming closer. The sounds clashed grotesquely with the sound of the pattering of raindrops, right outside the window.

"Cass, can you ring them up while I get some more pastry boxes from the back?" Ella was calling to her from somewhere in the bakery.

Cass hesitated, hearing again the approaching sirens. She turned away from the front window and headed back towards the counter, where two locals were waiting to pay their bill. After ringing them up and wishing them a good day, she went to the bakery to see if Ella needed help. Indeed she did, and soon Cass, being the taller of the two, was reaching to a high shelf to retrieve a bag of pastry boxes.

The two women walked together back into the café, where Ella started packing the boxes in drawers near the display case. Cass, meanwhile, found a clean cloth to begin wiping down tables that had been vacated by lunch customers.

As she was doing so, she heard the bell on the door ring with its usual greeting. She turned to see Deputy Chief Farley McSwain, dressed in plain clothes, hurriedly entering. He scanned the room quickly, finding Ella behind the counter and making his way towards her. Cass resumed her wiping as she heard Ella call out.

"Well, Farley, what a nice...."

As Ella's voice trailed off, Cass turned towards the woman. She watched as Ella, frozen in mid-sentence, turned to face Farley. He stepped slowly towards Ella and placed his arms around her. He leaned very close to her and whispered something into her ear. Ella's head was on the other side of Farley's, but Cass could see the woman's shoulders and back, could see them bend as if to collapse.

Cass continued staring at the two behind the counter, feeling herself a cruel intruder into some quiet secret that was being shared between them. She watched and waited. She willed herself to breathe even as she felt her breath catching and holding.

Soon Ella was pulling away from the embrace and staring into Farley's eyes. She then rushed past him and frantically headed towards the front door. Farley followed her, neither of them saying anything further or addressing anyone else in the room.

Cass watched Ella walk by, saw the wild look of fear and shock in her eyes. Ella and Farley then departed the café and were soon pulling away in Farley's squad car.

Farley's entrance into the café and Ella's abrupt exit out had all happened so quickly and unexpectedly that Cass felt herself frozen in place, questioning whether this exchange had really happened. The customers still in the café seemed to have not noticed it at all.

Cass spent the next hour refilling mugs of coffee and hot chocolate, ringing up customer bills, and cleaning tables after the meals and hot beverages had been completed. When the last customer left, Cass turned the sign on the front door from *Open* to *Closed*, but decided to leave the front door unlocked while she cleaned. She had noticed that Ella had left earlier with no pocketbook, which meant she had no keys. She thought Ella might return at any moment, and didn't wish for her to be left waiting outside in the rain, unable to enter into her own business.

She closed out the register and accounted for the cash, just as Ella had trained her to do. She cleaned, for the second time this morning, the entire kitchen and baking room, then proceeded to thoroughly wipe down the café tables and sweep the room thoroughly.

She finished the cleaning as police cars drove by the front window. She then decided to mop the floor for good measure. She took one more look around, hoping to find something else to clean or to do while she waited for Ella's return. Finding none, she locked the front door and turned off the lights. She found Ella's pocketbook in the cabinet under the counter and, taking it with her, she headed through the door that connected to the home.

She walked through the quiet, dark house into the kitchen and placed Ella's pocketbook on the counter. As she did so, she heard Ella's cell phone vibrate within.

She retrieved a glass from the cupboard and poured herself some tap water. The cell phone located somewhere deep in the pocketbook vibrated again. And then another time. Someone was trying to reach Ella. And they were being very persistent.

Cass considered whether she should find the phone in Ella's purse. Whether she should answer it and at least tell the caller or callers that Ella was not here. That Ella did not have her phone.

And then, she remembered. She forced herself to focus and remember.

I won't be staying for too long.

She walked to her bedroom, changed her t-shirt, and retrieved a hooded jacket. She turned the lights off in the home and proceeded out to the back porch, hearing the phone vibrating frantically even as she closed the door behind her.

The rain was falling steadily, but not as torrentially as it had been earlier in the day. She turned right and headed on her usual trek down the main road and towards Lake Lure. As she walked, she turned to occasionally peer into the front windows of the restaurants and shops that lined the road. Everything seemed eerily quiet. She passed an antique shop and noticed several women in the middle of the shop, engaged in what looked to be a somber discussion. One of the women reached out to another and offered an embrace. Cass continued to walk.

By this point, she was soaked through. The heaviness of her drenched t-shirt and fleece jacket added to the exertion she put forth as she quickened her pace. The rain continued to hit her, continued to absorb itself into her clothes and her hair. She continued to walk.

Two police cars approached and passed. Both were headed back towards Chimney Rock, but neither with sirens turned on. Cass focused on the passenger seats and peered through the windows to see if Ella was there. She wasn't.

She saw an older man, standing under an umbrella, talking on his cell phone. As she neared closer, she recognized the business owner. Walking quickly past, she overheard his words.

"I know it's loud out hear with this rain, but the reception inside is even worse," he shouted loudly, pausing as if to hear a response. "Yes, that's what I heard, that there were gunshots and some kind of struggle ... no, I haven't heard anything else in the last while ... I don't know what his condition is, or even if ...."

She continued walking, looking straight ahead as she maintained the cadence of her steps despite the added weight of the drenched clothes. She was now out of earshot of the sidewalk conversation she had just passed. She was again alone.

She rounded one curve in the road, and then another. She walked past Mrs. Stampshed's house and looked up the front steps. She remembered sitting on these steps, not too long ago. She glanced at the front window and saw Mrs. Stampshed standing there, appearing to look out at the rain. Cass saw an unusual expression on the woman's face, an expression that telegraphed sadness. She felt her pace slow a little as she considered stopping to see if the older woman was okay. She decided instead to continue walking.

She walked by Boys Camp Road on her left, where she remembered pulling up weeds from around turnip plants. She walked past the garden bridge, where she remembered sipping hot cider. She walked around more curves and bends and then found herself nearing the lake and the mountains and the Lake Lure Police Department.

There, at the police department, she saw cars. Many cars. She had never seen the parking lot so crowded. She saw people entering into the building in hurried fashion. She saw other small crowds of people huddled under the awnings that covered the building's front.

She stopped walking and watched the people, as they hugged and cried and held their heads in their hands. She calmly scanned the crowds and those entering through the front doors. She saw Farley, in a discussion with two other officers. She assumed that one of these might be Lucas, but from the back neither of their hair looked black enough for that to be so. She brought her gaze back to some of the other groups of people standing outside of the department, and then to others as they exited the building. They were wiping their faces with tissues and hugging each other. She looked among everyone. So many of them were on cell phones, talking to someone. She did not know what they were talking about.

She couldn't find Lucas, but then remembered that he had a busy schedule that day. He had told her as much that morning. She assumed that he was probably somewhere else. He was probably helping someone whose tire was stuck in the mud. Or assisting a motorist who had hydroplaned on the wet road. He was somewhere helping someone.

I can see him. He is somewhere helping someone whose car is stuck in a ditch.

The vision she had conjured of Lucas helping a motorist remained in Cass's mind. Eventually, though, it began to transform into a vision that was not welcome, but one that would come nonetheless. The freeze frame appeared.

A police officer is opening the door. He is dressed in uniform and his weapon is drawn. He has entered cautiously. He is alone. The girl is looking at him. She wants to cry out, "Danger", but her lungs will not find air.

The still picture moved, as if it was splashed with water, and another appeared.

The police officer is crouching now, crouching down beside the girl. He has taken off his shirt, his black police uniform shirt. His white t-shirt is showing his perspiration as he holds his black shirt against her back. He is applying pressure to something back there, something on the girl's back. His eyes look concerned. He is young. He is brave. No voices are speaking. There is silence.

Cass walked towards a tree at the parking lot's border. It was a tree with a large trunk and a canopy of thick branches that would shield the worn paper from the rainy conditions. She leaned her body against the trunk and retrieved her *peace*. She took it from the Ziploc bag that she now kept it in, tucked away in her pocket at all times. She looked intently at the drawing and then closed her eyes. Soon, she was back. Back to the village. Back to the rocking chair with a gentle breeze and soft wind chimes in the distance. She replaced the paper drawing into the Ziploc bag and then into its place of rest in her pocket.

She took one last look at the police department, at all the people around it. They looked troubled and frantic and sad.

I don't know anyone here. I won't be staying for too long.

She nodded her head. She felt relieved. Relieved that she had not allowed herself to become connected. To make friends. To become anything special to anyone. Relieved that she had been strong and had remained alone.

She pitied them. She pitied them that they, too, were not alone. As was she.

Cass walked on, and walked and walked. She walked miles and miles beyond, up and down side roads, up and down mountains. She walked for what seemed like hours, although it was difficult to know for sure with the sun hidden behind the massive grey clouds. Soon, the dark grey turned darker and she sensed that night was approaching.

She turned resolutely and headed back towards the village. The rain had continued and the air was chilly. The combination of the cold and the wet over the course of this long journey had crept into her muscles and bones, so much so that she was now shivering. She noticed her breath as she exhaled. It left her body in a cloud of condensation.

She increased her cadence, willing herself to walk faster. Her shaking subsided slightly with this renewed exertion, but not entirely. She was starting to feel very, very cold. The weight of the drenched fleece jacket felt heavy upon her shoulders. She lifted the hood, hoping that even in its soaked state it might provide some shelter and warmth to her freezing ears and chattering jaw.

She walked on and saw the police department again. The building now looked normal. It was relatively empty with few cars in the parking lot. She knew that from this point, if she walked quickly, she would arrive at Ella's house within the hour. She suspected that Ella would be there, probably with a hot pot of coffee and a pile of warm towels awaiting her tenant.

She walked and saw the road sign for Boys Camp Road. She moved her eyes to look straight ahead and kept her vision there as she neared the sign.

Just walk. Walk straight ahead.

She stopped. She turned only her head to look down Boys Camp Road. About a half mile down this road, turnips had once grown, in a garden behind a house.

From the little of this side road that Cass could see, it looked dark and grey. It looked desolate and abandoned. The main road she was on was illuminated with numerous street lights, but for some reason this side road appeared covered in shadows.

"You don't know anyone here."

Even as she heard the soft words spoken with her own shivering lips, her body turned. Facing the shadows fully, she took a step onto the darkened road ahead.

Twenty-Six

He continued staring ahead into the steady rain, feeling hidden in the darkness of his unlit front porch. The world around him seemed thunderous from the water hitting the grass and the asphalt. It was louder and more violent as the storm again gained momentum and made its way across the town. With every other raindrop, Lucas heard a gunshot.

He had asked to be alone. He had sent away Farley and the other officers. He had even asked his mother to leave. She had left him some food and had turned down his bed like he was a little boy. She had begged him to come to her home, to their family's home, to sleep. She had asked him to let her stay here, at his house, with him. But he had insisted he was okay, and they all had finally relented.

He wished to be alone.

The rain continued. This same rain that had started this morning as he sipped the coffee in the café. That moment in time felt to Lucas like a lifetime ago. A lifetime now filled with danger and blood.

The man's name was Michael Barrett. All of those times that Arlene had mentioned Mike, the man she had escaped from, this was the man she had described. This was the man she had feared. This was the man who had found her, after all these years.

He had entered her salon after waiting for the last morning customer to leave. He had thought he had locked the front door, but had not realized the dead bolt was broken. He did not know that Arlene had to secure the door each night with a chain and padlock.

He had found her alone in the break room, and had ambushed her from behind. He had bound her and had begun to strip her, muting her screams with tape across her mouth. He had chosen the perfect day for his attack, with a rainstorm so loud that neither screams nor gunshots could be detected against it.

What Michael Barrett had planned to further do was not yet known. What was known was that this was the point in time that Lucas had shown up and put on the robe. While disrobing had cost him precious seconds, having his identity as a police officer hidden had no doubt earned him additional time as well.

The gunshot hitting his arm, the charge by the attacker, the impact and struggle, and the maneuvering for weapons. All of these memories were battling for dominance in his aching mind. He could not yet process the decisions he had made and whether they had been right or wrong. But what he did know was for those few precious moments, he really just had one goal. To protect Arlene, at all costs.

He stood in silence on the porch, replaying the attack in his mind. As Michael Barrett had charged and tackled him, the man's weapon had fallen away from its owner. Lucas's own weapon had become disengaged from his hand, both trapped underneath the man's large frame. The ensuing fistfight had been an exercise in survival, with both men struggling to be the first to retrieve his own weapon.

As memories from the day assaulted him, Lucas again felt the sting of Michael Barrett's fist against his eye socket. He felt the ringing in his ears from the head butt which landed on and busted open his lip. He felt the bullet stinging through his arm, tearing muscle and scraping bone along the way.

He had fought back, and even though the other man was heavier and just as tall, Lucas was ultimately quicker. He had pummeled the man's face. He had broken the man's nose and bloodied the man's mouth. He had fought with the desperation of one fighting for his own life.

But, more importantly, he had fought for Arlene's life. For Ella's life and Farley's life. For all who would miss him once he was gone.

Lucas had reached his gun quicker than the attacker, grabbing and discharging almost simultaneously. The stranger, however, had done the same, just one split second behind. Even though Lucas's shot was first, it had not been quick enough to prevent the attacker from also levying his own bullet.

As he continued to watch the rain from the darkness of the porch, he thought again about the attacker. This time, however, he pictured the man in a hospital bed. Lucas's first shot had hit the stomach, and his second had pierced the man's lung. As he had left the hospital earlier in the evening, Lucas had been told that he would be updated on the man's condition in the coming days.

He had never killed a person before, and perhaps he never would. He hoped that would be the case. But if it weren't, he had done what he had believed must be done. He had tried first to save Arlene, and second, to somehow survive.

He had seen Arlene briefly, as they were being taken on gurneys to the waiting ambulances. She was crying, and seemed traumatized, but had luckily not suffered any serious physical wounds. Even through the emotions, she had reached her hand out to him, as if to touch him. She had whispered his name, *Lucas,* even as the tears and convulsions overtook her.

Lucas had been admitted to the hospital. Then, after a thorough exam and plenty of prodding eyes and hands and the proper attention to his gunshot wound, he had promptly discharged himself. There was no reason for him to stay in the hospital. He didn't believe in spending the night there just for the purpose of someone "keeping a watch" on him.

He was the Chief of Police. He would be *here*, in his town. *He* was the one who would keep a watch, a watch over those who called this place home.

He picked up the bottle of cold beer from the table beside him. He watched the rain fall as he lifted the bottle towards his lips. But his body and hand were shaking uncontrollably, making it impossible to steady the bottle enough for a quick sip.

Returning the bottle to the table, he looked back out at his yard. The rain was coming down in thick sheets. He felt almost hypnotized as he stood in the dark and watched it. He imagined how cold that rain must feel. He knew he was safe from its chilling touch, under the shelter of his porch.

Safe. From the rain.

He had changed out of his bloodied uniform earlier, intending to go to bed early once he had persuaded everyone to leave. He had placed a hooded jacket on just for temporary warmth, with no other shirt underneath. Now, he unzipped the black hoodie and removed it from his body. He stood there in his jeans and bare feet. He stepped down one step, then others, and walked out into the night.

Reaching well beyond his porch and its shelter, he stood still. He felt the cold drops fall upon his body. He was looking straight ahead, into the darkness, as he allowed the rain to cover him.

He slowly turned his head downward, and looked upon his chest. There, visible even under this darkening sky, was the black bruise. It was growing darker, forming hauntingly over the middle of his chest. He caught his breath and held it, then willed himself to breathe again. He stared at the bruise, then pictured his heart underneath. Pictured it sore to the touch and turning black. Imagined it with a pointed bullet lodged deep inside. The bullet that had been intended for it. The bullet his vest had stopped.

At that moment, his heightened senses were alerted. He turned his vision abruptly to the forested, vacant lot to his right. After doing so and allowing his vision to adjust to the lush darkness of the thick trees, he saw her.

She advanced slowly out of the wooded lot and then paused, her eyes never leaving him, never leaving the black target on his wet chest. The look on her face was anything but its usual stoic neutrality. She looked as if in shock, as if she was close to fainting. He could see her breath as she exhaled. It was coming out in hurried puffs, as if she were on the verge of hyperventilating. She started to double over, then appeared to steady herself.

He turned and walked quickly back to his porch. He returned the jacket to his body, zipping it up tightly to conceal any reminders of the day's violence. He started for his front door, to enter and to find the solace and isolation he had craved just moments before.

Yet, he turned and stood in the darkness, at the top of the porch steps. He looked out and saw that she was still there. Standing in the rain. Watching him.

She was walking towards him now. Slowly and cautiously. As she did so, he thought back to what he had told her that morning. *Something about being safe? With me? Here?*

She was now just a few feet from the first step of the porch. She was drenched, soaked through in her leggings and long-sleeved fleece jacket. Her hair had loosened from its tie and was dripping in wet strands around her face. He noticed how dark her hair was when completely soaked, as it was now. The wet hair gave her eyes a whole other dimension, one that made the topaz appear darker and deeper.

She stepped forward and onto the first step. Then to the second step, never taking her eyes from his. Now she was on the third, and then to the fourth. With each step she exhaled, her breath visible in the cold night air.

She was one step beneath him and now under the shelter of his porch covering. She stopped advancing and stood quietly. Her eyes were intense as they studied and bore into his own, so much so that he looked away, unable to take any more of the scrutiny.

He wished that he had told her that he wanted her to stop. He wished, as she was walking towards him, that he had told her he wanted to be alone.

Even as he looked away, she was still looking at him. Somehow, he knew this. It made him feel weak and vulnerable. It made him feel wounded. But there was something else. Some other emotion that was finding its way into his heart and into his mind. Something that was still forming, building.

He could tell that she was now studying his face. She was seeing his right eye, almost shut now, with black and yellow bruising all around it. She was seeing the huge whelp on the back of his jawline, and the busted lip that left half of his mouth swollen. She was seeing the puffed redness and tenderness across his face and neck and knuckles. He considered what a horrid sight he must be.

As he continued looking away from her, into the dark void of the night's storm, he sensed that he was facing the weakest moment of his life. He felt fragile, as if he might shatter. He felt exhausted, like he would never again be strong enough to wear his badge. To protect his town, or his mother's village, or his family and friends. Or even this person, this woman, standing close to him now.

She had trusted someone at some point in her life, of that he felt sure. He also knew, or believed he knew, that the person was no longer a part of her life. He believed that the pain and burden and sorrow of that void was with her, at every turn and with every step. It was with her at night when she tried to sleep, and in the morning when she awoke.

If not for his bulletproof vest, he knew that today he would have been another. Someone she had entrusted with part of her truth, and someone who was then no longer in her life.

He felt a single tear escape his eye and slowly start making its way down.

Let it fall.

He hadn't the energy to even reach up to wipe it away.

Let it fall. Can't I weep? Just once?

As the tear continued its slow descent down his cheek, she stepped up from the fourth step. She was on his level now, her face inches from his own.

He felt the slightest of touches, and her lips were suddenly there. They were soft, on his skin. She slowly kissed his cheek and absorbed the tear unto herself.

He turned and looked straight at her, at her face, so close now. At her lips, with his tear still shining and visible. At her eyes, with sadness and pain always hidden just beneath the sincerity of her gaze.

She was seeing all of the broken parts of him, but she would not look away. He felt it again, the same emotion he had felt before. A few minutes ago, when he had first seen her walking across his front yard. His breath slowed now, his heartbeat calmed. His hand and his whole body stopped its shaking.

He was standing at ease, in silence. With her. Still, no words had been spoken, yet something had happened. He was comforted. He had been led into a peaceful calm from an unexpected source.

He felt her hand take his own. She opened the fingers to place something into it, then closed it again. Whatever she had placed into his hand was light and small. She looked back into his eyes and smiled warmly.

"Rest," she whispered. Then she added, even more softly, "Heal."

She turned and walked down the steps and into the rain, walking across the yard and towards the direction that would take her back to her room at Ella's. He watched her from his porch, from the spot where she had been standing just minutes before. He watched her walk away until he could no longer see her under the sheets of rain plummeting to the earth.

He was suddenly sleepy, fully ready to close his eyes and to put this day behind him. He turned and went inside, closing the front door behind him. He took off his jacket and the rest of his clothes, then dried himself quickly with a towel. He fell on his bed without even bothering to pull down the covers. He lifted the spare blanket and covered tightly up beneath it.

Am I really going to sleep? Will sleep even come?

Then he realized that his left fist was still clenched. It had stayed clenched the whole time he had removed his clothes and dried off.

He was still holding tight to something that she had given him, right before she had left.

He opened his fingers slowly, revealing a tiny daisy. He wondered how it had survived into the winter. He pictured her stooping down to pick it in the forest on her walk to his house. He looked at it and remembered a similar one, placed behind her ear.

A blue dress. A breeze through her hair.

He clutched the daisy again and placed his hand gently over his chest, over the deep bruise that had formed just inches above his beating heart. As he felt sleep overtake him, he did so with the daisy held tightly, and with two conflicting pictures fighting in his mind.

One was of the deranged man who had tried to kill him hours earlier. The man who had charged, who had bloodied him, who had shot him and fought with him.

The other picture, however, was starkly different. It was the mental picture of her, and she was telling him to do something. She was telling him to rest. She was telling him to heal.

He watched her now, in his mind. He watched her walking away into the rain. And as he finally succumbed to his exhaustion, he watched her walk beyond the mountain ranges. Beyond his vision and beyond his life. He watched her walk into a dark abyss, one from which she would never return.

CHAPTER

Twenty-Seven

*O*n this last day of the calendar year, she passed many houses that still displayed the lasting remnants of holiday decorations. There were several Christmas trees visible behind living room windows, still lit with strings of light, and even some wreaths still hanging on front doors. Yet, even with the lingering decorations, like the rest of the world, the little village readied for a new year.

Ella's Christmas tree had been taken down for a few days now, but Cass still smiled just thinking of it. It had been a few feet tall and covered in handmade, wooden ornaments made by Walter. Some had been miniature baseballs and bats, others traditional stars and mangers. All had been carefully painted, with intricate details and vibrant colors. They were tokens of previous times which made them precious items of great value to Ella and Lucas. They had been placed upon the tree and later removed from the tree with extreme care and reverence.

The holiday season had been one of joyful celebration. The traditions and religious services and winter splendor had all seemed to take on more meaning in light of what had happened just days before. The locals had seemed in a state of endless rejoicing.

He had survived. He was still with them and his body would heal. He had survived.

Lucas had spent quite a bit of time at Ella's over the days leading up to Christmas Eve and on Christmas Day itself. He had arrived for the meals, as Cass had expected, but had also seemed more willing to stay beyond the last bite of dessert. On these holiday evenings, spent sitting around Ella's fireplace in her small living room, the three of them had talked freely and informally. The son and mother had exchanged memories of holidays past and the visitor had taken it all in with a calm study.

On Christmas Eve, Ella and Lucas had headed off to church for service. They had asked Cass to join them, but she had opted for a walk in the frigid night air. She had found herself sitting at the edge of the lake, peering out over the dark, still water. All had been quiet.

She had remembered then the story Lucas had shared about his people, about the mourning and cleansing of the Cherokee. She had looked at the night sky and tried to determine which direction was east and which was west. She had removed her jacket and then she had entered the lake, alone, on that cold Christmas Eve night. She had dipped down in the direction of the east and then turned and done so for the west, dipping and repeating for a total of seven times. And then she had returned to Ella's, walking slowly in her drenched clothes as she shivered in the cold night air. She had arrived back at the house late, after Lucas had left and Ella had gone to bed.

The following morning Cass had woken early, hoping to take an early morning walk before anyone else was encountered. She had been surprised to find Ella already up, baking fresh cinnamon rolls and humming a carol softly to herself. Soon afterwards Lucas had arrived, bringing with him a bag filled with gifts and sporting a Santa hat on his head. The three of them had enjoyed Christmas breakfast together, and then Ella had indicated it was time to unwrap presents.

Cass had volunteered to wash the dishes while Ella placed some last minute presents under the tree. While Ella and Lucas were busy in the living room, Cass finished the last of the dishes and took the opportunity to quietly leave out the back door. She had felt it only right to allow the little family to enjoy their holiday together, and privately.

As she had walked down the porch steps and onto the walkway, a voice had called behind her.

"You do know how disappointed she'll be, right?" It had been Lucas. He had stepped out on the porch and had closed the door behind him.

"It's Christmas," she had said while turning to look at him. "Your family should have some time together."

"She wants you to stay." He had held a serious look while saying this, then had relaxed his face and smiled gently. "Come inside, Cass." He had opened the door towards him, then stood and waited while holding it ajar.

Moments afterwards, Cass had found herself relaxed in one of Ella's recliners. It had been time for the official gift exchange in front of the roaring fireplace. Lucas had given his mother a blue, fluffy sweater and a new toboggan to match. Ella had given her son a thick scarf and a gift card to his favorite sporting store in Asheville.

Ella and Lucas also had gifts for Cass. From Ella, Cass received a package of hair ties as well as two new t-shirts. Lucas had wrapped his present to Cass in a light blue paper with snowflakes on it. Inside, Cass had found a Chimney Rock ball cap and a hand-carved walking cane, both from Billy's souvenir shop.

"I thought they might be helpful, on your walks," Lucas had said, looking into the fire as he did so.

As she tried on the ball cap on that Christmas morning, Cass had also found an envelope in the lining. Inside the envelope there was a handmade coupon, good for one "field trip" to the Cherokee Village – with him.

Cass, too, had bought gifts, although her original plan had been to quietly leave these on the kitchen counter for Ella and Lucas to open at a later time. But since she had been asked to join in, she had given these to their rightful recipients.

For Ella, Cass had picked a bouquet of wildflowers back in October. These had come from the field right behind Ella's house. She had dried and pressed these, then had placed them in a used frame she had purchased from The Treasure Chest. Ella had seemed genuinely touched by the gift.

For Lucas, Cass had purchased an umbrella at The Treasure Chest. The largest, sturdiest umbrella she could find.

Now, as she walked on this sunny but cold last day of December, just the thoughts of the Christmas morning spent with Ella and Lucas brought warmth to her face and body. Unfortunately, the blast of frigid air that swept across her startled her away from those memories of opening presents in front of a fireplace.

On this particular day, with it being New Year's Eve, she had closed up the café with Ella a little early and had headed out immediately for her walk. She knew that it was time to start putting more distance and time in. To focus more seriously on preparing her body and lungs and heart for the day that was coming soon, in just four and a half months. The day that she would walk out of this place.

She looked up at the road signs ahead and saw that one had come loose from its bolt. It was hanging perpendicular to the other. This looked odd, but also familiar. She realized too late why that was so. The frozen image approached...

The girl is tired and dirty. She is somewhere she doesn't know. On a street in a town that she doesn't know. She is hungry and she is alone. She has been walking all day, and now she wishes to rest. Her head is upturned, looking at two street signs. One has come loose and is hanging across the other.

A voice is asking her, "What is your name?" But she is looking at the signs. The sign that is secure says James Street and the sign that is hanging says Cassidy Street. She is ready to answer now. She is going to say her name. Her name is Cass.

The frame dissolved and transformed into another.

The girl, the one named Cass, is sitting alone in a shelter. It is a shelter for people who have no home. She is shivering, not from cold but from fright. She is alone. She understands now that being alone is real. It is finite, and it is done. This is her life now. Now and always. She assumes this is how her life has always been.

She is alone. Now she must be strong. Now she must survive.

Focused again on the present, through her own determination as well as a few minutes with her drawing, she continued walking towards the lake. The sun was now starting its descent behind the mountains and had taken with it the last remnants of warmth. There now seemed to be an icy shadow cast across the sheltered valley.

Cass considered how cold the water would feel upon her and how much her ears would ache that night as she laid her head down to rest. Those concerns were minimal to her, as compared to the potential for calm and peace. She had remembered the story he had told her, the story Lucas had shared about the cleansing and mourning and the ceremony in water. She had tried it on Christmas Eve and two other times since then.

Is it working? How will I know?

And then she thought about the key question, the one that mattered the most.

Am I in mourning?

She thought about the possibility that she was in mourning, then considered that she knew of no reason why she would be. Since coming to this place over seven months ago, she had no memory of any loss she had suffered.

She then questioned how that would even happen to her. She questioned how mourning could happen to someone who was all alone. She realized there could be no loss and, thus, no mourning. Not for those who were alone.

But even as she processed these questions against the clattering of her shivering jawbone and chattering teeth, she continued to walk towards the lake. She rounded the last curve and saw it up ahead.

She turned and made her way towards the outskirts of the beach area where she could easily navigate a way into the water.

She had anticipated that no one else would be near the lake on such a cold day, and found that her prediction had been correct. The temperatures were in the low thirties and the sun was absent behind the towering grey peaks.

She lowered the hood from about her head, then unzipped and removed her fleeced jacket. She took off her shoes and socks and pulled off the long sleeved, second shirt she had worn for warmth. Now, standing on the beach in only her t-shirt and leggings, she started to slowly walk towards the water. She imagined that the lake was beckoning to her. *Come and be cleansed.*

She made it to the water's edge and allowed her feet to enter. The water was freezing and a jolt of frost shot upward and throughout her body. She stood there for some time, trying to ready herself. Trying to regain her resolve.

Finally, she steeled herself, clenching her jaw and her fists. She focused her eyes and remembered the story. She lifted her leg to move forward.

"You can't do it alone."

The familiar voice was close, somewhere close behind her.

She turned to see him standing in the grass, very near. At first his expression was one of concern, then, as she met his eyes, the smile appeared. Gentle and kind. A smile on a face that was still bruised and healing. He took a few steps to reduce the distance between them, then he turned his attention out towards the lake.

"You can't do it alone," he said softly. "Remember? What I told you, in the story?"

He was waiting for her response. She followed his gaze out to the middle of the lake then turned back to him.

"I remember the story," she said quietly, feeling suddenly unsure.

He stepped even closer and looked into her eyes. "You have to have your tribe with you, Cass. Your tribe is part of your cleansing." He smiled reassuringly, and then he unzipped his jacket.

She looked away.

What is happening?

She readied herself to leave the water, to gather her items and walk away. But even as she considered the options, she looked back at him. He had removed his jacket and was now taking off his shoes. He pulled off the thermal shirt he was wearing, exposing a thin t-shirt underneath. Dressed only in the t-shirt and his jeans, he walked towards her, towards the water.

"Don't do this, Lucas. You'll freeze. It's not important. It's not worth…." Her words were halted as he walked by her and took her hand.

He was ahead of her now, in the water up to his ankles. She knew he was cold, but he never showed it. He tugged on her hand gently. He turned his head back and smiled, nodding his head to the side to encourage her to follow.

She started walking, willing herself to move. Her whole body felt frozen and exposed, all except for her hand. It felt warm and hidden, inside the palm of his own.

They made their way in silence, into the lake, until the water was just at her chest. They stopped, but he continued to hold her hand. They both turned towards the east. He looked over at her and smiled, and, through her chattering teeth, she smiled back.

He started to descend, into the water.

"Stop," she yelled out suddenly.

He stopped and turned towards her, seeming startled at her raised voice.

"You don't have to, Lucas," she said, trying to regain some semblance of control in her voice and in her mind. "I'm the one. The one that…I'm the one that needs…." She couldn't figure out what she needed or what she wanted to say.

"Cass," he said softly, keeping his eyes on hers. He moved his hand under the water, moved his fingers to intertwine with her own. "I'm your tribe," he whispered gently. "When you mourn, I mourn."

She watched him immerse himself into the water, and she

followed. As she came up from the darkness, she couldn't differentiate between the coldness of the lake and the chill of the winter air. The two of them turned in tandem, unlatching their hands as they did so. Once they were turned towards the west, she reached out and took his hand again. He threaded his fingers into her own and they dipped down together.

East then west then east then west, they continued their ceremony without speaking or looking at one another. With the final immersion to the east, they both remained underwater a little longer. They then rose to the frigid night air.

They turned towards one another, their hands still clasped. He looked at her, appearing to seek out something in her face. She wondered if he saw what he was seeking there.

Is there anything to see?

The two of them began walking back towards the beach now, sledging their way through the cold water. She gently pulled her hand from his. The ceremony was over, and she did not wish to impede any further on his good will. She walked a little ahead of him, exerting energy and willing her aching legs to move quicker through the heavy mud that lined the floor of the lake.

Reaching the beach first and emerging fully from the water, she headed for her dry outerwear and shoes. She unexpectedly found a towel laying atop them. She picked it up and considered it for a moment, then wrapped it tightly about her shivering body. She looked up just as Lucas was walking onto the beach.

His hair, usually combed back away from his face, was now draped across his forehead in dripping strands. His soaked t-shirt was glued against his chest and his pants were clinging to his legs in soaked clumps. He walked towards his own pile of clothes and picked up another towel that was waiting there.

"I just happened to have these in my truck," he said lightly, holding up his towel before wrapping it about his head and vigorously rubbing his hair. As he did so, she noticed his shirt and pants legs, both dripping with a rhythmic release of cold water.

They both replaced shoes and socks upon feet and shirts and jackets on torsos, then stood to face one another in an awkward silence. He started towards his truck, which was parked not too far away, and looked back over his shoulder.

"Come on, I'll give you a ride," he called out.

"I think I'll just walk," she replied, and started in the opposite direction. She walked away from the beach and the lake and the man dripping wet in the thirty degree weather.

She did not know if the cleansing had worked, or even why she had felt it was needed. But she knew the cleansing had come at a cost. The cost had been him, the man who was freezing even now in drenched clothes. He had joined her, had held her hand, and had dipped into the water alongside her. It was what he did, and who he was. He was someone who helped those who were hurting and saved those in danger.

But now he would feel the repercussions. He would feel the chill to his bones and the ache deep in his ears. That was the cost of trying to save those who could not be saved.

And so she went, walking again, alone.

But while her body was frozen and rigid, her mind was warm and moving. It was filled with a sliver of sunshine, and a subtle ray of hope. She resisted and focused on her shivering jaw and the chill in her heart.

But, still, her soul was sensing it. A truth that she wouldn't escape.

He is everything good.

And he.

He.

He…is my tribe.

Spring

CHAPTER

Twenty-Eight

The buds forming on the massive crepe myrtles were a welcome sight. They served as a visible indication that this unforgettable winter would soon be behind him. The unusually warm weather of two weeks ago had tricked the flowers into believing that spring would soon arrive. Lucas hoped the rest of nature would follow suit and simply push its way into the warmth of the approaching season.

After the shooting on December eighteenth, the weeks that followed had included questioning and paperwork, all led by the State Bureau of Investigation and focused on the incident that day. There was no question that Lucas had done what needed to be done. Even so, the protocol must be followed.

As for Michael, he had recovered from his wounds and was now awaiting trial in the county jail. Once the trial started, Lucas anticipated that even more of his time would be devoted to testimony and trial prep.

More strongly now than before, Lucas was feeling that time was a commodity that he simply did not have. He believed that he certainly did not have enough of it to be wasting. He had his job, his mother, his friends, his hobbies. And, of course, his projects around the house. Projects that needed to be completed, as quickly as possible.

At the end of his shift that day, Lucas headed straight to his home. He forced himself to lift a few weights and run a few miles, then quickly showered and shaved. He put on some loose sweats, a long-sleeved thermal shirt and some work boots, then headed out to his backyard. His intent was to put the finishing touches on an old lamppost that he had found the week before while antique shopping with Ella.

Upon first seeing it in the shop, Lucas had considered the possibility that the lamppost could add a certain charm to the end of a driveway. A lone beacon for a lonely traveler. It was about eight feet in height and a rustic, dark red color. Unfortunately, it also included some rust to add to the rustic element.

Leaning the lamppost up against the side of his shed, he made haste to begin on the rust issues. He sanded the rusty patches down and then closed his eyes to feel them with one or two fingers, as his father had taught him. He rubbed and rubbed some more, going back and forth across the area, trying to sense any bumps or irregular spots. He was pleased to find none.

Feeling quite satisfied and ready to begin painting, he opened his eyes and stood, scanning the ground around him for the painter's tape he had tossed there. He suddenly realized that the air had grown quite cool, which was typical for an evening in early March. He eyed the fire pit, sitting in the middle of his yard. He tried to remember the last time it had actually held a fire and concluded it had certainly not been this winter. He grabbed some sticks and logs from the wooded lot beside his house, and soon was enjoying a roaring blaze.

Quite satisfied with the warmth emanating from the open flames, Lucas stood by and warmed his hands a bit. He then turned his attention again to the lamppost. Although the sun was visible in the evening sky, the cooler air made for difficult painting weather. But considering the small area that needed to be painted, and the fact that he'd like to have this project done before the week ended, he decided to proceed nevertheless. After walking inside to retrieve the can of spray paint he had forgotten earlier, he walked back out to find two women admiring his antique lamppost.

"Well, that's coming along quite nicely, son." Ella exclaimed. "By the time you're done, I won't even recognize it as the same one you bought on our trip to Rutherfordton."

Lucas smiled modestly as he walked towards her. "Thanks, Mom," he said gently as he embraced Ella and gave her a tight hug. He looked over his mother's head and nodded at Cass. "And good evening to you, Cass."

Cass appeared to be tickled as he greeted her in this faux formal manner. She looked down, grinning. Looking back up, she returned his greeting just as formally. "Good evening, Chief of Police Montraine. How do you do, sir?"

"Oh, you two," Ella said with a laugh and a gentle push on Lucas's shoulder. Ella took the dish that Cass had been holding and offered it towards her son. "On these nights that you're too busy to stop by, I certainly don't want you to starve."

He eagerly took the plate, feeling suddenly famished. "I won't starve, Mom. I do have food and I know how to cook." He lifted the foil on the plate and took a whiff of what smelled like Ella's homemade chicken pot pie. "The problem is, I can't cook like *this*. Thanks, Mom."

Lucas walked over to the two chairs that sat alongside the fire pit and set the dish down on one of them. As he did so, he asked, "Are you two going to hang around and keep me company while I eat?"

"Sorry, son. I just can't. No matter how hot you make that fire or how many blankets you throw on me, I'm just not sitting out in this chill." Ella started walking towards her car.

"I think I'll stay," Cass called out to Ella's back, then added, "for just a while, if that's okay?"

Ella turned around with a surprised look on her face. "Well, of course it's okay. In fact, thank you for keeping my son company when his feeble old momma can't do so. Lucas, you can drive her home, right?"

He readied to respond. Cass beat him to it.

"I'm walking back. But it won't be too late, I promise." With this, Cass walked over to and sat down in the second chair.

After Ella had left and the two of them were left alone, the conversation commenced quickly and easily. Cass asked about his day at work and he shared the challenges as well as the funny things that had happened. Lucas asked her about the bakery and the specials of the day and the café customers and about what she had seen on her walk.

As she spoke, she looked into the fire, and he noticed, as she did so, the flames reflecting off the deep blue of her eyes. The fiery reflections created a color that he imagined was the color of the tropics. The clean, clear water that surrounded uninhabited islands unseen by man.

As she continued talking, he was also struck with the realization that the topics of their frequent discussions were always the same. His work. Her work. His stories, his memories. His town and family and friends. He was convinced that if he had described his conversations with her to someone, they would no doubt have assumed that his exchanges with Cass were stifling, boring and impersonal. But that assumption would have been wrong and would have been almost the exact opposite of what they really were.

Their conversations were easy. Gentle. They were funny at times, the times that both of them would chuckle softly and she would cover her mouth with her hand while her shoulders shook. They were interesting and they were calming. He would sit and listen to the soothing sound of her soft voice. He would watch the slight smile upon her face as he shared a memory of his childhood. He would see her look out into the distance, across the mountains, as he shared a story of his people.

He also knew that there was one word that would describe what their conversations weren't. One thing they never would be.

Enlightening.

He never asked, and she never offered up, anything about before. The time of her life that had transpired before she had walked into their lives, almost ten months ago. He had concluded that this was how it would remain between them, until the day she left. But there was another reality he had accepted, even as he sat around this fire with her on this chilly March evening.

I'm done trying to find out more. She is who she is.

Lucas took his final bite from the plate of pot pie and wiped his mouth. As he set the plate down on the ground beside of him, he took the opportunity to turn and look at her. She was stretched out in her chair, so much so that her legs were extended straight in front of her and crossed at the ankles. Her arms were also crossed across her chest, and her head was propped awkwardly back. Her eyes were closed.

He sat back in his chair and looked at the fire, feeling its warmth against his face and even through the material of his sweat pants. He looked up and saw the first twinkling of stars appearing in the light grey sky. He looked back over at her. Her eyes were open now, and she, too, was looking up at the night sky.

"I never thanked you," she said quietly, still looking at the sky. "For going into the lake with me, that day." She turned her head towards him and he turned as well to meet her gaze.

They had seen each other almost every day since that day. They had talked freely and casually. But just like the other seemingly significant interactions that had occurred between them over the past months, neither had ever brought up or addressed the day of cleansing in the lake. Not until now.

"You don't need to thank me," he said. "But how about we wait until summer for our next cleansing ceremony?"

She snickered a little to herself and grinned at him. Then, the grin slowly disappeared, transforming into a stoic expression.

She won't be here in the summer.

She spoke again, changing the subject. "I really do like the lamppost you're working on."

I forgot all about the lamppost.

"You do?" he confirmed. "That's good to hear."

"Is it going at the end of your driveway, or up close to your house?" she asked, seeming genuinely interested.

"To be honest, I'm still thinking about where to put it." He stood up and went to retrieve more wood. After stoking the embers a little and adding more logs, he returned to his chair beside her.

Cass.

She was a person who had come into his life, into all of their lives, and would remain there for a little over two more months. He thought about his list, presently sitting atop his bedroom dresser. His list about her. He pictured it in his mind, remembering every clue from his ten-month investigation.

<u>*The Drifter- May 19*</u>

Walked here (from where?)

Late teens, early 20s (correction: 27/update: 28)

5'8" (approximate)

Unkempt

Backpack

Hiding something (missing persons? parole? check with other municipalities and hospitals)

No database matches

No fugitive matches

No hospital matches

Lean, appears to be strong physically, but mentally?

When does she sleep? (encountered her again on porch after midnight)

No cell phone

Beautiful

Brave

Selfless

Tristan

Doesn't like beer
In Sylva two years ago
Something about a house in each place?
Prominent scar or scars on back
One year per town?
30–40 miles per trip?

He stood up and walked into his home, then returned quickly. He walked to the fire pit, folding the piece of paper from the note pad as he did so. He tossed it into the flames, and stood watching while it quickly caught fire and burned to ashes. Then he sat, a broad smile on his face.

She watched it burn as well, just as he had. She didn't ask what it was or why he was burning it. She just watched the flames leap up and the ashes as they drifted into the sky.

He turned towards her again. He watched as the embers reflected in her eyes and the corners of her mouth turned upward in a content smile. He watched as the wisps of her hair blew softly around her face.

She is who she is.

CHAPTER

Twenty-Nine

$\mathcal{W}$alking back from The Treasure Chest, Cass noticed the increased activity all about town. Groups of people were walking along the sidewalks, peering into shop windows. Cars full of sightseers were pulling into and out of the entrance to the State Park. Shop owners were replacing wintery flags and decorations with everything spring. Warmer weather had arrived, and she fully understood the uptick in everyone's outlook. She, too, felt something. Something warm.

Entering into Ella's home from the back porch, she dropped off the used tennis shoes and pairs of socks and extra leggings she had bought from Justina earlier in the day. She glanced again at the shoes as she set them down, turning them over quickly to once again check the tread. In just a couple months, she would need sturdy shoes with which to depart. She determined this pair would suffice.

She already knew the exact path she would take on that morning, the morning of her departure. She would wake early, grab her backpack, and be on her way. She would head east on the same road she had walked along at least a thousand times during the past year. She would take this road out of the village and into the town and then to Highway 9, where she would turn right and leave this place behind her.

Cass had considered on multiple occasions that in all fairness she should consider the village and the town in singular terms, each as their own place in her sphere of understanding. She considered that perhaps her goal on her day of departure should be to simply leave one – or the other – behind. Yet, just as quickly as that possibility had reached her, she had rejected it. When she thought of her time here, she thought of this *one* place, the place that included both. She would leave both behind.

And so, as she had thought about all of this, the route had actually been quite easy to determine. She would not leave the way she had arrived last year, for that would be in the wrong direction. Interestingly to Cass, for all this time, she had never even walked in that direction, the direction of the western part of the village. The part where her *peace* existed. She had never returned in that direction, and she wondered now if she ever would.

The route was chosen, and she already had most of the scant items that she would take with her when she went. Last minute things, such as a new toothbrush, could wait until the last few days. She would do all of this quietly, without any fanfare or anything to bring attention to her preparation. She had no desire to interrupt their days or their lives. It wouldn't be necessary. She could depart silently, without disturbance or detection. And certainly without goodbyes. She had come and now she would go. It was that simple. Now the only things left were to be strong and to survive, on her own, for just two more months.

Cass felt a sense of satisfaction as she again left the home, intending to walk some more before the day concluded. These plans were interrupted as she stepped onto the sidewalk and glanced down the street. Feeling a fluctuation in her pulse, she caught sight of Lucas standing next to his squad car, in front of Billy's shop. As she walked closer, she saw that there were others on the sidewalk, others whose names she knew.

"Cassie!" yelled Juney as Cass slowly approached them. The little girl started running towards her, and the rest of the group turned towards her as well. Cass anticipated a hug was coming, so she bent her knees in a deep squat so the little girl wouldn't hit her head on a hip bone. Juney was almost to her, so Cass held out her arms and Juney flew towards them.

"Cassie! Cassie! Cassie!" Juney seemed so happy to see her as she flung herself into Cass's waiting arms. *Cassie* was Juney's version of Cass's name made into a rhyme with Juney's name. She had started calling Cass by this nickname from early on and it had somehow stuck.

Cass stood up and took Juney's hand as they both walked towards Margie, Jacob, and Lucas.

"Hello, Cassie," Lucas said in a teasing tone.

Cass gave him her best "it's not that funny" grin before turning towards Margie. "Hey Margie. Hi, Jacob." Cass gave Jacob a gentle side hug as Juney snickered nearby.

The group stood for a while, chatting about various topics. The children excitedly talked about their new puppy, Sammy, and Margie shared some thoughts on Spring Break, which would be starting the following week. Then Lucas brought up the topic of a 10K he would be running that weekend in nearby Fletcher.

"Why don't you try it with me?" he asked.

Cass looked around and then concluded that he appeared to be asking this question of her.

"Try what? A race?" she replied, with disbelief in her voice.

The look on his face appeared serious, as opposed to its usual teasing mode. "Sure. Why not?" he asked. "It would probably be a piece of cake for you."

Lucas was pulling his radio from his belt as he spoke. Someone from the department needed him, and the group waited quietly as he responded to the radio call. A moment later, he returned his radio to its proper compartment.

"So, what do you think? The registration is still open." Lucas was waiting for an answer.

Cass chuckled a little and looked over at Margie and the kids. They were all waiting, waiting with anticipation. Then she remembered, they didn't know her. Not really.

Cass shook her head gently. "I'm not a runner."

Moments later, Margie was taking the children's hands amid their soft protests. "We have to get going," Margie said cheerfully. "Time to get home and do a little homework. Say goodbye, kids."

Cass and Lucas bent down at the same time and the twins hugged them both simultaneously, forming an impromptu group hug. Margie said her own goodbyes and headed towards their car with the children, when Juney suddenly broke away and came back to Cass.

"I forgot, Cassie. I made this for you." Juney pulled something from her pocket and held it up. It was a rope bracelet, adorned with yellow and purple beads, including one bead that looked like a butterfly. Juney pulled on Cass's left hand and placed the bracelet within, then kissed Cass sweetly upon the cheek. "It's for spring," Juney said. "It's a friendship bracelet for springtime." Then she giggled sweetly and returned to her mother.

Lucas and Cass stood silently and watched the family drive away.

"So, how does it feel?" Lucas asked quietly. "To spend time with someone whose life you saved?"

Cass thought about this for a minute, about this question that she had not really considered before.

I saved a life.

She looked down at her hand and at the colorful bracelet laid upon it by the girl. The young girl who had screamed, who had wanted nothing more than for her brother to somehow survive.

She thought about how precious and beautiful the bracelet was, against the scarred surface of her hand. The hand she had used as her anchor to pull herself over the jagged fence. The hand that had led her to Juney.

"On paper, I guess I saved Jacob's life," she responded. Then she added quietly, "But really ... the life I saved ...."

She hesitated for a moment, lost in thought as she pictured Juney as a young teenager, then as a high schooler, then as a woman in her twenties. She knew, beyond any doubt, that Juney would be lovely. That Juney would be loved.

She was jarred back to reality by Lucas's radio, once again summoning him. She listened as he responded, questioning and then deciding. She knew nothing about police work, but she knew that something about the conversation sounded serious. There was a town or city nearby, and someone needed backup. He was walking towards his squad car.

"See you later, Cass," he called back over his shoulder.

She watched him and willed herself to turn, to walk away. She heard his engine turn over and heard the radio from inside the car. She watched him put on his sunglasses and noticed that he was buckling his seatbelt. She walked to his car and knocked on the glass.

He rolled down the window. As he spoke there was alarm in his voice.

"What's wrong, Cass?"

Why did I come over here?

She looked away, trying to gather her thoughts. She attempted to figure out exactly why she was standing at his car.

"Cass?"

He left the car running while he opened the door and stepped out. He placed a hand on her arm. Suddenly, her arm felt warm. The spot where his hand rested felt protected. She wondered how her skin and body could change so quickly. She willed herself to walk away, but instead felt the sting of tears beginning to form in her eyes.

Why are you trying to console me? It is not me who needs protecting. It is not me.

She felt the slight moisture in her eyes now growing, forming a puddle that threatened to get out of control.

No.

She determined she would not do that. Strong people did not cry. *Do I even have a reason to cry?*

She squinted her eyes to contain the emotion, to push the tears back into their secured shelter. She then looked up, to his eyes. His sunglasses reflected only her own worried face, so she looked away again.

She readied her voice, prepared it to sound nonchalant and indifferent. "Will you be alone?" she asked quietly.

There was a brief pause before he answered. She took the silence to mean the question was out of bounds, or one he couldn't or wouldn't answer. She wondered why she had thought it was any business of hers. She wondered why she had even asked the question.

She looked back at him, wondering why he was still standing there. She took a step back, letting his hand fall back to himself.

Lucas removed his sunglasses. He was looking straight at her, and his eyes were dark and gentle. "No," he whispered. "I won't be alone."

He smiled gently as he placed the sunglasses again on his face and returned to his car. He backed out into the road as she turned and walked on her way.

Without looking back, she could tell. She could tell from the sound of his car engine, diminishing in volume as the distance between them grew. She could tell, he was gone.

She felt the spot on her arm, where his hand had just been. The warmth had left. It was just her arm again. Nothing had really changed about it after all.

CHAPTER

Thirty

*L*ucas walked slightly behind her, staying just close enough to make it obvious that she was being accompanied to the back door of Ella's home. He wouldn't be entering the home, not tonight. Ella was at a gathering of the Ladies Auxiliary, a regional meeting that was a half-hour away in Forest City. Without his mother there, he thought it best to say a quick goodbye and then be on his way.

They were both quiet now. He was thinking about different parts of the day and which moments may have been most enjoyable and meaningful to her. He wondered if she was thinking the same, about him.

He had given the day's trip to her as a gift, a "field trip coupon" tucked inside a ball cap at Christmas. For his part, Lucas had been surprised by how quickly the day in Cherokee had transpired and how differently it had transpired than what he had anticipated. As a young boy, he had visited the Cherokee museums and heard the lore and history many times. He had been thoroughly enthralled back then, but had somehow lost that interest as he entered his teen years. He had thought that connection had been lost for good, but after today, he felt that he had recaptured some of his youthful appreciation for his heritage. He had seen the familiar through Cass's eyes, and the pride and interest had all come pouring back.

He had split his time today between viewing the Cherokee village for himself and watching *her* as she viewed the Cherokee village. She had taken the time to read each and every plaque and description board. She had picked up every brochure and had seen every display. She had stopped at each expert speaker and asked what must have been a hundred questions.

Even after they had returned to his truck, she has asked to go back to the museum for the purpose of looking around some more in the gift shop. He had waited for over half an hour, and she had returned with bags and souvenirs and more questions. She had shared some of what she had bought with him, and had kept other purchases to herself.

As he now stood on the paver that was at the bottom of the porch steps, his thoughts of the day were suddenly interrupted by Cass's voice. It was projected down towards him, now that she had ascended the steps up.

"Thank you, Lucas." She paused as if to say more, but didn't. She was looking straight at him now, and their eyes met and held. He wondered if there was something more to be said, but even while wondering, she turned, walked several feet, and unlocked the door. She proceeded in with her three bags in tow. She turned and gave a quick nod along with a slight smile, and then closed the door behind her.

Entering his own home several minutes later, Lucas considered her simple words of gratitude. Words that seemed more than plenty to capture what today had been. He kicked his shoes off, peeled off his socks and plopped into the reclining chair in his living room.

He took a deep breath and willed himself to relax, but inexplicitly felt tense and unsettled. He got up and headed to the fridge. At first he pulled out a beer, then reconsidered and replaced it with water. As he closed the door, he noticed the small calendar held in place with magnets. He flipped it over by two months, to the circled date on his calendar. To the eighteenth day of May. Then he flipped it back. Today was March twentieth.

He opened the sliding door to his back patio and stepped out onto the concrete patio floor. He listened. He could hear the river that ran behind his mother's home. Even from his home, much farther away, he could hear it. There had been rainstorms the past few nights, and the river was rushing with a fury.

His thoughts immediately went to her. He wondered if she too was listening to the river. At this same moment. He wondered if she was standing at the window of her bedroom, his old bedroom, listening and thinking about the river. He wondered if the sound of the water crashing over rocks would help her to rest comfortably on this night.

Why am I so consumed with concern for her?

Whether he considered the whole situation logically or emotionally, he couldn't understand why he had taken her there today. Or why he had dipped into a freezing lake while holding her hand. Or why he had watched for her, almost every day, to walk around the curve of the road near his home. He couldn't understand any of it, which led him to ask the question. The only question that seemed to really matter.

Who is she ... to me?

———

Lucas stood at the foot of the stairs in the same spot where he had just been, just twenty minutes earlier. He looked upward towards the quiet porch and noted that there was no one there who happened to be on the lounge chair looking up at the sky. He walked up the stairs and to the back door. Although he had a key, he knocked.

"Cass."

His voice was so faint, and the knocking on the door so gentle, that at first he thought perhaps she hadn't heard him. Then, he saw her tentatively pull back the curtains on the door window.

Seeing that it was Lucas, she unlocked and opened the door. She greeted him with a worried expression. "Hey. Is everything okay?"

Instead of entering through the opened door, he walked to the back railing of the porch and turned to look straight at her. He felt ill-at-ease and nervous, although he had been on this porch at this house thousands of times before.

She looked around him, into the trees and growing shadows that surrounded the back of the house. The silence between the two of them was accentuated by the sound of water flowing beyond them.

She looked back at Lucas, and then stepped out onto the back porch. "Are you all right?" she whispered, lowering her voice to match the soft tone that his own voice had held as he knocked.

As she stood there in her sock feet, she brushed a strand of hair from in front of her eyes. Her ponytail was almost completely gone from the day's activities. Loose hair hung haphazardly around her face. Her eyes were wide with concern now. She took a step forward, towards him, and repeated her question.

"Are you all right, Lucas?"

He shook his head slowly. Back and forth, never taking his eyes from her.

"No," he whispered, and wondered, as soon as he said it, if he had actually said it aloud.

He unexpectedly remembered something silly from earlier in the day. He remembered the two of them, standing and listening to a story about the beginning of time and the spiritual beliefs of the old tribes. The stories were about how animals and man and nature had lived harmoniously, until man had become too powerful. At this point, the animals had held a meeting, with the bears and the deer leading the way.

He thought back to that moment, to the moment that he and Cass had listened to the story. At that moment, earlier today, he had wondered what animal she would be, standing there in the meeting of all animals. He had known almost immediately. She would be the gazelle, cautious and ready to flee.

Lucas stopped shaking his head. He inhaled and exhaled deeply. He knew the risk. He had known it now for a while. But finally, after all of this time, he was prepared to accept it.

"Cass...."

He thought of fancy words and eloquent phrases, but then remembered that he wasn't either of those. He looked in her weary eyes and decided just to ask the question. The same question. The one he had answered himself, before rushing over to see her. It was the one she would now face. The one he hoped she would answer.

"Who am I?"

He paused and noticed her eyebrow arch upwards. He decided he owed it to both of them to be clearer. "Who am I? To you?" He wondered why, on those last two words, his voice had faltered slightly, had become hoarse and cracked.

She stood silently, staring intently. Doubt crept into his heart and into his mind.

He looked away from her. It had been what seemed like an eternity. A long time for her to answer the question. He steeled himself to look at her again.

As he did so, he realized that everything was falling into place exactly as he had anticipated it would. He had known from the start. He had told himself, over and over. *Not her. Not her.*

"In fifty-nine days, I'm leaving," she said softly. "I'll never come back, and I won't ever think about this place again, or the people in it." She had emphasized this last part, and was now shaking her head gently. "Nothing will change that." She turned to enter back into the house.

"That didn't answer my question," he called out.

Cass stopped her progression towards the door, and Lucas continued.

"Please. Just answer this one time." His voice became soft, and he whispered, "You can trust me, Cass. Trust me that it's the last question I'll ever ask."

She turned around again and faced him, and as she did so, he noticed something in her eyes. They looked sad. Tortured.

"Lucas," she started, gently and hesitantly. "In fifty-nine days ..."

"I know what you're doing, on that day. On May eighteenth. You're walking out of here. Never to be seen or heard from again." His voice sounded hopeless, as hopeless as her eyes looked. "I know, Cass. I get it." He felt tense, and then suddenly bold. "But, Cass, wasn't it you?"

Her eyebrows lifted up. He had her attention.

"Wasn't it you, Cass, who said *now* is all you have? Remember? We were dancing, and I told you I would kiss you, if you wanted. That I would be there for your first kiss." He was pointing to his chest, pounding it for emphasis. "That it would be me." His voice was cracking, growing hoarser yet softer. "On the day and time of your choosing, Cass. And you chose *now*. That's what *you* said. You chose *now* because, you said, that's all you have."

He had the words now. He knew what to say. He knew what his question meant. "So I don't need to hear about the next fifty-nine days or a particular day in May or anything else." Lucas saw her head drop. Her eyes were now downcast. He lowered his voice even further.

"I'm not asking you to tell me anything about you, or anything from your past or your future. I know you don't want that." She looked up at this, and he thought her eyes looked moist. He repeated what he had just said, so quietly it felt like a whisper. "I know you don't want that, Cass."

Her eyes became more filled, even as she blinked in an apparent attempt to get herself under control. He was afraid she might bolt, might flee into the safety of the home. He would say it all, before she went. Before she was gone, forever.

"I know I'm just a random person that you happened to meet along the way. I get it, Cass. A person you met even though you're not staying too long." He said this gently, then continued more tenderly. "But I'm also a man. I'm a man who thinks about you. Every day.

Every moment of every day, quite literally." He chuckled softly and looked down, embarrassed for himself. "At first, I thought maybe I was just curious. You know, the whole not knowing anything about you. And then I thought, maybe, I was just obsessed. Obsessed with a beautiful woman, whose path kept crossing my own."

He looked back up and saw that she was watching him. "But then, I started wondering…." He stopped and allowed himself just a moment to breathe, to look into her eyes, for anything that he could read or deduce. "I started asking myself, who am I to her?"

He paused and watched a single tear fall to her cheek.

"Am I your friend, Cass?" he asked softly. "Am I your crush?"

He noticed a strange expression on her face, but she remained silent. He swallowed and looked away, feeling suddenly hopeless and regretting the decision to come to her like this. He started talking again, more to himself but aloud to her as well.

"I know that you will leave. I know that won't change. I know that now. But even knowing that, I couldn't pull away. I couldn't make myself forget that you're still here. That you haven't left yet." He looked back at her. "And when you are gone, I'll still be here. And I'll wonder. Who was I? To you?"

He looked down while running a hand through his hair, then slowly pulled his eyes back to her. They stood looking at one another. He waited for her response, any response, but she stood firm and silent. He suspected at that point that there would not be a response, would never be an answer.

But then, as he watched, he sensed a subtle change. Her stoic stare was gone. Her eyes lingered and fluctuated between warmth and determination, between cold steel and soft feathers. Her eyes were saying something. They were saying that she was asking herself the question. He imagined and even hoped that this was the case. That she was asking herself, *who is he, to me?*

Suddenly, as if her internal deliberation had concluded, the look turned to sadness and resignation. As if a great loss awaited her, she finally spoke, with a soft, weary tone that begged to be heard.

"No matter what happens, I'm leaving in fifty-nine days."

Then he watched as she turned and entered into the house, leaving the door ajar. He waited a minute or two, then turned towards the rail in frustration. He faced the trees and the river and the endless miles of mountains and valleys that stretched out beyond them and around them.

He thought about the fact that they were just two people in this vast place. Two people who had somehow ended up here. At this place in this time. He pictured the future and how he would think of her, how he would consider their time together. He thought that perhaps when he thought of this time in his life, he would remember that they had been nothing more than strangers. Two people who had just happened to intersect for one year of their lives and then had never crossed paths again.

Somehow this thought brought him comfort as he listened to the river below.

He heard soft footsteps behind him, coming closer in a hesitant cadence. He felt a touch to his shoulders. Something had been draped around him.

He looked to his right shoulder and saw the corner of a blanket, one that was now stretched around his back and in front of his left shoulder as well. He glanced down at the blanket corner more intently and saw that it was one of the Cherokee blankets that he had seen at the village shop. He turned slowly around and raised his eyes from the blanket.

She, too, had a blanket wrapped about her shoulders. It was a beautiful woven garment, the same deep blue as his own.

He stood as still as stone. He felt mesmerized. He looked deep into her eyes, those eyes that held all truth, all fear, all sorrow and courage.

Another tear fell, trickling down her cheek. He had never seen her cry, not before this night. But as he stood there, with his blanket draped around his shoulders, he watched the tear leave its precious trail across her lovely face. He thought that perhaps it was a tear of sorrow, or perhaps even one of joy. Or perhaps it was a tear that represented both.

In silence, she smiled sweetly. Then she walked forward to within a foot of him. She stopped with her eyes just inches from his own.

He forgot to breathe.

Finally exhaling, he watched as she took her blanket from her own shoulders and placed it onto his. She took great care to make the second blanket lie flatly against the first, brushing the corners down and pulling it here and there across his back. He kept his eyes on her face, just inches from his own, as she did so.

She stepped back and looked at him, at all of him. She seemed afraid, but determined. She focused her eyes on his face, into his eyes.

Another tear dropped upon her cheek as she took another step back. She moved her vision to the trees and forming darkness behind him. She squinted her eyes, as if remembering something. A smile formed on her lips, and she looked back.

And when she spoke, the softness of her sweet voice was such that it broke his heart, and linked her forever to it.

"We honor water." She blinked and gently brushed a tear from her cheek. She kept her eyes on his own as she continued. "To clean and soothe our relationship, that it may never thirst for love."

He felt frozen in place, unable to blink.

"With all the forces of the universe you created," she said softly, "we pray for harmony and true happiness."

She was smiling now, shaking her head gently even as more tears fell from her eyes. "As we forever grow young." The last word was whispered, yet he heard it clearly, even over the sound of nature all around them. "Together."

She seemed to be taking in the whole sight of him, his shoulders with the blankets draped upon them, his hair and legs and height. With every glance she always returned to his eyes, and each time with a soft smile on her lips. After what seemed like an eternity of her looking at him as he stood with the two blankets firmly about his shoulders, she concluded her answer to his one and only question.

"*This* is who you are. To me."

She started to step back again, but he reached out, quickly, and took her wrist. He held it firmly, but not tightly. He wanted to hold her in place, just long enough for him to think. He needed time to consider all of the implications of what she had just said. Of what she had just done. Of what it meant, for both of them.

She stood in place and he lowered his hand from her wrist.

His mind knew that she was leaving. He knew the date.

But his heart knew something entirely different. His heart knew that it would end in complete loss and sorrow, but the pathway was now set. There was no turning back.

He stepped forward, coming very close to her. He took the two layers of blankets and grasped them into his right hand. Watching her vulnerable eyes as they filled with longing and frailty, he wrapped his hand about her, and took her under the blankets.

As he did so, his lips found hers in a tender kiss. He pulled away and looked into her eyes, and there he found a gaze returned, one full of sweetness and beauty. He bent and kissed her again, a kiss that began as gentle, then gradually progressed into one filled with more. He pulled back and found that she had followed him, keeping her lips on his in a longer embrace.

She left his lips then, and he looked at her as he held her with his right hand under their blankets. His free left hand found her face, where he caressed softly while kissing her lips, her cheek, her forehead.

He had always thought of her as so lean and strong, but all he felt now was soft. She was soft and lovely, with lips that tasted like strawberries and flowers and tears. His right hand was still holding the blankets about her while his left reached up into her hair, holding her head as he kissed her again.

Her body was pressed tightly into his, not because of his own hold, but because she was holding him tightly. Her hands had wrapped about his chest and around his back. She was holding him so fiercely he could hardly breathe, or perhaps his lack of breath was due to the passion rising between them.

He stopped and pulled back a few inches, just to look at her. Her eyes were still filled with tears, and he took his thumb and wiped away the ones on her cheek. Her lips were wet and swollen. She smiled at him, then leaned her head slowly towards him. She kissed him gently on the lips, keeping her eyes open to watch his own. She pulled one hand from its place on his back and placed it on his face, on his cheek. She held it there as she leaned towards the opposite cheek and kissed it gently. Then she kissed his jawline. Then she lowered her face and softly kissed his neck, holding her lips there for too long.

Lucas took the other side of the blankets, the other corners draped over his left shoulder, and grasped them quickly into his hand. He wrapped them around her and now engulfed her completely under the warm coverings.

He now knew the answer to his questions, both the one he had asked her and the one he had asked himself for so many months. He knew now that she was his. And he was hers. They had chosen each other.

And as he continued to adore her and to kiss her and to embrace her while under the blue blankets, he felt a steady uneasiness. He felt an emotion that threatened to bring tears to his eyes, just as he saw in hers. He sensed a cautionary knowledge that lingered in the background of his consciousness.

The beginning of a sorrowful goodbye.

A fleeting warning.

A ticking clock.

Thirty-One

She looked over at the two blue blankets, folded neatly atop the table in the corner of her bedroom. It had been over two weeks since those very blankets had been draped about her shoulders. And since that day, she had felt cherished. And included and protected. She had begun to feel eager to welcome each day, and anxious for those moments when she might see him again.

She acknowledged that this transformation wasn't just about him, although he was a significant part. It was about them. They had somehow found a way, to start growing young. Together.

Tearing her eyes from the blankets, she returned to tying her shoes. Grabbing a clean t-shirt, she added this to the shorts she had on, and then worked on her hair. It was a wet mop of a mess, so she combed it gently and pulled it back in a loose ponytail. She lamented that she didn't have more time to let it air dry, but Lucas was waiting.

Walking out of the bedroom and into the kitchen, she picked up two of the Froggy Biscuits she had made in the bakery this morning. She gave a quick goodbye to Ella, and headed out of the house through the back. As she was closing the door behind her, she thought she heard Ella call out, something that sounded like "Don't ruin your appetite for supper."

Cass soon found the pathway that led towards the river. As she grew nearer, the sound of the rushing water grew more intense. She came into a clearing and searched for their rock, finding it quickly and him sitting upon it. Lucas looked as if he was watching for her, and waved heartily as he saw her approach.

He stood and started back across the rocks, apparently meaning to help her. But she was already to the third rock by the time they met one another. As she stepped onto it, he did as well, only to find his foot slipping and his body struggling for balance. Soon she was holding him, wrapping her arm around his waist and steadying him in one quick gesture.

With her arm still around him, both of his hands came up to her face. As he held his hands on her cheeks, he lowered his face slowly. He looked into her eyes, then down to her lips, then back to her eyes. He came very close as she watched, and then he stopped. He whispered something softly, too softly for her to hear over the water, and then his lips met hers.

With her other hand, the hand holding the bag of cookies, she reached up and hooked her wrist behind the back of his neck. She held his head to hers as the kiss between them lingered, becoming deeper and desperate.

Forty-four more days.

The thought came to her, even as his lips left hers and she leaned forward to find him once again. Soon, they were parting to catch their breaths. He held her to him and then giggled a bit, as did she.

Forty-four days.

She pushed it out of her mind, deciding resolutely to focus on him and on them. On this river and this sunset. They left the third rock together and proceeded to the fourth and then to the fifth. They sat on the large rock, the same one that they had sat on many months before.

On this day, similar to that day, they sat in quiet contentment.

They listened as the water spilled over the boulders all around them. But unlike that day, they sat in a tender embrace, with his arm wrapped around her and her head leaned into his chest.

I can hear his heartbeat. Is there anything more cherished than his heartbeat?

They sat like that, in stillness, for a long time. Then they made their way together back to Ella's house to join her for a supper of grilled pork chops and steamed broccoli. They all had Froggy Biscuits for dessert, which for Cass and Lucas was their second round. Then Ella retreated to the living room to watch a game show and Lucas and Cass proceeded to the back porch.

It was a pleasant early April evening, with the temperature in the mid-sixties and a light breeze blowing through the valley. Cass reclined on the lounge chair while Lucas sat at the table. Retrieving a wooden box from the middle, he took out a box of matches and lit two small candles that always remained outside. One was struggling to hold its flame, no doubt waterlogged from the recent showers. But the other illuminated a tiny fire that would burn on, even as the night sky advanced upon them.

He glanced over at her. She saw this and quickly shimmied to the far side of the lounge chair, patting the vacant space left behind as she did so. He smiled shyly then carefully reclined beside of her, stretching out his left arm under her neck and allowing her to snuggle close beside him. His left hand rubbed lightly up and down along her forearm as they both looked up into the twilight.

"Tell me something about you I don't know," she said, snuggling up tighter to escape a cool breeze that had sent slight shivers up her body.

"My favorite color is blue," he said quickly, as if expecting this very question.

"Which blue? After all, there's navy blue. And light blue. And... oh, I guess it would be Carolina blue, since we're in Carolina." Cass chuckled at her own cleverness. She nudged him with her right elbow, but he was all seriousness.

"Cass blue," he said. He turned and looked at her. "The color of your eyes. That's my favorite." He held the intense gaze as he inched his head forward and met her lips with his own. A tender, sweet kiss, followed by strong arms holding her tightly.

This is the man I look for. Every day as I walk these streets. These are the arms I long to be embraced by, and the lips I long to kiss. His is the smile that warms me.

She moved her face slightly upward, into the curve of his neck. It was warm and soft there, and smelled of musky cologne and strength and courage and everything good. She determined that she would keep herself there, nestled up against his neck, for all of her eternity.

As the sky darkened, they remained there in silence. Soon, she heard his deep breaths, a sign that he had fallen asleep. Just hearing his sounds of slumber suddenly made her own eyelids feel heavy.

She lay still, held in the embrace of his sleeping body. She listened to the soothing river below them, then felt her eyelids begin to close. She felt her eyelashes brush lightly against his warm skin.

Peaceful.

With no memories nor turmoil, she began to drift off. As she did so, she again thought of her existence.

I could stay here, in this spot, nestled up against his neck, for all eternity.

I could stay here, in this spot.

I could ... stay.

Thirty-Two

"Lucas," Farley called out again, with warranted impatience in his voice.

Lucas shook his head as if that would chase away the thoughts that were distracting him from work. He felt he needed desperately to get a handle on things, to get control again of his emotions and his outlook. But that goal had proven to be quite difficult to attain.

"Sorry, Farley," he replied. He quickly signed the two forms his deputy had been waiting on, then handed them over. Farley turned to leave, then hesitated.

"You forgot the date," Farley said while sliding the papers back on the desk. "Anything you need to talk about, Boss?"

"No, just a little tired," Lucas replied, and then completed and returned the papers again. Farley looked them over, gave an understanding nod, and then headed out of the office. Lucas set the pen down and folded his hands under his chin. He needed to close his eyes, just briefly.

The days, the nights. His whole world had revolved around work and family and friends and community, but all were now suddenly set against the backdrop of *her*.

They had gone swimming the night before, in the calm waters of the lake. Although it was now late April, the lake water seemed to still be shaking off the chill of winter. This, however, had not dissuaded them.

Lucas had bought her three bathing suits from a shop in Hendersonville. Two of them were one-piece suits, the third one a two-piece. He had realized too late that he had no idea what she would like, so he had bought the trio, hoping that at least one would work. He had grabbed three bags at the store and put each bathing suit in its own bag.

Arriving at Ella's late in the afternoon, he had handed Cass the three bags and had explained to her that he didn't know what kind she preferred. He had felt like a little kid, acting shy and awkward around the girl he liked at school. He had also felt uneasy, as he had stood there watching her with the three bags in her hand. Uneasy because he had known which bathing suit he wanted her to wear. He had felt ashamed for it.

"Hopefully you'll find at least one you like," he had said.

Without even looking into the bags, she had smiled at him.

I love her smile, he had thought.

"Thank you, Lucas. I'm sure anything you picked out will be fine," she had said. She still hadn't looked inside any of the three bags.

He had watched as she had randomly grabbed two of the bags and placed them on Ella's kitchen counter. She had then headed towards the bedroom to change with one of the bags still in her hand. As she left him she had called back over her shoulder. "We can take those two back to the store this weekend."

He had watched her close the door and had glanced over to the two bags on the counter. He had been tempted, but had decided against looking in them. *What does it matter?* He had thought.

Later on in the evening, after they had arrived at the outskirts of the lake, he had stripped off his outerwear to reveal his dark blue swim trunks. And she. She had removed her t-shirt and shorts and socks, and had revealed the two-piece bathing suit underneath.

She had dipped her toe in the water and had declared it too chilly. He had picked her up, slung her over his shoulder and then down across his chest and into his arms. He had walked out into the water, holding her tight and away from the chilly surface, then he had gradually lowered her while still keeping her cradled in his arms. She had spread her body out straight, in a plank, stretching her arms above her and pointing her toes. He had lowered her enough so one arm could touch the water, and he had slowly turned while she drew liquid circles around the two of them. At one point, he had stopped, and had just looked at her. He had bent his head slowly and had kissed her, even as she lifted her head slightly to reach his own.

They had driven to his house, after swimming, and had built a fire in the pit. They had cuddled up with flannel shirts over t-shirts and shorts, as the air turned cooler with the setting sun. She had sat on his lap, her wet hair tossed carelessly over one shoulder. He had inhaled as her hair touched his nose, then had lifted his face a little to move his nose and lips under her ear and into her neck. She had smelled of nature and fire and daisies.

Lucas was pulled away from the lovely memories of the previous night by the familiar voice.

"Do you want to see him now, or later?" It was Farley again, who had entered the office and was sitting in a chair in front of the desk. This time, Lucas was able to cover for the fact that he had not even noticed Farley's entrance.

"Now, please," Lucas replied, wondering who exactly it was Farley was referencing.

Moments later, he had the answer to that question. The newly hired Officer Colby Melton was entering the office, smiling broadly. It had been months since Lucas had first met this new recruit, and now he was finally here and ready to get started.

"So, I guess you got everything moved up here okay?" Lucas

asked this as he stood to shake Officer Melton's hand. He motioned to a chair and the new member of the team sat.

"Yes, finally. I'm all moved in to the apartment and ready to get to work."

Lucas looked carefully at Officer Melton, or Colby, as he had asked to be called. Although Colby reminded him of a younger Farley, the three of them were actually the same age.

"Well, how about you take the rest of this week to get situated in your new community, and we'll start you out with orientation bright and early Monday morning?" Lucas asked this while browsing through his calendar in order to pinpoint the actual start date of Colby's contract. "After all, we're still ahead of schedule, Colby. Today is only the twenty-third."

April twenty-third?

Lucas stared at the calendar, forcing himself back to the conversation as he heard Colby's voice.

"Monday it is. I look forward to it, Chief." Colby stood and shook Lucas's hand again. As he was doing so, he abruptly added, "Oh, one more thing. Remember during my interview, when you asked me about what inspired me to do police work?"

The two men dropped their hands and stood a few feet apart.

"Yes, I remember," Lucas replied. "You were inspired by a policeman who sacrificed his own life for others, somewhere around where you grew up, I think?" As Lucas was recalling this, he noticed Colby nodding his head.

"That's right, Chief. Well, when I left that day, after the interview, I felt pretty guilty. I mean, here I had made a big deal about how inspired I was, but then couldn't even remember any of the details or even the officer's name." Colby looked away for a second, then brought his eyes back to Lucas. "To be honest, I felt ashamed."

"I can appreciate how that feels," Lucas shared, in a reassuring tone. "Sometimes it's hard for me to remember everything that I should remember about my fallen brothers and sisters across the state. As the years go by, we start to forget important details when we shouldn't." Lucas was emphasizing certain words to clearly articulate his own shortcomings, hoping that Colby would know he was not alone in these feelings.

"Thanks, Chief. That helps to put it in perspective," Colby said. "But just the same, after my interview, when I returned back home, I thought a lot about that. About the same things you were just talking about. I was over at my parents' house one evening and I asked them if they remembered the incident that I was thinking about, and they did. Anyway, one thing led to another. My mom went digging in some boxes she had up in the attic which were filled with old newspaper clippings. And now, thankfully, as I start my new job, I know the name of the officer. I know his name. I know his age. I have his picture."

Lucas noticed how solemn Colby was as he said this. He felt a great sense of brotherhood with this new officer, as well as with the one who had inspired him.

"Well, done." Lucas said, and patted Colby on his arm. "You do honor to the fallen, Colby. I can tell that means a lot to you." Lucas reached for the bottled water on his desk, then continued. "Tell me a little about him. About our fallen brother."

"His name was Sergeant Bryan Canter," Colby began. "He was twenty-nine years old. Husband. Father of two daughters. He had been on the force for a little over three years. He had just gotten off duty and was actually headed home, to his family. He had stopped at a strip mall to pick up a gift for his oldest daughter, who was turning four the next day. He was in the wrong place at the wrong time. In the direct vision of a sociopath with a weapon. Caught in a trap while trying to help others." Colby paused, seeming to consider the horror of what he had just described. "Although, if he were here today, he'd probably say he was in the right place at the right time. He saw danger and he ran towards it." Colby paused and the two men stood quietly.

"Keep him in your heart, Colby," Lucas said. "Let his act of selflessness inspire you each day, as you put the badge on for the citizens of our town."

"It sure will, Chief." Colby responded. He was nodding now and looking out the window. "And I'll never forget it again. His sacrifice, nor him. In fact, I'm still shocked that I forgot most of the details in the first place, considering I knew one of the kids involved."

Colby stopped and cleared his throat. He looked down at his hands then back up at Lucas. Lucas sensed that he was done talking. Something seemed to have changed in his demeanor.

"Well, I hope your friend made it out okay." Lucas said this with genuine care as he watched Colby struggling with something unseen. A memory that seemed to have just resurfaced.

"Oh, he wasn't my friend. I mean, I knew him, but we never hung out or anything. He was a kid from a rival high school who I played against in football. He played linebacker while I played running back. And, he was…he was really good. I mean D-1 scholarship type of good. Everyone in the whole county knew him, or his name at least." Colby paused and turned his attention again to the window. "We were all just kids, seniors in high school. All of us were getting ready to graduate."

Lucas stood quietly, allowing Colby to process the images from the past.

"How could I have forgotten that?" Colby asked himself, then turned to Lucas as if the question had been meant for him.

"Some memories are just too painful," Lucas said, touched quite deeply by Colby's reflection. He had intended to say something else, but then decided no more was needed. He had said it all.

"Well, I didn't mean to dwell so long on that, Chief. I guess I just wanted you to know. I brought the clipping with me and I'm going to frame it and put it on my desk. That way, I'll see it each day, and I'll remember." Colby pointed to a folder he had laid on the desk while he was speaking, then opened the folder and pulled out a newspaper clipping. He looked at it briefly, then held it to his side as he dropped his arm.

"I'm glad you shared that memory with me, Colby. As difficult as that was, I'm glad. Because it's part of your story. And we all have stories. Our stories are what drives us to do what we do, and that's important." Lucas paused and let that sink in. He wanted Colby to always feel comfortable in sharing his fears and his inspirations.

"Hey, I have a few things I need for you to sign," Lucas continued, seeking to lighten the mood again. "Why don't you sit down behind my desk, read over these few pages and see what you think?"

Colby laid the newspaper clipping down on top of the folder and proceeded around the desk. He sat in Lucas's chair and started on the pile of official forms that Lucas had placed in front of him. Lucas sat down in the chair in front of the desk and checked his phone for messages. There was one from Ella about supper that evening and another from the mayor. There were none from Cass.

The girl who chose me doesn't have a phone.

He smiled as he thought about high school and the notion of a girl without a phone. He leaned forward to place the phone on the desk and then leaned back, catching a glimpse of something printed on the newspaper clipping as he did so. It was a single word, one that for some reason had alerted his brain and caught his eyes. He leaned forward slowly and read.

Tristan.

Time. Just moments earlier he had thought about time and how quickly it was passing and how badly he wished to stop it in its tracks. But now, in this moment, Lucas felt as if all time and movement and living had already stopped. He started reading at the paragraph in which he had seen the word.

Tristan Porter, star linebacker for the J.R. Emerson High School Rams, was pronounced dead at the scene. Porter, 17, had recently signed a letter of intent with The University of Alabama, and was scheduled to join the Crimson Tide on a full football scholarship in the fall.

Lucas stopped reading and turned his head away. He looked out the window at the blooming buds on the crepe myrtles and the dark and light greens popping up all along the mountains. He felt his heart beating quickly inside of his chest. As he stared out the window, he wondered what emotion it was he was feeling at that very moment, and he knew it could only be one.

It was fear. Fear that this Tristan was *her* Tristan.

He dropped his head as his mind raced. He closed his eyes and tried to focus. Then, he quickly opened them, having convinced himself that there was more than one Tristan in the world.

There is more than one.

"What was the date?" Lucas asked, lifting his head to look out the window at nothing in particular.

"I'm sorry. The date?" Colby replied as he continued with his signature on the papers.

"The date that Officer Canter died," Lucas replied softly.

"I should know that, but I'm afraid I don't. I'll check the news article when I'm done here. I know it was in May because I remember all of us were getting ready for graduation, all the seniors in the county. We were almost done. We were almost there."

Lucas closed his eyes again.

I already know the date. I don't want to know. But I do.

He looked back at the newspaper clipping and quickly scanned the words. There was no *Cass*. There was no *Cassandra*. He completed his quick scan and felt a sudden burst of encouragement.

She's not here. She's not part of this. This is not her Tristan.

He felt himself breathe again as his tense shoulders relaxed. He was feeling relieved, almost overjoyed, at the revelation that his instincts had been wrong.

Then, he turned his head back. Back towards the beautiful mountains and the still lake. Back to where just the night before he had held her in his arms. And as his head was turning, yearning to take him back to those happy memories with her, his eyes caught an image. It was a color picture in the article, placed low and in the corner.

In the image there was a young man dressed in a tuxedo. His hair was a little short of shoulder-length, and fell in sloppy, blonde waves around his face. He looked like the surfer boys who modeled for magazines, whose pictures were up all over malls and department stores. He was tall and muscular. He stood straight and proud. He was smiling, flashing white, perfect teeth. His eyes were bright and filled with confidence and charm.

And on his arm was a girl. A girl in a strapless pink dress. A dress that draped to the floor with a slit up the leg. There was a hint of her leg and her high heel that could be seen, as the image had captured her while walking. Her hair was long and was falling in loose waves about her shoulders. Her makeup was subtle but glowing, with light pink upon her lips. She had long black lashes on deep blue eyes.

She was smiling.

It was a smile Lucas had never seen before. It was a smile that said, "This is joy."

He stared at the picture, unable to turn his eyes away and unwilling to yet read the article with all the words and answers. He looked into the girl's eyes, at his favorite color of blue. He reluctantly lowered his vision to the caption below the picture.

Seen here, in her May 17ᵗʰ Prom Court Pageant at Emerson High School, is senior Alexandria Porter. She is being escorted by her twin brother, Tristan.

CHAPTER

Thirty-Three

*S*he jolted awake and then sat upright. There was sweat beading on her head and around her neck. The room was all darkness except for the sliver of moonlight that shown through the window pane. She found herself breathing heavily and consciously willed herself to calm down. But even as she thought it, she knew it wouldn't happen. She felt the impending eagerness of one who wishes to be ending something but realizes it is only just beginning. The freeze frame from her nightmare returned.

The teenager is smiling as he stands looking forward. His hand is on her hand. Her arm is looped through his. He is ready to escort her. He is dressed in a black tuxedo, with a white shirt and black tie. His blonde hair is combed carelessly about his face. His eyes are bright and his smile is wide. The girl on his arm is looking straight ahead as well, as if she is anticipating something. She is smiling, with lips of pink. She has long hair that is flowing in waves all about her shoulders and back. She is wearing a full-length pink dress, and she is standing straight, with her shoulders back. There is a banner behind her, on the auditorium stage where they are standing. It says "Prom Court Pageant". The two are frozen, yet there is a voice. It is the boy's voice, and he is whispering, "Stop shaking,

Alex. There's no reason to be nervous. I'm right here with you." His voice is gentle and filled with pride and love. They are frozen, and they are beautiful.

As if a slide on a computer screen was transitioning to another, the freeze frame then dissolved and morphed into a moving action. This action had real people and real voices and Technicolor blues and reds and greens and living, breathing details.

Cass stumbled out of bed, her feet catching in the sheets. She reached for the lamp with her weakened hand while fumbling for the drawing, for her *peace*, with the other. But even as she did so, she knew it was too late. She collapsed to the floor and pulled her knees up, gasping and begging in vain.

Stop.

As the moving picture barreled towards her, she buried her head in her hands. She didn't want to see them, these people whom she would soon see.

The two teenagers are walking now, through the front door of the jewelry store. They are smiling and giggling. There is only one other customer in the store, and he is heading towards the door to leave.

The girl is looking at the earrings. She is thinking, "Yes, they are very pretty."

As they stand together, waiting for a sales person to come out to help them, the boy is looking at the watches, which are displayed in a glass cabinet next to the earrings. The boy is speaking now. He is saying, "Mark this day and time, Alex...May the eighteenth, at 10:21 in the morning. This will be a day and time that you will always remember. Because this will be the exact moment that you realized that you have the most amazing brother ever put on the face of this Earth." The boy is looking at the girl and uttering a silly giggle. The girl is giggling back and lifting her right arm to embrace him.

As she is doing so, a slice of hot, searing pain enters her. It begins in the middle of her right shoulder, and then travels down towards her lower back. It is leaving a trail that feels like molten metal burning into her, rendering her speechless at first, and then screaming in utter terror. The boy is staring, first at her, and then at something directly behind her. The girl sees his eyes shift and expand as the searing pain now slices again, this time closer to her spine, and lower on her back. The second slice came within a second of the first. But now, between seconds, there is time for the girl to look over the boy's shoulder. She is looking into a large mirror that is on the wall. In the mirror the girl is seeing the reflection of a third person, a stranger standing right behind her.

The man is tall. The man is big and he looks confused and angry. His eyes are wild, seeing but not seeing. His hand is holding a large knife, the kind of knife that people use to cut watermelons on warm summer afternoons.

The man is bringing the knife to her again, ready to slice her in half and in quarters. The girl can feel where her skin has been cut open already. She can feel the air and the dirt of the world entering into her through the open slices. Even as the girl is doubled over from the pain of the last two cuts, she keeps her eyes on the mirror. She is preparing for a third slice. The girl sees in the reflection that it is coming. The knife is aimed towards her neck, aimed to slice deep down into her neck. The girl is on her knees now, helpless and pitiful.

The man's hand is now stopped, stopped by the hands of a teenage boy. His name is…his name is Tristan. The boy is struggling to stop the downward progression of the knife, to push the man away. But the man is angry, and his anger gives him strength. The man takes his other hand and uses it to grab the boy by his t-shirt. The man rips his hand from the boy's grip, and plunges the knife deep. Deep into something.

The girl does not know what it is. The body of the boy is blocking her view. The girl cannot see where the knife went, or where it is now.

The girl is laying on the floor, floating in a pool of red water. She is dizzy and confused. All is silent. She feels like she will sleep, but knows that she cannot. She knows that danger is here. She knows she mustn't close her eyes. She sees only the door to the jewelry store, and nothing else.

The girl is wondering if she is now alone. The door looks just like the door that she and the boy walked through mere minutes earlier. She is wondering, "Was that real? Is this real?" The girl is breathing heavy,

On the Eighteenth of May   267

yet shallow. She cannot find air to come into her lungs. She is wondering, "Where is the boy?"

The door opens and a police officer is entering cautiously. He is dressed in uniform with his weapon drawn. He is alone.

The girl wants to cry out, "Danger," but her lungs will not find air. Her eyelids are closing and opening and then closing again. She is feeling the pool of red liquid moving around her. It is warm and thick. It is growing.

The police officer is crouching down beside of her. He is saying something to her. She is watching him as he talks into his radio, as he puts his fingers on the inside of her wrist, as he holds his hand against her back and pushes against it with pressure. He is taking off his shirt now, his black police officer shirt. His white t-shirt is showing his perspiration as he holds his black shirt against her back. He is applying pressure to something back there. His eyes look concerned. He is young and he is brave.

The police officer is pressing on her back while holding his gun in his hand. He is talking again on his radio, but the girl cannot hear what he is saying. It sounds jumbled and far away. He is looking beyond her back, to something on the floor. The girl wants to see what he is looking at. She wants to cry out to him, "Please find my brother – I think he is here."

The girl is rolling ever so slightly onto her stomach, grimacing as the searing pain shoots up and down her back, through every muscle and to every nerve. The police officer is saying something to her, but the words are inaudible. Now, on her stomach, she is turning her head to see what the policeman has been looking at.

The boy's eyes are open, the bluest of sapphire. Blue and deep – as the ocean. The girl is waiting for them to blink, for his mouth to open and call her name. She is waiting to hear his laughter, for it to find its way to her waiting heart. She is waiting.

The girl hears a sound behind her. She is feeling the pressure of the black shirt as it suddenly subsides and disappears. She is feeling a body, the police officer's body, now suddenly draped across her own. The body is limp and listless. The police officer's chest is now laying across the part of her back that seconds earlier he had been hovering over.

The pool around the girl is growing bigger and deeper now, with red liquid streaming into it from channels and rivers of pain. The girl is lying there, on her stomach, with the policeman draped across her back and the boy to her side. Her face is still turned to the boy, the boy who is her brother. The girl is looking at a broken piece of glass. It is near her brother's face, on the floor. She is reaching her hand out to take it away, to remove it from its place near his beautiful, sweet face. But as she is doing so, the girl is seeing that it is not glass. It is a broken piece of mirror. And as she is looking into it, she gazes upon another face.

It is a grotesque face. It is a despised face. It is a face with smeared mascara and streaked eyeshadow and trembling, pink-stained lips.

CHAPTER

Thirty-Four

*L*ucas looked again at the map of the southeastern United
States, now spread out upon his desk at the station. He set
down his can of cola and picked up the black marker beside it. He
found Pell City, Alabama, the location he had read about from the
newspaper article, and drew a messy box around it. Then he looked
from the state of Alabama, north and east, to Chimney Rock, North
Carolina. He drew another box, then sat back in his seat.

He hadn't slept at all. He had stayed late at the office and then
had called his mother to let her know that he needed to work late.
He had asked her to let Cass know. He had gone home only to stare
at the ceiling, then had returned to the office before daybreak. The
fatigue was now catching up to him.

What he had known previously was that she had walked into
Chimney Rock on May eighteenth, that she had been in Sylva two
years earlier, and that she was twenty-eight years old. That was all
he had really known. Before.

But now, he knew more. He knew that she had been seventeen
years old at the time of the incident. He knew that something very
traumatic had happened to the woman whom he knew as Cass. And

he knew that it had happened on that day, the eighteenth of May, over ten years ago.

Considering all of it, he accepted that there were hundreds of explanations for what may have been the past decade of her life. He considered that she may have been living in her hometown up until just a few years ago, at which time she decided to explore the mountains of the western Carolinas. He thought about the possibility that she may have been working there, in Alabama, or perhaps attending college. He considered that maybe she had been living and working somewhere else, like Montana or Texas or Maine. He imagined her with a car, one that she sold right before he met her. He thought of her with a phone, a phone that she used in her work and her life. A phone that she had decided to do without – just for a year. Just as a challenge. He pictured her with a family, somewhere in some place. A family she had been with all of this time, right up until the point at which she walked into Chimney Rock.

He told himself that perhaps the situation was not so grim. Perhaps the best scenarios were actually possible.

Or perhaps. Just perhaps …

She's been walking. All this time. All these years.

He shook his head gently, terrified to acknowledge what his gut was telling him. Horrified to accept that this, of all the possibilities and explanations, was the one that was most likely the truth.

He drew a box around Sylva, where Cass had lived for a duration of one year. He thought back to the formula he had written and tested several months before, the formula that equated a day of walking to thirty-five miles. He checked the scale on the map, and once again tested his theory between Chimney Rock and Sylva. His formula applied almost perfectly.

But what about the other years?

With tired eyes, he looked at the vast expanse on the map between western North Carolina and Pell City, Alabama. He looked at the space which represented hundreds of miles between the two places. And as he did so, one person came to his mind. It was a person, walking alone. Trying to be strong. Trying to survive.

He took his thumb and forefinger and spaced them out to fit the scale for thirty-five miles. He found five different general routes that reached from Pell City, Alabama to Sylva, North Carolina, all of which led through random towns and cities in between. He used his fingers to determine if, in exactly eight years, any of these routes would support his theory.

His heart sank as the formula applied perfectly for the first one, then the second, then the third.

He stopped.

He knew there were hundreds of other route combinations that no doubt connected her hometown to Chimney Rock, but he had no desire to test any more of them. He knew what he had wanted to know.

Lucas looked up and away from the map. He couldn't stare at it any longer. It sickened him to consider that what he had been imagining and fearing was now exposed as the truth.

This has been her life. For almost eleven years, this has been her life.

The day before he had scanned the newspaper article quickly, but had not read every word. He had scanned it only enough to gather general information about the incident, the attacker, and the outcome. Upon arriving home after work, he had briefly considered, and then rejected, the idea of conducting internet searches to dig up any additional information that he could. He knew her name. He knew the date. He knew the location. Within a few minutes he could have known every last detail about her life and her family. Her hopes, and her dreams.

But he had decided that he wouldn't. He wouldn't secretly invade her privacy. He wouldn't investigate her or find out things that she had long kept from him. Those had been her choices, and he would respect them, until she left. Until the end.

He folded the map and placed it in the back of his bottom drawer of files. Closing it, he acknowledged to himself that there was still something gnawing at him, something that didn't seem to fit.

Almost eleven years ago, the attack had occurred. Cass had survived. The horror of it would have been enough to leave anyone in shock, to cause anyone to block out the memory and to run from it their whole life.

But what about the years in between?

He thought about how hard she worked to avoid talk of the past. Any past. She wouldn't even talk about where she was living last year, before she arrived here. Anything or anyone or any time that had come before the day she had stepped foot in Chimney Rock had been shielded.

Lucas put his head into his hands.

Why?

He lifted his head and retrieved a piece of white copier paper from his desk drawer. He picked the marker up again and drew a large circle on the blank paper. Inside and in the middle of the circle, he wrote a small initial. *C.*

The first wall would be the thickest, for the most terrifying memories. The memories that were most important to repress.

He used the marker to add thickness to his drawing. He stopped and stared at the circle, long enough to make his head start to ache. He decided to change his scenery.

As he turned towards the office window and looked out, there she was, walking along the road that ran in front of his building. She was looking up into the trees, and now pausing to watch two squirrels playing along the tree trunk. A car driving by beeped its horn, and he watched as the driver waved at Cass. She waved back.

She kept walking, never looking towards the department where he watched her from his window. He knew she wouldn't look back. She had told him many times that his job was important, that she would never disturb him. He watched her ponytail swing back and forth as she walked with a quick pace, stopping only briefly to pick a flower and place it in her pocket. He watched her as she looked up at the mountains and then down at the lake in front of her.

He knew he should feel pity or sorrow or shame at knowing what he now knew. And even though he felt slivers of all those things, there was something he felt much stronger. Stronger now than the day before, or the day before that.

I love her.

He was determined that he would love her. Nothing had changed about that. He was determined that he would protect her. As much or as little as she needed. And he was resolved that he would support her. If that meant she decided to stay, or if that meant she would leave as she had planned to do all along, he knew now that he would see it through.

He turned his vision away from the window and left Cass to continue the solitude of her walk without his prying eyes. He focused again on the circle, and suddenly felt a wave of helplessness wash over him. He admitted internally that he didn't know how to help her.

He chided himself for being a police officer who was incapable of helping. Incapable of saving.

He stared at the circle.

She represses the memory of the attack. And then ....

And then ....

She walks.

He picked up the marker and started to draw another circle, a circle to the inside of the first.

And when the eighteenth of May arrives again, she fortifies the first wall, with another inside it.

He stopped and considered the implications of what he was thinking. He started drawing again, another circle, this one on the inside of the two already drawn.

And when the eighteenth of May returns for the second anniversary, another wall is built.

He could picture it now, the young girl walking into one town, and then another. Each spread apart by exactly one year. Each departure and arrival on the same day. The day on which she walked and pretended that it wasn't a day. The day that she wouldn't count. He kept drawing. A fourth wall. A fifth wall. A sixth wall.

He drew walls, each inside of the previous wall and all inside of the first wall. The thickest wall. The one beyond which lived the memory of that day. The day of the attack.

The attack that had been wielded by a madman, one who had already tortured and killed his parents before heading to a random jewelry store. The attack that had left the massive scars seared along her back. The attack that had left the elderly jewelry store manager critically injured and hiding in the massive safe. The attack that had left a police officer killed in action. The attack that had taken the life of Cass's twin brother.

Lucas drew the eleventh circle, representing her last wall, the one she had built as she had walked to Chimney Rock last May. He then leaned back and looked at this drawing in its entirety.

It is a fortress. An impenetrable fortress.

He readied his hand to lay the marker back down, then hesitated. He looked at the calendar on his desk. Today was the twenty-fifth of April.

He looked at her initial. The *C* was all alone in the otherwise empty center of the circular prison.

He then wrote another initial in the center. *L.* He stared at the two initials, then felt his pulse quicken.

In twenty-three days, there will be another wall.

With hesitation, he slowly drew the final circle. As he drew it, he was careful to encase his own initial outside of it, while leaving hers to the inside. Alone.

He felt nauseous. He stood from his chair and exited the office, heading for the bathroom even as Farley called out to him. He didn't turn to look, afraid he might get sick on an officer's desk.

He made it to the men's room and bent over the sink, turning the faucet on and splashing cold water on his face. He willed himself to regain some composure. Turning the faucet off, he glanced up at himself in the mirror. Drops of water dripped off his chin.

I don't know what to do, Cass. I'm so sorry that I don't know what to do.

He dried his face with a paper towel, then turned the faucet on again to drink some cool water from his cupped hand. No longer feeling physically sick, he left the bathroom to head back to his office. As he walked through the large room where several officers were seated, he heard Farley call out from near the doorway.

"I told her to just wait in your office."

Lucas stopped.

Who?

He turned towards Farley with what must have been his classic *what the hell?* expression.

Farley went on the defensive immediately. "I told you she was here, as you were rushing by earlier."

Lucas walked towards the hallway that led to his office, then rounded the corner that exposed his office door. He opened it slowly, and saw Cass sitting in the chair in front of his desk. There was a small bowl of ice cream in her hand, one that she extended towards him as she stood.

Her smile melted him.

"I'm sorry to drop by unannounced. Ella told me you worked late last night and I've been thinking all day that maybe you could use a little surprise. Like a chocolate chip ice cream and hot fudge sundae surprise." She giggled slightly while looking at him expectantly.

He was on his job, and he was the Chief of Police. Yet, without thinking about either of those things, he walked towards her and kissed her. He kissed her passionately and deeply. He embraced her, even as she held the bowl of ice cream awkwardly to one side and held the back of his neck with the other. He lowered his hand to the small of her back and pushed her close to him. He ran his other hand into her hair, pushing the back of her head gently forward, pressing her lips against his as he continued.

I've missed you, Cass. I miss you. Please stay. Please stay.

He continued, unrelenting, and sensed that she had missed him as much as he had missed her. He concluded this assumption from the strength of her hold and the caress of her lips upon his own.

Finally, he stopped, pulling his lips back slowly and hesitantly. She watched him, following his lips and his eyes as he slowly lifted his head up and away. She was breathing hard, but still holding the ice cream steady and even. She hadn't spilled a drop. They both looked at the bowl and laughing simultaneously.

"Next time, remind me to set the ice cream down first," she said lightheartedly. She turned and laid it on his desk, next to a piece of paper that had been left there. Lucas saw it, even as she was removing her hands from the bowl.

She stopped her movement. She was turned away from him, so he couldn't see her face or her eyes, but he knew just the same. He knew what it was that she had seen.

"Look. It's our initials." She was looking at his drawing and was pointing at the center, where her initial was inside a circle and his initial was not.

He spent no time contemplating what to say or how to explain. He had already decided, when he saw her turn towards the paper on his desk. He would always, always, be honest with her.

He walked to the desk and stood beside her. He took her hand in his own, then took her forefinger. He placed his hand on top, aligning his forefinger with her own. He led her finger to lay on the line, the line for the final wall.

"This is the wall that you'll build. In twenty-three days." He was leading her finger around the wall as he said this, placing his head against hers as their hands traced together. "When you leave Chimney Rock behind."

He stopped his hand and hers with it. She stared at the drawing for several moments. Then, ever so slowly, she took her own forefinger and moved it from underneath to the top of his. She led their hands to trace not this innermost wall, but the one directly outside it. Then, together, with her leading, they traced the wall beyond that. And then the next one. In silence, she led him in tracing the walls. When she got to the thickest, the one that encased them all, she stopped.

"Do you think they are strong?" she whispered, turning to look at him with questioning eyes.

He returned her gaze, wanting to hold her and love her and take away everything that had ever harmed her. He wanted to know her. He wanted to know the person she was and the person she had been, from the moment she had been born until this moment.

He nodded slowly.

She exhaled deeply, as if relieved that he had affirmed this. She looked back at the drawing then again at him, seeming to have realized an important detail, one that appeared to confuse her.

"There's a wall between us," she whispered softly, making the statement sound somewhat like a question. "I wish we could tear that one down." She paused and looked up from the paper. "Just that one."

Without hesitating, he shook his head.

"We don't have to tear it down, Cass. Not that wall. Not any of them." He was struggling now that the moment was here, finding it difficult to find the words for what he wanted to say. "We just need ... we just need ...."

"Need what?" she asked, with wide eyes that seemed hesitant and afraid.

"We just need ... a way," he responded quietly. "A way through. We just need ... a door."

She was the one shaking her head now.

"A door?" she replied. There was a hint of frustration in her voice. "Why a door?" She was shaking her headed stronger now, as if hearing something she did not wish to hear. "So you can come through? So you can save me?"

Lucas looked at her, into those eyes that wanted to know. That seemed to want to believe. He put his arms around her tenderly and she returned the embrace. She rested her face into his neck while he stroked the back of her hair with his fingers.

"The door … it's not for me, Cass." He leaned his mouth close to her ear. "It's for you."

He felt her face against his neck, in hiding and seclusion. He felt the grip of her hands on his shirt grow firmer. Her body came against his, as if she were forcing her cells to disappear into his.

"I don't understand what you're saying," she said quietly. "I don't understand what…" Her voice trailed off as she leaned her head away and looked again to the drawing on the desk.

"What I mean, Cass, is that it's important. It's so important that …."

"What, Lucas?" she interrupted. She had pulled back to look at him, but had kept her arms around him. "What is so important?"

He took her face in his hands and kissed her forehead, slowly and sweetly. He looked at her again, up close and intimately. He was memorizing every line and every freckle, every scar and every strand of hair touching lightly across her cheek.

"Someday there will be a door, Cass. And it will be opened, for you." His voice was quivering now, sounding hoarse and tired. "And then, maybe, another door after that will be opened, and then another even after that. But the most important thing for you to remember, Cass, is that someday, it may be the last door."

He paused, still holding her face in his hands. He knew what must be said, but he worried how to say it. He had no wish to frighten her. He only wished for her to remember. He needed words that would come to her again, even if many years from now.

"Please, Cass. When that happens, walk through. Walk through while the door is still open."

Her face was now filled with a look of subtle despair. He cupped her scarred cheek, stroking it gently with his thumb as she stood in silence. He leaned forward and kissed her softly, then whispered only to her while his lips lingered.

"Even when I'm not with you … remember."

CHAPTER

Thirty-Five

She looked out the window, into the moonlit sky that was now showing the faintest hints of the impending sunrise. The alarm clock had not yet sounded, yet she knew that sleep would not return to her. She sat up and looked at the clock face. It read a little past four-thirty.

She had dreamt last night. It had not been the usual nightmare borne of images and pain, but rather, it had been a real dream. It had been made of the make-believe and things that had never happened.

In her dream, she and Lucas were walking along a sidewalk. They were holding hands and talking loudly, both at the same time. They were talking about dancing and running and turnips. Then, in the dream, she had stopped on the sidewalk and had looked around. She had been surrounded by a thick concreate barrier. She had been alone and all had been quiet. But strangely, in her dream, she had been content. She had been unafraid to find herself all alone.

She gazed out the window again, at the chimney on the mountain. It appeared as a jet black shelf, sticking out from the side of the massive structure that stood guard at all times over Ella's home. She thought about the afternoon she had spent there many months ago, sitting on that shelf with him. She smiled. She had found recently that she always smiled whenever she thought of him.

So why was I happy in the dream? To be separated from him?

She started to think about it more intently, then realized it wasn't worth it.

It's a dream. It's not supposed to make sense.

She emerged from the bed and quickly washed up, then dressed in a fresh t-shirt and shorts. After lacing up her shoes, she grabbed a small roll of cash from the backpack and a bag she had left near the closet. She turned off the lights and tiptoed across the hallway. She wanted to be sure that Ella was able to sleep as late as she needed, especially during these final days.

Much later in the day, after her shift at the bakery had ended, she headed out to complete her afternoon tasks. The first stop was Lake Lure Family Dentistry, the small office that she had visited back in November. Her teeth cleaning was scheduled for three, and Dr. Nixon had graciously agreed to again provide this service for a cash payment.

The dentist gave her an "all clear" and encouraged her to keep brushing and flossing. He told her that he would see her back in six months. She didn't bother to correct him. She felt sure that he wouldn't even think of her in six months or wonder why she hadn't returned.

Afterwards, she walked to The Treasure Chest, where she discovered a handwritten note taped to the front door. *Sorry – we closed early today. Come back tomorrow.*

She took the bag of leggings and shirts and placed it against the front wall of the shop. Through the opening in the top of the bag she could see a blue dress, the dress that she had worn while dancing with Lucas.

Now that her major tasks were done for the day, Cass walked by the Mountain Trellis Greenhouse and bought four small trays of Ella's favorite pink and orange impatiens. She quickly proceeded to Ella's back porch and planted these all around in the boxes attached to the railings. She finished and stepped back to admire the result. The porch now looked just as it had, that first time she had seen it almost a year ago.

Smiling to herself, she gently picked two blooms from the flowers, one pink and one orange, then proceeded quietly into the house. She took the small vase that always sat on the kitchen windowsill and filled it with water and then the blooms. As she set the vase down on the counter, Ella emerged from the bakery.

"Cass! You're back!" Ella exclaimed, seeming genuinely surprised. "Don't tell me you're getting slack in your old age. What? Did you only walk ten miles today instead of fifteen? How dare you?" The two women were chuckling as Ella approached and wrapped her arms gently around Cass. "Ah, my dear girl. I'm so happy to see you."

Your hug is warm. Your touch is comforting.

"You do realize you saw me just two hours ago," Cass teased, although she did not rush to escape Ella's embrace. The women stood there a few seconds longer, and then Ella stepped back.

"How was your dentist appointment?" Ella asked.

"I believe I'm his star patient," Cass replied. "I even got this new toothbrush and this little tube of toothpaste, just for keeping my teeth super clean." Cass was actually much more excited by the freebies than she made out. Having these in her possession meant she wouldn't have to buy them before she left in five days.

"What is this?" Ella had spotted the vase and was walking towards it. "Oh, Cass, how lovely," she exclaimed as she neared the blooms. Then, seeming to suspect something, Ella peered out the kitchen window and noticed the newly planted flowers.

She stood still for what seemed like a long time, then quietly said, "I love them, Cass. Each time I see them, I'll think of you."

Ella turned and Cass saw her wipe her hand across her cheek. Now walking towards her bedroom, Ella weakly called back over her shoulder, "Thank you, Cass."

Cass waited in the kitchen for a while, wondering if Ella was coming back out, then decided to pass the time appropriately while she waited. She eyed the green plaid pillow that was perched on the recliner, the one with the loose seam. She found the mending kit in the utility drawer and proceeded to carefully sew the seam tightly together, pushing the filling back in where it was attempting to escape. Once done, she plumped the pillow evenly and returned both it and the kit to their rightful spots.

She was headed towards her bedroom to pack the new toothbrush and toothpaste when she heard a light tapping on the back door. As she opened it she found Margie and the children waiting outside, Jacob with a large envelope in his hands and Juney with a small pie.

"The children and I wanted to be sure we had the chance to say goodbye, before you leave," Margie said as Juney and Jacob stared at Cass with wide eyes. "We know how busy you must be, getting ready and all that, but we also knew we wanted to see you, and hoped today might be okay."

Cass nodded gently and led them inside to the table. Juney and Jacob sat, folded their hands on the table, and commenced to staring at Cass.

Have they always been this quiet?

Suddenly, Juney spoke up. "How long are you going to be gone, Cassie?" Juney's tiny bottom lip started to tremble as she spoke.

Cass wondered how she should answer.

The little bit of time in which she hesitated was apparently answer enough. Juney dropped her head and Cass heard soft sniffles.

"Not long," Cass said kindly, placing her fingers underneath Juney's chin and lifting it gently. "Not long, sweet girl." Cass looked to her side and saw that Ella had returned to the kitchen. She and Margie were intently watching this exchange.

It's a lie, and they know it.

Now that Juney's tears had been dried and a smile was again upon her face, the mood of the room lightened a bit. Juney pushed the little cherry pie she had made over to Cass and insisted that she take a bite.

It appeared then to be Jacob's turn, and he shyly pushed the envelope over towards Cass. "Me and Juney made these for you," he stated proudly. "In our school."

Cass opened the file-sized envelope and found two drawings inside. Each had writing beneath them, with the title the same for both.

I love...

"They had this assignment for Valentine's Day," Margie explained, "but the kids wanted to wait to give these to you. They wanted to wait until springtime."

The first drawing showed Cass as a tall, extremely thin, stick figure. She had long hair in a high ponytail that reached down to her knees and an ensemble of black shorts and a yellow t-shirt.

Cass began reading the writing beneath the drawing, finding herself quickly captivated.

This is Cass. She is my friend. I was scared but she came to me. She helped me and I love her. I love her so much. I want her to stay. I want her to stay and come see my baseball games when I get to be in fourth grade.

Cass finished reading but kept her head bent, acting as if she was still reading but actually buying time. She looked up and found Jacob's expectant eyes.

"Thank you, Jacob. It's lovely, and..." Cass paused to find the right words.

Jacob was grinning from ear to ear, showing a gap where another tooth had fallen out. She tore her eyes from him and returned them to her lap, where she exchanged the top paper for the one that had been on the bottom.

In this one, Cass was a person with stubby arms, thick fingers, and long, full legs. She had her hair braided in two pigtails hanging on each side of her face, and she was wearing brown leggings and a red shirt. Her eyes were huge, and were solid blue with no pupils. She read the words under the picture.

I love my Cassie. And she loves me. I like her pretty long hair. But what I really love is how strong she is. I think she is the

strongest person in my town. I want to be like Cassie when I grow up. I want to be strong too.

Cass looked up at Juney and smiled. "Thank you, Juney," Cass said quietly, looking tenderly upon the lovely child.

Strong. Be strong. Survive.

The group talked and laughed and ate thin slices of the little pie with coffee and hot cocoa. Then Lucas arrived and joined in on the laughter and conversation. Cass showed him the two drawings and Lucas pretended to be heartbroken that the children had written about her.

"Wait! What? I thought I was the one you wrote about in school?" He grabbed Jacob in a pretend headlock to the squeals of both children.

Soon it was time for the little family to leave and for the children to return to their evening rituals of homework and baths. Margie gave Cass a big hug and leaned her lips close to Cass's ear.

"Goodbye, Cass," she whispered. "And thank you. I'll never forget you, or what you did."

Cass had heard this from Margie many times before, but this time, for some reason, she found a lump in her throat. There was a finality to it, and Cass felt Margie's shoulders shake as they embraced one another. Margie gently kissed Cass on the cheek, then turned and headed for the door.

Jacob was next, and he gave Cass a quick boyish hug and a sweet "Goodbye". She hugged him back and thought of him as a teenager, as an adult, and as an old man.

Live a happy life, Jacob.

As he pulled back and turned away, Cass felt assured that he would.

Finally, Juney approached. Juney had held it together quite well the whole evening, but Cass knew she was a tender-hearted child, and imagined how difficult this whole evening had been for the little girl. Juney walked slowly towards her and Cass bent down on one knee.

Juney stopped a few inches from her, and then whispered. "Cassie?"

"Yes, Juney?" Cass replied softly.

"Will you remember me?" Juney asked. The little child was staring into Cass's eyes, searching there for something. For an adult's assurance. And for the truth.

Cass took Juney into her arms and held her. She heard the child sniffle and then felt her tiny shoulders tremble as she wept. Juney's fingers were bracing into Cass's shoulders, holding on. "Will you?" Juney asked again.

Cass looked up and saw that Lucas was watching her. And she remembered a third drawing, one that she had seen almost two weeks ago. Not one with stick figures or blue eyes, but one with circles. Many circles.

Walls. Strong walls.

"Of course, Juney," Cass said sweetly, holding the child's shaking body against her own. "How could anyone ever forget you?"

Cass felt his eyes upon her, but she didn't look up. Juney continued her embrace a moment longer, then walked slowly to the door, calling back "Goodbye, Cassie" as she made her way to join her family.

———

Stretched out on her bed, Cass reflected on the day's activities as well as the emotional parting with Margie and the children. She was feeling drained from the many lies and tears and questions. Especially so from the last question, the one Lucas had asked her.

After Margie and the kids had left, and after Ella had retired to her bedroom, Cass and Lucas had retreated to the back porch. He had held her in his arms and had kissed her cheek. She had wrapped her arms around his back and had kissed his warm neck. They had stood there quietly, in a complete and peaceful ending to the day.

And then, he had asked. "Why didn't you say goodbye?"

"You promised," she had replied. "You promised no more

questions." She had turned her head upward and towards him, but he had been looking straight ahead, into the darkness of night.

"You said everything else to them, Cass. You told them everything they were hoping to hear. But you never said the word *goodbye.*" He had said it softly, in a voice laced with sorrow and defeat. "I wonder, in four days, the final time we stand together on this porch, I wonder if you'll say it then, Cass? If you'll say goodbye, then … to me?"

She had held him tight and laid her head on his chest. She had heard his strong heartbeat underneath the surface. She had remembered the night he had stood in the rain, the night the black bruise had been poised over that heartbeat.

She lay there now, in the dark, in the bed that once belonged to him. Her eyes were heavy and her heart was fatigued. She felt herself drifting into sleep, where a make-believe dream was awaiting.

I am walking on the sidewalk with Lucas. We are talking loudly and holding hands and laughing about dancing and running and turnips. Ella is there with us, and Margie. Juney and Jacob are walking in front of us, laughing and skipping. Arlene is walking with us now, and Justina and Billy and Mrs. Stampshed. Farley McSwain has joined us, and now Officer Abernathy and Officer Alexander. And we are all together. The sun is shining. I am turning my head to look at them, to find them.

But suddenly, I am surrounded. Surrounded by a thick concrete barrier. All is quiet.

Where is the laughter? I am alone. I search the perimeter. I look for a door. There is none. I begin pounding on the wall, pounding to break through, to find them on the other side. My fists are bleeding as I punch. I can feel the pain in my knuckles as the blood splatters against the barrier. I am scratching now, trying to claw my way through the thick concrete. My nails are torn and hanging from my bloodied fingers. There is no one to help me. I keep hitting and punching and clawing. I hit with all my might, and the wall collapses in front of me.

The concrete dust is floating in the air, slowly settling to reveal what was behind the wall. As the air clears in front of me, I search. I search for

Lucas and for Ella and for the twins and for the people. I search. And then, there in front of me, I see her.

A girl. She is turned away from me, so that all I can see is her back and her hair. I inch my way closer, slowly closer, walking carefully over the rubble left behind by the collapsed wall. I am reaching out towards her, inches away from touching her back. I need her to tell me where the others have gone. I must find them. I must remember where I left them.

As I reach towards her, she whispers something. It is something I can hear over her shoulder, something meant only for my ears. I hear what she says.

I hear what she says.

I stumble backwards, over the rubble, and quickly grab the larger blocks of concrete. I try to put them back in some order. I try to rebuild the wall. Each time I get it almost built, it falls back down again. I am crying out, yelling for someone to help me. Help me to build a stronger wall. And all the while I am screaming, the girl remains turned away. She will not look, for she already knows.

The wall will never be strong enough.

The girl already knows, and now she is speaking, because she knows. "The wall will never be strong enough," she says. "Because you and I ... We are one."

CHAPTER

Thirty-Six

$\mathcal{L}$ucas took another sip of the wine, then placed the stemware back down on the ground beside them. They were sitting along the riverbank, each of them perched on their own rock. "Sorry. I guess I'm just a beer guy," he said apologetically, watching Cass as she took a drink from her own goblet.

They had walked to the winery's tasting room earlier in the evening, a lovely building located just up the road from Ella's. They had spent an hour under the quirky chandeliers, surveying the hundreds of bottles named for mountain towns and villages close by. Cass had asked if she could try it, the famous apple wine made from the local crops that scattered throughout the area. They had purchased the bottle and then had walked out onto the wooden deck, with views of the rock chimney and the glistening waterfalls. But she had decided differently, that they would try the wine in another place. She had decided to return to the river.

He could tell now, from the way she sipped it, then sipped some more, that she liked it. She poured a little more into the glass then recorked the bottle.

He watched her as she looked out over the river. She appeared

lost in her thoughts, or perhaps soaking in the melodious splashing
of the water over the rocks. Suddenly, without turning her head, she
reached her hand out towards him. He took it into his own.

"Is there anything you would like to do, in your final thirty-six
hours here?" He tried his best to sound nonchalant and informal
as he asked it, as if she were a distant relative who had dropped by
unexpectedly to pay a visit and was interested in seeing a few sights
before leaving.

He knew there was no other way he could be, not in front of her.
He was feeling too raw, as if all emotion was lying right under the
surface of his skin. He felt as if he might lose his mind if he really
thought about it, about the fact that today was the sixteenth of May.
He considered the fact that for his entire life, this date had held no
meaning whatsoever to him.

*And now, it is the most despised of days. The most despised except for
the two dates that will follow it.*

She shook her head slowly in response to his question while
keeping her eyes on the water. Even from the side, she looked full
of sorrow. He wondered if she was regretting her decision to come
to Chimney Rock, or perhaps reconsidering the choice she had made
to leave.

Choice. Now that the word had crossed his mind, he realized it
was a word that had never been spoken between them. And, most
likely, never would. He promised himself that he would not give in
to any temptation to try to persuade her or to influence her, although
he felt certain she was incapable of being persuaded or influenced.
He felt certain that she would know what to do. Would know what
she needed to do.

But will I know what to do?

As much as he had prepared for this final week and these final
days, Lucas was now realizing the truth. He simply wasn't ready.

They walked hand in hand towards Ella's house, using the faint
moonlight to guide them up the bank. Then, without speaking, she
stopped. She took her hand and touched his cheek. It lingered there

as she stared at his jaw, the bridge of his nose, his eyes, and his lips. She took her other hand from his and did the same with the other side of his face. She reached her hands slowly to the back of his neck, and then kissed him. He pulled her to him, holding her so close that they lost their balance and fell against a tree. This disturbance went wholly unnoticed as they continued in the quiet splendor of the dark night.

Finally, she pulled back, staring again at his lips and then lowering her head. He reached his arm around her waist and she quickly came to him, resting her head against his shoulder and breathing deeply. She seemed mentally exhausted but physically alert.

I know exactly how that feels.

"I'm going for a walk," she said into his shoulder. "I'll never go to sleep like this. I feel so tired but I can't rest. I can't calm down. I need to..." Her voice trailed off as she pulled away from his embrace and headed along the path towards the road. "Thank you, Lucas. Thank you for taking me to the river." She said this while turning around and walking backwards. "I'll see you tomorrow," she added. Then she was gone, into the darkness ahead.

Lucas sensed turmoil. Turmoil where, for many months, there had only been determination. She had told them all the exact date she would be leaving. But now he sensed that she was wondering, considering. Perhaps even doubting.

Should I rejoice in that? Selfishly rejoice in the fact that she is doubting herself?

He wanted to ask her to stay. He wanted her to *want* to stay, without him asking. But he was haunted by the dilemma of whether or not staying was the best thing, for her. His head was splitting, just from constantly asking himself that very question.

Entering Ella's home a few minutes after, he found his mother seated in her favorite recliner holding her favorite plaid pillow.

"She fixed it," Ella said, staring at the pillow, then looking up at Lucas. "She fixed the pillow that had the ripped seam." Ella was smiling now, the kind of smile that comes before the tears. Her lips started to tremble.

He walked to her, intending to comfort her. But there would be no comforting. He could tell that his mother had been thinking, and now she was ready to act.

"Where is she?" Ella asked, standing as she did so.

"She went for a walk."

"Did you ask her?" Ella moved closer to him.

"Ask her *what?*"

Ella took his hands in her own. "Please, son. Ask her. To stay."

Lucas swallowed hard. He looked to his mother's expectant eyes, then away towards the fireplace.

"Please, son." Ella said, again. "She will, if you ask her. I know she will. She's just a lonely person who is looking for a family. She just wants to know that someone cares. Please." Ella sounded desperate, almost frantic.

That's not what she wants, Mom. That's not it at all.

"She knows that we care, Mom. She knows." He reached out to hug her, to ease her worry in some way. But she rebuked his embrace, as if exasperated.

"You'll regret it, son. For the rest of your life, you'll regret it." She said this as she turned, walking towards her bedroom as if she was done with him and the entire conversation.

"Of course I will, Mom." Lucas said softly, embarrassed to hear his own voice crack as he did so. He whispered then, almost to himself, "I knew I would regret it all, from the very first time. The time she wrapped her arm around me and raced down a field with our legs tied together. From the time she sat with me on the giant rock in the river, or the time we dipped down into the cold water together."

He shook the memories from his mind and looked up at his mother, who was now frozen, watching him. "I knew it all along. Knew that I would regret every moment of knowing her, of loving her. Because all along, Mom, I knew those moments would lead to *this* moment, to *these* days, when she would walk out of my life. Forever."

He was determined that he wouldn't lose his composure, not at this point. Ella was watching him, and he knew that she was taking her lead from him.

"And even if she didn't leave, Mom, even if I begged her and somehow convinced her to stay, I would always know." He shook his head now, resigned to the final hopelessness of it all. "Deep down, I would always know. It's not what she wanted. I would always know that she had wanted to leave." Lucas was feeling frustrated now, hurt and lost.

"So, yes, you're right, Mom." He looked intently at her, intending for her to hear him. For her to understand. "I will regret every bit of it. Every decision I made along the way. I'll regret not asking her tonight, just now when I held her in my arms. I'll regret not asking her to stay. I'll regret not telling her one more time what she means to me."

He hadn't meant for it to, but his voice was rising now. It was louder. Fiercer. "But most of all, Mom, I'll regret not listening. Not listening to the voice inside my own head. The voice that said *not her, Lucas, not her.* The voice that said, *caution.*" He subtly shook his head, wondering how it had all come to this. "I heard it, Mom. I heard it loud and clear. I just wouldn't listen."

He stopped talking and felt his shoulders shaking violently. His head was aching and his lips were dry. His eyes were tired, so tired he could hardly hold them open.

Ella's voice was gentler now, more empathetic towards their shared sentiments. "But how do you know, Lucas? How do you know that's what she wants?"

He considered that there were ways that he could shield his mother from the truths that he now knew. Ways to protect her from the real stories of real people. Stories that he knew would only break her heart. But he realized, in that brief moment, that he hadn't the strength anymore. He hadn't the strength to shield anyone, especially himself.

"She had a family, Mom. Cass had a family, long ago. She had a brother, whom she loved." He had turned to stare into the empty fireplace again. He pictured her in his mind. She was smiling. She was walking while holding her brother's arm, dressed in a gown with her hair flowing about her. She had been happy.

"But something terrible and tragic happened, Mom. When she was young. And Cass somehow ended up all alone. Walking. From one town to another. Spending exactly one year in each." He stopped and listened, but his mother was silent.

"You see, Mom, one year is actually the perfect length of time." He was thinking it all through, as the jigsaw now started to fit together. "In one year, you can find a job and feed and clothe yourself. You can contribute and help a community, while still keeping a comfortable distance."

He continued staring into the empty fireplace. In the dark void he saw a lone figure, walking alone towards the mountains. Walking alone in the rain.

"Cass didn't want to be loved, by anyone," he said. "And she didn't want to love in return. What she wanted all along was to simply be somewhere, somewhere where she could be strong, where she could survive, and where she could be alone."

He turned now and faced his mother, who was standing with a horrified look on her face. Her trembling hand was over her mouth.

"And because Cass is alone," he continued, "she must find ways to keep those nightmares at bay, to repress whatever traumatic images that seem to attack her and follow her, even after all this time. Because she is alone, she has to find a way to comfort herself. She has no phone, no pictures, no scrapbooks or videos or letters. So in each town, she finds a house." His voice suddenly caught, and he felt overwhelmed.

She finds a house.

"She finds a house that she thinks looks peaceful." His voice cracked as he said this, so he coughed to mask his struggle. "Even though it's a place in which she has never stepped foot."

Lucas continued to paint the picture for his mother, with words he had often thought but had never before verbalized. "She draws a picture of the peaceful house and she keeps it with her always. And when memories come to her, she uses the drawing to somehow ground her. To focus her back on the present. So that she might somehow endure, one day more."

In her darkest moments, she is alone, with only the drawing to comfort her.

He looked down and gathered himself. He pictured her outreached hand, scratched and cut, reaching out as she sat on the hospital floor.

"And then that day arrives, Mom. The day that she *must* leave. The day that marks that exact day when all happiness left her sweet life." He again looked up, this time at Ella. Tears were streaming down her face as she held tightly to the back of a chair. She was shaking her head, willing the story not to be true.

But there is more, Mom. And you will hear it. As much as I think you can hear. Because you and I must find a way to go on, after she is gone.

Lucas stepped a little closer to his mother, mentally preparing himself for what he would say next.

"You asked me how I know that leaving is what she wants. I know because, on the morning of May eighteenth, Cass can't be here. She can't be anywhere, Mom. She has to be walking, in the middle of nowhere, with no sense of direction and no faces that she knows and no phone or clock to tell her what the time is." He stopped and looked for something to stare at, something less upsetting than his mother's red, tear-stained face.

"So she keeps walking, all day, no doubt pretending and believing that the day doesn't even exist. And then by evening, after having walked thirty or forty miles, she walks into a random town. And there she starts her life anew. She starts her life again, with no memory of the year she just left, or the year before that, or every year that leads all the way back to that year. To the year when she was seventeen."

His voice was growing hoarse now, from talking and not swallowing and heaving for breaths each time he felt like he was choking from the words and the ache in his heart. "She wants to leave because she has to forget us." As he said it he still couldn't bring himself to accept it. "Because if she can't forget us, you and me, Mom, she can't forget the whole year she spent with us. And if she can't forget that, then she can't forget the year before that, and the one before that."

He walked to his mother and placed his hands on her trembling shoulders.

"You see it, don't you, Mom? It was all too close. She had to insulate herself, over and over. She had to fortify each barrier with another until it finally felt like she could live again. But that point never came. And so she tries to be strong. She tries…"

Ella lunged and hugged him eagerly. She held on tightly, the way she had when his father had died. He hugged her in return, wishing as he did so for a return to the days of his childhood. Those precious days when his mother could kiss away every hurt.

He talked over Ella's shoulder, into the wall where the old pictures of his parents and grandparents hung in frames. "If she stays here, she'll have to remember everything that happened here. She'll have to remember us. And she'll have to remember it all."

He stepped back and began rubbing his forehead. He looked down at his shoes, at the floor, at the edge of the throw rug that was behind the couch. He wanted to say something else, but had hesitated as he wondered to what purpose it would serve. It was a thought that had dwelled in his heart for some time now. A question that worried and enraged and gnawed at him, deep within his soul. He was speaking the words before he could ask himself whether he really should.

"I think the thing that bothers me most," he said softly, "is when

I think of her as a seventeen-year-old girl. All alone. Wandering. And I ask myself, 'How? How did she leave?'"

He heard his voice grow tenser as his heart became angry. "I mean, where were the police? Where were her parents? Didn't anyone know how to fill out a missing person's report?"

"Stop, son," Ella said tenderly.

But Lucas's mind was elsewhere. It was on whomever was responsible for the young, teenage girl. The beautiful girl with the smile on her face, walking on her brother's arm.

He ignored his mother's request and continued. "I mean, seriously, didn't anyone know how to search for someone? How to form a search party or how to get other towns and cities involved?" He felt like he was yelling, but it in no way rivaled the screaming in his head, the screams in his heart and mind. "I mean, hell, Mom, she had been stabbed." The word caught in his throat. He lowered his voice. "She was probably in shock. These were small towns. She should have been found in a matter of hours. She should have been found quickly and returned to her home and family. I mean was everyone incompetent? Or just ignorant? I just can't fathom how...?"

"Lucas!" Ella yelled it this time. "Stop."

He looked at his mother, with desperation and defeat in his heart, but she was not looking at him. She was looking past him, at something there. At someone who had opened the door and had entered into the room. At someone who was now standing silently behind him.

He turned and faced her. He saw that she wore an expression of stoic indifference, as if she had walked in on them talking about a person wholly unconnected to her. She looked at Ella and studied her tear-soaked face. She then turned her gaze to Lucas, and he saw in her eyes a silent reminder of a promise. He had promised there would be no more questions. He knew that she trusted him, trusted him to keep his word.

"Why, Cass?" he whispered softly, his dry throat aching as he did so. "Why wasn't there a missing person report? Why weren't you returned safely to your family, to be cared for? To be helped?" Watching her eyes as they bore into his own, he concluded his questioning. "You were only seventeen. And you were all alone. Why?"

He watched as her eyes shifted away from him. She reached her hand out slightly as if to hold back something that was approaching towards her, something invisible that only she could see. She swayed slightly, as if she would drop from exhaustion, then steadied herself.

She looked again at Lucas, and her lovely face took on an expression of shame and guilt. Her eyes grew pink around the rims, but no tears formed. She walked to him then, and placed her hand on his hand.

"We're both tired," she said while rubbing his hand lightly. "Go home and get some rest." She pulled her hand away and turned towards her bedroom.

"Rest?" He couldn't let it go. He couldn't let her go. "You told me once before to rest. To rest and to heal. Do you remember, Cass? That night?"

She didn't turn back nor respond as she continued walking towards her door. He watched her from the back as she reached her hand into her pocket and retrieved the paper.

"But when did *you* rest, Cass? When did *you* heal?"

She held the folded paper in one hand as she opened the bedroom door with the other. She closed the door behind her, whispering a response as she did so.

"If you knew the price of that question, you never would have asked."

CHAPTER

Thirty-Seven

*T*he girl is standing in front of a full-length mirror, wearing a pink dress. It is a strapless gown that falls to the floor with a slit up one side. It is the same dress she wore in the Prom Court Pageant just the day before. And now, tonight, it will be time to finally wear it to the event itself, to the Senior Prom. She is taking one last look.

Her hair and makeup are already done. The girl's long hair has been washed and dried, then curled into loose cascades that fall all about her shoulders and back. Her makeup is understated, but glowing, with golden hues placed on her eyelids to accentuate her blue eyes, and a light pink color on her lips.

Her mother has told her to be careful, not to mess them up. The early morning salon appointment was the only one left, the only one left because, as her mother said, the girl didn't call the salon soon enough. All of the other appointments were taken. All of the good appointment times, like ten o'clock or ten-thirty.

Here the girl stands, in her pink dress and her perfectly styled hair and her perfect makeup. And it is now ten o'clock in the morning. The Prom is still many hours away.

Tristan is walking up behind her. He is whispering as if sharing a secret. *"I'm sorry to inform you that when Jake sees you tonight, he may actually try to kiss you. You may actually get your first kiss." The girl has turned now, is slapping his shoulder. He is jolting back down the hallway towards his bedroom, laughing hysterically.*

The girl thinks about Jake. He is Tristan's friend, a fellow teammate on the football team. He is the girl's one and only senior year crush. She has never dated Jake. She has never dated anyone. She is shy and unconfident and awkward around boys.

The girl is looking again in the mirror and wondering. Will she really be kissed tonight? Will she be kissed, for the first time, tonight?

The girl hears a voice. She is wondering if it is one of her parents, then remembers that they have left for brunch at the Country Club. All of the parents are there with them. Parents who are busy planning Prom picture locations and predicting who will be crowned Prom Queen that evening. The girl hears the voice calling again, and realizes who it is.

"Come downstairs, Alexandria. I have a surprise."

The girl returns to her bedroom and gently removes the gown, being extra careful not to smudge her makeup or to touch even one strand of hair. She is hanging the gown carefully upon its velvet hanger. She is removing the high heels and placing them neatly on the carpet near the gown. She is looking through her closet now at all of the pretty dresses and high heel shoes and skirts and rompers. She chooses a pretty beige sun dress and is now putting it on along with a pair of jeweled sandals. The girl is hurrying down the stairs to find her brother.

The girl is looking everywhere to find him. She looks in the living room and the library and the dining room. She looks in the media room and the game room. She looks in every room, but he is nowhere in this expansive house.

The girl is opening the front door now and seeing his car. The motor is running and he is behind the wheel. She closes the door behind her but remains standing on the porch. He sees her out the car window and calls out.

"Come on. Get in!"

His voice is youthful and happy. She stands in place, on the front porch.

Tristan exits the car and advances towards her. He pulls her hand excitedly and teases. "You won't find out what my surprise is unless you get in the car." He is laughing as he opens his driver's side door and disappears into his shiny red Mustang convertible. It is a present, given to him by their parents after his football season.

The girl looks back at the house, the mansion that they call home. If she rides somewhere with him, to whatever surprise he has planned, her mother may get angry. The girl hesitates.

The girl is curious. She is wondering, "What is his surprise?"

Cass jolted upright, so suddenly she hit her head on the corner of the bed post. She noticed she was on the floor and wondered why, then remembered the evening before. She recalled the questions and the hurried retreat into the bedroom. She had closed the bedroom door behind her and had quickly sat on the floor, focusing on her *peace* and bringing herself back to the present. Back to the person she was in this village.

She had sat there for hours in darkness, checking the clock frequently, watching until it had passed the one o'clock mark. And then, she had felt the heavy weight of fatigue finally pulling her down. Down onto the floor, where she had curled up in a tight ball and willed herself to sleep.

She had known, though, that the night would not go undisturbed. The images and the unwelcomed were coming more frequently, now that she had hesitated. Now that she had doubted.

Go, just as you always planned to go.

She nodded to herself, feeling the resolve and the focus return. She pulled a blanket from the foot of her bed and wrapped it about her, then balled herself up tightly. She could sleep, now that she knew she would make it. Now that she knew she would leave.

Her eyes closed.

Tristan is blowing the car's horn. "Are you coming?" he is yelling out of the passenger's side window. "We won't have time before Mom gets back if you keep standing there."

The girl is walking quickly to the car. She has made up her mind, but Tristan is not one to take "no" for an answer.

"I'm staying here," she is saying through the open window. "I still have to get some things ready for tonight, and Mom really wanted us to stay close to the house."

"Are you serious?" he is saying with disbelief in his voice. "It's only ten o'clock. The Prom doesn't start until eight this evening. Even at the very earliest, we won't be taking pictures with everyone until six or so. Just get in the car, already. You're starting to ruin my surprise, and I've planned and worked hard for this." His voice is tender and kind and giving. "So please, just get in the car. For me?" Tristan is looking at her with those pleading eyes that so often persuade her to help him with his homework. "Please, Alex? Please?"

The girl is opening the door now. She is getting in the car.

Her brother is driving the car towards town, with her in the passenger seat.

The girl is asking, "So, what is this big surprise you keep hinting at?"

His eyes are on the road, but he is grinning widely from ear to ear. Upon hearing her question, he seems to consider for a minute his response.

"Alexandria," he is saying, with an unexpected softness in his voice. "There have been many times, as we've been growing up, that I've watched you stand on the sidelines and cheer me on. Times that I've been on the receiving end of your generosity and all the good and kind things you do for me every day." He has stopped talking now and is glancing over at her with a serious look. "I know how lucky I am and what a great sister you are. Really."

The girl is listening, her eyes welling up with tears. She thinks about her mascara and realizes that she simply cannot cry. Her mother will not be happy about that.

Tristan is turning now, into a parking lot. The store ahead has a sign – Bradford's Jewelry Store. Tristan parks the car and turns off the engine. He is turning towards her, speaking. "You never ask for anything, and you certainly didn't ask for this. But once upon a time, not too long ago, you and I and Mom were in this very store. We were here because Mom had to pick up her diamond bracelet. You know, the one with the broken clasp, and you and I had ridden along to pick up my vitamins from the pharmacy down there. Remember?"

The girl is nodding her head.

"And while we were in here, Alex, you saw a pair of earrings that you really liked. You never said you liked them, but I know you well enough that I could tell."

As he is speaking, the girl is thinking, trying to remember what earrings he could be referring to. She decides that whether she remembers them or not, she will play along as if she does. This gesture and his thoughtfulness are simply too precious for her not to do so.

Tristan is talking again. "That day, when I heard Mom basically tell you to not even think about it, that you already had earrings, I thought to myself, 'Here is something that I can finally do for her.' So, I've been cutting grass around the neighborhood, as you know. But instead of spending that money on energy drinks and dates with Sophie, I've been saving it. Just for this moment. The moment I buy you those earrings to wear to your Senior Prom."

Tristan is pausing now as the girl dabs tears that are falling from her eyes. She is stunned, rendered so by the overwhelming kindness of her brother.

They are walking now, through the front door of the jewelry store, smiling and giggling. There is only one other customer in the store, and he is heading towards the door to leave. This will be a quick trip, one that will be done and see them safely back home before their mother returns.

Tristan is so happy that he has pulled this off. The girl is amazed at all of the things that make him so good. They are walking up to the counter, and Tristan immediately points out the earrings. They are over one hundred dollars. He is reaching into his pocket and pulling out bills. She is looking at the earrings. Yes, she thinks she remembers these. Yes, they are very pretty.

They are standing together, waiting for a sales person to come out to help them. Tristan is looking at the watches, which are displayed in a glass cabinet next to the earrings.

"Mark this day and time, Alex. May eighteenth at 10:21 in the morning. This will be the day and time that you will always remember. Because this will be the exact moment that you realized that you have the most amazing brother ever put on the face of this Earth."

Tristan is looking at her and uttering silly giggles. The girl is lifting her right arm to embrace him, noticing the wall clock as she does so. The wall clock has just changed. It now reads 10:22.

She woke to whimpers, weak convulsions of pitiful groans that came from somewhere. She listened and then realized. The source was her own throat, the sounds from her own soul.

Cass, now covered in sweat and feeling overheated, sat up again and pulled the blanket away from her shoulders and back. She began to reach for her right pocket, and then realized how futile the effort would be to retrieve the drawing. She knew the *peace* would not be coming, not this time. She knew that some storms are too violent, and that even the strongest dam can be breached when the walls have been weakened. She lifted her hands to the side of her head and braced herself, as she sat in the dark, alone.

The girl is opening her eyes. She is in a stark white room, with noises that beep and something attached over her face. She looks to her side and then the other, but sees only sterile solitude all around her. She looks at her arm, where a needle is immersed into her skin, with a tube that connects her to something. She starts to sit up, then feels sharp pains shooting up her back, as if she is being stabbed with a thousand knives. She collapses in misery, whispering aloud, asking for him.

"Tristan?" The girl hears no answer as her body returns to sleeping.

The girl is opening her eyes, awakening from another slumber, another in a line of thousands of slumbers in this place. She realizes she is in a hospital. The voices in the room are hushed. They do not want to disturb her, but also have no desire to see her. To comfort her.

At first she is confused. "Why am I here?" she asks. And, finally, a nurse tells her, reminds her that she has been involved in an 'incident". It is something that involves her brother.

The girl is remembering now. A trip to a jewelry store. She asks, "Where is he? My brother? Where is Tristan?" But no one will answer, and she knows the answer anyway. She keeps asking because she thinks maybe things will change if she pretends she doesn't know.

Days become weeks, and the girl waits. Waits to see her brother.

The girl is in a wheelchair, being pushed through hallways and a lobby. The girl is leaving the hospital. Her father has come to drive her home.

Her father is walking her to her bedroom, asking if she needs anything. She is treated politely and respectfully, but no one is asking what happened. No one wants to hear. And the girl doesn't want to tell, doesn't want to believe. If she speaks it, it will be true.

The girl spends the night in her bedroom, but she doesn't sleep. She is wondering, "Is he down the hall, in his bedroom?" She is trying to sleep so she can get up early the next morning and ride with him to school. He is funny and warm. He is her best friend. He is the person she loves the most.

She is weeping now.

It is late in the next morning and the girl is walking downstairs to the kitchen. She is holding tightly to the railing. Her back is still tender and weak, and offers no strength to her arms or her body. It is difficult for her to move, to will her legs forward. The doctors said that she should finish her healing at home. That she should be surrounded by those who love her in order to heal completely. The doctors said it would take much time to heal, but that she was young and she was strong.

The girl is stepping carefully off the final step and is turning to her left. Her mother and father are there, sitting at the dining room table. Her mother's eyes are swollen and red and moist. Her mother has not slept.

The girl has not seen her mother since returning home the day before. The girl has not seen her mother since...since...for a very long time. The girl is happy to see her mother now, and walks towards her to embrace her. To be comforted by her mother.

Her mother is standing and taking several steps back. She is placing herself out of reach. She is staring at the girl. There is something she wishes to say.

"How can you be here?" her mother is asking. Her eyebrows are arched inward. She seems to truly be asking something that she wishes to know.

The girl is looking away and to her father. She doesn't know what she is being asked, or what to say. She begins walking forward again, towards her mother's embrace.

"Stop." The word is spoken with authority, and with disgust. "I told you that day, when we went to the jewelry store to get my bracelet. I told you that you already had earrings." Her mother's voice is quivering. Her mother's hands are trembling. The girl is no longer walking towards her.

Her mother seems to gain back her composure, and then continues. "I told you that you didn't need those earrings, but you can't ever seem to understand that. Your greed, your self-centered greed just couldn't let you forget about them. You just had to make sure your brother took you there for those damn, ridiculous earrings."

Her mother is shaking now, appearing as if filled with fury. The girl is looking at her father, but he is looking away, out the window. Tears are streaming down his face, but he will not watch.

"Mom," the girl is saying quietly, shaking her head gently. "I didn't...."

"Mom? Mom? You call me 'Mom'? You don't deserve to call me that. I WAS a mom. I had a boy, a son. And you took him from me. You lured him away from me, and into danger. I told you to stay here, but you just couldn't do it, could you? You selfish, selfish...." Her mother is pausing again and wiping her nose on the back of her hand.

The girl is uttering a too-quiet "But, Mom" and is interrupted by her own guttural weeping. "Mom, please, I didn't...."

*"Stop it! Don't stand in this house and open your mouth. There is nothing you can say. I had a son." Her mother is beating her own chest now with her open palm, beating her chest as if to say, **He was mine.***

"And now he is gone," her mother continues. "And when I look at you, you standing there, upright on your own two feet, I don't find any happiness in seeing you. In knowing that you are here. Alive. Because looking at you only reminds me of what I have lost."

Her mother is turning, as if to walk away. "I hope your jewelry was worth it. Because that is the price, Alexandria. For the rest of my life, I will detest the very sight of you." Her mother is opening a medicine bottle that is on the kitchen counter. She is taking out two pills and returning the cap calmly. She is walking up the stairs.

Her mother is no longer crying. Her mother is done.

Convulsing in deep sobs now, the girl is turning towards her father. She is looking at him, carefully, and noticing for the first time the deep bags under his eyes. There is a grey tint to his skin. All life and love and joy have now left him.

"Alexandria, try to understand," her father is saying. "She's in a very fragile state right now. And she needs my help. She needs our help." He is looking at his daughter hesitantly and then turning back to stare out the window. "She's not like you, Alexandria. You're strong. You can survive this. On your own."

Her father is walking over to the dining room table and placing two items on it, a debit card and a sealed envelope. "There's several thousand in cash in the envelope. And I'll keep the debit card paid off, so don't ever worry about exceeding your limit."

The girl is watching him. Her sobs have ceased and she is standing, facing her father as if in a trance. She is feeling her legs grow suddenly weaker. She is reaching for the top of a chair to balance herself.

Her father is looking into her eyes. Her lips are trembling as she awaits his hug, awaits the comfort of the human touch. She is wondering how long it has been since she has been touched and held. She is watching as several tears fall from his eyes and drop to the floor. She is waiting for him to say something and to embrace her, but instead, he is turning and walking up the stairs. He, too, is now gone from her sight.

It is dark now. The girl is lying in her bed, unable to sleep. She is turning to look at the clock. It is a digital clock that displays 4:07. She is rising from her bed, in this bedroom that she painted and decorated over the summer just for her senior year. It has strings of lights draped across the window and framed pictures. She is taking off her pajamas and putting on underwear and shorts. She is putting on a bra and a t-shirt. She is looking through her closet filled with dresses and high heels and sandals and rompers. She is pulling out a grey hoody. She is putting socks on her feet along with her running shoes. She is unplugging her cell phone from the charger and putting it in her pocket. She is walking towards the door.

Her dog, Penny, is hopping off the bed to follow. The girl is lifting the dog and placing her gently back on the bed. The girl is closing the door behind her as she departs the room.

The girl is walking quietly down the hallway and now passing her parents' bedroom. Her father will have to get up early for another day of work tomorrow. Her mother is sad and grief-stricken. They both need their sleep. She will not wake them nor disturb them. She is passing her brother's bedroom, but she doesn't turn to look at his door. She knows now. There is no one inside waiting for her.

The girl is walking down the stairs, softly and slowly, using the hand railing to prop up her weakened body. She is opening the refrigerator to get a bottle of water, then returning it to its place, unopened. She is drinking a glass of water from the faucet. She is gulping it down and looking at the refrigerator door. Attached to the door with two giant magnets are two official letters. One is to congratulate Tristan on his acceptance into the University of Alabama and to confirm his full-tuition football scholarship. He will be playing linebacker for The Crimson Tide.

The other letter is the girl's acceptance letter, to the Massachusetts Institute of Technology. She has been given placement in the Biomedical Engineering Program. The girl begins to read her acceptance letter, and then stops.

The girl is now cleaning and drying the glass and returning it to the cabinet. Turning, she sees the kitchen counter upon which sits her medicine, the medicine prescribed to help her heal. Two other bottles are there as well. They are pills that the doctors have given to her mother, to help her mother sleep. The girl leaves all three bottles untouched.

The girl is walking towards the table where her father has laid a debit card. She looks at it without picking it up. Her name is written across it. Beside of it is an envelope. It is thick and sealed. She leaves both where they sit.

The girl is pulling the cell phone from her pocket and placing it on the table, beside the envelope. As she sets it down, face up, her finger touches the screen. It is illuminated, with a screenshot of the girl and her brother. It is a picture taken on the first day of their senior year. In the picture, she is smiling. The girl is now picking up the cell phone and turning it over.

The girl is walking towards the front door. She is wondering whether or not this is real. She is wondering what she should be feeling, or if she should be crying, or whether she should be screaming out for someone to save her. For someone who can rewind the hands of a clock, all the way back to May eighteenth. Back to that moment that was right before the moment when she saw 10:22 on the jewelry store wall. To a time that she wasn't alone.

The girl is now feeling it. It is something inside of her, being built from a cauldron of despair and solitude. It is a wall. It is miniscule and weak but will grow to be tall and thick. It is slowly forming within her. It will continue to grow and strengthen, and it will separate the two parts of what would be her life. The girl knows now that she cannot exist in both parts. She knows now that she can survive in only one.

The girl is opening the front door of her home. She is stepping out, then, for some reason, turning back. She is listening. She is waiting and listening. She is hoping.

Is anyone calling out my name?

Is there anyone left who will miss me?

Is anyone coming to find me?

The girl is waiting for a sound, but silence is now her steady companion.

The girl's eyes are shifting to the right, to the oil portrait hanging over the living room fireplace. It is a portrait of a family. A father. A mother. A daughter. A son.

A son.

The girl is staring, seeing only his image. She is lingering on his smile. She is staring at every freckle, every strand of hair hanging across his forehead, and every sparkle in his bluest of eyes.

She is turning away and deciding. She will remember no more.
The girl is walking out the front door and closing it gently behind her.
She is walking down the front sidewalk. She is walking into the darkness.
And beyond.

Thirty-Eight

$\mathcal{H}$e pushed himself up into a seated position, grabbed the remote, and headed towards the bathroom, simultaneously pushing the *on* button as he walked. Standing in front of the running faucet and splashing cold water upon his face, he heard the news reporter behind him. "Good morning. It's May seventeenth, and here's your breaking news."

Moments later, he finished tying the shoelaces on his running shoes and proceeded out the front door. Instead of turning towards the main road that offered relatively flat terrain, he turned towards the mountains. As he ran, he felt himself accelerating. He took the inclines aggressively, feeling angry at the world and exhausted with himself. After four miles of running at a faster clip than he was used to, he headed back home and showered.

The day had started and was now well on its way, whether he wished it to be or not. Lucas had determined that he would spend the day as normally as possible, reporting to work as usual and staying busy with traffic, paperwork, and simple assistance to citizens around the town.

Regardless of his wishes, however, he spent the workday

constantly looking at the time on his cell phone. He kept wondering how the day was passing so quickly, and what Cass was doing at those very moments.

Is she also pretending like today is just a normal day?

Lucas transitioned his first shift of officers out and his evening shift on, then finally wrapped up his own day. He was reluctant to leave the normalcy of his job.

After showering again and changing at home, he headed to Ella's in his truck. As he drove, he glanced down to the passenger seat and saw the picture. He had taken many photos of them over recent weeks, photos he would have on his phone to scroll through as often as he wished. But she had no phone and she had no pictures.

He had found his favorite, the selfie he had taken while they both sat along the bank of the river on the rocks. She had left her rock and plopped down on his lap, unexpectedly. He had wrapped one arm around her waist and then retrieved his phone with the other. The picture was a freeze frame of them laughing and off balance, seemingly falling off the rock and not really caring. He had ordered two prints of this picture. One he had framed and perched on his nightstand beside his bed. The other was now in the seat beside him. This one would be for her.

As he arrived and parked, he remained in his truck. He thought about her, about what he knew of her life. And then he thought of what he knew of tomorrow, when she would walk away and not look back. He thought about how to say goodbye and how to put her needs in front of his own.

A selfish thought came to his mind, one he had considered several times over the past few days.

How can she leave us behind? So easily?

But each time he asked himself, he answered the question as well.

It won't be easy. She'll leave just the same. But it won't be easy.

He walked up the back porch steps and found her lying on her favorite lounge chair. As he approached he noticed that she looked tired, but calm. She turned her head at the sound of his footsteps and the expression on her face turned instantly anxious.

He readied himself to speak with some type of funny greeting or informal hello, but he hadn't the chance. She stood quickly and lunged to embrace him, hugging him hard with unexpected strength. She held her cheek against his as her arms grasped his back. He wrapped his arms around her in return, and they stood there together, in silence.

Please stay, Cass. Please stay.

"Thank you, Lucas," she said quietly, whispering it into his ear.

"For what?" he whispered back.

"For not asking me to stay," she replied. "For helping me to be strong, up until the end. If you had asked me, I couldn't have done it. I wouldn't have known how to leave."

He pulled back then and held her shoulders with his hands. He looked at her, deep into her eyes. He didn't need words, she would know from his eyes.

Please, Cass. Stay.

Recognition came to her eyes, and she appeared to wrestle with an understanding that she wished not to accept. She inhaled deeply and held his gaze.

"Do you remember the night we went souvenir shopping?" she asked sweetly.

"Of course I do," he said, remembering every step she took and souvenir she picked up and question she had asked.

"Do you remember the vase that I accidently knocked over with my shopping bag, in Billy's store?" She was speaking more slowly now, emphasizing the words towards some unknown purpose.

Lucas couldn't recall that part of the evening at first. Then, focusing in on the "Billy's" part, he remembered the shattered vase and Cass bending to pick it up and Billy calling her off. He sensed that she was being too specific for this to be some random thought. She was getting ready to make a point, and he had a feeling he was not going to like it.

"Yes, Cass. I remember." He took her hand as he answered and held it firmly in his own.

"On that night, Billy didn't pick up the pieces. He didn't try to figure out how to fit the pieces back together. He didn't do those things because some things are just too broken, Lucas. They are beyond fixing. They are the things in this life that you sweep up and toss away. And when you toss them away, you forget about them."

But you're not broken. You're perfect. Just as you are.

He continued to look into her eyes, and he sensed that she knew exactly what he was thinking. She turned and looked away, at first closing her eyes and then opening them again.

"You're a policeman. You're used to saving people. Fixing things that are broken. Keeping people safe."

She turned back to him and stared intensely, seeming to make it clear that she wanted him to hear what she was saying. "You don't know when you see someone drowning that they are going to drown anyway, no matter what you do. And because you don't know, Lucas, you continue to try, and try, and try, even as you are drowning yourself."

She leaned closer to him and placed her head against his shoulder. She whispered against his shirt, but loud enough for him to hear. "There are many more vases. Beautiful vases. And they are whole and unbroken and lovely."

He held her to him. His voice was soft. "How much lovelier could you possibly be, Cass?" He kissed the side of her head and smelled her hair. He kissed her forehead and her cheek. He found her lips and kissed her deeply, turning her head with his hand as he turned his own.

Why can't I help her?

He kissed her again, all the while feeling weak and pathetic. She was holding him tightly and kissing him just as forcefully. They were both desperate for time that would not be given. He knew now, with a finality he could no longer ignore, that he must let her go.

He pulled his head gently back, away from her kiss, away from her soft lips and beautiful eyes. She stepped forward and placed her head on his chest, turning her head sideways as she liked to do. He wrapped his arms around her and stared up at the mountain above them. He remembered then that he had the picture in his shirt pocket. He took his arm from her and pulled the picture out carefully, showing and then handing it to her.

She held the picture and stared at it. She smiled sweetly then brought her gaze back to his own. She reached her hand out, to hand the picture back. He took it from her then opened her shorts' pocket, slipping the picture within and then resuming his strong embrace around her.

They stood still and quiet, tightly entwined in one another's arms.

"I've thought a lot about tomorrow, about the date of the eighteenth of May," he said quietly, breaking the silence between them. "That day has been on my mind, actually, for many months now, Cass. A date on the calendar that I've dreaded."

He paused and took a breath, wishing to choose his words carefully. "And not just because I knew what that date meant for us and for our time together, Cass. But, more importantly, because of what I've come to know about what that date meant to you."

He stopped and looked down just as she was looking up at him. He looked into her saddened, dark blue eyes. The eyes he had gazed into so many times, with longing and compassion and love. The eyes he would soon see for the very last time.

She was steeling herself. He could see it upon her face. Her jaw was clenched and her chest was heaving in strong, controlled motions as she worked to control her breaths. He would make this quick. He would not put her through more than was needed. This hurried goodbye would be his last gift to her.

"I've never asked you to stay. And I won't ask you now. I trust you. I trust you to know what you need to make it through another day in this world. On May eighteenth and May nineteenth, and every day after that, and every year of your life. I want only for you to find some rest. To find some peace."

She was still looking at him intently, nodding her head ever so slightly.

He had asked her why she hadn't said goodbye to the children, and he suspected that goodbye was not in her vocabulary. Goodbye was for people with whom you had a strong bond, a tight connection. Her aspiration with every day was to try to avoid the connections and relationships and "goodbyes" of this world. She wouldn't say goodbye.

But he also knew, from her eyes, that she wouldn't turn away first.

"It's okay that you won't remember me," he whispered softly. "I'll remember enough, for both of us."

He leaned down and kissed her tenderly, and held his lips to her own. He opened his eyes as he did so, and found that hers, too, were open. He held her gaze and he held their kiss, and then he slowly pulled his lips from hers.

He took one last look, trying to commit the face, the eyes, the lips, the scars…trying to cement it all deeply into the fabric of his mind and his memory. His eyes were blurring now. He must hurry to capture the essence of her as she stood there in front of him. Her hair was braided loosely and tossed carelessly over her shoulder. Her eyes.

The eyes of the woman I love.

"Goodbye, Cass."

He turned quickly and began to walk away. At the top of the stairs that led from the back porch to the ground, he stopped. He stopped and listened, thinking that perhaps he would hear her say it as he walked away. But he had known. He had known from the very beginning. There would be no goodbye from her.

He walked away quickly, down the porch steps and across the pavers. As he entered into and sat in his truck, he looked ahead at the front of *Walt's Bakery and Café.* He looked through the window at the small table for two that was placed right in the front. He pictured himself and her, sitting with two mugs of coffee, talking about rain and umbrellas.

I'll remember it all, Cass. For both of us.

Feeling frustrated and hopeless, he began his drive home. He passed one of the local restaurants and slammed on his breaks. Cutting his truck hard to the right, he barely pulled in between two parked cars. Entering the bar area a few minutes later, he spotted a familiar face at the far end. He made his way to the empty barstool beside his best friend.

"Well, what a surprise," Farley exclaimed over live music that was blaring from the adjacent room. "I haven't see you in here for months." Farley took a swig of his beer and appeared to be waiting for a response.

Lucas gave a slight nod and waved down the bartender. "I'll take a shot of Jack."

Lucas could feel Farley's eyes boring into the side of his face, but he didn't feel like talking. He felt like sleeping, but he was reluctant to close his eyes. Afraid of facing the void that would come at the end of this day.

"What did she say?" Farley asked with interest, turning his body to face Lucas in a supportive gesture. Lucas appreciated the effort, so he offered up an answer.

"She wished me all the best," Lucas said in a fatigued tone. "And I wished her the same. And then we parted ways. She needs to get some sleep."

The bartender approached and set a shot glass full of brown liquor in front of Lucas, then placed another beer can in front of Farley. Farley ignored it as he continued facing Lucas.

"So … are you going to meet up with her in the morning?" Farley appeared to be confused at some missing detail of this story.

"No. She made it clear that this is something she does on her own. Without fanfare or companionship or anything like that." Lucas stopped and considered all he had processed over the course of the last forty-eight hours. "I do know that she's going by way of

Highway 9. So, I would predict she'll be gone pretty early so as to avoid any of us as we're going in to work." He shrugged his shoulders. "Or, at least, that's my guess."

"Yeah, but what did she say, when you told her?" Farley opened the newly arrived can of beer and waited expectantly.

Lucas pulled the shot closer to him and wrapped his fingers around it. He sat quietly as he stared at the small glass and the alluring liquid.

"Wait. Don't tell me ... you didn't tell her?" Farley's voice betrayed a hint of frustration mixed with disbelief. "So what, exactly, has the last seven months been about?" Farley took a long gulp of beer and set his can down forcefully.

Lucas thought about Farley's reaction and reflected on the wisdom behind the words.

Why didn't I tell her?

But he already knew the answer. He knew he had done the best he could, with what he had known. He pictured himself gulping down the shot, feeling the cool smoothness slide down his throat. He pictured another shot after that, and then another.

He lifted the glass towards his lips, then quietly shared, "I don't know."

"Bullshit."

Lucas stopped his hand and turned towards Farley. "What was that, Deputy?"

"You heard me, *Chief.* You know exactly why you didn't tell her." Farley took another gulp of beer and shook his head. "You didn't tell her because you're scared. You're scared of not doing the exact right thing to support her...or to help her."

Farley paused and ran his hand aggressively through his hair, exhaling in an exasperated manner as he did so. "If there's one thing I've learned in these past seven months, it's that you're worried. You're worried to the point of being obsessed. About being unfair to her or confusing her. But because you were so afraid of doing the wrong thing, you actually missed the opportunity to do the good thing. To show her what she means. To you."

Farley took another frustrated gulp. He was mumbling something under his breath. Suddenly, he set his beer can down and stood from his chair.

"What would you do, Lucas, if you could see her, one more time?"

"But I won't see her. Not one more time or ever again. I said my goodbye and I let her go. It's done." Lucas had said this so softly that he wondered if Farley could even hear him over the crowd.

Farley took his wallet out and threw a twenty-dollar bill on the bar.

"Oh, yes you will, Chief," he said, with determination in this voice. "You will see her. You can take that to the bank." Farley turned then and looked Lucas in the eyes. "Tomorrow morning, I want you sitting on that front porch, in that blue rocking chair. And I want you to be ready. And the only thing you have to ask yourself, as you spend tonight staring up at your ceiling, is this: What will I do, with one more moment of time, with her?"

Farley patted Lucas encouragingly on his shoulder, and then left hurriedly through the front door.

Lucas sat alone and considered what Farley's parting words had meant. He glanced at the shot glass, still held in his grasp. He placed it on the bar and pushed it back towards the bartender. He wouldn't be drinking tonight.

He caught his reflection in the mirror behind the bar, and he focused. He felt a sliver of hope, but was hesitant to give it any credence. And then one thought pushed all doubt away. He set his focus on that thought, the only one that now mattered.

What would I do?

If given one more moment of time ... with her?

Departure

CHAPTER

Thirty-Nine

*B*its of light sleep intermingled with images dreamt up from distant memories had interrupted any chance at restorative slumber. It was still dark outside, with just a hint of the impending grey of early dawn. She glanced at the clock and saw that it was a little past five, quite a bit earlier than her planned departure time of six o'clock.

She didn't really want to walk in the darkness, but then considered that by the time the sun rose and weaved its way across the sky and then set, this day would be concluded. She would be somewhere, starting anew. Just thinking about the journey ahead gave her a sudden jolt of strength, a focused energy to reach her anticipated rest at the end of this day's walk. There was nothing more to think about.

It was time to begin.

She quickly rolled off the bed and grabbed her backpack from the floor. She had slept in her traveling clothes the night prior, for efficiency. She quickly brushed her teeth and washed the sleep from her eyes. She combed and braided her hair. She threw away the toothbrush and then packed the toothpaste into her backpack. She briskly made her bed then folded up the blanket Ella had loaned her and placed it on top.

Has it really been a year since Ella handed this blanket to me?

She took another glance at her calendar then flipped quickly through the last eleven pages of months. Each day had a large X drawn atop it, all leading up to departure. She laid the calendar down on the corner table and unzipped the middle section of her backpack for one final inspection. She had a pen, a piece of paper, a new unopened desk calendar, some protein shakes, and one change of clothes. She also had some cash, rolled up into a tight cylinder with her second hair tie pulled around it. She would possibly need this for a deposit or the first month's rent or to buy some "getting-started" items. But she would need no more than this. The other money she had would be left behind.

Including the clothes and shoes she was now wearing, and the sunglasses she had propped on her head for later, Cass now had everything she would take. She looked around the room. She did so not to commit it to memory, but rather to make sure she had cleaned it appropriately and left it in good condition. Ella had been nothing but generous and kind during the past year, and Cass was determined that she would not add any additional work to Ella's full schedule for the day.

She looked again to the corner table, where she had just laid the used calendar moments earlier. On it sat the trophy for the three-legged race, among other items she had placed there the previous evening. She walked over to the trophy and read the fine print on the nameplate. Lake Lure Founder's Day Festival – First Place – Three-Legged Race. She remembered his arm wrapped around her waist and the screams of the crowd as they raced together down the grassy field.

She took the straps of the backpack and clipped them over her shoulder and about her waist, making the fitting snug and impossible to easily slip off in a moment of heated exhaustion. She wished to make good time and to cover a great distance today. She had already determined there would be no time for breaks or moments of hesitancy.

She took one last look around the small room, then turned off the lamp on the bedside nightstand. With the light bulb no longer illuminated, the room was quite dark. She stood quietly and still. She felt like a seasonal tourist, like someone who had completed her stay in this mountain village and was now ready to leave.

She tiptoed out of the bedroom and into the hallway. She looked to her right, towards the door that led to the bakery. She considered going to it, to see it one last time, but rejected this idea as quickly as she had thought it. The time for last glimpses had passed.

She tiptoed quietly through the home's kitchen and left through the back door, guiding it to close gently behind her. She walked across the porch and down the steps and along the pavers, being careful with her footing in the darkness. She reached the sidewalk and turned right, then proceeded forward without looking back.

Silence enveloped the street and homes, and only crickets provided company as she walked. She had walked this road hundreds of times over the past year, and had long ago planned out the general route she would take out of *this place*. She would head east, then turn right. The opposite direction from the way she had come.

As she walked, she once again thought of her *peace* and the drawing she had kept with her this past year. She had never seen it again, after that day, but she resisted any urge to feel melancholy. Soon, she would be well outside of *this place* and on her way to... wherever. And it would all happen before anyone here had even woken up.

As she walked further down the road, she was well aware of the familiarity all around her. The house on the left that belonged to Mrs. Stampshed. The one across the river where the Kearney family lived. Ahead, on her left, she saw the green street sign for Boys Camp Road. She walked by it quickly, keeping her vision straight ahead.

With each passing moment, the dark grey sky began to gradually lighten. And as it did so, she suddenly felt it.

She felt a new wall. Tall. Growing taller.
She felt other sensations as well. She felt resilient and prepared.
She felt shielded and empowered, as she shed thoughts and memories.
She felt strong.
Focus.
Her day of departure had arrived. Her journey had begun.

CHAPTER

Forty

She walked out of her bedroom and towards Cass's room, the room that had belonged to her son.

She had been up all night, unable to sleep due to anxiety and sorrow. Around two o'clock in the morning she had perched herself near her back bedroom window, aware that regardless of which route Cass took, this was the most advantageous point by which to see her leave. She had waited there, silently, until about quarter past five, at which time she had heard some activity in the second bedroom. A while later, she had witnessed Cass closing the back door and walking quickly away.

The prior evening, Ella had begged Cass to let her make a hot breakfast or at least a "to-go" bag of biscuits before Cass's morning departure. Cass had insisted, however, that she depart in silence and solitude. Ella loved Cass too much to go against these simple requests.

Cass had been well out of sight for over an hour now, but Ella still held out hope. Hope that as she entered the bedroom, Cass would be there. Hope that perhaps she had changed her mind and returned. Hope that she was in the bakery at this very moment, taking fresh croissants out of the oven.

As Ella opened the door to the bedroom she immediately noticed the neat condition of the dwelling. The bed was made and the blanket was folded neatly on top, with the pillow placed squarely to the side. The floor had been swept and mopped and the sink and toilet were scrubbed and sparkling. If anyone had walked in at this very moment, they would have found it hard to believe that a human being was actually living here as recently as an hour ago.

Ella shivered and tried to picture Cass, right at that moment, wherever she might presently be. She tried to conjure the image, then became too sorrowful to continue.

As she prepared to leave the bedroom, she caught sight of the corner table. She approached and immediately recognized an item, the trophy from the Founder's Day Festival. Under the corner of the trophy was a sealed envelope. She picked it up and gently tore it open, revealing a pile of bills. Ones, fives, tens and twenties. Dozens and dozens and dozens of bills.

She saw that there were other items left on the table as well. There was a small beaded bracelet, Cass's desk calendar, and the two papers that Juney and Jacob had brought over just a few nights back. Looking beside the table, Ella noticed a brown paper bag sitting on the floor. Peering inside, she found souvenirs from Billy's shop, and the ball cap and walking stick that Lucas had given Cass for Christmas. She also saw two blue blankets, folded and placed neatly at the bottom.

Ella reached to the table and picked up the familiar desk calendar, with each day of the past year marked out with an X. She had seen this calendar on many occasions while restocking Cass's towels. It usually sat upright on the night table, but now had been left lying flat, with the other items that had been left behind. As Ella studied the calendar, she noticed something at the bottom of the page for May, a message that had been written in small printed letters.

Thank you, Ella.

With a single tear now slowly making its way down her cheek, Ella set the calendar down. As she did so, a folded piece of paper fell from within its pages. Unfolding the crumpled, stained paper, she saw that it held a hand-drawn sketch of a house. It was a very rough rendition of a place somewhere that had apparently meant something to Cass. Looking at the drawing a little longer, Ella wondered if this was a place she knew. As soon as she asked herself the question, however, she immediately answered as well.

What does it matter?

This, too, had been left behind, which put this drawing and this place in the same category as everything else on this table and in this room. Ella grouped them all together in her mind, and included herself.

With the drawing still clutched in her hand, she turned to leave, then caught a glimpse of a speckle of white. As she looked around the table, she realized she had almost missed it. It was nothing more than a very small, white rectangle. Picking it up, she immediately recognized the heavy photographic paper from the many prints she had collected over the years.

She turned it slowly over and began to feel the deep and dark emptiness of the room. The air was thick and the silence was dreary.

The other side of the photo was now fully in view, and Ella was left to stare at the two familiar faces. A man and a woman.

A woman who was no longer here.

CHAPTER

Forty-One

The sun was finally starting to peek its rays across the horizon. Cass glanced upward and told herself that she was making good time through *this place*. Soon, the residents would start making their way outside, to greet their neighbors or to check their mailboxes or to head off to their work or hobbies or favorite breakfast spots.

She was encouraged that she had not yet encountered anyone on the sidewalks or streets aside from the occasional drivers who gave her no more than a wayward glance. Thanks to her earlier start, she was confident that she would be out of *this place* and on her way well before mid-morning. She anticipated that she should be approaching the important right turn very soon, the turn that would put her on Highway 9 and the route leading away.

She considered stopping for a minute to retrieve a protein shake, then quickly changed her mind. Once she was clearly departed out of *this place*, then she would stop. But not before.

As she rounded the next curve and looked ahead for any sign of the highway, she was surprised to see flashing blue lights. While the image was an unexpected one, and her gut reacted with anxiety, she never slowed or adjusted her walking. Nearing closer, she recognized

Deputy Chief McSwain. He was standing behind his car with his radio in one hand and his signature sausage biscuit in the other.

She determined that she would not stop for pleasantries or conversation. A smile and a wave was something she could do while still maintaining her progression.

Walking in the grass beside the road, she passed by the police car. As she did so, she noticed for the first time the wooden roadblock beyond the car, which was covered in a large reflective sign.

Road closed.

Cass processed the two words while continuing to walk past them. She considered the fact that if she were driving this would indeed be an unfortunate turn of events. But she was walking.

The voice calling out to her sounded muted at first, perhaps since it was the first and only human voice she had heard this morning. Coming back to her senses, she turned towards its source.

"Good morning, Cass!" Farley said again in a friendly tone.

She smiled and waved at him, as she had planned, without losing a step or slowing her pace.

"Hey…Cass," Farley called out as she walked past.

She stopped, her first stop since walking out of Ella's home earlier.

"Yes, Deputy McSwain?"

"You may have missed this sign," he said while pointing to the blockade, "but this road is closed."

She stared at him while attempting to process what he was communicating. She heard the words he was saying, but could not fathom what he meant or what it meant to her.

She finally managed a response. "But just for cars, right?"

She silently told herself that the gentle shaking of his head back and forth was just an optical illusion, brought on by the early rays of sunshine and the lack of nutrients in her body. She questioned whether perhaps she should have stopped for a protein shake before getting this far.

"I'm afraid it's closed to everyone and everything," Farley said while finishing a bite of his biscuit. "A potential rock slide that's just a little too dangerous right now. You can check back later on today and hopefully it will be all clear by then."

Focus.

She widened her stance for balance as she felt a wave of dizziness and nausea barreling towards her. She exhaled deeply and, as she did so, she realized she had been holding her breath for what felt like an eternity. She looked up to the sky.

What time is it? Seven? Maybe a little past seven?

She already knew what she would do and how she would do it. She had walked and trained and learned *this place* for almost every day for the past year. She knew another way out, and she knew how to get there.

She estimated it would take her about two hours to retrace her steps and then make it to the alternative option. She realized she would not have much time to spare before getting to and across and away in the other direction.

But she knew she could do it. She determined this recalibration could work. She told herself that it must work. Once she was well away of *this place,* she would figure out a way to veer her trajectory back in the right direction, towards the east and the north.

She nodded to Farley and turned back. She glanced quickly towards the sun then resumed her walking, now on her new path of departure.

—∾∾—

The excursion brought on by her unexpected rerouting had not gone as quickly as she had projected. Now that residents were up and moving, she had found herself either going out of her way to avoid people who may wish to talk to her or actually stopping to greet people when avoidance was not possible. She was polite but curt with all of her responses, never disrespectful but also clear in her quick explanations that she must be on her way.

Cass had significantly gone off the simpler route just for the purpose of avoiding any area around the Police Station. This had added considerable steps and time to her journey. She had also happened upon Mrs. Stampshed loading groceries into her home and had stopped to assist her. This help had then led to Mrs. Stampshed's story about her latest bout with Shingles and her recounting of getting up three times during the night to take pain relievers. Cass had stood and listened with an anxious interest and empathy.

Finally, she was back on the main road, and headed once more towards her intended destination, the revised exit out. Unfortunately, on this stretch of road, there were no backroads that could be used in avoidance. She resolved that she would walk quickly and hope. Hope that no one was outside.

She approached the sign for Boys Camp Road and quickly walked past it with a steely focus straight ahead. She walked on, past everything she had already passed once before on this day. She resisted the urge to feel frustrated or impatient.

Focus.

She somehow made it past the shops and homes without encountering any challenges. She was now on the segment of road beyond the downtown area. This was the segment of road that led away. Away from *this place.*

She realized that she was now in unfamiliar territory, having only walked on this particular part of this road once before. It had been exactly a year ago. From what she could remember, there were only a few turns left before she would come upon some campgrounds, and then her *peace,* and then finally the sign indicating the end of *this place.*

She glanced upward towards the sun, just like she had so many times since turning around at the roadblock. She was anxious and worried, but then convinced herself there was no need. By her estimations, it was still only nine-thirty or, even at the latest, ten in the morning.

Could it be ten already? Is it even later than that?

She steadied herself and breathed deeply. She reached in her pocket to pull out the drawing, then remembered leaving it on a table this morning. *It's okay*, she told herself. She knew she would soon be seeing it in person.

The house. Her *peace*.

The thought calmed her, even while she quickened her pace. She knew it couldn't be far. She knew she was strong and she could walk quicker. She knew everything she needed to know.

Focus.

She looked and saw what appeared to be a large tree overhanging the road. She remembered this tree. It was the tree she had seen right after the town limits sign. It was the tree she had seen right before finding her *peace*. She could barely make it out, but it was there. She saw it. She knew.

I am almost there.

Sweat now covered her face and dripped down her back, sticking the inside of her t-shirt against her shoulder blades. She glanced at the sky and knew instinctively that it was still mid-morning. Yet, the stronger pace and heightened urgency were beginning to take its toll. She imagined she was tiring, even with a full day's journey still ahead.

She reminded herself over and over, *all is well*. She was close, and the sun indicated that she still had time. She nodded and told herself that she could deal with a little sweat and exhaustion. She had prepared and trained for those very challenges, for sweat and fatigue and heat.

She thought now of her *peace*. She recalled how, on this very day a year ago, she had first seen it, here on the outskirts of *this place*. She had seen the massive tree first, then she had spotted it. She remembered how she had studied it carefully, committing enough of its details in her empty mind to recreate it in sketched form.

Cass smiled slightly with pride at her ability to pick out the most peaceful place. A place where she imagined a person rocking in a chair and looking out over vast rolling hills of nothing.

She examined each side of the road and spotted a clearing up ahead, one with a gravel driveway leading from it. She was walking very quickly, so she determined to take only a few brief glances as she passed the house. She did not wish to trip on a rock or hinder her pace in any way. Not now, when leaving was imminent. She began quickly turning her head every few seconds so as not to miss the first view of it.

Through the gaps in leaves and trees she finally spotted the structure, up high on a faraway hill, just as she had drawn. Without stopping or even slowing her pace, she caught several quick glimpses. The long, curved driveway ran over a flat brown bridge then dipped up and down small hills, finally ending at the front porch. There were trees and bushes lining most of the driveway, not tall enough to block the view of the hills beyond, but lush enough to form a lovely walkway. It was like nature's red carpet leading up to a haven of restfulness. There were wildflowers as well, growing all along the driveway. Yellow and white blooms on thin green stems.

Other than these few quick observations, however, she could make out very little about the house itself, for it was perched on its hill and stood a considerable distance from the road. The house itself appeared to be so small that detecting details was close to impossible. She took another quick glance at the wildflowers, set her sights on the curve in the road ahead, and moved forward quickly.

Approaching the far side of the gravel driveway entrance, she looked for and finally spotted the town limits sign. It was located at the beginning of the next curve, ahead of her on the right. Her heart leapt at the sign's proximity. While not yet close, it was now within her vision. She calculated that she would be there in a matter of minutes.

She walked on, across the last few rocks of the gravel driveway, then back onto the grass. There, quite close, was a brown mailbox bolted to a wooden post. The black paint that indicated numbers and letters was flaking off in several places, which made the address hard to read. The mailbox was void of any name.

She thought to accelerate her cadence for the final few hundred

334 Jordan R. Samuel

feet, but actually slowed dramatically as she noticed something unusual on the mailbox. It was a wooden crate, hanging from the back of the mailbox post. She turned slightly and took one slow step towards the crate, and then stopped.

The crate was low and flat, which made it quite easy to see the contents contained within. There were small cans of pink and blue and yellow paint. There were packages of craft gemstones and sponge stamps, all in a multitude of colors and shapes. And, in the corner of the crate, there was an assortment of paint brushes.

Some of the brushes were thin and some were thick, but all were neatly arranged in a small vase. It was a vase that had somehow been put back together, from a thousand broken pieces of glass.

CHAPTER

Forty-Two

He had been here all morning, since way before the sun had risen. He had sat on this front porch, just as Farley had instructed, and he had waited for the possibility to see her one more time. He had watched her quickly walk by and then pause at the mailbox.

Although the distance from the porch to the end of the driveway was significant, Lucas knew it was her. She was standing at the crate, the one he had attached to the mailbox while it was still dark outside. Perhaps she was now looking at the vase, the broken vase that had been rebuilt from a thousand broken pieces of glass.

Billy had been happy to meet him at the shop for an urgent after-hours purchase. After bringing the small vase home and shattering it in a small box, he had then stayed up all night with glue in one hand and his hair dryer in the other. The intricate process was finally completed around four in the morning, and resulted in a mismatched mosaic that Lucas found even lovelier than the original.

Cass's brief pause at the mailbox allowed him to think, once again, about the question Farley had posed to him at the bar. It was

a question he had repeated to himself over and over while working
all night on the vase.

What would I do if given just one more moment, with her?

Lucas stood from the blue rocking chair in which he had been
sitting since before dawn, the very chair he had spray painted just
a few weeks earlier. He stood on the porch, the same porch he had
sanded and painted during March. He looked past the lamppost, the
one he had refurbished in his back yard. The one she liked. It was
now firmly set in concrete just a few feet from the front porch steps.

He thought back to the end of summer and remembered his
frequent visits to her hospital room. He had seen the drawing on
the crumpled paper as it lay beside her bed. The first time he had
looked at it, he had felt a sense of the familiar. The second time, as
he had studied it, he had known exactly which house it was. It was
a house he had seen many times in his lifetime. It was a house in
Chimney Rock.

Standing here now, on the expansive front porch, he remembered
those anxious days in the hospital, and one visit in particular. On
that day, she had crawled on the floor, calling out for a boy named
Tristan. He could still see her in his mind, covered in hundreds of
red, raw cuts and blackish bruises. She had sat on the floor with her
head bent down, reaching out for something.

He recalled the moment that he had placed it in her hand, the
drawing on the paper that he had folded back up for her. In that
moment, she had somehow escaped the torment that she endured,
always, on her own.

That very day he had visited Margie at her real estate office and
had told her of his intent. He was going to buy the old house that
had been abandoned for years, the one on the western outskirts of
the village.

Margie had gotten to work on the real estate end of things
while Lucas had worked on the financial end. He consolidated the
cash he had in savings with some stocks he had purchased long ago.
Soon, the paperwork had been signed and filed, the money had

been transferred, and Lucas had gotten to work on the tiny house on the hill.

He had completed much of the difficult work in the fall, spending most of his evenings after work at the old house. He had gutted much of the plumbing system, replaced the hardwoods in the living area, and had bought new appliances for the kitchen. He was surprised and pleased to find that most of the windows were adequately sealed and still functioning, leading to only a few necessary replacements along with a new back door. He had relied on Farley's assistance for most of the larger projects, and his friend had proven to be quite generous with his time and talents.

Lucas had bought some inexpensive but cozy furniture from a value store in Forest City, and had done his best, with his limited fashion sense, to match curtains and valences in colors he thought Cass would like. He had painted the living room in a light beige and the kitchen in a light yellow. He had also painted the bedroom, but only after searching through magazines for soothing color and bedding ideas. In the end he had chosen a deep greyish-blue. It was the color of the lake on calm, quiet days.

As he had worked on the house in the cool evenings of fall and the cold evenings of winter, he had done so with a certain image always playing in the back of his mind. It was the image of him telling her, of him showing her.

In his mind, he had conjured up all sorts of ways this could happen. He had thought of bringing her here on a picnic, and then revealing to her that the place was actually now hers. He had considered a dramatic scenario, where the house was hidden by a huge tractor-trailer that suddenly drove away to reveal to her the waiting home. He had even thought about a quiet, romantic dinner at which he would put the key into her hand and tell her she didn't need to walk away. Not anymore.

But as the seasons had come and gone, both in the little village and in their two intertwined lives, Lucas had come to feel quite differently about the house, this house that he had bought for her.

He had been given opportunities to tell her, like the day she had come home from the hospital and he had helped her to sit up in her bed. She had been so weak and frail, and he had considered that it may give her something to look forward to as she healed. But he had remained silent.

Or the day he had found her alone at the lake and had taken her hand and had dipped down in the freezing water beside of her. He had almost told her then. He had almost told her that her mourning could end. That some respite was waiting for her, just up the road.

Or the day she had seen the lamppost at his house, and had asked him where he would be putting it. He had almost said it then. *I am putting it at the end of your driveway, to light your way. To lead you home.* But he hadn't.

He had come to question himself as to why the house was so important, and whether it was more important for her, or for him. He had begun to analyze his intentions and to wonder in what ways the ownership of the house might confuse her. He had worried that by giving her the house, he might unknowingly persuade or manipulate her into staying when in reality she very much wanted to leave.

As he had sanded and painted and hammered, these were the troubles and concerns that had floated through his mind. He had eventually reached the conclusion, even as the wet concrete was hardening around his refurbished lamppost, that he didn't have a plan. He had realized, finally, in those late spring days, that he would prepare the house for her, and then he would stop.

The house was small, with one bedroom, a bathroom, a living area, a kitchen, and a tiny screened-in back porch. The star attraction of the house was the front porch, which ran the entire length of the house frontage as well as wrapped halfway around the side. Lucas had long considered the views from the porch to be spectacular. From the front porch one could see an expanse of green hills and woodlands, as well as the thousands of daisies that he had planted along the driveway. Around the corner of the house, from the vantage point of the wraparound porch on the side, were more hills as well as the summit of Chimney Rock Mountain, visible in all its glory.

Lucas had known when he had stood on the porch, for the first time, what the name of this house would be. He had found a large piece of white oak, lying on the grounds near the house, and had cut it into a flat slab. He had visited the specialty shop in town and had watched the craftsman carve and burn the name of the house into it.

He momentarily pulled his gaze from the road and looked over his shoulder to the front door of the house. Over the door frame, a wooden sign was placed.

Tohi.

It was the language of his people. It was Cherokee...for *peace.*

He brought his eyes again to the road far away, and to the woman he loved. The woman he had said goodbye to, the evening before.

She was here, at the mailbox. And now it appeared that she was looking up, towards the house. He wondered if she could see that there was a person here, on the porch. He wondered if she could see that the person was him.

It was time. Time for him to decide.

What would I do if given just one more moment?

The front door to the house was already unlocked and pushed fully ajar. But in front of this was a screened door. It was one of those old, squeaky doors that pulled open slowly and closed back even slower.

Standing to one side, he reached for the handle and brought the door outward. He turned his head and looked towards the road.

And then he stood very still, and held the door open.

CHAPTER

Forty-Three

*S*he tore her eyes from the vase and the crate and back to the gravel driveway. She followed the driveway as it reached to the little house. On the porch, there was a person. A man.

I know this man.

He walked now, towards the front door, as if to enter through it. But instead, he pulled on the handle, and then he looked to her. She was too far away to decipher any other details. To determine what the door looked like, or how it sounded as it moved on its hinges. These were things she could not know.

But there was one thing about the door that she did know.

It is open.

She kept her eyes on the door as she felt her leg muscles instinctively twitch and tense, readying for movement. She took a step towards the driveway. And now another, onto the driveway itself. She could feel the uneven gravel through her shoes and beneath her feet.

She readied to take another step, then felt a bead of sweat fall down her forehead and across her cheek. And through the small drop of sweat, she felt the heat intensified. The heat from the strong morning sun that was now beaming over her left shoulder.

She turned her head gradually while realizing the sun's location. As she saw it, higher in the sky than she expected, she felt fully the consequence of stopping, of her hesitation and doubt and even hope.

She felt her breath quicken as she turned back towards the main road, the road that would take her past the town limits sign and around the curves. The sun was hitting her back and shoulders as she walked away from her *peace*. The strong rays were trying to warn her that the time was now very late. And that warning now came with pictures. Images and sounds and movies.

She walked as quickly as possible, moving her legs at a rapid cadence up the gradual incline of the road. She had veered off a little onto the asphalt itself, and had heard a car blow its horn as it rushed quickly by. She was surrounded now, bombarded with painful thrusts into her mind. She felt as in a trance, trying to focus on walking while bearing the attack. Trying to survive against the onslaught while still rushing onward. She felt herself weakening.

She was still here. She was still in *this place*. And because she was, she felt the approaching tsunami of the most painful and the most unyielding.

She saw the town limits sign ahead. She walked towards it and braced herself. Mentally braced for the storm from the past.

The girl's arm is looped through her brother's arm. He is escorting her as she walks proudly in a dress made of pink …

"Come on, Alex," Tristan is calling. "You won't know what my surprise is unless you get in the car" …

Cass shook her head as she walked. She shook it uncontrollably as she spoke, softly and only to herself at first, then louder and out into the world.

"Don't get in the car. Don't get in the car."

The girl and her brother are standing together and looking at the jewelry display case. He is pointing at the earrings …

"Mark this day and time, Alex," her brother is saying. "May eighteenth at 10:21 in the morning. This will be the day and time that you will always remember"...

And then ...

The girl's cheek is being kissed, kissed by a little girl, a smaller girl, with blonde hair and wide eyes. "It's for spring," the little girl is saying....

Cass stopped walking and bent over, placing her hands above her knees for support. She suddenly felt exhausted, even as the images and voices continued to find her. The assault was strong and the waves were damaging, but there was something else.

The girl's father is laying an envelope down on a table, next to a debit card. "She's not like you, Alexandria," he is saying softly. "You're strong. You can survive this. On your own"...

The girl's hands are being touched, are being rubbed and patted. There is a woman, with silver hair, who is patting her hands. The woman wants her to rest, the woman wishes for her to heal ...

The girl's mother is crying, she has grown weak from sorrow. She is saying to the girl, "I don't find any happiness seeing you. Knowing you are here, alive. Looking at you only reminds me of what I have lost" ...

A man is standing in front of her. His shoulders are covered in blue blankets. He is reaching his arm out to take hold of the blankets. He is coming towards her, to take her under his blankets.

She took a few deep breaths, and then slowly stood upright.

She looked ahead of her, at the road that went straight then disappeared behind a curve. She saw the sign just ten feet from her. She focused on the road and the sign while she stood in place. She thought excitedly *it is right there.*

"So please, just get in the car. For me?" Tristan is looking at her with those pleading eyes. "Please, Alexandria. Please." ...

Her mother is screaming, heartbroken and sad. "I was a mom. I had a boy, a son. And you took him from me, and into danger."

She felt the sun against her back, taunting her, reminding her. The day and hour were near.

10:21 in the morning, on the eighteenth of May.

She remembered that moment, the one that her brother had told her that she would always remember. She remembered it, and she wept.

She forgot time as she stood there, doubled over and convulsing with the sobs of a decade of tears. She had remembered what he had told her she would, even through the many years that now separated them. Even with so many walls that had been built just to shield her from that day. From that time. From that life.

And then, there was another. Someone else was speaking. There was something else she had been told to remember. From another time. From another life.

Lucas is standing in front of her. He is saying, "Even when I'm not with you, remember." But she is confused. She doesn't know what it is. What is it that she must remember?

Cass stood and wiped the tears from her cheeks. She looked forward, towards her unknown destination. And towards the one beyond that. Towards the years and decades that awaited her, right beyond that curve in the road.

And then, she turned.

She walked towards the trees and into the vast greenness that lined the road and hid the mountain behind it. As she pushed back small limbs and walked clumsily over bushes and brush, a lone voice led her towards the house.

"... While the door is still open."

She walked on through the forest, but much quicker now. She had suddenly realized how long she had stood looking at the sign. How long she had stayed there, bent over and struggling.

Through the gaps and holes left among the leaves, she could see a white structure in the distance up ahead. She kept walking, ducking under large limbs and navigating around dead logs and crevices in the ground. She heard the river running to her right. She was getting closer now.

She willed her legs to move faster but fatigue and uneasiness were slowing her progression. It seemed to have been a lifetime since that moment that she had seen him, holding the door open on the porch. So much time had passed since she had turned away and left the mailbox and the house behind. So much time. Too much time.

She looked ahead and saw more of the house and the driveway through the vacant space in between the trees. But she couldn't yet see the porch. Or the man. Or the door. She kept pushing and progressing, fighting her way through the thick foliage. She reached for a thick limb with a mass of leaves emerging from it, then grabbed it and pulled it back.

Hidden in the shadow of the forest, she looked up to the house. She could now see from this closer range that there were blue rocking chairs on the porch, and a sign over the door, and daisies planted all around. And she could see that there was a man, still on that porch. He looked dejected and defeated. His head was held into his hand, and his shoulders were bent in despair. But, yet, even still, his other hand remained on the door.

He was holding it open.

He had held it open this entire time. As she had walked away, as she had struggled and fought. Through her loneliness and grief and sorrow and abandonment, he had somehow held it open. Through it all.

She watched him as he stood there, unaware of her presence.

And then she heard herself speak. It was the voice of a frightened seventeen-year-old girl. A girl with raw, stitched-up gashes along her back. A girl with a tender, broken heart. It was her voice, her *own* voice that now whispered ...

"Don't close."

She pushed the limb behind her and began to walk past it. She wished at that moment to be energized but suddenly felt physically weak. Her legs were moving slowly, as if weighted down by years of guilt and regret. Her body was hesitant, as if afraid to leave the dark veil of the leafy shelter around her.

She thought then of a race, one from long ago. A race that she had run with a stress fracture at her right ankle. A race that she had finished in pain and triumph. She remembered the state champion she had been. She remembered.

I'm not a walker.

She took a deep breath and felt herself accelerate. She emerged from the forest and hit a quick stride as she entered the driveway, unbuckling and dropping her backpack as she did so. The roughness of the tiny gravel felt sharp through her used, worn shoes, but this discomfort only propelled her to run faster.

The runners on either side of the girl are gasping for deeper breaths. They are all leaning inward to run the curve in the asphalt ahead. The girl is slightly behind them, gaining her strength and speed as she blocks out the searing pain. The girl is focusing on her place of peace.

Cass approached and ran across the small bridge, keeping her eyes on the porch, and the door, and him. She noticed that his own attention had been on the door this entire time. She watched the side of his face, growing a little closer now, a face she had thought she would never see again. She pictured the front of his face and his smile. She ran harder and faster.

The girl is glancing into the stands and is seeing her family. They are standing and cheering, yelling for her to run. To try. To be strong. The girl is close to the leader now, pumping her arms with every fiber of strength in her body. The girl is willing her legs to run faster, to be stronger. She sees the finish line ahead.

She will go, now. She will fight. She will fight to make it to the end.

Cass sprinted along the gravel, running up and then down the gentle hills. She slipped and fell, and then quickly stood again and regained her fast pace. She ignored the blood now trickling down her knee and the scrapes along the palm of her hand. She ignored the exhaustion that was screaming from her body. She focused only on the front porch ahead.

Perhaps he had detected a movement, or perhaps he just had a feeling. Either way, she saw Lucas turn and look towards the

346   Jordan R. Samuel

driveway. Her heart leapt at his expression, as he reached out his free hand towards her.

She felt a steady incline as the driveway started up the last, steep hill, but she was now feeling strong and fast. She could see it now, the door and the house, up close with details. Painted porch railings, and blue rocking chairs, and the deep brown of his tender eyes. She could see the lamppost now, not far away, the one he had been working on at his house just last month. She could see the steps leading up to the porch. Only fifty or sixty feet to go.

With her eyes still on his, she suddenly stopped.

His face dropped. His left hand, held out for her, stretched further towards her as his right hand remained on the door. His eyes were pleading.

She kept her gaze upon him. And on the house. And on the door, the door that she would very soon walk through. But not before ....

Kneeling down, she reached her scarred hand towards the hundreds of daisies growing wildly along the driveway. She picked one, plucking it carefully along its thin stem.

It's just a flower, growing along the side of the road. There is nothing elegant or special about it. It was not cultivated or sought after or cherished. All it did was live.

Catching his eyes again, she placed the daisy behind her ear. She then stood and walked the rest of the driveway, holding his eyes with a joyful smile.

As she walked up the first step, and then the next, her eyes filled with the tears from a decade of journeys, those filled with lost hopes and forgotten dreams. But as she found the last step, and his hand waiting just beyond it, for her, she knew that this journey had been her very last.

She took his hand and looked into his eyes, then looked up, above the door frame, at a sign that read *Tohi*. Then she faced and looked in through the door itself.

Straight ahead was a wall clock. It was old and worn, with giant hands that ticked away at the fleeting seconds of each of their lives. She looked upon it and she saw the time.

She pulled him gently behind her as she stepped forward, over the threshold and through the door.

Epilogue

She poured another glass of the sweet tea and then placed the pitcher back in the refrigerator. As she closed the refrigerator door, she smiled at the photo being held in place by two small magnets. It was a photo of the two of them, laughing near the river in springtime.

She walked into the living room, past the two "I Love" essays that Juney and Jacob had written for her. These were in glass frames and hanging on the wall, right above a framed picture of the two children which was displayed on a side table.

Sitting on the couch, she slipped on her moccasins, a gift from Lucas for her birthday three months ago. He had meant it as a novelty, until he had seen how much she loved them and actually wore them. She loved the feel of the soft leather and the look of the fringe and the beaded tassel on the top. Each day, when she got off of her shift at the bakery, the thing she most looked forward to was slipping on the moccasins.

She took one of the two blue blankets that were kept on the back of the couch and headed towards the front door. It was a little chilly today, probably too chilly for the short wrap dress she had put on after work. But she had worn it anyway. She had decided she would be plenty warm under the blanket.

As she walked towards the door, she passed two identical trophies, both for the Founders Day Festival three-legged race. In June, she and Lucas had repeated as champions. They were already discussing when to start practicing for next year.

She looked up at the wall near the door and saw a small frame, within which was a plain white paper with a drawing of a house. The paper was worn from folding and unfolding and rain and blood. But here it was, nonetheless.

Nearing the door she passed the antique wall clock, the one Lucas had been given when he was in sixth grade. He had now given it to her, which made the clock her very first antique.

She walked out onto the front porch, where she sat in her favorite blue rocking chair. She set her glass of tea beside her on a wicker table that held books and candles and a vase.

She rocked and she gazed out across the hills and mountains of this place.

There were many days, in quiet solitude, that she thought of her brother and of the young police officer who had died that day. She thought about them and wondered how different their lives and her life might have been had she not made the decision – the decision to get in the car. But the blame and guilt that she had carried for so long were both gradually starting to fade. They had given their lives to save hers. And now, she was learning how to honor their sacrifice. She was learning how to save her life as well.

And in those quiet moments, she saw Tristan's face. But it was not the face of grief and horror. It was the face of a boy, her brother. It was the face of her friend, her companion, and the person she had loved the most. When she remembered him, now, she remembered him as smiling, as he escorted her across a high school stage.

She remembered, also, the truth of the last words he had ever said to her. She remembered that, indeed, she had been blessed with the most amazing brother in the whole world. And when she remembered that, it wasn't with tears or mourning. It was with a smile and a nod. She had come to understand that a blessing of that magnitude cannot be forgotten or hidden. It cannot be locked behind walls. It must be remembered with a heart of thanksgiving for all that it had been and meant.

She continued rocking in her blue chair as she studied the trees, with their leaves of gold and orange. The breeze blew gently and a shower of leaves floated down from the branches. With the hundreds of trees that stretched before and around her, she felt that she was in the middle of a heavenly autumn shower.

Rocking steadily, she heard the soft melody of the wind chimes hanging nearby. She picked up one of the books from the table, the one that she had started reading several days ago. It was a book she had found on a random shelf at The Treasure Chest, a book of old poems.

She found her leaf bookmark and opened to the page, then began reading as a gentle breeze blew across the porch. It loosened several strands of hair from her ponytail, and these now flittered playfully across her face.

Removing her hair tie, she let her long hair blow in the wind as she laid back her head. She closed her eyes.

Tobi.

A familiar sound met her ears. She opened her eyes and peered in the distance, to a car that was pulling into her driveway. It was a police car, from the Town of Lake Lure Police Department. Her heartbeat quickened as she pictured the man who would soon emerge from the car. The man who would embrace her and hold her and love her.

Most importantly, though, he was the man who had opened, and kept opened, her door. She understood now how he had worried, how he had been tormented from not knowing what to do. He had been cautious to become too attached, then careful not to hurt or confuse her. He had second-guessed himself and struggled, right up until the very end.

And at the end, when he had held the door open, he had let her know that it was her decision. That only she could determine her path in this life. That only she would know when the door being held was, indeed, the last door.

She looked back at her book, intending to finish one last poem on the page she had marked. She read the title and author and saw that it was a poem by Robert Frost.

A voice said, Look me in the stars
And tell me truly Men of earth
If all the soul-and-body scars
Were not too much to pay for birth

She closed the book and stood from the chair. She was thinking about the question posed by the poet, and considering what the answer might possibly be.

She looked out over the beautiful world, across the trees and the mountains. She saw leaves blowing in the wind, and a blue sky with billowy white clouds. She heard the river running close by, and saw it shimmering in the glowing, glorious sun.

She set the book back upon the table, then glanced at the vase that was sitting there as well. It was made from a thousand broken pieces of glass, and it was holding a single daisy.

And, she knew.

She knew the answer to the question.